Dillian could see
she had the resolv
bargain. She coul
woman, trembling with fear of him and what
he might do to her.

The trouble was, he was half right at the
very least.

Fighting for control, she said defiantly, "My
mother died when I was twelve. After that, my
father's idea of a companion for me was anyone who owed him a favor. I can ride a horse
like a man, shoot like one, fence with the best
of them."

She stopped then. He didn't move. He just
waited. Dillian moved one foot forward, then
the other. She was within arm's reach of him
now. She thought perhaps he was not as calm
as he pretended to be. His knuckles appeared
white where his hands bit into the upper parts
of his arms.

She didn't jump when he finally reached out
one hand to tilt her chin upward. She just held
her breath until he lowered his mouth to meet
her own.

She had to hide what was happening to her
now, as her lips parted, and she found herself
melting. Dillian had to pretend she knew it all
already . . . this passion . . . this bliss. . . .

The Marquess

by

Patricia Rice

A TOPAZ BOOK

TOPAZ
Published by the Penguin Group
Penguin Putnam Inc., 375 Hudson Street,
New York, New York 10014, U.S.A.
Penguin Books Ltd, 27 Wrights Lane,
London W8 5TZ, England
Penguin Books Australia Ltd, Ringwood,
Victoria, Australia
Penguin Books Canada Ltd, 10 Alcorn Avenue,
Toronto, Ontario, Canada M4V 3B2
Penguin Books (N.Z.) Ltd, 182–190 Wairau Road,
Auckland 10, New Zealand

Penguin Books Ltd, Registered Offices:
Harmondsworth, Middlesex, England

First published by Topaz, an imprint of Dutton Signet,
a member of Penguin Putnam Inc.

First Printing, December, 1997
10 9 8 7 6 5 4 3 2 1

 REGISTERED TRADEMARK—MARCA REGISTRADA

Printed in the United States of America

Prologue

March 1816

In the weak light of the carriage lanterns, the cloaked figure pulled his hood more securely around his face and climbed from the aged vehicle into the pouring rain. The driver leapt from his unprotected seat, following his passenger toward the lighted inn.

"You could have taken the public coach," the driver pointed out, continuing an old argument.

"I could have flown in on vampire wings," the cloaked figure growled irascibly, with a distinctly un-British accent.

Hugging his jug and lingering beneath the overhang of the roof before heading out into the wet night, Tipplin' Tom heard this last and blanched. The lumbering black barouche had captured his attention upon arrival. The nobility seldom risked their lives and their vehicles on the rutted path to this humble village, not in a few decades or so, anyway. But the terrifying words of the carriage's occupant rang loud and clear. Gulping, Tom scurried back to warn the tavern's inhabitants.

Unaware of their audience, the driver responded vehemently. "This has gone far enough, Gavin! You've hid at sea these last years, nearly killing yourself to earn our passage and then some. Now's the time to assert yourself. You're a highfalutin marquess over here! Just glare at the villagers and toss a few coins. They'll bow at your feet."

"I don't want anyone bowing at my feet. I don't want the damned title. I want a roof over our heads and a chance to earn something besides wormy biscuits for a change. What I do with myself the rest of the damned time is no one's business but my own."

With the hood pulled low to disguise his features, Gavin cautiously entered the dimly lit, low ceilinged tavern.

The few inhabitants at this late hour cowered in far corners. None came forward to greet them or offer ale. Scowling, Gavin glared at this reaction to his presence. They didn't even know him here, and already they acted as if he had three heads instead of just one slightly damaged one. Someone must have seen him down the road earlier and reported back here before they arrived. He'd grown used to averted gazes in the dismal seaside taverns he'd frequented these last years. He'd learned to walk alone. He didn't need these puling, ignorant villagers. He just needed directions.

"And you wanted me to act the noble aristocrat?" he hissed at his driver, turning around to stalk back out.

"Coward," the slighter figure returned disrespectfully. But he strode into the tavern to ask directions while his cloaked passenger retreated to the waiting carriage.

The clouds opened, and rain fell in torrents when the barouche finally returned to the road. A different driver now perched upon the open outside seat, while the slighter one of earlier shook out his soaked hat in the interior. No one had bothered relighting the carriage lamps, and they could only see dark silhouettes through the gloom.

"You'll need servants," the slighter man answered the silence as the wheels hit a rut and they bounced off the walls. "He's a half-wit, but he knows how to find the manor."

Gavin made a choking noise that might almost be a rusty laugh. "An auspicious beginning: a half-wit for manservant. I like your thinking, Michael."

This time, the man called Michael made the growling reply. "If you mean to bury yourself out here in the middle of nowhere, I won't be buried with you."

The cloaked figure threw off his hood and nodded understandingly. The pale blur of his face against the darkness revealed little as he rubbed at the irregularities of his jaw. "You'll do as you wish, as always. When have I ever interfered?"

Both of them could write volumes into the silence that followed, but they knew the words by heart and had no need of repeating them aloud or recording them for posterity. As the rain pounded overhead and the carriage lurched and righted itself, they watched for the first sight of their new home.

Soaked and overgrown evergreens brushed against the carriage doors as they jounced down an even narrower road. Gavin clung to his walking stick and winced as the right forward wheel hit a deep hole, then propelled itself out by the sheer force of the blow. He had the rather awful suspicion they traversed the drive to his inheritance.

Not even Michael's vivid imagination could have conjured up the monstrosity looming before them as they rounded the curve. Silhouetted against the horizon, gabled roofs soared with medieval turrets, mixing with Roman arches atop a structure that sprawled across the hillside. Unused to English architecture, both men stared at the storybook fantasy as the carriage lurched to a halt before it.

Concurring with Gavin's unspoken thought, Michael whispered, "Even I couldn't have dreamed that up. Do you think we'll find a sleeping beauty inside?"

Dropping his gaze from the outrageous roofline to the more mundane elements of land and foundation, Gavin shook his head. "If we do, she's covered in thorns, and I'm too damned tired to hack my way through." With a sigh, he threw open the coach door, ignoring the etiquette of allowing his newly hired servant to do it for him.

Instead of hitting a paved drive, his boot sank in foot-deep mud.

Torn from a long-rotted trellis, a rose cane swung out and snatched his hood.

In all that vast monstrous exterior, not a single light flickered with welcome.

Later, staring into a fire created from a particularly odious bric-a-brac shelf and a kitchen stool, Gavin morosely contemplated the inheritance for which he'd spent these last years earning passage to England and some semblance of respectable wealth. He'd thought he would arrive in style so as not to shame his unknown family. He'd wasted both time and money on that endeavor. The family solicitors had informed him he had female cousins of some sort. He'd notified the solicitors of the date of his arrival. Not only had his unknown and unacknowledged family departed, they'd taken with them every servant and every sign of life, leaving him only this deteriorating shell requiring more wealth than he possessed.

Kicking at an elegantly carved and extremely filthy wing chair beside the fireplace, Gavin wondered how long the place had lain empty. Michael's comment about finding a sleeping beauty didn't seem far off the mark. Filth coated every surface. Vines had crept in through windows. So far, he'd not discovered any evidence of leaking roofs or cracked walls, but the night was young and the rooms were dark. No doubt mice scuttled about in the walls and wind blew down chimneys. For this he'd bought a new suit of clothes and a carriage. He'd have better invested his limited resources in return passage.

Firelight gleaming off his auburn hair, Michael wandered the towering library with fascination, staring at the elaborately carved moldings layered in cobwebs, admiring the dusty thick oak paneling of the walls. Books filled the shelves, and by the light of a candle, he pulled them off randomly, dusting them off and examining their contents. Gavin could tell from his soft exclamations that he thought the place a treasure trove, but Michael had never been the practical type. One couldn't eat books.

"In the morning, we'll survey the lands," Gavin said aloud, although he might as well talk to himself. Michael had no interest in land. "It's early enough in the year to put in a crop. The solicitor's letter said the main estate had no mortgage."

"The solicitor's letter said the estate had no funds," Michael reminded him vaguely, lost in a tome of ancient origin.

The solicitor's letter had left Gavin more than underwhelmed. Merely noting the estate had spent some years locating the closest heir to the title, it announced Gavin Lawrence as the eighth Marquess of Effingham and the heir to Arinmede Manor, as the late marquess left only a female descendant. The letter invited him to visit at his convenience. Gavin had known then that he couldn't expect much. He had only to look to his father and grandfather to know the Lawrences of Arinmede and Effingham had little going for them beyond charm and good looks. But through the years of war, in the aftermath of disaster, Gavin had clung to that foolish letter. He had a family in England, a titled family and a home. He'd thought his father a liar. He knew his father a liar. But he hadn't lied about his origins. The solicitor's letter proved that much. The solicitor's letter hadn't lied any more than his father about the family inheritance. It had just left out a few pertinent facts.

Arinmede Manor not only did not contain any female cousins or dowager marchionesses, it had no inhabitants at all. Arinmede Manor might provide a roof over their heads, but the rest of it had deteriorated to a rotten shell needing two personal fortunes to restore. And for the previous marquess to have left his home in such a state, he must have possessed the same rotten luck and wastrel habits as all the rest of the Lawrences Gavin knew.

He had spent these last years captaining ships and trading in foreign ports so he could earn enough money to put him right back where he was before, bankrupt and without family, except now he was faced with a foreign country and strangers with odd habits who knew nothing of him. He would have been farther ahead if he'd stayed in the States.

Glancing up at the coat of arms engraved in the wood above the fireplace, Gavin lifted his glass in salute to his long line of ancestors. At least this time, they'd left him a roof over his head.

One

Flames shot through the lower windows and licked at the eaves. Smoke billowed in thick black clouds blending with the night sky. Women garbed only in cotton nightclothes hugged each other in horror and screamed hysterically from the lawn as a beam crashed somewhere in the interior. All eyes turned with despair and helpless anguish to the slender female materializing in the upper-story window. Fire ate slowly at the old wood just below where she stood. Smoke curled and blew around her, sometimes hiding her entirely as she calmly lowered another bundle of valued possessions to the ground.

"The woman's mad as a hatter," an auburn-haired footman exclaimed in disbelief as the servants dived to sort through the rescued valuables.

Dillian ignored the obviously new servant's comment as the fallen blanket woke her to a sudden possibility. Even as someone handed her the rescued bag of coins representing all her worldly goods—outside her father's useless papers—her mind leapt to the wrappings of that last load. Blanche played the role of martyred heroine well, but Dillian had no intention of allowing her best friend, cousin, and employer to die a heroine's death. She had no intention of allowing her to die at all.

"Grab a corner of that blanket!" she yelled to the footman and the burly butler. "Hold it out flat so Lady Blanche can jump!"

A wail of joy replaced the earlier cries of distress as several people at once grasped Dillian's idea. When the lady next appeared in the upper-story window, they had the sturdy blanket spread between the fingers of a dozen servants yelling, "Jump!"

Dillian's stomach knotted in fear as Lady Blanche hesitated. She knew fire had already destroyed the old wooden stairs. It charred all the downstairs windows and worked its way through the centuries-old floorboards. Only Blanche's quickness had seen the household roused and sent to safety, but she hadn't been quick enough to save herself. Blanche had always been too good for this world, seeing to others before she saw to herself. Selfishness was not a concept Blanche understood. Sometimes, it made Dillian want to scream. Right now she could scale that wall and wring her cousin's neck.

"Jump, Blanche! Now!" she shouted over the roar of fire and hysteria.

For a brief instant through the swirl of smoke, Dillian saw Blanche turn her despairing eyes in her direction. Then the wind caught the flame and sent it flying upward.

Screams pierced the night air as the figure in long blond tresses disappeared behind the inferno.

The flaming figure leaping from the upper window was barely recognizable when it finally soared through the air in the direction of the tightly held blanket.

Tears rolled down the cheeks of the liveried footman as he hastily wound the blanket around flaming night-clothes to smother them. Auburn hair gleaming like the fire behind him, he lifted his slender burden gently, and a path opened through the crowd.

Hysterical shrieks died to quiet sobs.

Refusing to resign herself to the inevitable, Dillian furiously fought her way through the crowd after him.

Blanche couldn't die. She would slit her own throat and stake herself in a lion's den before she would let Blanche die.

And if Dillian discovered Neville responsible for that fire, she would throw the grand and glorious young duke into the lion's mouth ahead of her.

Clinging to the rear postilion of the gleaming black barouche, Dillian shivered in equal parts fear and cold as the vehicle swayed through the darkness concealing the rutted, overgrown drive. Taking a curve at a reckless rate, the carriage tilted precariously, and she grasped the rail in white-knuckled terror, not seeing the edifice looming ahead until the carriage rumbled straight for it.

Violet eyes widened in disbelief at the gothic monstrosity silhouetted against the starlit sky, like some fable from a storybook. Nothing else was visible. Not a single light glowed in the whole of that black sprawling monolith. Where in the devil was the madman taking them?

Already so terrified she could scarcely unbend her fingers from the rail, Dillian watched in horror as the carriage rolled to a stop at this improbable destination. As the driver leapt down and pounded on a massive oak door, she hurriedly glanced around for a hiding place. She found no lack of concealment in the rambling thorns and untrimmed shrubbery at the base of the mansion. She had only to concern herself with keeping her gown from being torn from her back.

The gown was the last of her worries as she pried her fingers free and darted into the bushes. The worst of her fear centered on the helpless occupant of the carriage. She need only focus on Blanche and all else seemed trivial.

The insistent shouts and knocks of the carriage driver on the massive doors of the manor brought a creaking groan of aging wood. Beyond terror now, Dillian watched in astonishment as a tall lean figure appeared in the opening, the folds of his cloak flapping slightly in the cold spring wind as he listened to the driver's hushed arguments. Not until this grim specter loped down the stone stairs to remove Blanche from the carriage did Dillian realize her peril.

As the black creature carried Blanche through the gaping maw of this gothic cavern, Dillian realized she would have to enter after him.

The eighth Marquess of Effingham didn't notice the slight shadow slipping in behind him as he carried his sleeping burden into the manor. One more shadow among many didn't disturb him. He'd lived with shadows long enough to welcome their privacy.

He cursed under his breath as the doddering clock on the landing struck eleven chimes and one expiring whistle. He cursed the clock, cursed the purloined coach, cursed its driver who now raced up the dust-coated stairway ahead of him. He cursed the stairs as he climbed them carrying the helpless bundle in his arms. He cursed the generations of Effinghams who had sunk all their spare capital into expanding this hideous architecture into a gothic village one needed a horse and carriage to traverse.

He hadn't begun to exhaust his extensive repertoire of curses when he saw Michael disappear down the entire length of the hallway and enter the farthest room. At times like these he suspected Michael of seeking subtle revenge for the differences in their heritages, but he knew Michael too well to believe that for long. His appearance here now with this unconscious woman meant he'd embarked on another of his harebrained adventures. Were it not for the fact that his brother had a heart wider than his chest, the marquess would have turned around and gone back to the carriage. He and Michael had been through too much together, however, for Gavin to disregard his brother's summons now.

Besides, Michael acted as Gavin's eyes and ears to the outside world, so the marquess indulged his idiosyncrasies. The old war wound in his side ached as he carried his light burden to the end of the hall. The woman wore a voluminous nightshift that trailed on the floor and a nightcap that left her long blond hair falling over his arm. In the furtive shadows of this unlit hallway, Gavin couldn't see more than that.

She stirred as he reached the room where Michael already knelt at the fireplace. Laying her down on one of the few whole mattresses left in the house, the marquess relinquished his burden and strode toward the window to pull back the draperies.

"Don't!" Michael warned, turning from his task. "Light might endanger her eyes. It's freezing in here. Where's the coal?"

Gavin swung around to confront the smaller man speaking so peremptorily. Dragged from his slumbers by Michael's knocks, he wore only the breeches and stockings he'd fallen asleep in. The cloak and hood he had pulled around him before answering the door served both as blanket for warmth and protection from prying eyes. In the darkness of the unlit room and the encompassing shadows of the hood, his eyes went unseen, but his voice was cold when he spoke.

"It's May. I haven't bought any. I wasn't precisely expecting guests."

"You have one now. I'll find some firewood."

Cloaked Gavin remained in the shadows as Michael departed, watching as the woman on the bed stirred. She would no doubt waken soon. He'd known Michael to go for firewood and disappear for weeks. The marquess wondered if it cost anything to commit a relative to Bedlam.

The soft moans from the bed tore at what remained of his softer insides, but he could do nothing. He didn't dare light a candle or lamp—even should he have one—to examine the extent of her injuries, for injured she must be for Michael to bring her here.

Gavin sighed with relief when he heard Michael's footsteps pounding down the hall. His bloody aristocratic stockinged toes had practically frozen to the floor while waiting. Gavin had half a mind to slip out through the secret passage and leave Michael to his patient, but then he might never get his questions answered.

Michael carried a candle and a coal scuttle filled with wood chips and kindling when he returned. Holding the candlestick high, he searched the darkened corners until he found his brother's frozen shadow. "Damn you, Gavin, she's waking. Get out here and make her comfortable."

"She's comfortable clinging to the ceiling and screaming?" Gavin asked dryly, not moving from his place in the shadows as Michael arranged his fuel in the fireplace.

Michael uttered a few pithy phrases of his own as he threw the cloaked marquess a glare. "Her eyes are bandaged. She can't see a thing. She may never see anything again. You'll just be a voice and hands to her. You needn't worry about your pretty phiz."

Perhaps one-tenth of Michael's tales contained some portion of truth. This particular tale had the sound of tawdry drama from beginning to end. Still, the fact remained that a real woman lay in that bed, apparently moaning in pain. Reluctantly, Gavin stepped forward to see to her comfort.

"Who in hell is she?" he muttered as Michael struggled with the fire. "And why the devil did you bring her here?"

The figure on the bed lay suddenly still. Gavin suspected she could hear him, and he cursed his uncouth tongue. He had lived too long from civilization.

"Her name's Blanche Perceval. She's an heiress. Someone set her house on fire. She made sure all the servants escaped, then found herself trapped. So she rescued her companion's life savings and flung it out the window for lack of anything better to do." Michael's tone didn't hold the same sarcasm as his words. "By the time the servants found a blanket for her to jump into . . ." He shrugged and turned away from the fireplace to watch the woman on the bed. "The surgeon says she's lucky to be alive. She's a heroine. I thought you'd appreciate the irony."

With small flames finally burning in the grate, Michael carried the candle to the bed. Its flickering light made a ghostly gleam across the figure on the sheets. For the first time, Gavin realized she wore bandages and not a nightcap. The linen covered her eyes, but not the raw burns on her cheeks. His fingers involuntarily traced the scars on his own jaw.

"She belongs in a hospital," he said curtly, turning away, leaving Michael to adjust the pillow beneath her singed hair and draw the sheets over her.

"I told you. Someone set her house on fire. I couldn't take any chances."

Gavin knew he didn't want to hear more. If it weren't for Michael, he'd lead a relatively peaceful existence in this decrepit hermitage he'd burrowed into. Michael, however, had never been one for staying quietly at home. He had always kept his brother on a permanent carriage ride to hell with a lunatic for driver. Not for the first time, Gavin considered exiling his younger brother to one of their distant American relatives.

Not that any of those stuffy Puritans would take a man of twenty-six years who routinely masqueraded as anything from a gentleman's gentleman to a street magician. This time, he'd apparently taken on the role of footman, judging by the sooty livery. Gavin never knew what caused Michael to behave as he did. He just knew his brother operated under his own peculiar sense of morality, which had nothing to do with society's. Their relatives had disowned him at an early age, which had only reinforced Michael's tendencies to behave as if spawned by the devil.

But Gavin knew the man behind the deceptive facade. For that reason, he didn't throw his brother out now. Gavin had sheltered untold legions of Michael's homeless, maimed, and starving creatures before, but this was the first time in recent memory he had hauled home a grown female. Gavin had a niggling remembrance of a grimy waif brought home in the middle of a blizzard once. Unfortunately, Michael's propensity for rescuing the needy didn't differentiate between the honest and the villainous. Once the snow cleared, that same waif had disappeared with the last coins for their food. Gavin clung to his wariness now.

Suspecting the invalid feigned sleep, the marquess gave a jerk of his head and indicated the hallway. Michael obediently followed him out of the room.

"Are you telling me you brought her here to protect her from arsonists?" Gavin demanded, not concealing the incredulity in his voice.

"You'd rather I leave her to be murdered in her bed?"

"I'd rather you find somewhere else to take her! Bloody damn hell, Michael! What am I supposed to do with her? The servants think the place haunted as it is. That silly chit of a maid would take off screaming the first time the wind blew around the corner if I asked her to come up here."

"We can't tell the servants she's here. They'll spread it all over town, and the wrong person might hear it. You'll have to do it yourself, old chap. I've got to get that carriage to Dover or somewhere and lead them off the track."

Gavin swung around and paced the hall, cloak flying behind him as he flung his arms wide to emphasize his words. "You're a bloody lunatic, that's what you are! What in hell am I supposed to do with her? Send her shrieking into the night the moment she catches sight of me?"

Ignoring the Lawrence penchant for dramatics, Michael tilted his head to listen for any sounds from his patient. "You don't listen well, my noble lord," he answered dryly, once satisfied the woman in the other room still slept. "She's an heiress. She's most likely blind and probably more scarred than you. She's in desperate need of protection. What more can you ask? Protect her. Woo her. Earn her undying affection. Marry her, and save her and yourself. I expect you to speak politely to me for all the rest of our lives in return."

Michael's audacity shouldn't surprise him anymore, but Gavin still found himself caught off guard by his stupendous gall. His brother was quite capable of entering a hospital and kidnapping the poor woman in the mistaken assumption that what he wanted was right and therefore the rest of the world could go to hell.

"I suppose I can expect a Bow Street Runner and the militia on my doorstep by morning," Gavin replied gloomily, imagining the invasion of his privacy to come.

"Nary a bit." Michael produced a bottle of laudanum from his pocket and handed it over. "I took her out of the physician's house in his own carriage while the physician slept. No one had any reason to follow. He makes late house calls all the time. I just need to remove the carriage before anyone sees it. All you need do is hold down the fort a day or two while I'm gone."

The woman in the other room moaned softly. Michael instantly slipped from Gavin's grasp, disappearing into the bedchamber to look after his patient—or victim, whichever the case might be. Still fighting his temper,

Gavin slammed his fist into the wall, then in a swirl of his long cloak, stalked after his brother.

The bedchamber was empty of all but the restless invalid in white. Michael had disappeared.

Dillian cringed and clung to the wall as she heard the muffled roar of rage from the room where the monster had taken Blanche. A draft blew around her feet, and the old walls surrounding her creaked and groaned in the stillness. The rage in the next room, however, didn't frighten her so much as their circumstances.

She heard the sound of pounding feet outside her doorway. Stockinged feet, she'd noticed earlier. What manner of man or beast traversed these drafty halls in stockings? Or hooded cloaks, for all that mattered. Whoever had abducted Blanche had brought her to a lunatic asylum.

But the conversation she had overheard relieved some of her fears. She had feared one of Neville's men lay behind this abduction. Now all she need fear was a simpleton who thought a woman as wealthy as Blanche should feel grateful for the protection of a moldering ruin.

She had the oddest suspicion that this Michael had been one of Blanche's myriad footmen, but she had seldom given them much notice, and she hadn't seen him in a good light now. She'd heard the cloaked one leave, but she hadn't heard Michael depart. From the roar of rage, she suspected Michael had slipped out before the other finished ripping up at him.

She hesitated. She needed to see Blanche. But she didn't want the men knowing of her presence. If they were Neville's accomplices, Blanche could be in worse danger than before. Brushing disheveled curls from her face, Dillian rubbed her hands together for warmth. She wished she could just walk into Blanche's chamber and warm herself at the fire, but she'd learned patience and a cynical suspicion over these past few years. She had learned she had no physical strength or power with which to fight men. She had no wealth or fame. She had only her wits, and her wits told her the element of surprise was her best weapon right now. If they didn't know of her presence, she had some small advantage.

Listening carefully, she could hear no more sounds coming from the other room. She must take the chance. Blanche would be frightened by now. They needed to talk.

Cautiously, Dillian lingered in the shadows as she slipped into the hall. The fire threw a flickering light across the bare floors and wall. No shadow passed before it. No sound emanated from the chamber. Taking a deep breath, she entered.

Blanche was prying at the bandage over her eyes.

"Stop that!" Dillian hissed. "Do you want to ruin your eyes for certain?"

The figure in the bed turned quickly toward the sound of her voice. "Dillian! Thank heavens. Where am I?"

That was an excellent question, but Dillian couldn't answer it. In the dark, all country roads looked alike to her, and she couldn't read the signs while clinging in terror to the back of a carriage. She just knew it had taken hours at hair-raising speeds to get here. She didn't tell Blanche that.

"We'll figure that out later. I've only got a few minutes before one of them returns. I just wanted you to know I'm here. Make them go away, and then we can talk."

Even as she said it, they could hear the floor creak beneath approaching footsteps. The monster still hadn't donned his shoes.

"I'll be in the wardrobe," Dillian whispered. Without hesitation, she slid into the narrow musty darkness of old clothes. She left the door open just enough to hear.

"Stop that!" a male voice roared from the other side of the door.

Dillian stifled a grin. Blanche must have been fiddling with the bandages again.

"I brought you some water."

He didn't sound like a monster, more like an irritated male. She suspected men didn't much like being woken in the middle of the night to nurse invalids they didn't know. But this man lived in a moldering Gothic ruin and dressed like a madman. She wanted to know his story. Her imagination had already taken flight when Blanche's weak voice prosaically asked the question Dillian preferred making up answers to.

"Could you tell me who you are and where I am?" Blanche always spoke politely, even when frightened out of her wits. Dillian held her breath as her cousin continued, "Your accent is odd. Are you Canadian?"

The man didn't answer immediately. Dillian considered his hesitation suspicious. His reply didn't entirely relieve her.

"Close enough," he answered the last question first. "I'm Gavin Lawrence. The house's official name is Arinmede Manor. I'm more inclined to call it Arinmede Ruins."

The man's wry tone indicated a sense of humor, but Dillian wasn't in the mood for laughing. The description seemed apt enough from what little she had seen of the place. She wondered where the servants were. Surely, he didn't live alone in this sprawling monstrosity.

She listened to the battle of wills now taking place in the room beyond her hiding place. Blanche used her best little-girl voice trying to send her host away. Neville always fell for that childish tone of voice, until recently anyway. This man didn't seem impressed. Dillian gritted her teeth as he insisted on sleeping in the next chamber in the event that his "guest" needed him.

"Oh, no, sir! Not on my account, please," Blanche responded sweetly. "It would be highly improper, in any event. If you have a bell, I can just summon a maid if I need someone."

Blanche's innocent posturing had fooled many a male before, but Dillian didn't think it would work on a man bent on seducing an heiress. Of course, a man trying to do what was proper would be caught in another sort of bind. Blanche obviously could not attend herself. Just as obviously, she could not have a man as attendant. Dillian found herself listening with interest to how the monster would resolve that problem.

The growling answer emanating from beyond the door indicated he didn't resolve it willingly. "The bell pull rotted long ago. Just fling the water glass when you need someone. It's bound to hit something loud enough for me to hear. The maid is too far away, and Michael indicated some need for secrecy, so it seems you're stuck with me."

Dillian bit back a giggle at this highly original system of summoning help. She could imagine Mr. Gavin Lawrence wanting to strangle this man Michael right about now. She almost felt sorry for the poor misanthropic chap. Almost. The fact that Mr. Lawrence needed a wealthy wife and couldn't obtain one through normal means squelched any real sympathy. Remembering the rugged cloaked form carrying Blanche through endless corridors quenched any other thought of giggling.

"Will you send for my companion in the morning?" Blanche inquired hopefully. Dillian waited for the reply with interest.

Again, their host hesitated before replying. She didn't like it when he did that.

"I'll look into it," he answered slowly, "but if there's some danger, it might not be the wisest course."

"Dillian wouldn't hurt me!" Blanche replied indignantly.

"Someone could follow her," he pointed out implacably.

Even Blanche couldn't come up with a suitable reply to that. How did one say, "Open the wardrobe, and she'll appear" without causing no end of complications? They would come up with a better solution later. Right now Dillian wanted to find out more about the Lawrences of Arinmede Ruin.

Blanche and her host apparently reached some understanding with little more discussion. Dillian listened with relief as the man's footsteps disappeared from the room. She wished she'd dared peek at the monster, but the darkness was too complete.

She leaned against the back of the wardrobe to untangle herself from a moth-eaten shawl and a ball gown with a train apparently designed to be carried by a dozen pages. She couldn't believe women had trapped themselves in all that frippery in her mother's time.

Impatiently, she brushed it aside, but before she could reach for the wardrobe door, the panel behind her gave a lurch, and she nearly fell backward into a gaping black hole.

Stifling a gasp, she steadied herself by grabbing the ball gown, then gazed in amazement at the opening where the back of the wardrobe should have been. A strong draft already wrapped around her ankles. So that's where the mysterious Michael had disappeared.

"Dillian, are you in there?" Blanche called from the bed.

Unable to see anything but blackness, Dillian opened the wardrobe door. "I'm here. I think I just found a secret passage. I don't suppose he left a candle?"

"How should I know?" Blanche's irritated reply warned that pain had worn her patience thin. Dillian hopped down from the wardrobe and hurried to test her cousin's brow for fever.

"You're just a little warm. Drink some more water, then I think you'd best take more laudanum. There is no sense in suffering more than you must." She spoke gently, wishing she could take away the pain. A lot of people owed this slip of a girl their lives, but Blanche would never acknowledge it. So Dillian said her thanks without words.

"I suppose that means you'll have all the fun exploring secret passages and this rambling ruin while I lie here like an old grandmother," Blanche fretted. "Well, you had best locate a chamber pot or something before you go. Or take off this ridiculous bandage so I can look for myself."

Dillian caught her cousin's damaged hands before she could pry at the bandages anymore. "I think our host has some aversion to anyone seeing him. That bandage makes him feel safe with you. Leave it on for now, until I can scout things out a little more. Let me look for the chamber pot."

She couldn't find one in the washstand or under the bed. Cautiously, she checked the door in the west wall.

"Like in the *Beauty and the Beast* story?" Blanche asked with interest. "Perhaps he's a prince in disguise?"

"More likely a wolf in sheep's clothing," Dillian muttered, discovering a nearly bare sitting room behind this door. The owner certainly had spared the expense when he decorated this place. She crossed to the other side and a second closed door.

"Do you have any idea where we are?" Blanche asked as Dillian opened the door to let in the flickering firelight.

"Wherever it is, it's only a few hours from home. They have a water closet!" she announced with delight. "The place may be a ruin, but it's a modern one."

"He called it a manor, but it feels more like a castle. Castles have garderobes. Is there a moat?"

Dillian grimaced as she helped her cousin from the bed. "This is neither a fairy tale nor Sir Walter's medieval fantasies. It's a great sprawling lump of bad architecture and outlandish expense. I suspect this wing is relatively modern. I just can't figure out why a modern structure would have something so medieval as a secret passage."

Blanche apparently had time to think about it while she was in the water closet. When she came out, she announced with satisfaction, "So the lord of the manor could visit his mistress in secret. I read that in a Minerva novel once."

That sounded highly unlikely to Dillian, but she didn't argue. Despite her normally good nature and enormous energy, Blanche was tiring rapidly. She helped her cousin back to bed and tucked her in before pouring her more laudanum.

"I'll be right here while you go to sleep," she murmured as Blanche obediently drank the sleeping draft.

And right after Blanche went to sleep, Dillian amended silently, she fully intended to explore this odd household. First, she would find the monster's lair so she could avoid it in the future.

Then she would look for a weapon with which to protect Blanche. No matter how confident their thoughtful kidnapper sounded, Neville would find them within days.

She had every intention of being prepared for her cousin's would-be murderer this time.

Two

"**S**he what!"

The immaculately dressed young duke stared at the disheveled elderly physician with shock and fury. Behind him, an equally well-dressed man listened with impatience, exhibited by the tightening of his thin mouth.

"The young lady and her companion ran away, Your Grace," the physician insisted. "They took my carriage and disappeared during the night."

Removing his beaver hat, the duke ran his fingers through his neatly cut blond hair in a gesture of frustration and bewilderment. He glanced at his comrade as if expecting some explanation from him. At the older man's irritated expression, he hastily returned to interrogating the physician.

"You said she was seriously burned. You said she might be blind and could lose the use of her hands. A gently nurtured female does not take up carriage driving while blind and handicapped. What have you done with her?" Both fury and frustration underscored with worry choked the words nearly into incoherency.

The physician could add little more to his story despite all the young lord's rantings and ravings. By the time the two noblemen departed, the younger had reached a state well beyond coherency.

"There is nothing else you can do, Neville," the older man suggested. "If your cousin has chosen to run away rather than receive the treatment she ought, you owe her nothing else. If we don't return to London directly, we will miss the debate on that bill. Your vote is too important to neglect your duty."

"It wasn't Blanche. It had to be that blasted companion of hers. The wench is too sly by far. She's a scheming baggage if I ever saw one. I should never have let Blanche hire her. What in Hades does she think she's doing by stealing Blanche? What can she possibly gain?"

He'd finally caught the older man's interest. He looked thoughtful as he replied, "Money? Perhaps the lady's companion sees your upcoming nuptials as a threat and seeks to gain sufficient income so she need not worry about her position any longer."

Neville didn't look placated. "Miss Reynolds is too cunning for something so simple as that. She has convinced Blanche to put off our announcement for months. She has something planned. She is behind this. I'll set Bow Street on her."

The young duke looked up with an air of decision only to find himself suddenly confronted with a slight auburn-haired man in a rather eccentric pink waistcoat and gray frock coat. The duke tried walking around this apparition, but the man swept off his tall beaver hat and made a polite bow.

"Michael O'Toole at your service, Your Grace. Might I suggest we walk along to your carriage as we talk so as not to attract attention?" Boldly, the eccentric apparition caught the young duke's elbow and steered him down the narrow village street in the direction of the carriage waiting at the bottom of the hill.

Neville jerked his arm away. "You may not suggest anything. Remove yourself before I whistle up my servants."

The tall hat returned to cover auburn curls gleaming in the sunshine. O'Toole didn't look in the least concerned by the threat. "Bow Street is good for locating stolen goods and known thieves," he informed the air at large. "They have their sources in all the dens of iniquity in the city. They are of little use out here in the countryside, and you can be certain the Lady Blanche did not run to a den of iniquity."

The young duke scowled. "How did you know about my cousin?"

The dapper O'Toole shrugged. "The carriage was last seen heading south on the main highway about nine of last evening. I have men checking the way stations now. I am extremely good at what I do. The origins of that fire were suspicious, you know."

Neville clenched his fingers and stopped before they reached the carriage. The older man beside him presented an expressionless visage as he stared at the intruder.

"If you know that, then you know the magistrate is a sapsculled idiot who thinks an unhappy employee set it. Blanche's servants are never unhappy. The house was nearly two centuries old. It was a firetrap."

"The magistrate arrived in time to observe that the fire came out all the downstairs windows before moving up. A fire started in one place goes directly up before spreading out. I have enough experience to have observed that on any number of occasions myself. That fire must have started in several downstairs locations at once to spread in that manner."

Neville stared over O'Toole's shoulder at the narrow village town houses leaning up against one another. Had Blanche's house not been separated from the village by a narrow park, the whole town could have gone up in flames. He gritted his teeth and returned his glare to the man whose face now disappeared in shadow beneath the wide brim of his hat.

"What in hell kind of business are you in that you have such wide experience with fires?"

"Military, Your Grace," O'Toole answered snappily. "Until the end of the late war, I was an officer on the Continent as well as the Americas. You have heard, of course, of how we burned the capital of that country to the ground? I learned a great deal from that event which I found useful when Napoleon came out of hiding later. But that is not my specialty."

"I suppose your specialty is finding runaway heiresses?" Neville asked snidely.

O'Toole shrugged. "I would not say offhand that she ran away. She could have been stolen. As injured as she was, I would say that the most likely answer. My specialty is finding people who are considered unreachable."

Neville strode impatiently toward the carriage again. "That is faradiddle. The military does not run a lost and found."

O'Toole made a polite cough as he unhurriedly kept up with the duke's longer strides. "I did not say people who are lost. I said people who are considered unreachable."

The duke stopped and stared. Growing impatient, his older companion continued on down the hill to yell at the coach driver.

"You're saying you were a spy. Do you have references?"

O'Toole gave a deprecating smile. "I could give the name of my commanding officer, but he only handed me my orders. You don't really think anyone in the ministry would willingly admit to my existence, would you? You need only pay my daily expenses if I fail. Such a sum is trifling if I have a chance of succeeding, and I can assure you, I have a very good chance of succeeding. I have already told you more than you knew before." O'Toole removed a card from a gold carrying case and handed it over.

At this point Neville was prepared to pay the devil himself if he offered to find Blanche. He glanced at the card, scowled at the Mayfair address, and reached for his purse. "How could a scoundrel like you have a nobleman's address?"

O'Toole turned his face up to the sun and smiled. "I live a charmed life, I suppose."

Neville didn't have time to ask more. The damned earl had set the coach in motion. He had to get back to London. With an air of resignation, he handed over a hundred-pound note. "This should be sufficient to set the entire countryside on fire. I want her found, do you understand me? If you don't, I'll have your head on a platter. If you do, I'll see you amply rewarded."

O'Toole whistled as he tucked the note into his pocket and watched the duke hurry down the hill toward the waiting carriage. A hundred pounds was a hundred pounds. The duke could spare it. He knew others who could use it more.

Smiling cheerfully, Michael strolled back up the hill in the direction of the now cold ashes of a once lovely Elizabethan cottage.

Exhaustion finally overcoming her need for exploring their new circumstances further, Dillian slipped back through the secret passage to check on Blanche. She tripped on a misplaced piece of lumber and caught herself on the filthy wall, cursing lightly under her breath. She wouldn't remain a secret for long if she kept this up.

A distant female squeal made her grimace. Someone had heard her. Now they would send a squadron of servants to flush her out.

Quickly dashing to the end of the passage, she listened at the wardrobe door. Hearing only Blanche's rustlings, she stepped into the early morning light. Apparently, gathering an army of servants took a while. She heard none rushing up the stairs. She found Blanche sitting up in bed, her singed hair tumbling across a wealth of pillows.

"I must look for a place to sleep," Dillian whispered. "I don't know when I can get back to you, but I won't be far. Just scream if you really need me."

It made her heart ache watching Blanche's proud head nod sadly, but she could do nothing about their predicament now. Blanche had more courage than ten people. She would hold up for a few hours more. Carefully examining the burns on Blanche's palms, applying the unguent Michael had apparently stolen, Dillian did all she could to make Blanche comfortable before leaving. Then slipping into the hall, she headed for the servants' stairs to the upper stories before the hounds could catch her.

On second thought she needed food to fortify her for the day ahead. Instead of taking the stairs up, she hurried down them. She'd already discovered from the layers of dust that no one used these back stairs. If they sent an army looking for her, they'd have to climb up stairs wider than these. She hadn't grown up in a military family without learning the meaning of outflanking the enemy.

She heard two women murmuring to each other in the

kitchen but no more shrieks of alarm. She had located the pantries and cellars earlier. Dillian knew how to reach them without walking into enemy territory.

Capturing one of the pastries that she hadn't seen in the prior night's darkness, she almost made it back to the stairs when she heard the sound of someone coming down the passage. Obviously not their host, she thought dryly as she slipped into the dumbwaiter and pulled the door. This intruder wore shoes.

"Ach, no, child, ye'll not find one to deliver it here. The cowardly lot of them would see us starve first. Now, go and ask Mac to go down to the village for ye. I've not heard of one objecting to taking the master's money yet."

Dillian's sleepiness faded beneath this more interesting topic. She listened eagerly as the voices drew closer.

"I heard the lady walking last night," a faint voice whispered. "They say she walks before disaster strikes. Perhaps we'd best do like the others and leave this place."

The voice of the older woman scoffed. "And where would ye go, then? Enough with the foolishness, child. Leave the ghosties to theirselves and go about yer business. The master doesna' ask ye to go about where ye dinna want, does he, now? My lady says he is a good man, and I've seen nought to say otherwise. It's a good position, and ye're lucky to have it. Now, go away with ye."

Dillian held her breath as the steps came closer. She had thought the dumbwaiter unused, but perhaps the master even now waited in the deserted dining hall for his breakfast. Remembering the mess in the formal dining room, she shook her head. No one in their right mind would eat there.

The steps passed on by. Dillian settled down to eat her pastry as she heard the sound of the "master's" voice rumbling through the wall on her other side. The monster kept early hours.

"My lord, ye should have knocked me up if ye wanted something to help tide ye over the night. It's my duty

to see that ye're proper fed," the cook remonstrated as
she set out platters of eggs and toast on the billiard
table that had been converted to breakfast table with
the simple expedient of throwing some boards and a
cloth over it. He'd sold the Queen Anne breakfast table
long ago, but the billiard table had warped to worth-
lessness for its original purpose.

At the cook's words Gavin turned his gaze with apparent interest to the crack sifting plaster dust over the
linen, hiding his laughter at the British expression that
would have had his American friends howling. Considering the cook was fifty if she was a day, and round as she
was tall, knocking her up in the American way would
have been extremely difficult, if not outright unnatural.
Besides, he would never take advantage of a woman so
blind she couldn't see his face. He grimaced at the image
that raised.

"I will remember that in the future, Matilda." Gavin
refrained from mentioning that he hadn't raided the larder. No doubt Michael had stolen a pasty before taking
the carriage out for its long ride.

"Young Janet said she heard the lady walking last
night. The lady always walks in time of trouble. Is there
aught I should be telling the others?" the old woman
asked wisely, her eyes narrowing with concern.

Startled, Gavin brought his gaze back down from the
ceiling. "The lady?"

Blind to the falling plaster, Matilda stepped back from
the table and wrapped her plump hands in her apron.
"The ghost of the fifth marquess's wife, my lord. She
died in the master chamber, before the sixth marquess
added those new rooms. She only haunts the old part, I
understand. They say she walked the nights the seventh
marquess suffered with the toothache that killed him."

Gavin glanced suspiciously at the wall, which sounded
as if it had emitted a muffled giggle. He must see about
getting another cat if the rats had entered this far into
the house. Returning his attention to the subject his
cook had introduced, he rather suspected if any ghost
walked these floors, it was the last marquess. In the year
since his arrival, he had found his female cousin and her

mother, the marchioness. He felt sympathy for the seventh marquess's young widow and daughter, but any man who would die of an abscess rather than have a tooth drawn deserved his fate. He didn't mention his opinion to the loyal cook. Matilda still considered the marchioness the lady of the house, and he was more than grateful for the lady's influence in persuading her personal chefs back to this rotting mansion. He didn't much care about dust and disorder, but he had gone hungry too many times in his life to like doing so again. He saw nothing extraordinary in employing both cook and pastry chef since both were willing to work in this reportedly haunted mansion when others would not.

"I'll look into the matter, Matilda. No doubt one of the sashes has come loose up there. I'll not have Janet's sleep disturbed again. She has trouble rising as it is."

Matilda snorted in mixed reproof and agreement. When she left, Gavin gazed at his breakfast with less than interest. How could he transport it upstairs to the invalid without inviting all sorts of interesting questions? His conversation with Matilda made it evident that the servants knew everything that went on in this house even when they slept.

Maybe he should encourage their fear of "the lady." Of a certainty that would keep them out of the upper story. They seldom strayed up there as it was since he didn't use those rooms. Janet had all she could do to keep the library, study, and billiard room clean. He could sleep on his couch in the study as well as anywhere, and he certainly had no need for salons and drawing rooms. He didn't employ but Janet, the maid, and a man of all trades, in any event—outside the eccentricity of employing both a cook and a pastry chef. Janet and Mac weren't likely to go exploring of their own account. They didn't even like entering the front rooms when he was about.

He found it hard to believe that his wanderings during the night had awakened his lazy staff, but he would be more careful. And he would find a cat to chase any noise-making rats from the walls.

Deciding he was master of this household and could

do anything he liked, Gavin lifted a tarnished silver tray from the liquor cabinet, which served as sideboard, and slid his morning fare onto it. The invalid should be ready for some company about now.

When he stopped in his study to put on what remained of his shoes, he noticed the book on family history had moved from its usual place. He wouldn't have noticed such a small thing anywhere else in the house, but that particular moth-eaten volume rested on a high pedestal in a place of honor. Janet had removed the cobwebs at some point, but disregarded the dust that had gathered since. He hadn't complained of the neglect. Family history meant little to him under the circumstances. Apparently, it meant a little more to someone else. The dust had been disturbed, and he could see a clean square of wood where the book had originally rested. It had changed angles over night.

He narrowed his eyes with suspicion. He didn't believe in ghosts. He didn't believe "the lady" had chosen last night to walk and examine her ancestor's lineage. But he also found it difficult believing that a seriously burned and possibly blind invalid could find her way down here. That led one to question the extent of the "invalid's" actual injuries.

With less compassion than he'd originally intended, Gavin carried his breakfast tray up the stairs.

He found Miss Perceval sitting on the edge of the bed, fiddling with the bandage over her eyes again. He'd deliberately left off his shoes after his discovery. He had entered softly, but she looked up at him with expectation.

"Mr. Lawrence?" she asked eagerly, blindly turning her face from side to side in hopes of pinpointing his presence.

He didn't want to believe it an act. With the heavy draperies still drawn, the morning sun lent only a vague golden aura to the room. The filtered light enhanced the highlights of his patient's hair and made her slender figure in the bulky nightgown look very young and helpless. Maybe Michael had disturbed the volume for one of his many mysterious projects.

"I brought breakfast," he said gruffly. He wasn't accustomed to company and shied away from it at any cost. His social skills had never been of the best and had deteriorated to nothing of late.

"That's very kind of you, sir," she said uncertainly, finally focusing on his location by the sound of his voice. "Will you share it with me? It is rather lonely sitting here by myself."

She tried hiding the plaintive note but she was too young to do it well. Her social skills, however, possessed everything his did not. Gavin scowled and placed the tray on a table he drew up beside the bed. "You will find some difficulty managing cutlery with your palms like that. I ordered the eggs scrambled so you needn't cut them. Tell me what you would like on the toast."

"I can't see the cutlery to pick it up," she reminded him gently. "Perhaps if I tried taking the bandage off . . ."

"No!" He reached across the table and curled her fingers around a fork, then led her hand to the plate. "If the physician says your eyes must remain bandaged to prevent damage, then you must listen," he said with a little more politeness than his first shout.

"I think I would like a second opinion," she answered with irritation, carefully maneuvering the fork through the eggs. Blindly managing fork and food required a delicate sense of balance but she accomplished it. "I cannot see how these bandages accomplish anything except to conceal this place from me. Mayhap I have truly been stolen and hidden away, and you don't wish me to see your face to identify you."

Gavin certainly didn't wish her to see his face, but that wasn't the reason. He didn't even bother fingering the scars that ravaged his once handsome jaw and drew one corner of his mouth up in a permanent smile. He merely forked a mouthful of eggs from his plate and added jam to his toast. Once he swallowed the eggs, he'd found a reply. "As I told you last night, you're free to leave. But perhaps you could tell me your story before you do so. Michael thinks that you're in some danger. Why is that?"

Blanche shrugged and delicately clung to her bread. "I don't know this Michael. I cannot imagine what he is thinking. My house burned down and nearly took everyone in it. That is a very frightening event in itself. I would like assurance that my staff escaped safely. I must see that they have places to go, that they are not hungry in my absence. I cannot do that while trapped here."

That was an exceedingly mature viewpoint from one who couldn't possess more than eighteen or nineteen years, at his best guess. Gavin frowned some more, but she didn't flinch. He didn't know about her blindness, but her bandages obviously protected her from the sight of him. Since she couldn't see enough to fear him and apparently didn't have sense enough to understand the danger of residing secretly with a strange man without protection, he saw no purpose in frightening her with words.

"When Michael returns, I will send him out to check on your servants. Do you have a man of business who might see that they are paid?"

She hesitated, then stared down at her plate. "Only my cousin Neville's solicitor. He handles all my funds. Dillian always told me that was a mistake. Perhaps I should have listened." She looked up with an air of defiance. "But he always handled the family affairs. I cannot believe he would betray me, not anymore than I can believe Neville would."

Gavin found that an interesting starting point, but he didn't know if he ought to take advantage of it. He didn't want the chit harmed, but he didn't want to become permanently entangled in her affairs, either. He didn't possess the Good Samaritan instincts of his brother. He had enough problems of his own without looking for more.

"Perhaps if you could pen a short note, we could have it delivered without anyone knowing its source. Your solicitor would recognize your signature and obey your wishes?"

She thought about that. "I believe so. He's never refused anything I've asked of him." She lifted her damaged hands uncertainly. "I cannot say how recognizable my signature would be."

Gavin felt dubious, too, but he didn't mention his doubts out loud. It was the only solution that occurred at the moment. "I'll write the note that you dictate so all you need do is sign. Perhaps if I hold your hand lightly while you hold the pen, we can keep it legible enough."

He suspected she was giving him a skeptical look. Her reply confirmed it.

"I will make the note very brief, but I will write it myself. Will you bring me pen and paper?"

If he really meant her harm, he just wouldn't mail the note. Gavin didn't impart that bit of information as he trailed off, shoeless, in search of the required instruments.

The rustle of slippered feet on the old stairway behind him went unnoticed.

Three

After sleeping the better part of this second day away while the marquess of Arinmede Ruin reluctantly entertained Blanche, Dillian felt more equal to the task of keeping her protégée protected. At twenty-five, she considered herself firmly on the shelf, but Blanche deserved to have the entire world laid at her feet to pick and choose from. Dillian fully intended that she have those choices, Neville and his obstinate family notwithstanding.

Patting the cat the marquess had so thoughtfully provided to feed on his purported rats, she crept from the bed wearing the boy's shirt and breeches she had confiscated from an attic trunk. She would dearly like a glimpse of the man who hid in shadows, but she needed to avoid his notice more than satisfy her curiosity. Stifling her overactive imagination, she ran her fingers through her dark curls as a substitute for a comb and tiptoed downstairs to check on Blanche, before setting about finding food.

She had to fend for herself if she wanted to eat. Blanche had only hidden a few rolls and a chicken wing from the marquess's eagle eyes. Dillian no longer worried about that problem. If she had learned nothing else about this poor household, she had learned it contained a plentiful larder. The marquess might live in ruin and grime, but he didn't go hungry while doing so.

Snacking on a perfectly delicious meat pie, Dillian carefully navigated the back steps rather than the front ones near his lordship's study. She had discovered to her dismay that his lordship preferred sleeping on his couch rather than in a bed. She'd had to leave the family history volume rather hurriedly that first night.

But she'd learned enough from that brief foray to know Arinmede Ruin had housed generations of Lawrences, and the eldest sons were marquesses. Judging from the study littered with account books and tomes on modern farming, the hooded beast ran this place. She couldn't see the feckless carriage driver as a titled aristocrat, but the eccentric monster suited her fancy. Only they ought to call him the Beast of Effingham and not the marquess.

She carried the rest of her stolen food up to the third floor, where she had made a chamber for herself. She'd used Blanche's washstand for freshening herself. Now she decided to hunt for something more suitable to wear than the breeches she'd found in the trunk beside the bed. Clinging to the back of a carriage, collecting all the dust of the road, hadn't improved her only remaining gown. Deciding if the wardrobe in Blanche's chamber contained ball gowns, perhaps others contained something more sensible, she set out to explore.

Humming softly, Dillian ravaged one wardrobe after another, claiming a shawl here, an old-fashioned gown there, a petticoat elsewhere. She even found delicate silk stockings in the bottom drawer of a dresser in Blanche's room. Blanche really should have those, but she was doomed to wear nightclothes for a while longer yet. Perhaps this obviously bachelor household would eventually recognize that their patient needed clean clothing. She would remind Blanche to request some when she woke again.

Dillian felt much better once she discarded her improper attire for a gown, even if the clothing did come from a different century. She felt certain the gown must be French, from the Directoire period. The long tight sleeves were a bit of a nuisance, but the simple skirt with its slightly high waist felt familiar enough, and the light blue silk suited her, although the scooped neck did not. The gown sported a gold corded belt and a long fringed tassel hanging at the side. She wondered idly if she couldn't find sandals somewhere to match it. She felt like Marie Antoinette playing shepherdess. Or was that Josephine? Her history left something to be desired, but she knew good clothes when she saw them.

She slid her own dirty slippers on over the stockings and after stirring up the fire to keep Blanche warm, she slipped back into the hall. Blanche had told her about the note to her solicitor. Dillian feared that had not been a smart thing to do, but she understood her cousin's fear that the servants might come to harm otherwise. The village was a small one, after all. The parish couldn't support them for long. Still, she wished she could determine if the marquess had actually sent the note.

She also wished she had figured out some way of exploring the marquess's study while he went about his work during the day. Certainly, she couldn't go in there at night while he slept. That room must contain information about Effingham. She would like to find a few more secret passages.

Instead, she explored the library. Large gaps showed where someone had removed volumes and never returned them. At least in here, as in several of the downstairs rooms, the dust and grime had been eradicated and some semblance of normality restored. But, as in every other room she'd explored, this one, too, had the appearance of a room stripped of its valuables. Magnificent mahogany shelving and elaborately carved display cases sat empty of the generations of trinkets that should have adorned them. She was familiar enough with the houses of wealthy noblemen to know what belonged on their shelves.

She deduced that the marquess had systematically sold anything of value not entailed to the estate. She didn't like the sound of that. What was the current marquess's vice? Gambling? Women? Or just dereliction of duty and general incompetence? The only consolation she could find in the dismal state of affairs was that it had gone on much longer than any one man could have accomplished on his own.

She couldn't locate any more family histories or volumes of interest. The marquess apparently didn't use the library for anything but a financial resource. The only novel she could find had been printed in the late 1700s. The Effinghams weren't given much to fiction, it seemed.

Frustrated, she tried locating a panel that might lead to a secret passage into the study. If she could slip in and out during the day, she might learn a few things to help her current situation. A man as financially desperate as the marquess could very well be driven to kidnapping. Did kidnappers keep correspondence on their vile deeds? She really didn't want to move Blanche if they were truly safe, but she didn't feel particularly safe as yet.

Growing bored with her inability to discover anything, Dillian finally returned upstairs to her current means of entertaining herself. Blanche slept much of the time, and she didn't dare disturb her rest. But the blasted beast seldom ever slept. She found his attempts to chase the rats out of the walls amusing, but it didn't seem quite fair continually annoying the poor man. So far, he had done nothing but bark gruffly and keep Blanche comfortable. She owed him a debt for that. She leaned over and patted the cat following her about.

She still wondered about the story behind this crumbling manor and the villagers who wouldn't come near the place. She had counted only four servants maintaining this rambling monstrosity. She could understand why the owner stayed in the few rooms downstairs rather than seek comfort in the spacious chambers above. But she had time on her hands and an active mind that wouldn't let her sit idly. Whistling under her breath, she returned to the task she'd set herself.

"I tell ye, my lord, I heard her myself. The lady is walking again. Som'at's dreadful wrong. Could ye talk to her? Do ye think she's warnin' us?"

Sleepily, Gavin ran his hand through his tousled hair. It was a damn good thing he slept in his breeches, he concluded, or Matilda might have got the shock of her life. Maybe he could take to wearing nightshirts, and *he* could haunt these halls at night. A few glimpses of him at midnight should scare a few people into keeping to their rooms, where they belonged.

"I think we have a serious infestation of rats, is what I think," he growled to placate his cook. "If you'd not feed the wretched cat, he'd earn his keep around here. But I'll take a look around. Just go on back to your room. If the house is in imminent danger of caving in on itself, you're safe enough back there."

"Rats! I dinna allow rats in any house I live in, my lord. I know better than to leave food where those rascals will find it. Those dinna be rats walking up there."

Gavin left Matilda shaking her gray head and muttering while he took the stairs two at a time to the upper floor. The only rats he suspected were the two-legged kind. He still didn't want to believe Blanche anything but innocent. Perhaps Michael had come home without telling him. That was a hundred times more likely.

He saw nothing at the top of the stairs or down either hall, but the wings stretched into eternity and contained more doors to hide behind than he could check in one night. In stocking feet, he hurried down the east wing to Blanche's room. He found her sound asleep with the fire dying to embers. He stirred it and added more of the coal he'd ordered up from the village. She tossed restlessly on her pillow but didn't wake.

Annoyed, he wandered back to the hall and stood still for a minute, listening for whatever the servants heard. As a military man, he'd learned how to keep silent and observe the enemy. They hadn't taught him how to hunt ghosts, however. A cat meowed in the distance, and he felt some grim satisfaction in blaming the feline for his discomfort.

Feeling like an idiot standing here listening for something that didn't exist, he finally gave up and returned to the main portion of the house. A board creaked somewhere, and Gavin jerked around, trying to locate the sound. In a house like this, boards creaked all the time, but he couldn't help feeling jittery. If an arsonist meant to destroy Blanche Perceval, then he could very well have followed her here. This house might be an atrociously expensive ruin, but it was the only ruin he owned. He didn't mean to lose it.

Deciding the servants' stairs in the back deserved consideration if someone were sneaking about the place, he carried his candle in that direction. Another board creaked, and he hurried a little faster.

Thinking he heard a soft footstep in the chamber behind him, Gavin stopped and flashed the candle around. Cursing the darkness, the heavy draperies, and his decision to leave this chamber intact, bed hangings and all, he scoured the room before discovering the damned cat licking its paw in the corner. Cursing, he continued toward his original destination.

The servants' stairs leading up to the third floor were narrow, dark, and made of wood that creaked with every step he took. He didn't know how he could have imagined an arsonist sneaking up here. The man would be insane to even try. He started back down again.

At the sight of a suspicious light flickering on the downstairs landing, Gavin hastened his steps, nearly breaking his neck as he tripped on a loose board.

He could almost swear he heard a ghostly voice calling, "Careful now!"

Dillian sat cross-legged behind the wall, petting the cat and listening to the monster storm from room to room in search of rats or ghosts. She had disturbed his terribly light sleep three nights in a row now. She thought him most probably ready to strangle whatever he found. Or whomever.

The idea didn't disturb her too terribly. Dillian had led a boring life on the whole. Playing the ghost of Arinmede Ruin tickled her fancy. The boy's breeches and shirt allowed her freedom of movement. And she had to feed herself somehow. She didn't want Blanche giving up her nourishment to keep her from starving.

And her mischievous streak rather enjoyed the challenge of outwitting the Monster of Effingham.

Even in his stocking feet she could hear him creeping down the hall, intent on discovering her lair. She'd left a little surprise for him in the master chamber. She hoped he appreciated the sentiment. In the meantime, as much as she would like to see his face when he found it, she'd best remove herself from this passage. As long as there was any doubt as to Blanche's safety, she had to retain the element of surprise.

Gavin gave a vile curse as his lantern light caught on the perfect red rosebud set in a crystal vase beside the bed in the master chamber. He swung the light around to search the room's deep shadows for hidden prey. Instead, he discovered the furniture newly dusted and polished, the linen changed and fresh, and the rotting draperies torn from their rods to expose mullioned bay windows. He had no idea where "the lady" had hauled the material, for no evidence of it remained in here. For the first time since his arrival in this ruin, the master chamber appeared a welcome haven instead of a home for rats.

"Why roses?" he yelled in frustration at the hollow walls.

He thought he heard drifting laughter, but by now, his imagination could easily conjure up entire leagues of floating ladies in ghostly apparel.

Frustrated, disbelieving, Gavin knew the foolishness of following a phantom, but he refused to believe in ghosts. Hitting the panel hiding the secret door, he entered the dark passage beyond, immediately tripping over the abandoned draperies on the other side. His recently acquired cat purred and snaked around his ankles.

He didn't even bother cursing this time. He caught his candle before it fell and examined the pile of moldering velvet as the cat bolted back to the bedroom. No ghost had done this. He held the light up to the passage, but it didn't pierce the length of the long hall. Could Michael have returned and hid himself for some reason?

He dismissed that notion quickly. Michael wasn't inclined to dusting and polishing furniture. And if he stole draperies, he would do it for profit and not for aesthetic purposes. It had to be Blanche.

But every time he sought the invalid's room, she slept soundly with the laudanum. He had dressed the wounds on her hands and face, and knew their painful reality. He had caught glimpses of other, lesser burns, but she had modestly insisted on caring for those herself. Still,

he didn't think her capable of moving as swiftly and
silently as this intruder, even could she see. Gavin
wished Michael would get his scrawny ass back here so
they could send for a better physician than the local
quack. Someone needed to address the problem of the
lady's vision soon.

In the meantime he would tackle the dilemma of their
newly arrived ghost.

He slipped back to the hall, knowing the passage behind these walls came out in only one other place—
Blanche's bedroom. If the ghost hid in the walls, it could
only run one of two directions. It could slip past a sleeping Blanche easily enough, but it wouldn't slip by him.

Gavin carefully lit the lamps he'd set at intervals all
down the hall. He had the ghost trapped now.

Silence had never sounded so ominous. Dillian waited
behind the hidden panel. The monster usually stormed
into Blanche's room by now, certain the poor thing led
him a merry dance. She heard no sound of his approach.

Curiosity driving her more than sense, she slipped
through Blanche's darkened room and peered into the
hall, hoping to glimpse the monster marquess. All she
saw for her effort was a large cloak striding down the
hallway, lighting lamps. Other than noting his height and
the overlong length of black curls, she could discern
nothing abnormal. Muffling a giggle, Dillian slipped back
to the secret passage. She had feared he might get clever
and set a trap. Well, she had prepared for that
eventuality.

Swinging the small lamp she had confiscated from the
lower floor, she cautiously crept down the secret passage
toward the master chamber. Those old draperies would
make an excellent bed. She need only outwait him. She
hoped he hadn't found her bowl of soup. He really did
have the best cooks she'd ever encountered.

Gavin woke to someone kicking the soles of his feet.
Growling as he stretched aching limbs, he grudgingly
opened his eyes to discover he slept in the upper hall
with only his cloak for a blanket.

"You needn't take your guard duty quite so personally," a voice said reflectively above him. "You could have slept in the bed in the next room. Or had you meant to present Sleeping Beauty with that rose as soon as she woke? I hadn't thought you so romantic."

Gavin scowled at the perfect red rosebud between his fingers. The damned little witch! He would catch her one of these days, and then there would be hell to pay. His hand instinctively checked the hood of the cloak he'd used for warmth. He felt an odd relief that it remained in place. Realizing that he'd feared scaring a ghost, he gave a mental curse.

He glanced at the lamps burning their last oil up and down the hall. He'd wasted all that for nothing. Maybe he should just give up the chase and let the witch wander as she would.

"Your confounded invalid walks in her sleep," he grunted, pulling himself to his feet. The old wound in his side made him wince, but he kept his face turned away, as was his habit in any case.

"So you thought you'd light her way?" Michael asked quizzically. "That's an odd approach. Does she walk in the gardens, too? You must have amazing healing powers."

Gavin shoved the rose in his pocket at his brother's glance. "Never mind. Where the hell have you been? It doesn't take this long traveling to Dover and back. We need a decent physician to look at the lady's eyes. And she's worried about her servants. She wants to send her solicitor a note. Since you haven't seen fit to tell me who you suspect, I didn't dare send the note she wrote."

Michael shrugged. "I delivered one for her. The solicitor has sent the lady's servants to one of her other homes to air it out and make it comfortable for her return. Why don't you take her the rose? She can smell it, at least. You'll need to hurry with the wooing. The duke is half frantic and prepared to take all of England apart. He'll start on the Continent next since I've told him I found the carriage in Dover, and I'm currently supposed to be checking ship bookings."

"Damn you, Michael! I don't need any damned dukes

breathing down my neck! If the lady is in some danger, why don't you just call in the authorities?" Gavin didn't even question his brother's other statements. He knew Michael's devious methods too well. He didn't want to know which scheme his brother employed to delude the poor duke, or how he'd forged the lady's signature.

"Dukes *are* the authority around here. Neville's too involved in government to spend much time looking for a lost cousin on his own. He might spread his wealth around and hire another investigator or two besides me, but you can handle those pennyweights. Just concentrate on wooing the lady. In six months time she'll be rich as Croesus. You'll make her an excellent husband, far better than the arrogant duke."

Michael started drifting off in the direction of the stairs. Gavin caught his shoulder and shoved him up against the wall.

"Are you telling me that the lady really isn't in any danger except from an amorous cousin?"

"Someone burned the house down," Michael pointed out logically. "The duke is her only close relative. If she has a will, I'm certain their solicitor has appraised him of the contents. She has put off his requests for a decision on their marriage for over a year. The date when she comes into her own wealth is drawing closer. You may draw your own conclusions."

"I conclude this is all humbug to throw the heiress in my direction," Gavin announced stiffly. "Go find a physician for the lady. Once she can see again, her desire to remain under my protection will end quickly enough."

He strode off toward the master chamber, leaving Michael whistling, unperturbed, at the head of the stairs.

"Dillian, is that you?" Hearing someone enter, Blanche looked up from her listless contemplation of the square of yellow light that represented the window.

"Expecting that she-devil, are we?" The voice contained a mixture of laughter and annoyance.

Blanche strained to remember where she had heard that voice last, but her memories of this past week were so jumbled she couldn't place it. "Who are you?" she demanded sharply.

"Arrah, now, and here I thought you would be remembering the likes of Michael O'Toole after that delightful evening in the gardens of your grand house while we searched about for your little pussycat. I'm that hurt, I am."

"Michael O'Toole! What in the name of heaven are you doing here? How did you find me?" Worriedly, she asked, "Did Neville send you?"

"And you think I would have aught to do with a spalpeen like that? Faith, and you have little opinion of me. 'Twas me what brought you here, my lady. His Grace was that set on moving your lovely self to the Hall, and I thought as how you spoke so harshly of the place, that I would bring you here where you might reside in comfort instead."

"Comfort! O'Toole, you have maggots for brains. I have no maid. I've been deprived of my companion and kept in less than respectability by a strange man who is excessively reluctant to carry on a civil conversation. I want these infernal bandages off so I might write my solicitor with better instructions. I can do nothing but sit here and vegetate! This is your idea of comfort?" She was not one to normally berate her servants, but she remembered O'Toole quite clearly now. Insufferably obnoxious and ingratiatingly clever, he was also too damned good-looking for his own good. The maids had nearly swooned every time he turned that charming Irish smile on them. She couldn't imagine why she had hired him in the first place. In fact, she couldn't remember hiring him. He'd just appeared one day wearing her livery and helped chase her cat through the kitchen garden.

"The master of this household has waited upon you personally, my lady!" O'Toole replied in a voice of outrage. "He would have no one know of your whereabouts for fear others would do ye harm. The poor man is nearly white from lack of sleep, and him a lordly marquess and all. He is that worried about you. The poor man was by way of being smitten from the moment he set eyes on your fair face, my lady, and that's the truth of it."

"O'Toole, I am not a ninnyhammer to take your Spanish coin. Go spread it elsewhere."

"Yes, O'Toole, take your gaff and stuff it."

A coldly masculine voice intervened before Blanche could loose any further invectives at her footman's head. She recognized the tone of her warden, as she'd come to style him. He certainly didn't have the sound of an ardent suitor. "Wait!" she ordered before she could lose this one contact with the outside world. "What of my servants, O'Toole? Have they found places? Has my solicitor acted yet in their behalf?"

O'Toole's Irish brogue softened slightly as he replied, "That he has, my lady. They're airing out the Hampshire house for you, preparing for your return. I took the liberty of assuring them of your safety."

"Thank you," she said gravely. "Now, if you would be so good as to fetch my companion from wherever she is abiding and have my maid pack a trunk of clothes from Hampshire and send them to me, I will be most appreciative."

Blanche listened to the silence that fell after this command. She wondered how they would explain Dillian's disappearance. Dillian hadn't found any good way to announce her arrival. They couldn't know where to find her. Perhaps she could work something around O'Toole's visit. She grew exceedingly bored sitting here twiddling her thumbs while Dillian lurked in the walls and her host grudgingly read to her a few hours a day. O'Toole might call him a marquess, but he didn't behave like any nobleman she'd ever met.

"Yes, O'Toole," the supposed marquess responded gravely, "go fetch the lady's companion and her garments while you are also finding a good physician. And see that you return in good time for a change, no more gawking at maids or lifting an elbow at taverns."

Blanche wished she could see O'Toole's face at this command. She did not possess the boldness to speak her opinion of the man's excuses, but the marquess had nailed him quite succinctly. She waited for the glib reply, the laughing rejoinder, but she only heard a curt "Aye, aye, your lordship" and the sound of departing boots. He left her feeling rather bereft. The marquess might be all that was proper, but he was deadly dull also.

She heard the "thunk" of something hard hitting the table beside the chair where she sat.

"I've brought flowers, my lady. The day is warm, and they have a pretty smell. Shall I open the window for you?"

She almost laughed at his awkwardness. As daughter of a marquess, granddaughter of a duke, and an heiress in her own right, she was accustomed to a great deal of male flattery. Men bowed and kissed her hand and quoted passionate verses for her amusement. This man just thunked what was probably a pewter cup on the table and said the equivalent of "there you are."

"I would like that very much, my lord," she murmured politely. If nothing else, she was always polite. The fact that she wanted to scream and stamp her feet with frustration had nothing to do with anything.

She felt the warm spring breeze rush in as he pushed open the squeaking window. She longed to be outside, grubbing among her flower bulbs, playing with her kitten, laughing at Dillian's nonsense. She supposed she would never do those things again. Even if she were not blind, she must start facing facts. She was almost twenty-one years old and the possessor of a great fortune. She would have to marry and accept her responsibilities.

With wistfulness, she inquired, "Is the scar very bad?"

He hesitated before answering. He was the most cautious, irritating man she had ever met, but she waited patiently for his reply. She had little choice. She couldn't see the mirror herself.

"What scar?" he asked uncertainly.

That seemed an idiotic question, but she answered, "I can feel how it pulls at my skin. It must look terrible."

Gentle fingers traced the line of her jaw. "It seems a sin that anyone should wish harm to such beauty, my lady. I can tell very little of how it will look when it heals. Wounds such as these look far worse when fresh. I would not concern yourself about it unnecessarily. Even should a mark remain, your inner beauty would erase it."

Startled by the sudden switch from gruff bluntness to gentle flattery, Blanche didn't dismiss his remarks as she would have if O'Toole had made them. Remembering that Dillian had told her this man hid himself in darkness and behind cloaks, she thought she understood some of the depth of his feelings. Cautiously, she placed her fingers on his rough hand as he started to withdraw it.

"I thank you for taking me into your home despite your reluctance to do so. I hope someday I can reward you in kind."

He made a noise deep in his throat that may have been a grunt of approval or disbelief, she couldn't tell which. She didn't cling when he withdrew his hand.

"You can reward me now by calling off your witch. My servants are convinced she is the ghost that portends terrible consequences. I have no desire to lose my cook."

Blanche fought a smile at this abrupt change in mood. The Monster of Effingham had returned.

She couldn't betray Dillian. Dillian was the only weapon she possessed. But if the marquess already guessed that she existed, then she would be weapon for not much longer. Still, she would prefer talking it over with her cousin before revealing anything.

Rather than give the reply he sought, she merely answered, "Had I a witch of my own, sir, I would have her transform me into health again. Perhaps my presence is in some way disturbing your servants? Shall I come down and meet them? I cannot know how isolated we are out here. Would it not be safe just to meet a maid or your cook and reassure them?"

The marquess growled and slammed a hand against a paneled wall. She could hear the loud clap the sound made and shivered inwardly. Her host evidently was not a small man, nor a physically frail one. What in heavens name had O'Toole got her into?

"They gossip. All servants gossip. It will soon be out that we have a ghost. How long do you think it will take before your duke hears the rumors and wonders if the truth beneath them might relate to his missing cousin?

You and your witch have nothing to fear from me, but if O'Toole is correct, you have something to fear from the duke. I leave you to consider it, my lady."

Gavin didn't leave her to consider it long. By tomorrow morning, he fully intended to have all haunts trussed and bound and brought to rest if the lady didn't give him what he sought soon.

Four

Dillian carefully dusted the charming watercolor she'd found in the attic. She'd never had a house of her own to decorate or putter around in. She rather enjoyed applying her imaginative tastes on this lovely chamber. She particularly enjoyed knowing she drove the monster mad every time he discovered another adornment in the master bedroom he had never used. She hung the painting next to the vanity, in a white space where another painting must have hung. 'Twas a pity she couldn't find wallpaper or paint.

Carefully checking the dark expanse of hallway outside the master chamber, she slipped toward the servants' stairs. Blanche had fallen asleep hours ago. She couldn't find the monster anywhere. The game of hiding from him grew a little thin. Blanche was right. She would just have to appear on the doorstep and say O'Toole had sent her.

Unfortunately, unless she showed up in the bedraggled and filthy gown she'd worn while clinging to the carriage, she would have to appear in one of the unfashionable and outdated gowns from the attic wardrobes. Men might not know a great deal about ladies' attire, but even Effingham would suspect something if she arrived in that French gown with no carriage in sight.

Her mind nibbled at the puzzle as her feet found the places on the stairs that didn't creak. She'd worked out the progression over these last nights: first step to the right, second to the center edge, third to the inside left. She thought it much like learning a dance routine, but the next to last step was a little tricky. Her legs had some difficulty reaching from the right side of one tread to the far left side of the next.

She winced and grabbed the wall as her slippered foot slid on the tricky step. She froze, waiting for the monster's heavy footsteps to come running. He had not gone out once in all these nights but lay awake waiting to catch her. Didn't the man have any social life at all? What did he do for women? All men kept women in her experience, except for the ones who were a little strange. The Monster of Effingham might be odd, but she didn't think him the type to dislike female companionship.

Surprised when she heard no rush of running feet, she shrugged. Perhaps he'd finally given up the game. She meant no harm. Surely, he understood that by now. She'd tried showing him by decorating his chamber. Now he could sleep in comfort instead of on the narrow sofa in his study.

Not that he'd slept in the bed yet. If he had any brains at all, he should have known he would put an end to her best escape hatch by sleeping in the room where the secret passage ended. Perhaps he grew bored with the game also.

Deciding no one had heard her misstep, Dillian gently pushed open the door at the bottom of the staircase. Her tallow candle blew in the draft through this back hall, but it illuminated no hulking giant in the shadows.

That was an unfair description, she thought as she slipped down the hall in the direction of the kitchen. Effingham didn't really hulk. She winced at the grammatical sound of that but let her thoughts continue. The monster wandering these halls did it with a certain flair and elegance. She rather liked the swashbuckling sight of his cloak billowing out behind him as he raced down the stairs in an effort to cut her off. For a man so tall, he moved gracefully. She wished, just once, she could dance with a man like that.

Dillian blew out the candle as she stole through the kitchen doorway. The cook slept as lightly as her employer. She didn't wish to disturb her sleep any more than necessary. She just wanted to see what delicious fare she could scavenge from this night's dinner. She wondered idly if Blanche could steal this cook away should she ever return to her proper place.

"Aha! Caught you!"

A large shadow materialized from the hidden alcove behind the stove, directly in her path. Dillian gasped, dropped the candle, and fled down the corridor beside the pantry.

Gavin cursed as he ran down the corridor after her and saw nothing but closed doors. He stopped and listened, but he could only hear himself breathing. He'd been so damned close . . .

She was just a slip of a thing. She couldn't possibly outrun him. She had to be hiding behind one of these doors.

He opened the shutter of the lantern he carried and threw its beam into the first doorway on his right. A closet of cleaning equipment. He could see no possible hiding place in there. He crossed the hall and threw open the next door. An empty chamber, no doubt intended for some lower servant. The same with the next one. Cursing now, he continued down the hall. She had to be here somewhere.

Gavin swung around at a loud groan and creak behind him. What in hell?

He raced back the way he had just come, but he could find no source for the noise. He stared at the wall from which it emanated. The creak of ropes and pulley came from over his head now. That little witch!

Taking to his heels, he raced up the servants' stairs. He thought he knew this house inside and out, but he'd spent little time in the servants' quarters. He didn't know where she'd found the dumbwaiter, but he knew what one was and where it would go. This time, she couldn't escape.

The servants' stairs led to the main block of the old portion of the house. A maze of corridors led behind the walls of the salons and public rooms in this section. Ingeniously hidden doors opened into all the main rooms so the servants might come and go without guests seeing them in the public hall. Gavin knew exactly which door opened into the huge, drafty formal dining chamber.

He burst through and nearly fell over a broken chair laying carelessly in front of the never-used door. Even his cousin-in-law, the antique dealer, had given up any hope of selling the enormous and unwieldy furniture in here. Carved pediments representing dozens of Greek gods supported a massive table long enough to seat a starving army. From the scars in the old wood, a starving army must have dined off it without benefit of plates. Then they'd had a free-for-all with the heavily carved, hideously uncomfortable chairs. Gavin stumbled over another one on his way around the room, searching for the door leading to the dumbwaiter.

There had to be one. Food would have arrived icy cold if maids had carried it up the way he had just come. And he knew the sound of ropes and pulleys when he heard it.

He heard the sound now. Going down.

Damn! He didn't have a hope of getting back down there before her. He'd had little enough hope of reaching here in time. He'd just thought he could see which direction she took. She must have waited somewhere in between the floors to see where he went, then gone the opposite way.

Gavin didn't know why he bothered, but he slipped back down the stairs again. He didn't even know why he assumed the ghostly intruder was a she. From what little he had seen in the darkness, the apparition wore breeches. Idly, he wondered if Lady Blanche had a younger brother, but he couldn't remember mention of one.

To his surprise, he discovered his blood running with anticipation as he avoided the main corridor to the kitchen and took a back one he'd learned in his days of exploration. He thought it most likely years since he'd felt this kind of excitement. The only thing he could remember running close to it in recent memory was receiving the letter saying he'd inherited this estate. That excitement had worn off quickly once he'd figured out that an estate which couldn't send him the fare to England couldn't be much of an estate.

He'd probably find disappointment at the end of this adventure, too, but for the moment, he enjoyed the chase. Lurking in this great hulk of a palace bordered on tedious most of the time. He found some satisfaction in squeezing profit out of every little asset he possessed, but despite his circumstance, money had never been his driving force. He didn't have a driving force anymore. Chasing ghosts came as close to satisfaction as he'd found in some time.

That said volumes about his life, he supposed, but he set his lips in gratification as he saw candlelight dancing beneath the door ahead. He had counted on his ghost's penchant for good food.

With quiet care, Gavin locked the door to her escape hatch. Then, following the back corridor to the front of the house in his stocking feet, he waited at the only other route to the upper floor. Perhaps one of these days he'd brave the stares of the villagers and go in to be fitted for shoes, but in the meantime, saving his boots for outdoor wear made sneaking around easier. If his resident "ghost" tried the dumbwaiter trick again, he'd hear her. He thought her a little too clever to use the same trick twice.

When he saw her finally emerge from the same corridor he had taken, she moved warily, as very well she ought, Gavin thought grimly while keeping an eye on her progress. Wrapping his fingers around the rope tied to the door behind her, he lingered in the shadows behind the ridiculous suit of armor guarding the main hall to the public stairs. He thought he just might enjoy seeing if he could turn a ghost's hair white.

Holding the sandwich she had prepared hastily and not attempted to eat, Dillian crept down the towering enormous hall. She cursed the beast for locking the door on her. She should have stolen that key long ago, but it had never occurred to her that it could be used against her. She'd rather thought of the key as an escape for herself should anyone come chasing after her.

She hated this monstrous hall. Perhaps in daylight, when the sun came through the stained glass dome in the foyer, it might seem a friendlier place. At night, it rustled with shadows and tiny unseen creatures. Or it echoed menacingly empty, as it did now.

The silence didn't fool her. The creatures of the night knew when a human presence came among them. The monster waited out there somewhere. He'd come too close to give up easily. She contemplated finding a downstairs room and enjoying her meal until he went away, but it was late. She feared she might fall asleep before she knew it was safe to come out. She hadn't developed any warning signals down here to let her know when he approached as she had in the upper halls. She had to get upstairs to safety.

She couldn't see him anywhere. How could a man as tall as the marquess hide himself in that great expanse of empty space? The moon must be out. Light filtered into the foyer from the glass dome. She could see nothing but the silhouette of the grand staircase and the few tables that still graced the entryway. He must be waiting at the top of the stairs.

Stealthily, she stole toward the crossroads between the front entrance and the corridor to the side entrance. She could go outside and sleep in the barn. The spring night seemed sufficiently warm. And if he'd locked the side entrance, she could just slip into the library and find a place behind the curtains in one of the window seats. He couldn't search the entire downstairs for her. He'd grow tired of waiting after a while.

She'd almost made that choice when the door behind her slammed closed. The rat! He'd sneaked up behind her somehow.

Without another thought, Dillian took to her heels and flew down the front hall in the direction of the main stairs and safety.

And slammed directly into the broad chest of the towering form stepping out from behind the suit of armor. Her sandwich smashed between them.

"Gotcha!"

The voice boomed over her head as powerful arms wrapped around her back and dragged her up against an elegantly lean body. Dillian felt crushed, suffocated—

and something else she couldn't quite name as she realized for the first time in her life she stood in a man's strong embrace, her chest pressed against his.

Fighting the paralyzing effects of this imprisonment, she shouted, "Let me go, you big oaf!" She squirmed, dropping her sandwich to shove at the encompassing bars of her prison, but she might as well shove at stone walls. Her petite stature had never particularly concerned her before, but she felt dwarfed against this monster. She found her face buried against his shirt ruffles in distressing intimacy.

"Let you go?" he asked with some trace of gruff amusement. "So we could play this game another week? I think not."

He lifted her easily from the floor and hauled her in the direction of his study. Dillian squirmed some more, but it only made her appallingly aware of the differences between her body and his. Lord, but she'd never considered how hard a man's chest could be! Or thighs. Or all the places in between.

She froze as she realized the strangeness of some of the bulges pushing against her. As if recognizing the reason for her fear, her captor adjusted her easily to fit beneath one arm. Now she practically rode his hip. She tentatively pounded a fist against his back, but as she thought, it cost her more pain than him. He just dug his fingers in tighter.

Dillian closed her eyes in mortification as she realized how intimately he held her. She didn't open them again when he threw her onto the couch. She waited for the beast to light the lamp and expose her in boys' breeches and shirt. A hot flush spread across her cheeks before he could even see her.

To her surprise, the lamp didn't come on. She sensed his terrifying presence looming over her, preventing her escape. Cautiously, she opened her eyes and looked up. Cloaked shoulders blotted an enormous expanse of her vision, but she could see nothing of his face in the darkness. She realized he had his hands on his hips and his legs spread aggressively. She didn't like that stance at all.

"May I have the honor of an introduction?" he asked with sarcasm when she said nothing.

Dillian thought about it. She didn't know if he'd believe her if she told him the truth. It did seem a trifle ludicrous for a twenty-five year old staid lady's companion to hide in walls and steal food. He had only to light a lamp to see she wasn't a boy, if he hadn't surmised that already. Perhaps she could draw some sympathy if she gave some story about a nobleman enclosing her father's tenant lands . . .

Impatiently, he interrupted her creativity. "If you're going to lie, do it quickly. Otherwise, you're wasting your time. I can guess where you came from in any event. I'll just wait until the lady wakes to confirm it. Until then, I'm keeping you someplace safe. I have no intention of spending the next week setting more traps."

Dillian gasped as the marquess jerked her back to her feet by grasping the neck of her shirt and hauling her up. She swung her fists and kicked, but he seemed impervious to her blows. Fear finally crept over her. She didn't know this man. He could do anything he wanted to her and throw her bones out for the wolves if he wanted. Or just stash her corpse in the walls, for all anyone would know.

Blanche would know. Blanche could set the duke on him, but it would be far too late to save her by then. Dillian squealed as he dropped her into a new seat, this one a wing chair beside the fireplace.

"You have no right to treat me like this, you monster!" she protested, jumping to her feet as he moved away.

The cloaked marquess jerked something off the draperies and effortlessly pushed her back into the chair. "I believe the punishment for breaking and entering is transportation, at the very least. Since the Americans have very disobligingly refused to receive any more British riffraff, you may contemplate the climate of Australia for a while."

He jerked the drapery cords around her chest and arms, securing her firmly against the back of the chair. He worked methodically, and Dillian shivered again as his knuckles briefly brushed the side of her breast. She fought her terror with words. "This is ridiculous! You can't do this. I'm a lady. I have powerful connections. You can't treat me like a common thief."

"Oh? Who says?" The aggravating creature knotted the cord securely and wandered off in the direction of another window, apparently in search of further rope.

Now that he no longer stood near her, her terror dissipated, and Dillian wanted to scream with fury. He wasn't even listening. The beastly man had made up his mind and didn't have any intention of listening to reason. When he approached again, she kicked her foot furiously at his midsection.

The marquess merely caught her ankle and wrapped the silken cord around it. He didn't handle her roughly, just matter-of-factly. His hand was almost gentle as it held her still. No man had ever touched her leg like this. Dillian didn't like the sensation. She squirmed uneasily, trying to slip beneath the tie binding her. His grip tightened and rode a little higher on her leg.

"I wouldn't, if I were you," he informed her casually. "You don't have a chance. I'm prepared to be lenient at the moment, but not if you give me any more trouble."

"I was only protecting Blanche," she said sullenly as he kneeled on the floor and fastened her ankle to the chair leg. His proximity made her nerves crawl. Strangely, her leg felt cold when his grip loosened. She understood the indecency of breeches when she realized he knelt between her knees to tie her other ankle to the chair. She shivered with the raw vulnerability of this position.

He seemed carelessly unaware of his prisoner's tension until he had the last knot tied. When he raised his head to examine the adequacy of her binding, she felt him hesitate, and she gave thanks for the lack of illumination in here. She still couldn't see his face, so he couldn't see the fear in hers. The cord strained beneath her bosom as she tried slipping her arms out from under it. When his hand came down to rest on her thigh, she nearly leapt out of her skin.

Amusement tinged his voice as he used her leg as a

support for returning to his feet. "I think I like my women this way," he mused. "Shall I bind your mouth, too, so I can get some sleep?"

"Don't you dare," Dillian answered with venom. "I'm trying to tell you, you're making a mistake. I am not a thief."

"You're not a guest," he pointed out prosaically. "I didn't invite you. You've raided my larder every night this week. You've ruined my sleep, caused no end of havoc among the servants, and picked my flowers without permission. I think I deserve some recompense."

When he moved away, obviously intent on making himself comfortable on the couch, Dillian kicked at her leg bonds and struggled against the upper ones. "I cleaned your blamed bedroom, your royal lordship! What else did you want me to do? Scrub your kitchen? From the looks of the filth around here, I thought someone might appreciate my gesture. Obviously, you're the beast you seem and prefer the dirt of your lair."

He turned to glare at her for that. "I have reason for what I do. You are in no position to comment on it. Now, get some sleep. Morning will come soon enough."

She gave a scream of frustration when he settled himself on the couch, covering himself with the cloak. The scream didn't disturb his position in the least.

Refusing to give in, Dillian shifted her shoulders and started the process of releasing her arms.

Five

In the light of early morning, Gavin leaned against the staircase and stared at the locked study door across the hall. He'd left his prisoner sleeping with exhaustion, one arm free of the ropes but the other hopelessly knotted in place. She must have spent the better part of the night trying to free herself.

With the draperies drawn against the day, he hadn't seen a great deal of her when he left the study, but he'd seen enough to guess the rest. He'd known last night that she wasn't large but nicely curved. He could still feel the firmness of her thigh beneath his palm when he so foolishly used it for support. He preferred not remembering how long it had been since he'd touched a woman's thigh.

But his thoughts kept straying to chestnut curls falling across a creamy brow. Gavin's fingers stroked the mangled side of his face as he remembered the flawless perfection of her cheek. He'd sold all the ornamental mirrors in the house long ago, but he need only cast a brief glance in the shaving mirror in the mornings to remember how he looked, if he needed reminding.

Perhaps Michael had the right of it. Perhaps he should woo the damaged woman upstairs. Even should she see again, the Lady Blanche would find it more difficult to shrink from his scars when faced with her own. The lovely woman in the study would only shriek in horror if exposed to his disfigurement. It had happened once too many times in the past to doubt her reaction. Beautiful women in particular reacted unreasonably, and the woman in the study was a picture of loveliness.

She was also a clever, willful, deceitful little saucebox.

Gavin couldn't imagine what she was about hiding in his walls and driving him to madness. But he pretty well figured it had something to do with the Lady Blanche.

He could hear the chair in the other room topple with a thud. She must have woken while he lingered here. She would hurt herself if she kept it up. He had to go in there, confront her with her perfidies, and drag the truth out somehow. But going in there meant showing himself to her. He showed himself to very few people, for good reason. Only half-blind Matilda faced him willingly. And his cousins, but they were another lot of willful baggages. He couldn't expect the same from a stranger.

He could wear the cloak and hood, he supposed, but damn it, this was his house. He didn't feel inclined to go about in costume in his own home. He used the cloak for warmth rather than wear out his good coat, but the days grew increasingly warm. Meeting her in the garb of hooded beast didn't appeal. Gavin supposed listening to her shrieks of horror when she saw his uncovered visage would give him some perverse pleasure after she had spent so many nights frightening his servants.

With that malicious thought in mind, Gavin unlocked the study door and strode in.

She had both arms free and struggled with the ties at her ankle as she lay sprawled on the floor where the overturned chair had left her. The fall should have bruised her from head to toe and left her screaming bloody murder. Instead, she looked up as far as she could—about the height of his kneecap Gavin calculated—and began a stream of imaginative invectives that encapsulated his ancestors as a combination of vile insects and field rodents. He'd never heard anyone swear so inventively without using a single curse word.

He waited patiently until she ran out of adjectives, then grabbing the back of the chair, he said, "Hang on, I'm pulling it upright."

This time, she cursed bluntly, but she grabbed the chair arms as he tilted the chair. Gavin considered remaining behind her, where she couldn't see him. With all the heavy draperies drawn throughout the house, light seldom made much progress through these chambers. She could just avoid looking at him as the servants did. But his own perverseness made him cross the room and open the curtains even as she bent to untie her ankles.

"If you try running away, I'll catch you," he informed her calmly as the sunrise penetrated the room, sending its warmth over his face.

"I'm not running away. My feet are asleep. Have you gone up to see Blanche yet? She'll worry when I don't check on her."

Gavin turned with surprise at the tone of concern in her voice. He expected to find her still bent over her task, but she had turned her head to watch him with curiosity. He should have known. He winced inwardly, waiting for the automatic scream as full sight of him registered. Instead, his beautiful prisoner's eyes widened slightly, and she tilted her head, avoiding the shaft of sunlight hitting her full in the face so she could see him better.

"I had wondered, my lord. The way you skulk around, I'd expected a deformed beast. I'm disappointed. It's just rapier scars. Is there some significance to the design?"

The rotted drapery he clenched in his fist ripped from its moorings. Gavin swung around and jerked it viciously from the rod, flooding the room with morning light.

Behind him, a liltingly mischievous voice taunted, "Very good, my lord. Will you swing from the chandeliers next? Or have you sold them all?"

Gavin wanted to growl and jerk another drapery down. He considered flinging whatever came to hand to reduce her into quivering terror. He was perfectly capable of terrorizing her. He'd done it before. Even the servants stayed out of his way. All except Matilda, of course. But he had the unnerving feeling that he would have to actually physically molest this one before she would get the message.

Instead, Gavin swung around and gave her an evil smile. He knew it was an evil smile. The muscle on the scarred side of his face didn't work properly. It created a sardonic look that at best caused people to look away.

"Good morning to you, too," he replied in his most

unctuous tones. Maybe she would think he meant to eat her for breakfast.

She returned to untying her ankles. "I'm glad you think so. I'm starving. I suppose the rats made a feast of my dinner last night."

He had the infuriating urge to laugh. Even Michael couldn't make him laugh much anymore. It took a certain level of lightheartedness to truly relax and make the chest and throat open up enough to laugh. He used to do it. He couldn't precisely remember when he'd stopped. He didn't start now.

"No thanks to you, we don't have rats. I threw out that disgusting concoction before the maids found it. If you're truly concerned with Lady Blanche, you may breakfast with her while I decide what to do with you." He stood with his back to the window, diluting the effect of his appearance by casting it in shadow.

"No matter what you do or say, you won't force her to marry you, you know," she said conversationally, rubbing her ankles. "So if that's your plan, you may as well give up on it and let us go now."

An undertone of amusement laced his voice as he replied, "By all means, toddle on. This place isn't exactly equipped for guests, as you may have noticed."

Her head jerked up then, and he could see the flushed color of her cheeks beneath those brunette curls. Damn, but she had the most delicate nose he had ever seen, and sooty black lashes that curled nearly to her eyebrows. Gavin wanted to lick her and taste her and bite into her apple cheeks. That wasn't all he wanted to do. He grudgingly acknowledged the almost painful surge of lust in his loins. He remembered more precisely why he didn't keep company anymore. Only paid whores would allow him to do what he wanted to do with this female now, and he never paid for his women.

"Your hospitality has been enchanting so far," she answered with a heavy tone of irony that stirred his blood even more. "I particularly enjoyed the tied-to-a-chair bit. But now, if you will excuse me, I have need of freshening up. I'll be happy to join you in Blanche's room shortly."

Gavin watched with interest as she stood and nearly fell again. The damned woman had more courage than sense, he decided. She caught the chair arm and balanced there precariously while the blood rushed from her feet. It probably hurt like the devil, he surmised. He could carry her upstairs, but he wouldn't. He knew better than that.

"I'll tell Lady Blanche you're coming." Ignoring her predicament, he crossed the room and let himself out.

Dillian dropped back to the chair, cursing. She pulled an ankle onto her knee and massaged it, still cursing the filthy beast who'd left her here to suffer. She should walk out and disappear again just to spite him. She had the uneasy feeling he hoped she would.

She couldn't drive the image out of her mind of the proud marquess standing there in front of that window, displaying his ravaged face for her to see. He was tall, but not in the least bulky as she had expected. He wore only a loose shirt and trousers that defined his lean grace and aristocracy. The Marquess of Effingham had long, elegant bones that practically made her drool. The width of his shoulders filled his shirt comfortably, and she'd felt the strength of him the night before. This marquess knew the meaning of physical labor. He hadn't developed that physique by lurking in dark corners.

The unmarred side of his face had handsome deep-set eyes and an aristocratic nose almost too pretty for a man. His strong jaw and dark black eyebrows could intimidate even in repose. Even without the scars. The scars—well, a face like that would have driven women mad if seen in perfection. The scars added a character she wagered hadn't been there before. In his youth he'd probably been one of those handsome twits who thought their pretty looks should buy the world.

Of course, she wasn't too crazy about the character he'd developed now. Feeling her feet returning to normal, Dillian attempted standing again. If she meant to eat in company today, she would have to prepare herself accordingly. She'd be damned if she would wear these breeches to breakfast.

Half an hour later, gowned in her French creation, Dillian entered Blanche's room the proper way, through the doorway instead of the wardrobe. She couldn't do much with her hair without a bath and a maid—not that she could do much with it even then—so she had pulled it back from her face with a ribbon. Curls still bounced against her cheek, but they didn't fall in her eyes for a change.

Her gaze instantly swung to the tall man sitting quietly by the window. Blanche had drawn the draperies so she might see the light of morning through her bandages. The sun fell on the marquess's scarred visage, but Dillian noticed the dark defiance in his eyes more than the surface damage to his skin. She felt that look like a knife in the stomach. She couldn't tell if he wanted to murder her or do something else unspeakable, but it made her insides crazy.

Then his gaze fell to the long-sleeved, low-necked French gown, and his mouth twisted into a caricature of a smile. Dillian wished for a concealing shawl.

"Empress Josephine, I assume?" he asked caustically.

"I don't believe they called her empress during this period." Refusing to let him intimidate her, Dillian pulled the skirt of the gown out to examine it more closely in the morning light. "I don't think it's more than twenty or thirty years old."

"What? Are you wearing the French gown you told me about? Come here, let me feel it." Sitting in the chair on the other side of the window, Blanche reached her hand out in the direction of Dillian's voice. As she ran her fingers over the smooth silk, she said wistfully, "I wish I could see it on you. It feels lovely."

"I'm sure you'll see it shortly, after Michael returns with the physician. Suffice it to say that your companion looks quite exquisite in blue, although the neckline is a trifle daring for this hour."

Several things struck Dillian at once. The marquess had evidently figured out who she was, and Blanche had completely given her away by speaking of prior conversations. The uppermost thought, however, revolved around the tray of food on the table between Blanche and their host. She had never developed a lady's delicate appetite.

Since the room had no additional chair, Dillian helped herself to a muffin and perched on the edge of the bed. She wished for a good cup of tea, but the marquess evidently preferred coffee and hadn't bothered bringing up a cup for her. Daring him with a look to make an objection, she bit into the muffin.

"You don't mind about Dillian, do you?" Blanche asked him anxiously. "She's been afraid that you meant me harm, and she wanted to be free to help if necessary. I told her she was foolish, but . . ." She shrugged elegant shoulders wrapped in a shawl Dillian had found for her.

"Does she have another name besides Dillian?" the monster asked, as if Dillian weren't present at all. He buttered a roll and politely faced Blanche as if they sat properly at the dining table.

Too consumed with hunger to object, Dillian merely helped herself to some sausage, rolled it up in a piece of toast, and continued eating. She'd learned a great deal about eating without plates or cutlery this past week.

"I'm sorry. My manners have gone begging. Dillian Reynolds Whitnell, the Marquess of Effingham, Gavin Lawrence. Dillian is my c . . ."

Dillian reached over, knocked Blanche's hand as she reached for her cup, and helped herself to some jam. "Blanche's companion. Her father was in the military and spent a great deal of time from home. I'm rather a substitute mother." She cringed inwardly that Blanche had so carelessly revealed her full name, but the marquess seemed oblivious of the notoriety associated with "Whitnell."

Blanche took the hint and blithely continued, "My mother died when I was very young, and Father never took the time to seek another wife, much to the despair of his family, I believe. But I think of Dillian as the sister I never had. She's scarcely old enough to be my mother."

The marquess followed this conversation without expression, but Dillian could almost hear the wheels of his brain clicking. She considered most men mindlessly one-sided, but she had the nagging feeling that this one had a positive labyrinth for a brain.

But the conversation was quite innocent, and he couldn't make more of it than was there. As a good companion should, Dillian merely smiled and nodded polite agreement. The marquess immediately sent her a withering look. She continued smiling. He'd never really introduced himself as a marquess. She had assumed it from the family history, and Blanche said Michael had confirmed it, but for all they knew, this man had simply taken over an abandoned derelict of a mansion, hired an accomplice, and kidnapped an heiress. For all she knew, they could work for Neville. So she smiled and let him think what he would.

The monster listened politely to Blanche's chatter as the meal disappeared, but Dillian sensed his attention lagging. If he meant to woo an heiress, he had a lot to learn. She scarcely blinked when he spoke into a lull in the conversation.

"Perhaps I could persuade the two of you to explain why Michael feels it necessary to keep you hidden here? I understand there is some question of someone deliberately setting the fire, but I find difficulty in believing a young lady could have made enemies who would dare do such a thing. I think it's time we have a frank discussion."

Even though she couldn't see, Blanche turned to Dillian for help.

Dillian longed to hand the problem over to someone stronger, more experienced, and more powerful than she. She wasn't at all certain this reclusive monster fit the description. She liked what she saw in his face, but she couldn't trust her instincts. Neville had always seemed innocent enough also.

The silence grew embarrassingly longer. Effingham raised an eyebrow. Dillian clasped her fingers into her palms and stared down at them.

"We don't wish to slander an innocent man," she hedged, finally. "But the fire wasn't the first incident. It would seem far safer if Blanche disguised herself until she comes of age in a few months. Then she would have control of her own affairs, and there should be no further interference."

"I see." He glanced in Blanche's direction.

Dillian could see the path his thoughts had taken. With her face scarred by burns, her eyes wrapped in bandages, and with all that long blond hair, Blanche would be rather hard to disguise.

He cleared his throat without expressing his opinion out loud. Instead, he suggested carefully, "I cannot keep the two of you hidden from my servants much longer. I employ only four, but they move about in the village frequently. Everything that happens here is known in town within hours. You might find it safer staying in a much smaller place that can be guarded by professionals. Michael made mention of another estate. Could it offer adequate protection?"

Dillian tried to hide her surprise. She had assumed the man had fallen in with Michael's suggestion that he woo and win Blanche. The match was nearly irresistible on his part. He would have a wife who couldn't complain of his scarred visage, one who brought considerable wealth to salvage his obviously bankrupt estate, one with a title and background matching his own. Besides all that, Blanche had beauty and brains, even should the disfigurement of the burns not go entirely away. Any man would want her. This one wanted to send her away. It made no sense.

But Blanche responded eagerly. "I have my estate in Hampshire. There are others, but this one is close by. It belonged to my mother. It is small, but surrounded by good woods and a wall. The gate is seldom used, but I could have it staffed. Is that what you mean?"

The marquess frowned. "I would have to see it to know. Woods could conceal intruders. Even a good patrol couldn't find them at night. Perhaps when Michael returns, I could leave him here while I take a look at the place."

The door to the sitting room drifted open, revealing a slender, auburn-haired figure in shirtsleeves lounging against the frame.

"You plan on leaving me where? With all this loveliness?" He winked in Dillian's direction. "Hello, shedevil. Found you finally, did he?"

Six

Blanche heard O'Toole's voice, but the Irish accent had mysteriously changed. She frowned and remained silent while the others argued around her.

"I'm not inclined to address foul villains who abduct helpless women in the middle of the night." Dillian apparently ignored the intruder and spoke to the marquess. "I think it best if you escort the rogue from the room."

The marquess, as usual, had his own ideas and ignored Dillian's waspishness. "Where's the physician?" he asked O'Toole.

"I couldn't very well bring one here now, could I? Unless you wished to hold him captive, of course. While I find that a compelling notion, you tend to scowl when I use my own initiative in such a manner. I didn't want you frightening the ladies with your scowl, so I called on Cousin Marian."

"Marian! What in the name of the devil does Marian know about burns?"

"Nothing, nodcock, but she knows the best physicians in London. She's to ask them the best treatment for a maid who accidentally set fire to herself. We should hear from her shortly. Marian is the most efficient of creatures."

Blanche listened to the marquess grumble under his breath and felt a surge of irritation. They talked about her eyes while ignoring her presence. She wanted these bandages off. She wanted to know the extent of the damages now. While attempting to follow conversations through the medium of her other senses challenged her, she would much rather look the marquess in the face when he grumbled like that. She hadn't had an opportunity to talk to Dillian alone since the marquess had found her. She wanted to know what the man looked like.

"Couldn't I disguise myself as this Marian's maid and go with her to the physicians?" Blanche asked calmly. The notion seemed the most practical one to her.

O'Toole laughed. She wanted to fling something at him. He was a servant, for pity's sake. How dared he laugh at his betters?

"London physicians may be quacks, but they're not fools, my lady. One look at you, and they'll know you're no maid. And since the duke is tearing the country apart looking for his injured cousin, they'll surmise quickly enough who you are. The only reason I felt safe in asking Marian to do this much is because she and that hard-headed husband of hers seldom travel in ducal circles, although they could, should they so desire. She has never met Neville, although she's ready to take his spleen out at your command."

Blanche still didn't see why she couldn't disguise herself as a maid, but she didn't like causing harm to a lady so willing to help a stranger. O'Toole's attitude irked her, however, and she reprimanded him. "His Grace to you, O'Toole. Whatever suspicions you may harbor, you have no right speaking of your betters like that."

She heard O'Toole start to reply, but Dillian talked right over him. "Did you bring my lady's clothing? She cannot travel to Hampshire dressed in a nightgown."

"Hampshire?"

"You're not going to Hampshire yet!"

O'Toole and the marquess responded at the same time. Again, Blanche noticed, O'Toole gave the floor to the other speaker. She thought that extremely odd behavior for a smooth-tongued Irishman. But today, he didn't seem Irish. With a face and hair like his, he could scarcely be anything else. Of all the assorted strong characters in this room, his was the enigma. Yet he was only a footman. Or was he?

Blanche almost missed the marquess's response while she pondered the problem.

"There is no sense in traveling to Hampshire if the

estate can't be protected adequately. If someone is looking for you, they're bound to look for you there."

"I fail to see why we can't just stay here for the duration. Who in their right minds would come looking for us here?" Dillian spoke with irritation.

"I would much rather see that my servants and my home are safe," Blanche answered implacably. "I would not impose on Lord Effingham more than is necessary. We owe him a great debt as it is. I don't see why I couldn't arrive quietly at night and slip in the back way. No one would need know I'm there but the servants, and they're all loyal. I can't believe anyone would bother us so far out in the country."

Her calmness cast a pall over the angrier voices. O'Toole used the momentary silence to advantage.

"I fear you are wrong in that, my lady. Radicals are stirring unrest across the country, but I fear it is more than Radicals burning hayricks near your home. The surrounding countryside is in an uproar. They set fire to a neighboring barn last night. If someone means you harm, the atmosphere is perfect for it."

Even Dillian grew silent as she swallowed that, Blanche noticed. She had good reason. The estate in Hampshire rightfully belonged to Dillian as much as to her. They had their own reasons for keeping that quiet.

"Michael, you can stay here with the women. I'll go investigate. We can't expect Lady Blanche to live in this miserable hole until she comes of age. We have to get to the bottom of this."

"What do you intend to do, my lord?" Dillian asked scathingly. "Terrorize them into behaving?"

O'Toole answered for the marquess. "Gavin is a military hero of sorts. He'll make an army out of your servants, no doubt."

Dillian's reply was an exceedingly impolite and unladylike invective. The marquess made a similar comment as he pushed aside the table and evidently started toward the door. Knowing Dillian's thorough condemnation of anything military, Blanche sought some way of defusing the situation, but she didn't think fast enough.

Dillian called after the departing marquess. "I'm going with you!"

"I'll tie you to a chair first!" was his reply as he slammed the door after him.

Unable to see her cousin's face, Blanche could envision the frustration and fury on it now. Dillian not only despised military men, she didn't take well to threats. O'Toole's comment following the marquess's departure didn't surprise Blanche in the least.

"Here, let me throw it for you."

The unmistakable sound of a teacup smashing against the door followed.

Again, Michael's voice spoke casually, "It was an abominable piece of porcelain anyway. We wouldn't want Lady Blanche encountering such a monstrosity once her bandages are removed would we? There's no sense in keeping the saucer now that the cup's gone, you know."

A second angry shattering of fragile porcelain broke the quiet.

"I hate leaving you, Blanche, but I don't know what else to do." Garbed in breeches again, Dillian paced up and down the floor. The wretched O'Toole had brought only Blanche's gowns, none of which fit Dillian. She felt quite certain the aggravating footman had known of her presence, but he was more concerned with Blanche enticing the marquess than in seeing Dillian suitably dressed. It didn't matter. Once she returned to Hampshire, she could find her own garments.

"I agree with you completely, Dill. You have to go. If you could find some way of smuggling Verity back here, I would be eternally grateful, but your idea of pretending I'm in residence at the Grange is excellent. I just hope you won't endanger yourself in the process."

"I'll pretend Verity is spending night and day in the chamber, nursing you. She can walk to her mother's and have one of her family bring her here by wagon. I don't know how O'Toole will get her in here, but I'm sure he'll think of a way. Are you sure you're safe with him? I trust him even less than the beast."

Dillian watched her cousin with concern. She knew mentally Blanche denied the possibility of the fire having harmed her vision, but sometime, they must deal with it. The fact that Blanche could see light gave hope. Dillian felt a lump form in her throat at the thought of permanent damage. She knew personally how unfair life was, but she had hoped she could keep her cousin from that knowledge. Words like "virtuous" and "noble" sprang to mind whenever she thought of Blanche. So few people in this world could truly claim heroism. Blanche was one of them. She had to protect her cousin from her own innocence somehow. Leaving her in O'Toole's dubious care did not lend itself to her peace of mind.

Blanche tilted her head thoughtfully. "Did you not think O'Toole Irish?"

"I thought him a rogue and a rascal. That's close enough."

"He didn't speak like one earlier. He's much kinder than the marquess, actually." Her lips turned upward. "I particularly liked the smashing china. He seems to know you very well."

"Yes, well, anyone would want to smash china around a tyrant like that. I'm certain he's had plenty of experience in the matter. Just keep that knife I found under your pillow. I'll get Verity here as soon as possible. Are you certain there are no papers I need to send back with her?" She didn't want to add, "Just in case the Grange burns," but they both knew what she meant.

Blanche shook her head. "I've gone over it and over it in my head. Most of the papers are at Anglesey or with my solicitor. Your father's journals and things are in London. I keep nothing at the Grange. We've been fortunate."

Dillian didn't consider the loss of a house and serious injuries fortunate, but she held her tongue. Clasping her hand around the door latch, she cast one last look back at Blanche sitting in the dying sunlight of the window. She truly hated leaving her. But she didn't protect just the Hampshire property by leaving, she protected Blanche's life.

"Are you certain you can persuade him to take you?" Blanche asked anxiously.

"He won't have any alternative." With a determined set of her lips, Dillian slipped from the room.

The Marquess of Effingham really had no clue how persistent she could be when she applied her mind to it. He should have realized it by now, but men so easily gave into the prevailing belief of the helplessness of women. Often enough she cursed the celestial irony that had hidden the steel trap of her mind behind a small, soft body. But at times like this, the disguise gave her an advantage.

She slipped out the side door to the stable. Someone had saddled one of the ancient carriage horses. She wished whoever it was had harnessed it to the decrepit barouche, but the mighty military man evidently meant to make good time. That made her duty tougher, but not impossible.

She had reason to be grateful for the inferior quality of his stable a few minutes later. She couldn't have saddled anything more active than the other glue pot the marquess called a carriage horse. Feeding the animal a handful of oats from a sack, she kept it quiet at the sound of boots crunching in the gravel. At least he wore boots when he rode.

She would have to follow him fairly closely until she figured out where she was. She knew the area around the Grange, but the ride from Hertfordshire to Hampshire could take a couple of days on horseback, depending on weather and road conditions and just exactly where this crumbling manor was located. She didn't want to get lost before she even left the county.

She waited until she heard his horse walking down the drive. She wondered if the beast wore his cloak and hood in the warm May sun or just contented himself with scowling at the passersby to keep them from looking too closely. Personally, she thought his disfigurement more in his head than on his face, but her opinions didn't count.

Mounting her passive nag, Dillian cautiously rode it from the barn. She had never tried riding in breeches

and without a sidesaddle before. It made her oddly uncomfortable, but she wouldn't worry about it. She had
to find some way of following Effingham without his
knowing it.

She went over the wall and rode on the field side of
the trees, letting the marquess think himself alone on
the road. She didn't know what she would do when she
reached planted fields, but his estate seemed to lie
mostly fallow. She could see a few sheep in the distance,
but no tenant farms or tilled soil. She supposed he had
his reasons.

Dillian caught glimpses of him through the fence row.
He didn't wear a gentleman's long forked-tail riding coat
but what appeared to be an ankle-length canvas coat,
similar to a greatcoat without the layers of capes. She'd
never seen such an odd garment, but it would successfully keep the dust from the road off him. Instead of a
tall beaver hat, he wore a broad-brimmed slouch hat low
on his forehead. If he kept out of everyone's direct line
of sight, they wouldn't see much of his face. She would
expect such a strange outfit on someone like the mad
O'Toole, but not on the elegantly aristocratic Marquess
of Effingham. Obviously, he was a creature of many
disguises.

Of course, he would choose to ride at night. She
couldn't keep her horse in the field once it got dark. As
the sun gradually lowered in the sky. Dillian nervously
looked for some other alternative. Neither horse had
much inclination for friskiness. They made a steady,
even pace but nothing more. She could safely stay well
to the rear unless they came across a crossroads. If he
got too far ahead, she wouldn't know which route he
took.

Finding a gate, she waited until the marquess disappeared around a curve before leading her mount back
to the road. Trees on both sides of the road threw it
into premature darkness. That aided her cause, she supposed, but it also made her nervous. Visions of highwaymen, looters, and rioters immediately peopled her
imagination. The faceless murderer who had burned
Blanche's home came next.

She wished she had a better disguise of her own. Boys' breeches might confuse someone for a brief glance, but no more. She wasn't precisely built like a boy. She wore the bulkiest coat she could find in the wardrobes, but the outdated fashion and the bright blue silk gave even more cause to stare. She felt like a scarecrow. Perhaps *she* should have worn the cloak.

The moon had reached a high point in the sky when she saw the marquess finally take advantage of a small inn to stop and water his horse. Every bone in her body felt as if it had been taken apart and beaten and put back together crooked. She waited until he'd gone inside to refresh himself before climbing down and watering her horse at a stream behind the inn. She didn't dare go inside, although her stomach protested vehemently and her mouth felt like talcum powder. Instead, she tried stretching her stiff muscles.

The marquess appeared behind her as silently as any wraith, causing her to jump half a foot when he spoke.

"You'll have to be satisfied with ale. I couldn't ask for tea at this hour."

Dillian stared up at the shadow outlined against the trees. He towered over her by a head, easily. In that ridiculous coat he looked at least three feet across the shoulders. She gulped and hesitantly reached for the mug at the end of his outstretched arm.

"No excuses, I see," he said gruffly, pulling something wrapped in brown paper from his pocket. "I figured it was almost time for your midnight supper." He handed the greasy package over.

She smelled the delicious aroma of meat pie and unwrapped it gratefully. Holding it out to him first, she asked, "Have you eaten? Would you like some?"

"I've got one for later. I just wanted to make sure you were fed before I tied you to that tree." He nodded to the leafy willow behind her.

She froze in mid-bite. Fury clogged her throat, and she jerked the pie away, glaring at him through the murky darkness. "I'll kill you if you try. I swear I will. I'll come after you with a pistol if I have to, but I'll kill you."

"Nobody raised you to be a lady, did they?" he asked

casually. "How did you fool the very proper, very noble Lady Blanche into believing you'd make a suitable purring kitten?"

"She believes no such thing," Dillian spat out, shoving the package of pasty into her capacious pocket. "Blanche isn't a fool. Neither are you. You know perfectly well you can't ride up to the Grange and start ordering servants about without some authority. I'm that authority. I can hire the guards we need. I know who should be there and who shouldn't. You need me."

He drifted deeper into the shadows. "I don't need anyone. But if you want to wear yourself out pretending otherwise, fine. Just stay up with me so I needn't ride to your rescue if someone takes a liking to your pretty blue coat. I don't believe in heroics. I'll let them have the coat, and you, too, if it comes to that."

Oh, a fine gentleman he made, Dillian fumed as she remounted—without his assistance. she could well imagine he didn't believe in heroics. Of course he didn't think he needed anyone. The Beast of Arinmede Manor could scale the Tower of London and leap burning bridges if necessary for his own sake. He could no doubt terrify a household of servants into anything he desired. Why bother with guards and fences at all? Just set the Magnificent Marquess in the drive like a gargoyle and dare anyone to trespass.

She was in a towering rage by the time she rode up behind him. She wished she had kept the knife for herself. She could just imagine the pleasure of running it through his shoulder blades.

"I despise military men," she informed him coldly.

"Good." He rode on without looking at her.

"I suppose it was a Canadian regiment. The Canadians were useless in the war with the states."

"Granted."

She glared at him. "The Americans didn't even have a decent army or navy, and they defeated what Wellington so rashly calls the finest forces in the world."

"They did that," he answered with a measure of satisfaction.

A niggling suspicion raised its ugly head. "You are Canadian, aren't you?"

"Nope."

Dillian let her horse fall slightly behind as she stared at his broad back. He claimed to be a marquess. He lived in one of the largest country houses she'd ever seen, even if it had nearly crumbled to the ground. Damn it, he *looked* like a bloody aristocrat.

"What regiment did you fight in?" she demanded.

"American navy under John Paul Jones," he replied with gloating satisfaction. "Want to make an issue of it?"

Seven

She utterly loathed, despised, and detested military men. Her mother had fallen in love with a feckless soldier who had wed her and left for war, leaving her alone, disowned by her family, carrying a child, and practically destitute. Blanche's father had done the same, although in his case, money was no matter and her mother had the protection of his powerful family. No amount of pleading had ever persuaded either man to stay home and tend to family affairs. Foreign lands and adventure called them more strongly than the trifling responsibility of home and family. And she could just imagine the damage the American navy must have inflicted on innocent civilians along the English coast, which should condemn John Paul Jones and his crew to a soldier's place in hell.

Dillian glared at the marquess's broad shoulders beneath the ridiculous coat. "It's a wonder you have the nerve to set foot in this country," she finally responded with irritation. The complete irony of an American navy officer claiming the title of British marquess stunned her, but since she doubted the truth of much of his story, she didn't enjoy the joke as much as she would have liked. "I wouldn't bruit that fact about much in society."

She could see the motion of his head as he looked over his shoulder at her, but the darkness was too complete to see more.

"I'll remember that the next time I appear in the halls of Parliament." He turned around again and for all practical purposes, ignored her existence.

Her rebellious mind delighted in the image of a black-cloaked Marquess of Effingham sweeping into the staid

halls of Parliament, glaring his peers into retreat, and
denouncing the entire British navy from his American
point of view. She almost laughed as she thought of him
confronting Neville and his powerful friends. Stuffy, arrogant, narrow-minded, and inbred, they couldn't conceive of a society where anyone but those like
themselves ruled. What would they do with a man like
Gavin Lawrence in their midst?

She liked the idea so much she could almost forget his
miliary background to entertain the thought of Blanche
marrying him and giving him the wealth to go with the
power of his title—provided he really possessed it. Even
Blanche would enjoy the joke, if marriage weren't such
an intimate union. Dillian avoided thinking of the day-
to-day details of married life. She preferred the wider
scope involved in setting the American marquess loose
in polite society, like a rapier in a hothouse full of delicate blooms. It made a much more entertaining topic for
her speculations as they rode deeper into the night.

Apparently suspicious of her continued silence, the
marquess allowed his horse to lag until she caught up
with him. Not seeing any reason why she should continue riding in his dust, Dillian fell into place beside him.

"I've learned to keep my adversaries where I can see
them," he mentioned enigmatically as he spurred his
horse to a faster pace once again.

"It's your own attitude that makes all the world an
adversary," she responded with irritation. Everything
this man did or said set her teeth on edge. "I'm perfectly
willing to work with you. You're the one shutting me
out."

"What can you possibly do to safeguard the estate
except get in my way? And don't give me that nonsense
about knowing the servants. Lady Blanche should know
her own servants. She can get rid of strangers when
she arrives."

He offered the opportunity she needed to explain her
plan, but she would much rather take that abominable
hat of his and stuff it down his throat. How did women
ever endure that sort of stiff-necked arrogance long
enough to marry and beget children? They had to be

mad. She had yet to meet a man who would listen to a woman long enough to understand her intelligence.

Instead of answering his question, she asked blithely, "Did you ever interpret the significance of the rose?"

"Unless you wish to spout the Latin origin of the phrase sub-rosa concerning the secrecy of speaking under the rose, no, I cannot imagine the significance," he answered curtly.

Since that was exactly what she wished to "spout," Dillian found herself at point nonplus. Disgruntled, she manufactured, "Blanche's family traces her ancestry back to the House of Lancaster, once represented by the red rose."

"Hogwash," he said succinctly. "Or as you British say, fustian."

With a sigh of exasperation, Dillian surrendered. She had to get her plan through his thick skull, and it wouldn't come about with this nonsensical argument. "I want to sneak into the Grange without anyone seeing us. I can enlist the help of Blanche's maid once I'm there. We'll pretend outwardly that I've just arrived to look after things while Blanche is staying with friends, but at the same time, we'll convince the staff that Blanche is actually hiding in her room. Then I'll send Verity back to Blanche and tell everyone that she's visiting family, while Verity will give out that she's actually nursing Blanche around the clock. Do you see what I'm trying to do?"

He didn't answer immediately, but apparently worked through all the details in his head first before accepting that she'd come up with a viable plan. He didn't glance at her as he replied. "It's an interesting ruse. Tell them what you want them to give out publicly and let them gossip among themselves about the alternative. The loyal ones will bend over backward protecting their lady, immediately making the disloyal ones believe the gossip. Anyone wishing to harm the lady will believe you've hidden her here and quit looking for her elsewhere. The only drawback being that you are once again placing her estate and servants and yourself in danger."

"Yes, but this time, we're prepared. We'll pretend

you're just a visiting friend but let it get about that you're actually an officer in the army come to guard Blanche."

He held up an arm to stop her eager improvisations. "I have no intention of letting anyone in the household see me."

Dillian sent him a look of frustration. "Then, how in the name of heaven do you intend to find the murderer?"

"I don't. I only intend to secure the premises. I had thought to forward the information to Michael and Lady Blanche so they might hire whatever work needed doing or take whatever action deemed necessary. But if you mean to place yourself in jeopardy by remaining here, I'll simply notify you of the actions to be taken. You can act on them as you see fit. It's none of my concern whether you do or not. When I return home, I'll ship the lady back here. That is the end of my part in this."

Outraged, Dillian sent him a scathing glare, to which he would undoubtedly have been impervious even had he seen it. "Your generosity is overwhelming."

"Thank you. In light of my prior experience with British gratitude, I think so."

"You are nursing some grudge and taking it out on Blanche?" she asked with incredulity.

"I am merely protecting myself and my interests, as any sane man would do."

Adding coldhearted and unfeeling to the list of epithets to throw at his head, Dillian refrained from commenting. Instead, she asked, "If you do not plan to be seen by the staff, where will you stay? Surely you cannot accomplish everything in the course of a single day."

He shrugged. "I've lived off the land before. Do not concern yourself."

The idea of a marquess living off the land opened her eyes a little wider, but she knew better by now than to give her opinion to this man. She merely said, "We will need some means of communication."

She almost heard amusement in his voice when he responded, "I can assure you, I'll find some way."

She didn't like the sound of that at all. She almost

liked him better when gruff and stiff-necked. Amusement did not bode well at all.

"Why are you doing this?" she demanded with suspicion. "Why don't you just throw us out of your grand
palace and let us solve our problems ourselves if you
despise us so much?"

He gave that irritating shrug again. "Because, regardless of what anyone might think, Michael is important
to me. If he wants Lady Blanche protected, I will do
what is necessary—within reason—to protect her. Michael and I occasionally disagree on what is reasonable,
but he understands my position. He will accept it when
I send Lady Blanche home."

Dillian shook her head, unable to fathom the workings
of this man's mind. He found an impertinent footman
important but would send away an heiress who could
make his fortune? For the first time it occurred to her
that she might be traveling in the company of a madman.
She sent him a surreptitious glance, but she could see
only the silhouette of his improbable hat and long coat,
with its collar turned up to conceal his face.

"Your priorities are fascinating," she said dryly, then
proceeded to ride the rest of the way in silence.

"The gate's closed," Gavin informed her quietly, riding back to the clump of trees where he'd left her.
"There's a guard asleep in the guardhouse. The sun will
come up shortly. Is there another entrance?"

He imagined her raising those expressive exclamation
points she called eyebrows, but he couldn't see her face
clearly in the predawn darkness. She had told him the
front gate would in all likelihood be rusted and unused.
Someone had obviously seen to the security of the gate
without the lady's orders.

"The postern gate," she answered without hesitation.
"With decent horses, we could jump several sections of
the wall where the stones have fallen, but I wouldn't
want to attempt it with these nags."

She urged her tired mount into the woods surrounding
the estate. Gavin followed and found himself focusing
on the sway of Miss Whitnell's breeches in the gray light

of dawn. She had well-rounded hips with ample flesh for a man to bury his fingers in. It didn't take any effort to imagine sinking his fingers into those soft curves. The memory of holding her against him had burned indelibly into his mind. He knew this obsession had more to do with the fact that he'd abstained from women for too long than the desire for this particular woman, but he was tired and his mind found this path easiest to follow. He ached with the need to take some comfort there.

He would keep their meetings limited to darkness, where he couldn't see so much of the lady's splendid figure. That hideous coat couldn't conceal the swelling temptation of her breasts beneath. They had dawdled too long on the road. The sun would rise soon. Just the idea of seeing golden rays caressing her curves sent a surge of lust to his loins. Gavin gritted his teeth and concentrated on the path they took.

When they reached the gate, he dismounted and opened it for her, then caught the reins of her horse. "Leave it here if we're to enter unnoticed. You can say you sent the carriage back easier than explaining why there is only one horse in the stable."

She nodded and without thinking, Gavin hauled her down. He knew the moment he wrapped his hands around her waist that he had made a mistake, but he didn't falter. The heat of her burned through his gloves, but he merely set her down on the ground. He couldn't tell the color of her eyes in the shadows as she stared up at him. He didn't want to know. He stepped back and gestured for her to proceed.

"I can walk the rest of the way myself," she said without inflection.

"I will see you safely inside." He didn't know why he said that. He had better things to do than make certain this obstinate wench stole into the house without mishap. Some remnant of his upbringing must have intruded through his weariness.

After tying the horses, they slipped through the shadows of dawn in silence. Dewdrops wet their boots. An occasional overhanging branch dripped moisture on their heads. In the distance, birds sang a cheerful wake-up call to the sun. The May morn already held a warmth that heated the fresh scents of grass and wildflowers and promised sunshine. Gavin need only reach his arm out to draw her womanly form into his embrace. He couldn't remember ever wanting a tumble in the spring grass so badly.

The urge to procreate must come naturally with the rising sap of spring, he thought sourly to himself as they finally reached the back of the stable, protected by the new leaves of an apple tree.

"You will send me some word this evening?"

Gavin thought she almost asked that anxiously as she searched his face, but he knew concern for himself didn't reckon into her question. He scanned the expanse of drive and yard between their hiding place and the house. He doubted if the servants had even risen to start the fires yet. The house wasn't overlarge but a pleasantly sprawling vine-covered brick with classical features. He eyed the old vines and nodded, hiding the amusement at the interesting images they wrought.

"Which room is yours?"

Gavin knew she didn't trust him, but not for the reasons she should. She merely gave him a quick glance, then counted the windows until she worked out which one was hers.

"The fourth from the back. Each room on this side has a double casement except the corner rooms. The rear corner belongs to Blanche."

"Go, then. When you reach your room, open the window so I'll know you're safe."

She relaxed at once at what must seem to her as a friendly admonition. In moments, she was across the yard and entering by a side door with a key she found under a jardiniere. Gavin shook his head in disbelief at this lax procedure. He marked the second item needing correcting on his list. The first was the guard at the gate.

He waited patiently, keeping his eyes trained on the fourth window. She shouldn't dally. If she had any sense at all, the servants would find her firmly ensconced in her own bed when she rang for them. For some odd reason, he had confidence in her sense.

Gavin slid back into the shadows of the trees as soon as that window flew open. He could see her slight figure outlined against the opening. He gave no indication that he'd seen her. She would just have to guess at his whereabouts from now on.

She hadn't realized yet that he'd just turned the tables on her.

Eight

She and Verity had done their work well, Dillian decided as she looked at the heavy tray on her dressing table, discreetly loaded with enough food for three people. After a week of scavenging whatever leftovers she might find, she was now presented with the opposite problem.

Gazing ruefully at her far from svelte figure, she didn't think she needed to make up the lost meals. Glancing over at the window, which had darkened with nightfall, she wondered if she could somehow get this surplus to the mad marquess.

Deciding he could very well figure out how to get his own meals, she carried the pot of tea and some of the food down the hall to Blanche's room. She might as well make this pretense as realistic as possible. If one of the maids should wander down the hall and see her room empty, they would believe her dining with the invalid.

Balancing the tray carefully, Dillian turned the latch and edged the door open with her hip. Swearing under her breath for not thinking of bringing a lamp or candle, she closed the door behind her and more or less found her way by memory to the table by the corner windows. The view of the gardens from here was lovely in the daytime. During the evening, the spot became chilly. She pulled the heavy drapery and lit the lamp.

A powerful arm grabbed her around the waist, and a hand smothered her mouth. Screaming into a hard palm, Dillian kicked backward and tried to drive her elbows into her captor's stomach. He merely held her tighter, not painfully so but with an almost gentle caress that brushed upward, freezing her more assuredly than anything rougher.

"Remind me never to sneak up on you in the dark again," a familiar voice murmured with mocking amusement. "As much as I'm enjoying the pleasure of holding you, I'd rather keep what hide I have left."

Dillian bit spitefully at his palm, but he removed it before she could cause harm. She swung around and glared at the bane of her existence. The marquess wore his black cloak and hood again, but he had the hood thrown back. Lamplight flickered over the faint scars on his jaw, but she noticed the heat of his dark gaze more than the scars. She backed away.

"You had some good reason for startling me out of three years' growth?"

He shrugged, and she thought she saw his lips twitch in what might have resembled a grin. Her imagination was getting the best of her. This black-hearted scoundrel wouldn't know how to smile. She glared at him until he replied.

"I've noticed a tendency for people to scream when I appear. I didn't want all the servants running up here."

"Fustian!" She threw the word he had used earlier back in his face. "You just wanted to get even. And I'll thank you to keep your hands to yourself from now on." Not knowing how else to deal with that disturbing look in his eyes or the way his hand had made her feel just moments before, she hastily changed the subject. "Have you eaten? The servants have brought me enough food for three people."

The look he sent the tray of food almost equaled the one he had given her. Any man who employed two cooks obviously had an appetite. Dillian lifted one cover to reveal a steaming bowl of nourishing broth, suitable for an invalid. She nearly laughed at his frown and lifted a second. Lamb pie was obviously more to his liking.

Knowing she'd left a considerable dinner back in her own room, she merely poured herself a cup of tea and watched as the marquess took her place at the table. She let him make hasty inroads into the meal before inquiring, "Have you looked over the grounds?"

He grimaced at the pitcher of water that was the only beverage left. "I don't suppose you could convince them that an invalid needs coffee?"

"I might convince them that I would prefer it. Blanche detests the stuff. Are you planning on making a habit of breaking and entering?"

He raised his eyebrows mockingly. "Like you?" Without expecting a reply, he sipped gingerly at the water. "The place is certainly easy enough to break into. Country houses are never sufficiently protected. If I made thievery a habit, I would forget working in the city. No one ever locks doors in the country. Or if they do, they keep the keys under flowerpots." He sent her a look that made Dillian grind her teeth. "There are more holes in your security around here than there are trees in the woods."

"All right. I'll give the butler a stiff warning about checking all the doors and windows downstairs before he retires. There's only the one key outside. We've always kept it there. Certain members of Blanche's family had rather irresponsible habits of losing keys and coming home at an hour when the staff slept."

He didn't comment on this, but continued, "That's just the tip of the iceberg. One guard cannot stay awake twenty-four hours a day. The gate needs either to be locked or staffed around the clock by people willing to stay awake. The walls are hopeless. Anyone but a three-legged cow can climb over them. You'll need guard dogs running loose at night to warn of any unexpected visitors. In addition, although this may sound ridiculous, I recommend buying a flock of geese."

"A flock of geese?" Dillian almost laughed, but the stormy expression on the marquess's formidable visage prevented it. Aristocratic brows formed black clouds, and his scowl forewarned of thunder and lightning if she did not take heed. Impossible man. Glaring back, she set her cup soundly back on its saucer. "Why geese?"

"A truly determined intruder can locate and distract the dogs. He couldn't possibly get past a gaggle of geese without causing a commotion and getting himself pecked

to pieces first. Most wouldn't even think to try before
the geese were upon them."

That made sense. She'd had the experience of riding
down the road when a gaggle of geese decided to cross
it. They didn't move for anyone, man or beast. She nodded thoughtfully. "All right. The geese are easier arranged than the dogs. I don't know where I'll find dogs
trained to guard the property who won't eat geese."

"Make inquiries. It shouldn't be difficult. Have you
gone over the staff yet? Have they hired anyone new?"

She would like to take umbrage at his arrogant assumption that she could handle everything with a sweep
of her hand, but the fact that he so casually accepted
her ability to carry out his commands weakened her ire.
Dillian poured herself more tea and watched him slice
happily into Cook's best pudding cake. He didn't eat as
if starved but more as if he savored every bite after a
long period of deprivation. She would order wine as well
as coffee for tomorrow. She wanted to see a look of
ecstasy on those harsh features. It might almost make
him human.

"The guard at the gate is the only person I don't
know. Blanche only kept a skeleton staff here and
brought her personal staff with her when she visited.
They're all here now, and I'm quite certain they would
walk on water for her if she requested. She saved most
of their lives the night of the fire. They'll sit up nights
and watch the windows if I so ask."

"It won't hurt having one of the footmen patrolling
the ground floor regularly when everyone else is asleep,"
he said thoughtfully, helping himself to her cup of tea
now that he'd finished the cake. "Give strict instructions
about keeping all strangers outside, although I can't
imagine an arsonist coming to the door."

"No," she answered gloomily. "If they mean to burn
us out again, it will come as you feared. I've already
heard all about the riots and the hay burnings. The staff
is terrified that the radicals will send the mob here. No
amount of geese and dogs and guards can stop a mob."

He gave her a sharp look. "Does a mob have reason
to come here?"

"Does a mob have reason for anything they do?" she asked caustically. "I have seen them rampage through the streets of London, overturning carriages with old ladies in them, breaking windows and stealing anything available. Out here in the country they cannot lay their hands on as many goods, but on the other hand, there is no one to stop them. They can set the entire countryside aflame if they so choose. I cannot say that they have no reason for anger. Now that the war is over, the army has dumped thousands of men into the streets without pay, without jobs, without hope of finding employment. The poor rates are soaring as high as the price of food. Only the rich benefit from the Corn Laws. The economy is in a crisis, and our government sits on its hands and claims everything must stay as it always has been because change is worse than revolution. I can't say setting hayricks on fire serves any purpose, but I understand their frustration."

He gazed at her thoughtfully. "You're as angry as they are, aren't you? I keep forgetting you're hired help. You have the manners of a lady. You remind me a great deal of one of my cousins. She was raised as a lady but knows the curse of poverty."

Dillian waited for the inevitable question about why a lady hadn't married instead of becoming a paid companion, but he didn't ask. Asking questions indicated interest. The marquess had no interest in a penniless dependent. She would do better to remember that before her imagination flew away with her.

"I doubt that your cousin knows what it is like having seven children in a one-room hovel, starving to death while her husband is gone daybreak to sundown scraping together enough pennies to pay for the roof over their heads. Enclosures have robbed the poor of their ability to raise their own food, and no one pays enough so they can buy their own. On top of that, the poor tenant farmer must pay the poor rate out of his meager sales while the wealthy landowner who collects rents instead of selling crops keeps his hands in his pockets. The situation is outrageous. Blanche has done what she can, but her powers are limited until she comes of age. Everything she suggests must be approved by her trustees. So far, they haven't agreed to her desire to pay her tenants' taxes."

The marquess sat back in his chair, seemingly relaxed as he listened to her tirade. His shirt gleamed white in the candlelight, contrasting with the darker coloring of his skin. Dillian couldn't believe that she sat here actually talking to this madman. Despite the starkly aristocratic structure of his face and the elegant lines of his figure, she knew this man as a reclusive eccentric at best. A demented American came closer. What interest did he have in the economic and social disasters of a country he so blatantly despised?

"And this Neville you mentioned is one of the trustees?" Long, thin fingers peeled at an apple with a fruit knife.

Captivated by the sensuous grace of his movements, Dillian answered without thinking. "No, but his solicitor is. Neville and Blanche are first cousins. Their grandfather was the fifth Duke of Anglesey. He had three sons. The eldest, of course, was expected to take over Anglesey. Blanche's father, the second son, made a career of the military, so her mother stayed mostly at Anglesey. Her grandfather had a falling out with Neville's father, the youngest, who wanted to make changes that no one else thought necessary. So Neville's family moved to London when Neville was quite young. Blanche's grandfather doted on her. When the heir apparent died without issue before his father, the old duke made out his will leaving Blanche's father everything, but Blanche's father died at Waterloo shortly after he became the new marquess. The old duke could not stop the title or the entailment going to his youngest son, Neville's father, but he refused to change his will leaving everything to Blanche's family, making it nigh on impossible for Neville's family to make any changes in the estate without the cooperation of Blanche's family."

The marquess grimaced. "I need something stronger than tea to get me through this. Why don't we get to the point? Tell me who is responsible for the fortune Lady Blanche has apparently inherited?"

Dillian gave him an impatient look. "That is what I'm trying to tell you. Blanche's grandfather outlived all three of his sons. Neville's father died of small pox a few years ago. The old man was not only distraught, but furious. He distrusted Neville. He wanted Anglesey to go on as it has always done, and the estate came before anyone or anything. He knew Blanche loved Anglesey and would take care of it, but only Neville could inherit it. So he arranged it so her inheritance and Neville's are so entangled and guarded by the same trustees that the only way either of them can get anything out of it is to marry each other."

"Unless one of them dies," he summarized dryly.

Dillian made a face. "That is one way of looking at it. If Blanche dies without marrying, her inheritance reverts to Anglesey. The old duke didn't want to bankrupt his estate, he merely wished to force Neville into accepting Blanche."

"But once he married her, what power would she have to prevent him from doing what he wished? I understood that wives have no rights of possession."

Dillian grinned. "That's where the old man made a mistake. He had it in his head that lovely, docile Blanche wanted Anglesey so much that she would marry Neville without question. He meant only to force Neville. So he set Blanche's inheritance up as a trust which her husband cannot touch. Neville would have to beg for every penny. If she marries before she comes of age, the trustees will most likely grant her husband a large dower. But once she comes of age, she can control her own fortune. She would very much like to have Anglesey, but not at the cost of marrying Neville and giving up her independence, not to mention a large share of her fortune. They have reached an impasse."

"When does she come of age?"

"In October."

The marquess stretched out his long booted legs and stared at his toes. "That gives Neville nearly six months to either persuade her into marriage or kill her."

"Well, she could marry another. He couldn't touch her inheritance, then. Her husband would have control of the dower amount. She would have the power to will the remainder to her husband and children if she so chose."

Dillian didn't mention the estate Blanche's mother had left her, the one they currently occupied. That wasn't protected by a trust but would instantly become her husband's property if Blanche married before she had control over it. It was also Blanche's strongest reason for not marrying until she turned twenty-one. Dillian worried about the consequences of Blanche's determination not to marry until then, but since Blanche had found no suitor she madly desired, Dillian had not concerned herself greatly until now. The possibility that marriage was the only way to save Blanche's life concerned her deeply indeed.

The marquess continued frowning at his boots. "It all sounds like a bucket of sheep dip to me. Let Neville go find another heiress to support his fancy estate. I'm sure there are many willing to buy a duke."

Dillian made a slight moue of puzzlement. "Neville has never shown much interest in any woman but Blanche. He enjoys politics. Even when they attend a ball together, he spends all his time in dark corners and smoky rooms, talking to his political cronies. I don't think he has the time or interest to look elsewhere."

"But he has time to hire arsonists? That doesn't make sense." The marquess stood up and pushed the heavy velvet draperies aside. "I'd better go. I want to keep a lookout on the grounds at night until you find those dogs."

"You will have to wait until the servants retire if you don't want to be seen," she reminded him.

He threw an enigmatic look over his shoulder at her. "I can hide as well as you. Take away your tray and pretend your invalid is asleep. I'll talk to you tomorrow."

She didn't like being ordered about. She might play the part of Blanche's paid companion, but that had never been her role. Still, although she had little regard for propriety, lingering alone in Effingham's presence suddenly made her nervous. She would do well to remove herself before he remembered how easily he had overpowered her earlier.

Picking up the tray, she left the marquess contemplating the nighttime.

Neville arrived at the door two days later. Dillian had purchased the geese just the day before. They squawked noisily around the carriage when the visitor climbed down, but the footman chased them from their employer's impeccably polished boots. Dillian watched from an upstairs sitting room as the butler hastily opened the front door before the duke even reached the bottom step. The long-suffering servants weren't any more fond of the birds than Neville, but they hadn't offered a complaint.

Dillian debated refusing to appear when summoned, but she saw no benefit in declaring war on Blanche's powerful cousin. Not yet, anyway. She checked to make certain her cap held her wayward curls in place, then dawdled just long enough to irritate him.

When she entered the salon where the butler had placed him, Neville glared at her without his usual bland countenance. "Where is she?" he demanded.

Dillian crossed her hands in front of her and asked innocently, "Who?"

She thought for a moment that he might take the stick in his hand to her. He hadn't even allowed the butler to take his hat or cane. He didn't mean this as a polite visit, then.

"Where is Blanche? What have you done with her? I hold you entirely responsible if anything happens to her! I'll have you up in assizes if one hair on her head is harmed."

Dillian gave him her best irreproachably missish look. "Her hair has already been singed. I have trimmed it. Will you have me transported?"

He shook the cane in his hand at her. "Don't give me that faradiddle, Miss Reynolds. Don't think you have me fooled for a minute. I know you're the reason she refuses to marry me. I can have you removed anytime I want. I am trying to be patient, but I want to know how my cousin is. Let me see her at once."

Dillian fluttered her lashes. "She isn't here."

Furious, Neville shoved past her and toward the door. "I've had enough lies. I'll see her now."

Dillian stepped out of his way and let him pass. He knew little or nothing of this house since it had belonged to Blanche's mother. She watched as he started up the stairs. "I wish you luck," she called after him.

From his position at the back of the hall, the butler sent her a questioning look. Unsmiling, Dillian shook her head. Neville didn't vaunt his power carelessly, but she wouldn't risk the position of any of Blanche's staff should he choose to do so now.

She heard him flinging doors and cursing. A footman and maid peeked through a door at the end of the hall but darted back at a frosty look from the butler. Biting her lower lip, Dillian merely waited for the duke's rampage to lessen. Neville seldom worked himself into a rage. She doubted if he knew how to control one. She had no intention of getting in his way until he returned to some semblance of normality.

By the time he bellowed "Where is she?" with more frustration than fury, Dillian had her story composed. Climbing the stairs where they could speak out of range of the servants, she waited for him in the main hall. The lovely old wood gleaming in the sunshine from the windows on either end gave her a degree of confidence. The old woven carpet had withstood the feet of generations. It would withstand the wear of many more if she had her way. She loved this house, and she would protect it any way she could. She just wouldn't exchange it for Blanche's life.

When Neville finally stood before her, he no longer looked his complacent, arrogant self. He looked thoroughly shaken. Dillian might have felt sorry for him had she not been there the night the house went up in flames and Blanche nearly died in the inferno.

"Where is she?" he demanded again, but in a less forceful manner.

"Safe," Dillian answered calmly. "As safe as anyone

can be knowing an arsonist wishes her dead. Did you think she would endanger her staff a second time?"

The duke's lips tightened in frustration. "That is specious nonsense. Why would anyone kill Blanche? I want to see her. How do I know you haven't harmed her for some sick reason of your own?"

"You don't, not any more than I can believe you aren't the one who harmed her in the first place. So we are at checkmate. You know she is alive. Your solicitor must have told you of the message he received. That's all you need know. You can do nothing else for her but worry her to death."

He slammed his fist into the old paneling. "I want to marry her, not worry her to death. She needs the best physicians. You must return her to London."

"How do you know she isn't there already? I have no control over Blanche's actions. It's not my place. I'm simply here to supervise the staff."

"Then, she's coming here or she wouldn't have sent you ahead. I want to know the instant she arrives." He looked at her shrewdly. "I'll pay you well. I'll double the money she saved for you."

Dillian gave him a pitying smile. "I hope someday you'll learn that friendship and loyalty buy more than all the gold on earth. Good day, Your Grace. I'll have Jenkins see you out."

Nine

Dillian frowned at the empty bedchamber. She'd found the marquess waiting here these past nights. She'd offered good food, wine, and coffee as lures, and he'd neatly fallen into the trap. Without Blanche, she found the house unbearably lonesome. The marquess had given her a few hours of interesting conversation and company of an evening, in return for her culinary offerings, of course.

She couldn't believe he would miss his supper unless something dire had happened. She set the dinner tray on the table and pulled back the drapery. The night looked innocent enough. She saw no mobs, no lurking intruders. But the woods beyond the neatly cultivated lawns could hide an immensity of evil.

She sipped at her tea and waited. As the hour grew later, she paced. The food on the tray grew cold, and she didn't notice. She had no appetite. Where could he be? What could have happened?

It was idiotic worrying about the madman. Just because she had lured him in here a few times didn't mean the marquess would behave in any orderly fashion. By now he could have found an inn with an accommodating serving girl. He might have found an old friend on the road and gone home with him. Or he may have tired of the game and gone back to Hertfordshire. Anything was possible.

But none of the above seemed logical from what she knew of the reclusive marquess, and something in her rebelled at thinking he would have deserted her without good reason. She glanced out the window again, but there was even less to see than before. The servants had started turning out the lights on the lower floor.

She didn't hear the geese. The guard dogs wouldn't arrive until tomorrow. She had no way of knowing if anyone lurked out there. Perhaps she should go out and see for herself.

Dillian dropped the drapery again, knowing the foolishness of that notion. If the marquess had found trouble, he would come here if he could. She was useless roaming around lost in the dark.

After another hour, she left the tray of cold food in Blanche's room and returned to her own. She told herself she had no reason to worry over a grown man who could obviously take care of himself. Any man who had survived whatever he'd gone through to earn those scars could defend himself. She would do well to look after her own concerns.

Unable to sleep, she slipped downstairs to check the doors and locks. She found the footman she'd assigned guard duty and made him test the fastenings also. He didn't question her orders but immediately took the east and north sides of the house while she took the west and south. They met again in the middle with no signs of disturbance anywhere.

Deciding she was being ridiculous, Dillian trudged back upstairs. The marquess had no obligation to report to her every evening. He was under no obligation at all. He could have gone home now that he'd done as he'd promised. She didn't like that idea.

Surely, he would have told her that he had everything under control and meant to leave. Wouldn't he have waited for the guard dogs? And what about the walls? Didn't he want to hear about the stonemasons she'd hired?

The argument careened back and forth inside her head, but she could discover no means of satisfying it. Instinct told her the marquess would have come if able, but instincts were notoriously unreliable. She didn't know the man well enough to trust her instincts around him.

Reluctantly, Dillian unfastened the buttons of her

round gown and folded it neatly over a chair. She must find some way to dispose of all that food before she took the tray down in the morning. The servants hadn't sent up as much as usual tonight. The duke's visit had thrown some doubt over the plausibility of Blanche's presence. She didn't know if she could continue the charade any longer. That was one of those things she had wished to discuss with the marquess. She really should get over this foolish notion that she could rely on the man, that she could rely on any man. She knew better.

She blew out all but the candle at her bedside and unfastened the ties of her chemise. Perhaps she ought to take a horse out in the morning and search the grounds. The head groom could search the woods. She didn't like thinking of the mad marquess lying wounded somewhere. She wished she could go out now, but in the dark, the search would be fruitless.

She frowned at her own perversity in continuing to allow her heart to war with her head.

The candle threw long shadows across the walls as she reached for the nightshift left lying across the covers. She felt the draft before she heard the window casement click. She'd scarcely opened her mouth to scream before the draperies parted and a dark cloaked figure stepped through.

The thrill of relief so flooded her that Dillian didn't remember her state of undress until she caught sight of the marquess's taut jaw and the direction of his stare in the candlelight.

Her unfastened chemise revealed the full curve of her breasts and the valley between. Even the cool breeze from the window didn't lessen the heat flooding through her as she swung around and presented him with her back.

Dillian wrapped her arms across her chest. "What on earth do you think you're doing coming in here like that?" she asked crossly.

Effingham didn't answer for what seemed like eternity. She hated it when he did that. She wanted to swing around and scream at him, but she was belatedly aware that she didn't have a robe at hand, and her nightshift lay on the bed behind her. She wore only her chemise, and the candle undoubtedly accentuated that fact.

The folds of his dark cloak dropped over her shoulders, and Dillian grasped them gratefully, pulling the heavy material around her, understanding he stood entirely too close to give her this aid.

"I've caught a trespasser," he murmured near her ear. Why hadn't she noticed the stirring rasp of that low voice before? Or the way it sent shivers down her spine? "I thought you might like to see if he's anyone you know before I dispose of him."

Dillian heard his wry tone as he moved away, but she didn't try to determine if he directed it at her or himself. If she had learned nothing else about the marquess, it was that he held no high opinion of himself like some others she could name. Still, his proximity made her nervous. She clutched the cloak tighter as she felt him back away.

"I will have to dress." To her dismay, her teeth chattered. She wanted to blame it on the cool air from the window, but she knew better. Goose bumps ran up and down her arms, but not from the cold. Her breasts felt swollen and tight. She could barely speak past the lump in her throat. She wished he would get out of the room now. His presence had her nerves jumping.

"Of course. I'll wait for you outside."

She heard the coolness in his voice. She wanted to swing around and read his expression, confront him somehow, but she couldn't. She stood frozen, not even caring how he meant to get outside just so long as he went.

The window clicked, and the breeze stopped. She didn't wonder how he'd entered a second-floor window. If she'd needed proof he'd been in the navy, she had it now. She couldn't imagine any other but a sailor climbing those vines outside the window.

She still held his cloak around her. She shivered inside its comforting confines. A moment later, she realized the cloak smelled of him, of the elusive male fragrance that identified the marquess in her mind. She had never thought about a man's smell before. Now she couldn't get it out of her head.

She checked to make certain the room was empty, even though she sensed its emptiness now that his strong presence had gone. But she didn't trust her senses any longer. She scanned the darkness, then continued clinging to the cloak as she sought out her clothes. She felt stark naked and embarrassed right down to her toes, but he hadn't said a word about her state of undress.

Had she not seen Effingham's eyes, she could almost pretend that he hadn't seen her. He had brushed aside the whole incident as if it had never happened. But she'd seen his eyes. She'd seen the way they focused hungrily on her breasts. He hadn't even looked at her face. She could still feel the intensity of his stare. She burned with shame—or something else.

Dillian wouldn't think about that something else. She hadn't reached twenty-five years of age without learning a little something of human nature. At sixteen, she'd had a passionate crush on the vicar's son. His every casual touch had sent her into paroxysms of joy. She'd sneaked off to meet him in the woods, behind haystacks, anywhere they could steal a few moments together. He'd been the same age as she. Neither of them knew anything they were about, but pleasure had mixed with the excitement of the forbidden, and they had learned a great deal together. Fortunately for her, she'd learned more about his character than his physical body before they'd gone too far to go back. No man had so easily led her astray since.

But she'd been the recipient of enough hungry looks over the years to know what they meant. She had no fortune, no name, nothing with which to gift a man but her body. Most of the time she succeeded in ignoring the fact that she possessed the build of a tavern wench. She was small-boned and not stylishly attractive, so she could hide herself easily behind demure round gowns in unfashionable drab colors. Mostly, men didn't notice her. When Blanche accompanied her, they didn't even know she existed. She preferred it that way. But other times Blanche's suitors had sought her out when they found

Blanche unavailable. They might act the gentleman around Blanche, but they saw no need for it around Blanche's hired help. Dillian hadn't mistaken their ardor as she had mistaken the vicar's son. She knew lust for what it was now.

She had seen lust in the marquess's eyes. Hurriedly pulling her riding jacket around her and fastening it tightly, Dillian tried not thinking about it. She had rather enjoyed their suppers together. She couldn't exactly call them pleasant. The marquess had a caustic wit and a bitterness that spiced their conversation somewhat heavily, but he also had a quick mind and an appreciation for intelligent subjects that she seldom found in society. She didn't want their intellectual converse polluted with the physical weaknesses of the flesh.

She played the fool. The marquess had no reason to continue their late night suppers once he caught the arsonist, and it seemed he had. She would have no reason to ever see him again. He could take his lust elsewhere, and she and Blanche could return to their normal humdrum existence.

Except, even as she hurried down the stairs to meet the man who'd thrown their lives in turmoil, she knew their lives would never return as before. Blanche would wear the scars of that fire forever, in one form or another. Her cousin's need for a husband had become all too apparent at the same time the field of suitors would drastically narrow. Once Blanche decided on a husband, Dillian would have to venture into the world alone.

She couldn't think about that just yet either. She had enough on her mind just dealing with the madman waiting for her out in the night.

She waited for the footman to pass the bottom of the stairs and disappear into the further reaches of the ground floor. Then she darted into the foyer, down the hall, and out the side door to the stables. She hadn't asked Effingham where they would meet, but she imagined he would watch this door for her appearance.

She imagined correctly. Without his cloak, the white of his neck cloth gleamed against the dark outline of the barn. He wore a dark frock coat and vest, as he had these past nights when they'd shared their supper and a few hours together. She knew very well how elegant he looked in a gentleman's clothes, no matter how out-moded. She also knew how dangerous he looked when he flung the cloak around him and ventured into the darkness again.

Silently, she handed him the cloak she held over her arm. He took it and pulled it on, concealing his features with the hood as he started briskly down the path to the woods. She thought he wore the hood more out of habit than necessity or any real need to hide himself. She wished she could hide her features quite so neatly.

"What was he doing when you found him?" she whispered, unable to bear the silence any longer.

"Skulking." The reply was succinct and without expression.

She felt the thread of tension between them tighten a little more. She thought they'd gone beyond their earlier disagreements to find some degree of understanding. To-night's incident had evidently rendered their truce null and void.

So be it. She could be as rude and curt as he when she so desired. Without another word, Dillian stuck her nose up in the air and strode forcefully beside him.

Except her legs weren't as long as Effingham's, and she kept falling behind. She had to race to keep up. Swearing under her breath as she tripped on a tree root, she deliberately stopped running and strolled leisurely, forcing him to look for her.

Dillian could almost hear the curse on the marquess's lips, but he refrained from speaking the words aloud. He forced his pace to hers as they left the beaten path, and he held branches back so she could pass.

"In here." He made a gesture with his head indicating the overgrown gazebo some long-ago generation had built out here. Dillian had nearly forgotten its existence. She wondered if the marquess had used it as his chambers these last few days. If so, he should be grateful it hadn't rained. Even the mass of rampant vines couldn't prevent the wind from blowing through the holes.

To her surprise, he had a lantern. He threw open the

sliding door and let a crack of light illuminate one corner of the interior where a trussed and sorry figure lay curled upon the floor. The man turned his face from the beam of light, but she caught sight of his features well enough. She didn't recognize him at all.

She stepped out of the gazebo, forcing Effingham to follow. He had the lantern closed when he did so.

"Well?" he demanded.

"He's not from around here," she informed him coldly. "Did he say why he was 'skulking'?"

"He said he's a soldier looking for work. I'd believe him had he slept by the road instead of hiding in the bushes at the rear of the property."

Dillian clasped her fingers in front of her. She had little enough sympathy for the military and a very low opinion of military men, but she wasn't completely narrow-minded. Many of these men had thought to find a better life by joining Wellington's forces. Instead, they had returned home with missing hands and feet or worse and were left to fend for themselves. She didn't wish any man harm, but she couldn't allow a possible arsonist to destroy Blanche or the Grange.

"What will you do with him?"

"Take him to the local magistrate for questioning, I suppose. The threat of transportation for trespassing might loosen his tongue. When will those dogs you bought arrive?"

He'd almost forgotten to act cold. She could hear the reasonable man with whom she'd spent these last few nights in the tone of his voice. She didn't want to hear that man. She wanted him gone. At the same time, she knew she didn't dare let him leave. The Grange could become ashes without his help.

"The dogs arrive in the morning. I've hired a trainer to teach them the grounds. How will they differentiate between you and an intruder?"

"They won't need to. I'm returning to the manor once I deliver your intruder to the authorities. I'll send Lady Blanche and Michael back here as soon as I arrive. I've done all I can. Michael is sharp enough to do the rest."

Dillian panicked. Somewhere in the back of her brain,

she knew what he was doing. He was running away from her. What had happened tonight made continuing their casual dinner conversation impossible. She knew that, somehow understood it, but she couldn't accept it. She needed him here. The Grange needed his protection. She had nothing else besides Blanche, and Blanche was safe in Hertfordshire. No one would look for her in a moldering castle without servants or society. If Blanche came to the Grange, Dillian would lose them both.

He was a marquess. She couldn't ask him to stay as a guard dog. She couldn't demand that he let Blanche stay as a guest in his home when he so blatantly discouraged guests. Damn.

"Will you at least come back and tell me what the magistrate said before you return to Hertfordshire?" she asked quietly, not knowing how else she could stall him.

He didn't reply immediately. She held her breath as he deliberated. If he would just return on the morrow, perhaps she would have thought of some way of holding him by then.

"I hadn't considered lingering to hear his verdict," he admitted gruffly. "I have no use for British authorities."

Of course. That was true. Dillian took a deep breath and tried again. "I would send Blanche some traveling clothes and a message before you go. I cannot believe it safe for her to travel, nor for her to stay here. I would warn her of the consequences and suggest other arrangements. Perhaps I should return with you."

She felt rather than saw his sharp look at this suggestion.

"That is not the brightest thing you have ever said, Miss Whitnell," he said stiffly. "I will return here for any messages you wish to send, but that is all."

She disliked it, but she understood it. She still found it unnerving being addressed by her father's name instead of her mother's after all these years. Blanche should never have revealed so much. Unable to argue, however, she nodded and started back toward the marked path without a word of farewell.

She heard him following at a discreet distance, but she didn't acknowledge him. She must have been all about in her wits thinking she could hold a marquess here to protect her home. It was Blanche she worried about now. Blanche could find no safety here. The episode tonight proved that. Somehow, she must force the miserable man to let Blanche stay in his Gothic ruin.

Without power or money, she had very few means of coercing him to do anything.

Ten

"Will there be anything else this evening, Miss Reynolds?" the butler asked with all the deference accorded the mistress of the house.

Dillian didn't know what Blanche had told the servants when she first came here as Blanche's companion, but they had always treated her in the same manner as Blanche. The understanding between the cousins might make that appropriate, but the servants knew nothing of their familial relationship. Or supposedly, they didn't. Just because Dillian's mother had grown up here should not ensure that the servants knew Dillian's identity. Her mother had never returned here after her marriage.

There were any number of people named Reynolds in this country. She hoped no one knew her real identity. Neville would choke on his fury should he learn Blanche had hired the notorious Colonel "Slippery" Whitnell's daughter as companion, even if she was Blanche's cousin.

But that was all water over the dam now. They had only six months more before they could do as they pleased. Dillian made a gesture of dismissal at the butler. "Go on to bed, Jenkins. Make sure Jamie is summoned to patrol. I heard some of the Radicals were in the village today."

They have no reason to come here, miss," Jenkins replied indignantly. "The Grange has always been good to its people."

She had no desire to explain that other forces might be at work besides rebellious farmers. She thanked him and wandered up the stairs.

The marquess hadn't returned to report what had happened with the magistrate. Now she not only had to worry over Effingham's whereabouts, but if the intruder might have escaped. Would he have had confederates who might have freed him, harming Lord Effingham in the process? She should know better than to worry, but she had little else to do.

Perhaps she should go back to Arinmede and look after Blanche. She would feel much better if she knew Blanche was all right, that her sight was recovering, that they might escape somewhere safe shortly. Once Blanche recovered, they could tour the Continent for the next six months. Neville would have a hard time finding them there.

If she returned to Arinmede, would the marquess really throw her out?

She avoided contemplating it. Instead of going to her own room, she wandered down the hall to the front corner chamber. These front rooms had been furnished as family rooms with a library and salon and dining parlor. The front corner provided a lady's study, with a delicate Queen Anne writing desk, chairs for reading and sewing, and several shelves of books. She had need of a good book tonight.

She dismissed Sir Walter Scott and picked up one of Miss Austen's social satires. She'd read it before, but she'd read everything in here at least once. Miss Austen was always worth reading again.

She still couldn't force herself back to her room. If the marquess climbed any more vines, he would have to look for her here instead of her chamber. She felt morally more secure in this proper setting. She also felt better with a view of the road. She settled in a window seat with a lamp, and occasionally peeked behind the draperies to see if anything had changed.

She just felt uneasy. The dogs had arrived with their trainer, but they were new to their job. She couldn't rely on them yet. She couldn't imagine the geese patrolling the yard with any regularity. How had the marquess passed by them last night if so? She just felt better if she watched for herself.

Hours later, her head nodded over the book, and she

had to jerk herself awake. Yawning, she admitted she couldn't manage this vigil any longer. Feeling a vague sense of disappointment that the marquess hadn't returned, Dillian peeked out the window again before giving up for the night.

She blinked and rubbed her eyes. Surely, she didn't see . . .

She did see. She saw a line of blazing orange flames marching up the drive, held in the hands of a mob of men.

She wouldn't panic. The Grange was all she had, even if it wasn't hers. She would protect it at any cost.

Dropping her book, Dillian flew down the hall, screaming at the top of her lungs. She didn't scream from panic but as the fastest way of arousing the household, both upstairs and down. She heard one of the maids in the attic fall from her bed with a thump at the noise. She hit the stairway and raced down, yelling for Jenkins and Jamie.

Fully garbed for his rounds, Jamie waited for her at the bottom of the staircase. "What is it, Miss Dillian? What is it?"

"Outside! Get everyone outside! They're coming with torches."

To a household of servants who had already been burned from their home once, that cry sent shouts of fear and fury careening through the hallways. Jamie raced to the back of the house to wake the cooks and kitchen help; Dillian raced up the back stairs to make certain all the maids had heard her.

The chaotic sound of dogs barking and howling, mixed with the outraged squawks of a gaggle of geese and the gonging of the alarm bell turned the silence into a nightmarish cacophony. Dillian didn't need the hysterical screams of the maids adding to the chaos.

"Quiet! Run to the kitchen and fetch pails and kettles, then get outside. No one has set fire to anything yet, and I'll be blamed if I let them. I need your help. Now, hurry."

As her calmness and orders sank in, they raced to obey, chattering the whole time but no longer screaming.

The Grange staff had always been orderly. She gave thanks for that now. They helped quiet some of Blanche's town staff who were convinced they would all burn in their beds this time.

Grateful she hadn't changed into her nightshift, Dillian grabbed one of her grandfather's old hunting guns from the study. Jenkins came running up with his shirt only half on and his trousers partially buttoned, a far cry from the staid and respectable butler of earlier. She handed him another of the hunting guns.

"Hand out the rest of the guns to any of the men you trust. I'll see that mob dead before one inch of this place is burned," she said furiously.

Jenkins grabbed a handful of blunderbusses and shot-guns, and handed them out as Jamie and the other foot-men joined him. When Dillian flung open the front door herself, he offered a vocal protest, but she ignored him. She didn't have patience for arguing over propriety.

The mob had already reached the last curve in the drive. She could see the torchlight flickering over black-ened faces. She couldn't recognize anyone in the dark-ness, let alone with disguises. It didn't matter. She fully intended to kill them if they came any closer.

She felt Jenkins and the armed servants filing out of the house behind her. She hoped the maids had run out the back as ordered. She had enough militant Whitnell in her to see the Grange burned over her dead body, but wisdom enough to know death was always a possibility.

"What do you want?" she shouted over the howls of the dogs. The trainer held them back at the corner of the house. She didn't want the animals hurt by gunfire. She hoped he kept them there unless needed.

The mob ignored her. Seeing the armed servants be-hind her, they veered in the direction of the stable. The horses! She hadn't thought to rescue the horses. Torn between guarding her house and protecting innocent animals, Dillian hesitated.

Incredibly, into that moment of indecision rode a hor-rifying specter of silver and black. Dillian gasped and stepped back as the specter's huge horse rode between her and the mob. Even with torches lighting the night

sky, she could only discern the rider's shape and mass—
and the bright arc of a shining sword.

The mob screamed as the huge beast rode down on
them, scattering them across the lawns, sending them
flying down the drive in front of him. The sword arced
and flashed and torches flew into the dew-damp grass,
there to sputter out, abandoned as their owners took to
their heels.

"The stable!" Dillian screamed, pointing in the direction of a few brave souls who sought the flammable
straw and hay. Her staff ran where she pointed, but the
cloaked figure on horseback got there first.

The cloaked figure on horseback.

The marquess.

Dillian almost melted with relief. He hadn't gone away
and left her alone after all. He still looked after the
Grange. She still had a chance to persuade him to stay
or take her with him.

If he didn't get himself killed first.

She screamed and ran toward the stables as remnants
of the mob surrounded him, threatening horse and rider
with their torches. Unable to aim her weapon with any
degree of accuracy, she shot it into the air, drawing their
attention. The black shadow on the horse didn't hesitate
as he used the distraction to cut a swath through the
mob with his deadly sword. Cries of pain filled the air,
and the men with torches fell back, seeing for the first
time the servants running toward them with guns. The
man in black used his magnificent beast to cut off those
few still attempting to reach the haystacks. They flung
their torches wildly and ran. Dillian watched in relief as
a few of the grooms stomped out the torches before
their fires could catch.

"A most unusual sight," Jenkins murmured from beside her, a slight note of puzzlement in his voice. "He
appears some knight of old coming to the rescue."

Dillian tried to see the dashing cloak and upraised
sword from the servant's point of view, but she saw only
the mocking smile and the flat black of the marquess's
eyes. She shook her head. "More like a corsair, Jenkins.
Beware he doesn't claim the sinking ship."

The mob had deteriorated to a rout, with ragged shadows darting hither and yon in belated attempts to escape the caped monster bearing down on them. The sword whistled over their heads, Dillian noted. He could have decapitated dozens of them, but he only scared them into running. As furious and terrified as she was, she wasn't at all certain that she wouldn't have cut off their heads. But she supposed in the morning she would be grateful for not finding the lawn dotted with headless bodies.

Behind her, the servants had begun gathering again, whispering among themselves as they watched with astonishment the sight of the black specter chasing the mob out of sight. She heard their speculation, the whisper of ghosts, but sensible heads prevailed. Jenkins was all for sending a delegation to invite the chap in. The cook wanted to bake him a cake. The maids simpered in admiration. Dillian found herself torn between the desire to strangle the bloody marquess for scaring her like that and the equal desire to throw herself into his arms and kiss him all over.

She doubted if she would have the opportunity for either. The cloaked figure had disappeared into the shadows of the trees along the road. She didn't think the reclusive marquess would return to play the conquering hero. With quiet decision, she turned and ushered the household back inside.

"Jenkins, I'll need to speak with the dog trainer and the grooms. And you'd best assign another man to help Jamie. We have no guarantee that some of them won't return later," she said quietly to the stiff butler, who had rearranged his clothing and now waited for instructions while the rest of the staff returned to their rooms, chattering and giggling.

"Yes, Miss Reynolds." He turned and left her standing there all alone in the lamp-lit hallway.

The warm wood paneling of the Grange, the carpeted floors and polished fixtures, all gave out an aura of security and welcome, unlike the monstrosity of Arinmede Manor. Dillian loved this house. Her mother had told her tales of sliding down the banister as a child, of snow fights on the front lawn, of games of hide-and-seek beneath those very tables she could see scattered down the hall, draped in silk and tapestry. This was the only real home she had ever known, even though she had only lived here off and on these last five years since she had come to Blanche. Still, the attachment was strong, even more so for one who had never thought to have a home of her own. She owed its safety now to the mysterious Marquess of Effingham.

She gave the dog trainer orders to patrol the grounds, arranged for the grooms to take turns standing watch over the stable, made certain everyone had returned safely to their beds. And then she waited.

Dillian didn't bother undressing. She pulled back the draperies in her room, lit a lamp in the window, and opened the casement. She couldn't make the invitation any plainer. Propriety had no place in what she felt right now. She owed the marquess a debt of gratitude and she would repay it, whether he wished it or not. No doubt he preferred returning to his reclusive existence in that crumbling pile of dust that was his home, but Dillian didn't think she could let him waste away like that. Whether he liked it or not, she would save him from himself. She had no other means of repaying him.

As she sat there waiting, she debated means of returning the marquess to society. It was quite apparent that he needed Blanche. She had opposed the match from the first, but now she understood the sense of it. The irritating O'Toole had it right. Effingham could take care of Blanche the way she should be taken care of. The marquess would love her as everyone did. And Blanche had a loving nature. She would love any man who would accept her as she was.

The perfection of the match satisfied Dillian, even though she felt a nagging sense of loss at the thought. She would find it lonely without Blanche, she supposed, but she would find other interests in time. This was a lovely village. She would involve herself in village activities. Perhaps she could solve the farmer's grievances. Maybe she would even fall in love with the vicar. Anything was possible.

The gray light of dawn spread across the horizon before the marquess finally took advantage of her invitation and heaved himself across the windowsill. Dillian thought he looked weary as he closed the casement and leaned against the wall farthest from where she sat. He still wore his cloak, but she could tell he'd crossed his arms across his chest, no doubt glaring at her in disapproval. The single lamp didn't reach his face, so she couldn't tell for certain.

"I'll send down for a hot bath and breakfast," she murmured when he said nothing. "You must be exhausted."

"I'm fine. I'm returning to the manor. I saw the light and thought you might need something. You have that letter ready for Lady Blanche?"

"Your horse needs a rest even if you don't. Where did you find him, anyway?" Ignoring his words, Dillian pulled the bellpull to summon a maid.

"Stole him. You have a neighbor with an amazing stable. I'll return the horse before I leave. Their groom will wonder, but there's no harm done." He eased away from the lamp, slipping into the shadowy corner when she pulled the rope. "I'm not staying," he reminded her.

"You have some pressing business that calls you back?" she asked with a trace of scorn. "I'm certain O'Toole is entertaining Blanche much more successfully than you would. They can wait a few more hours."

After the excitement of the evening, a maid was slow in answering, but they could hear the footsteps coming up the stairs in the early morning silence. Dillian donned a dressing robe and pulled it around her to conceal the fact that she still wore yesterday's gown. The marquess said nothing. The low rumble of his voice would carry and reveal his presence.

Dillian opened the door just enough to speak to the maid. "Alice, I'm sorry to disturb you at this hour, but I have to leave this morning. Could you have someone draw a bath and bring up some breakfast? Something substantial, if you would. Tea and toast aren't enough after last night."

"Of course, miss." The maid curtsied and hurried to

do as ordered without questioning. Dillian blessed
Blanche for hiring such efficient help.

"Do you intend to wash my back?" the marquess
asked behind her, his tone almost carrying a hint of
amusement.

"No, I intend to go in Blanche's room and get dressed
while you're washing. If you're leaving without resting,
I'm going with you." Dillian opened her wardrobe and
removed her riding habit from the interior.

"You'll do no such damned thing," he whispered furiously. "I'm sending your lady back here, where she belongs. I don't need your help to do it."

"Sending her back here so we can all die in our sleep?
How very generous of you." Unmoved, Dillian opened
her dresser, removing the other items needed for her
ensemble. She wished she could enjoy the bath she had
ordered, but she would make do. Still, she couldn't help
thinking that it would be the last one she would enjoy
for some time to come. Baths didn't come easily in Arinmede Ruin.

"They'll not dare attack again. Everyone saw you
order the servants instead of Lady Blanche. They know
she's not really here. This is the safest place for her
now."

"Fustian. She wouldn't be back a day before the
whole village would know of it. You've lived too far
from civilization for too long, my lord, not to know that.
We'll only stay until Blanche is well enough to travel.
Then we'll take the first ship to France and be out of
your hair."

The sound of someone coming up the stairs halted the
argument. Dillian gestured for the marquess to hide in
her dressing room while she opened the door for the
footmen carrying a tub. She would like to see bathing
rooms added to the Grange, but that would require
money. The trustees still controlled Grange income.

When a maid offered to stay and help her, Dillian
shooed her away. The cook sent up a pot of hot coffee
and a platter of warm muffins to break the first pangs
of hunger while she bathed. The rest of breakfast would
follow later. The marquess would have to bathe quickly.

As soon as the servants departed, Effingham returned. He had shed his cloak and stood in the first rays of dawn in his unbuttoned frock coat, loose trousers, and wilted shirt. Even so, she thought him the most elegant man alive. A shock of black curls fell across his dark brow. The coat fit snugly to wide shoulders and lean torso, even though he stood slumped and weary, leaning against the wall to observe the proceedings. He was all length, she decided. Long arms, long legs, long everything in between. His clothes clung to him as if molded to his measurements. Blanche deserved a husband as elegant as this one. The scars scarcely mattered.

"I smell coffee."

Dillian gestured toward the tray. "It's all yours. Be quick though. They'll return shortly with breakfast. I told them to put it in my dressing room, but they still might come in and offer to help me dress. They're extremely efficient."

He crossed the room and poured himself a cup of the black brew, taking a healthy swallow without any additives. Dillian grimaced. She detested the bitter taste, but he looked as if he could use it. "I'm sorry I couldn't figure a way to have your clothes freshened."

He set the cup down and peeled off his coat. "I'll survive. Unless you mean to wash my back, you'd better run and hide."

As the coat fell to the floor, she could see his sweat-soaked shirt plastered to his broad back, and she almost wished she could stay and help him bathe.

That thought sent her fleeing in a panic. She meant the Marquess of Effingham to marry Blanche. She shouldn't think such thoughts about her cousin's future husband.

Eleven

"Have you found that cousin of yours yet?" the Earl of Dismouth inquired as he and the Duke of Anglesey strolled down the steps of the Parliament building to their waiting carriage.

Neville clenched his fingers into fists and declared crossly, "No, but that confounded companion knows where she is, I vow. We should never have banned the rack. Drawing and quartering are too good for her. In the meantime, even my best investigator has disappeared. I'm wondering if there isn't a conspiracy. Blanche would never pull this kind of stunt on her own."

The earl stroked his graying side-whiskers. "There might be something to that. Lady Blanche's father served with Wellington, didn't he? I heard he had some relationship with the notorious Colonel Whitnell?"

Neville climbed in the carriage without looking back at the earl. "That was all before my time. I was still up at Oxford when my uncle died. What has that to say to anything?"

The earl settled on the seat across from him and crossed his hands complacently on the golden head of his walking stick. "There's a few rumors going around the foreign ministry about Whitnell. Nothing solid, you realize, but enough to raise questions. He's said to have held information of vital importance to His Majesty, information that never came to light. I just thought if there were any relationship . . ."

Neville waved a careless hand. "That's too far-fetched for me. My uncle was a pompous old fool. He wouldn't touch anything less than aboveboard. In any case, what would that have to do with Blanche? She was still in the schoolroom when her father died."

"Not a thing, I'm sure," the earl responded equably, leaning back in his seat. "I just thought you mentioned her companion's name as Reynolds. It may be far-fetched, but Whitnell was said to have married a distant relation of the Reynolds family. I do believe your cousin's mother came from the same branch?"

And so it was, now that he thought about it. Pulling his hat down to hide his eyes, Neville sank into a black study.

Gavin woke to a soft bed and the welcome scents of fresh coffee. It took a moment to overcome the sensual pleasure of enveloping feathers and a cool dusk breeze drifting through the windows. He couldn't remember the last time he'd felt such comfort. He couldn't remember the last time he'd slept the day away.

Hell. Slept the day away. What had the damned woman done, drugged his coffee?

Warily, he opened his eyes a crack to note the familiar tray and pitcher. The coffee aroma wasn't so pleasant with the prospect of drugs tainting it.

"Oh, good. You're awake. I've been having difficulty explaining why no one could come in and freshen the room after I roused everyone from their beds with plans for an early journey. They think I'm ill."

Gavin groaned and returned his head to the pillow. Gazing upward, he could see a bouquet of bright flowers embroidered on the underside of the canopy. He didn't know one flower from another, but this seemed a colorful assortment. It suited the little gamin. She ought to wear scarlet and emerald and sapphire. Fire colors.

His mind wandered. It had to be drugs. He dared a sideways look. The wretched elf sat composedly in a chair by the cold fireplace, some respectable-looking tome in her hands. She wore the riding gown she had taken out earlier in the day. He remembered she had pulled her hair back tightly earlier also, but it had escaped its pins now. A thick dark strand curled in front of one ear, and wisps hung about her neck. He fought back a grin at the sight. She looked about eight years old.

"I don't think I dare risk the coffee," he mused aloud. "I remember bathing. Do I dare hope I dressed again afterward?"

She blushed. A woman who could blush. How amazing. He truly hadn't gone about much in society these last years. He couldn't remember blushing women. He just remembered screams and horrified looks and heads turning away.

But this one gazed upon him fearlessly. He rather admired that, although he had to wonder about the motive behind it. He had embarrassed her unnecessarily. He could feel his shirt and trousers now, remembered lying down, waiting for her return. He'd enjoyed a bountiful breakfast, too, but his stomach felt empty again. He'd spent too many years going hungry to appreciate the feeling now.

As if she read his thoughts, she rose to the bellpull. "I'll have them send up some dinner. Would you like something besides the coffee, then?"

He didn't know why she had decided to use patience with him. She'd obviously spent the entire day guarding him against invasion. He'd just accused her of poisoning his coffee and embarrassed her with the notion of his nakedness, and she still stood there patiently awaiting his orders.

His orders. Of course. She thought of him as a bloody marquess, and she was naught but a lowly employee. He'd never get used to this British class system. Frowning enough to make her flinch, Gavin sat up.

"Coffee is fine. I've got to leave. Has anyone made inquiries about last night?"

"The squire was here. He apologized and said he'd called for militia, but none arrived in time. They're patrolling the village square right now. It's not a healthy situation, but I'm not in a position to do much about it. As far as I'm aware, Blanche's tenants are treated fairly."

Gavin rose and started shoving his shirt back in his trouser front before he realized he did so in the presence of a lady. He cursed his bachelor habits and turned his back to adjust himself more discreetly. "A mob follows where it's led. The rabble-rouser in town practically ordered them out here. I doubt if your tenants had any say in the matter."

"That is not reassuring. You are saying someone sent them out here to burn us out. And you meant to leave us here on our own?"

He wanted to tell her it wasn't his problem. He had more problems than he could deal with on his own. But she got so rosy-cheeked in her outrage that she diverted his wits. He welcomed any diversions at all. "As I told you before, they'll not try that tactic again. You have enough safeguards in place now that you shouldn't have to worry. Why doesn't your Lady Blanche simply tell her noble duke that she'll marry him come October and pacify him for a while?"

Gavin could hear the maid coming. He wondered what his nemesis would do if he refused to hide. The possibility that his dinner might end up all over the floor when the maid caught sight of him settled the matter quickly. He slipped through the open door of her dressing room as Miss Whitnell let the maid in.

The cook here wasn't as good as his Matilda, but the tantalizing aromas of roast beef and pudding overcame Gavin's reservations. The lady hadn't poisoned him so far. He would just make certain she shared the meal with him.

They'd shared other meals together. She had as much appreciation for good food as he did. He remembered young ladies as picking delicately at their meals, striving to make conversation or to flirt and catch his attention. Miss Whitnell had no such foolish notions. She merely ate what was set before her and allowed the conversation to dwindle or spark as it would. He liked that. He didn't feel any pressure to converse. He'd lost the habit years ago.

But somehow they always found a topic. As he came out of the dressing room and actually remembered to hold a chair out for her, she returned to their earlier one.

"I suppose you are of the opinion that Blanche should

give up all that is hers to a man's care, as if men were any better at taking care of things than women."

"In my experience, most people don't take care of what they ought, be they male or female. It would behoove a lady to choose a careful man." Gavin took his seat and watched her serve him the largest slice of beef. He offered her the little new potatoes dotted with something that smelled enticing. Matilda didn't make efficient use of herbs. Perhaps he should get the recipe.

"That's an easy thing to say, coming from a recluse like yourself. How is a woman to know if a man is careful until it is too late?"

This was a ridiculous conversation. Snaring a piece of potato, he answered, "By asking his friends, I assume."

She gave him an irritated glance and didn't interrupt his meal again. Gavin could almost see the wheels of her brain clicking and turning and smoking as he ate. When he was almost done, he said carefully, "If you're thinking of following me again, don't."

She glanced up at him with an innocent expression that wouldn't fool a fool. "Of course not. I wouldn't dream of it."

As if she had said nothing, he continued. "Your duke has the roads and the house watched. You would lead them directly to Lady Blanche."

She paled slightly and sipped at her tea. "Then, they'll know if you return her here. You can't send her back."

"I'm still not convinced your duke means her any harm. That mob last night was meant as a distraction. Those farmers wouldn't have burned the Grange. They've never burned anything in their lives. Somebody was behind it, somebody who no doubt meant to drive you screaming from the house, but you had plenty of warning. You could see those torches for miles. It wasn't the same kind of attempt as before."

The color still hadn't returned to her cheeks, but Gavin watched with a certain amount of fascination as she wrinkled her pert nose in thought. She had the gamin features of a thoughtless child, but he had learned to respect the active mind behind them. She would make a terrible sailor, never obeying orders if she disagreed with them, but as an officer capable of thinking for herself . . . That was a silly speculation. Who would listen to a half-pint termagant?

"What would they accomplish by driving us from the house? Do you think they meant to kidnap Blanche?"

He'd considered that possibility. He'd kept a careful eye and ear out for the instigators behind the mob. He knew little of English accents, but he could tell which belonged here and which sounded vaguely out of place. He had a good eye for character, too. Those with the odd accents didn't seem like farmer material to him. Had they been wearing slouch hats and raccoon vests, he would classify them on the same level as the two-bit outlaws he'd seen west of the Allegheny Mountains. Flat caps and frock coats didn't quite fit the image, but he reckoned English villains dressed a little differently. That still didn't mean they were kidnappers.

With his plate empty, Gavin sat back and contemplated his answer while sipping at his coffee. "I can't imagine the duke sending thugs like that to steal his cousin, unless, of course, he truly wished her murdered. I have difficulty picturing proper English aristocrats dealing in murder."

Since she remained silent, Gavin assumed the lady had the same reservations. He couldn't imagine the lackluster creatures he'd met over here even committing a crime of passion. The cold-blooded murder of a beautiful young heiress seemed equally far-fetched. A little poison to hurry on a dying old harridan, maybe, but not cold-blooded murder. Since she apparently waited for him to continue, he tried out one of his theories.

"Is there some possibility the duke might try terrifying Lady Blanche into marrying him?"

Miss Whitnell made a wry grimace and shrugged. "I believe him perfectly capable of murder. Terrorism wouldn't surprise me."

Gavin had seen the duke from a distance when Anglesey had arrived in his fancy carriage. He couldn't judge a man from that distance. He hadn't been impressed with the elegant clothes or the duke's youth or less than athletic physique. Pity he wouldn't have a chance to meet the man in person. But terrorism?

"Let me put it this way," Gavin said cautiously. "Would anyone have reason to believe Lady Blanche so easily terrified that she might turn to her powerful relations for help?"

Miss Whitnell's delightfully arched eyebrows rose with this new perspective. "I should think not. No, definitely not. Blanche has played simpleminded innocence for years for Neville's benefit, but even he must see that she has kept out of his clutches quite determinedly. He no doubt blames much of it on me . . ." Her eyebrows rose even further. "Perhaps he meant to terrify me!"

Gavin grinned. "Then, the man must have rooms to let in his upper story, as Michael would say. Any man in his right mind would know you would just get meaner and more stubborn if terrified."

A perfectly enchanting grin tugged at the corner of her mouth. Had Gavin not learned to protect himself against feminine wiles long ago, that grin would have left him utterly annihilated. Even now, inured as he was to feminine charms, he felt a tug at long dead heartstrings. He understood his lust for the first female in a long time that he'd encountered for any duration, but he didn't like or understand this other sensation. The obstinate Miss Whitnell wasn't at all the kind of woman he'd once admired.

Although—Gavin cocked his head and stared at the ceiling as he remembered those long-ago days—he had always had a certain inclination toward women with ample curves. He just didn't credit most of them with the same sort of brains that Miss Whitnell possessed, nor the same sort of character, he had to admit. The lovely, graceful swans of society he'd once courted had the constancy of barn cats. Miss Whitnell showed her devotion to her employer with every word and action. Perhaps this stirring of his insides was merely admiration for her character. Her irritatingly obstinate character.

"Perhaps you're right," she admitted with a smile. "Although it isn't at all the thing for you to say so.

Neville would not be so foolish as to believe he could scare me into persuading Blanche to marry him."

"Which leaves us precisely where we were before. What could they hope to accomplish by driving you from the house? Did you notice if anything was disturbed? Did the servants guard the doors? Could anyone have got in without notice?"

She stared at him wide-eyed as she worked her way through his questions, then answered slowly. "They panicked so, I doubt the servants paid much attention to the doors. . . ." She dropped her voice as she thought some more. "I really haven't looked to see if anything was disturbed. I've been too busy keeping them out of here. But certainly Jenkins would have reported it if anything were missing. Surely, you do not think them common thieves?"

"Not common. Thieves do not ordinarily set mobs on a household to drive them out. I just cannot quite find the connection between an arsonist burning down an entire household and endangering all within and this mob simply attempting to drive you from your home or terrify you into leaving. It seems as if there may be two different purposes at work here."

Miss Whitnell's expression changed to one of excitement. "Do you think possibly . . . If someone wanted to destroy something in Blanche's possession, they might have thought it kept in town and so burned the house down to remove it? Now, for some reason, perhaps they're uncertain as to whether they accomplished their goal and wish to verify this object is no longer with her?"

"That's beyond far-fetched. It would be simpler and less risky to simply steal the object in the first place. Do you have reason to believe Lady Blanche possesses something of importance that anyone would destroy dozens of lives to remove?"

She shrugged and frowned. "Blanche has access to immense amounts of money, legal documents, family papers, any number of things, not to mention the usual sort of jewels, objets d'art, and so forth. She even keeps my father's papers for me. She does not use the Grange much, so most everything was kept in London or the village house. We have not even begun to consider what was lost in the fire. Blanche's safety came first."

Gavin reluctantly admitted to himself that he had become more involved in this tangle than he had ever intended. He wanted nothing more than his privacy back. He had no desire to gallop about the countryside solving a mystery without any clues. His own estate needed constant tending, and his financial needs were much more dire than the Lady Blanche's. Still, he could not write her off as a useless parasite of society and condemn her to arsonists and mobs as just deserts.

Damn it all, he would have to help them.

Twelve

"I feel like a poacher," Dillian muttered, ducking under a low-lying branch near the wall she climbed across.

"You look like a poacher," the marquess responded agreeably. "The homespun smock is an artistic touch, if I do say so myself. Far better than that blue monstrosity you wore here."

"I'd rather be an unfashionable dandy than a poacher, thank you." Besides, the smock itched despite the linen chemise she wore under it. She didn't feel inclined to tell the wretch that, however. He occupied himself entirely too much with watching how she got about in these ghastly boy's breeches. She couldn't very well bind her hips as she did her breasts. Even the ill-fitting smock barely disguised what she couldn't flatten. Thank heavens the marquess was not the kind of man who acted upon his lusts. She would make certain he only drank coffee and not liquor in her presence.

She would make certain *she* didn't drink liquor when he was about. Those unsettling dark eyes made her quiver like no other man's had. She didn't like being stared at. Or she hadn't until this infuriating man came along.

"How will we keep Neville's men from seeing us?" she asked, more to divert her own thoughts than with any real desire to know his nefarious plans.

"What difference does it make if they do see us? They don't know who we are. They can't follow everyone who comes along the road. Just keep your hat pulled down over your face and slump a little if we meet anyone.

They're looking for you or Lady Blanche, not a Yankee and a poacher."

He looked the part of a Yankee well enough, wearing that same ridiculous coat and hat as before. He looked the part of a dangerous Yankee, if the truth be told. He ought to have a pistol in his belt and a rifle in his hand. Neville's men would stay clear of him, for a certainty.

"How much farther until we reach the horses?"

"I've stabled them in the next village. Cutting across these fields is fastest and will throw off any pursuit. I can't imagine the duke posting men this far out, but they will just think you from around here and not question too thoroughly if we do run across them. If we're fortunate, they'll believe you're holed up in the Grange and terrified out of your mind."

Dillian made a snorting noise. "Neville won't believe such idiocy. I've been ever so polite to him for years, but he still calls me a dragon."

The marquess gave a muffled laugh as he reached the road and held back the shrubbery to help her through. "A fine dragon you'd make. Insufferable mosquito, I allow, but you could scarcely swallow a gnat whole."

"Oh, you're a fine one to make jokes about appearances, my Lord Beast. I suppose you think you fit the fire-breathing dragon description, don't you? I saw you with your fine sword last night. You didn't remove a single head."

"I'm not inclined toward beheading misinformed farmers. I saw enough of that in the war. Blood and guts do not make a pretty sight; I'll thank you to remember that the next time you want me to run a man through. Just because I look a beast doesn't mean I need behave like one."

"On the contrary, you behave more like a beast than look like one. I think you like skulking in corners and behind cloaks. I think you are inherently antisocial and use your appearance as an excuse to hide."

His laugh this time was mirthless. "What a busy little mind you have. Have you ever considered the effect on society should I introduce myself as a captain in the U.S. navy? I daresay I have turned cannon on any number of British man-o'-wars in past years. That should make me a welcome member of society, particularly since I have no wealth with which to distract them."

Dillian followed him down the road, keeping pace with his longer legs only because he amended his stride to suit hers. She gave him a surreptitious look, but in the darkness and with his hat pulled over his face, she could see little of his expression. "With a title, you could no doubt attract a wealthy cit. Many families would pay a great deal to call their daughters marchionesses, as long as you're not interested in marrying into the aristocracy."

"I am very definitely not interested in marrying into the aristocracy. I am not interested in marrying at all. I have no desire to marry for wealth and spend the rest of my years avoiding my loving wife's look of horror every time she turns her head toward me, thank you very much. And that's quite enough of this conversation."

His stride picked up pace, leaving Dillian practically running after him. Neville didn't consider her a dragon for naught. Once she dug her teeth in, she didn't let go. She didn't mean to let go now. "How did you come to be raised American if you were in line for a title?"

That brought another of his humorless laughs. "They ran out of male heirs and got desperate, I suppose. I was never supposed to be a marquess. Had the family any choice, I would not even be a Lawrence, but my father and grandfather very properly married their doxies once they got them with child. My branch of the family never held a very high opinion of aristocracy and bloodlines. Actually, they never held a very high opinion of the law of any kind. You really don't want to know more."

After a line like that? She wanted to know it all. Dillian sent Effingham a curious glance, but he didn't much look like an outlaw. Even in that ridiculous garb he looked the part of aristocrat. It was in his tall, lean elegance, the way he held himself, the arrogance of his tone, the carelessness with which he dismissed the opinion of the rest of the world. No one would mistake him

for anything less than a nobleman no matter what guise
he wore.

"I should like to hear a great deal more, if you please.
I have never been farther from home than London. I
should like to know about the Americas and the navy
and your family. You ride a horse magnificently, but
you say you're a sailor. How can any one man be so
many things?"

"Easy. Be poor and desperate for any work at all.
Have a younger brother and a sickly mother to support.
The tale is not a romantic one. I have done many things
of which I'm not proud. I'm quite content just staying
at Arinmede and working the land, once I claim it. I
don't need society or annoying mosquitoes or lovely
heiresses."

His dismissive tone made it obvious the conversation
had ended. Since the lights of the village came into view,
Dillian gave it up for now. She didn't know why she
wanted to know more about this man who so obviously
wished to be left alone. For some reason, he just fascinated her. She would get over that quickly enough.

They found the horses at the inn, where the marquess
had boarded them. Dillian insisted on paying the shot
with the money she had taken from the Grange's household cash. The marquess quietly put his hand back in
his pocket and let her proceed. After all, Blanche was
the reason for their presence here. She had enough
wealth for all of them. Dillian saw no reason to put the
bankrupt marquess out of pocket. She just found herself
pleasingly surprised that he had followed her train of
thought and not objected. Not too many men would
lower their pride so. Of course, not too many men traveled with women dressed as poachers.

They quietly took a back road out of town. Dillian
knew this part of their journey. She knew the road they
took led away from Arinmede. She returned his courtesy
by not questioning. Surely, a sailor could read the stars
and know they took the wrong direction.

She received her reward for her silence when he
pointed out the crossroads ahead.

"Militia. I'm heading for Plymouth to take ship.

You're my tenant come to take my horse and some cattle I've purchased back to my farm. Don't name any names if you can avoid it."

Dillian glanced nervously at the soldiers rising up from their lounging positions in the grass. A moment later, she gulped with more than nervousness. She recognized one man wearing the uniform of her father's troop—surely, Neville hadn't set the Queen's Hussars to search for Blanche!

Thirteen

Dillian peered through the darkness, searching for familiar faces. Except for the officer, the motley group wore only ragtag remnants of uniforms. She'd met most of her father's troop at one time or another, but after the war, the faces had changed. When she'd changed her name and moved in with Blanche, she had lost track of those few she knew, except for those listed as fatalities at Waterloo. In the darkness, except for the man in uniform, none of these men looked particularly familiar.

She thought she recognized Reardon as the officer lounging against the signpost, letting the others do his work for him. She didn't know how to warn the marquess. Not only did she think it would look suspicious if she suddenly rode up beside Effingham, whispered her message, and rode back, but she didn't know what she could say to him. He didn't know this country very well. He had probably never heard of Colonel "Slippery" Whitnell. Even though Blanche had let slip Dillian's real name, it had made no difference to this man. She liked it that way.

"Who goes there?" called a man wearing the blue cape of a hussar but without the royal red shako. Dillian found it difficult imagining the dashing cavaliers of the Napoleonic Wars reduced to standing guard duty at country crossroads. Reardon must have got himself on Neville's wrong side to find himself in this humiliating position. She wondered how he came to be in charge of such a motley lot.

"Who asks?" the marquess asked complacently.

"An officer of the Queen's Hussars, sir. Dismount and state your name and destination!" the guard barked.

Effingham remained mounted. His Yankee accent assumed that tone of idle amusement Dillian wished to trounce him for upon occasion. He was asking to get himself killed. She didn't think these men any too happy with their duty. They would take him apart first and ask questions later if pushed too far.

"As far as I'm concerned, you could be a pack of damned horse thieves, my friends. And since I'm a United States citizen, I'm not much accustomed to bowing and scraping. I'd suggest you let me pass before I start another war just for the pleasure of seeing His Majesty's royal forces cut to ribbons again."

A couple of the other men sauntered over to stand behind their comrade, but Reardon remained where he was, watching the episode with boredom. Dillian bit her lip in an effort to keep her tongue still.

"A damned Yank," one of the men muttered.

The guard who had halted them spoke nastily. "It seems we won the last war. If you want to get beat again, go ahead and try it."

"Bloodthirsty, are we? You must not have been in New Orleans when General Jackson and his men cut down the 'world's finest fighting force' by the thousands," the marquess answered with the same dry amusement. "And we have a real navy now. Just imagine what John Paul Jones could do with more than one ship this time around. However, I'm not eager to slay my cousins. I'll hold the peace if you'll just let us pass. Even in this foolish country you can't stop innocent citizens without a purpose when they travel public roads."

For some reason, the marquess's languid air of authority and bored amusement worked on the soldiers, or ex-soldiers, as the case seemed likely. Their stances relaxed, and they seemed to regard the conversation as a challenge. Men! Dillian thought with disgust. This could evolve into an all-night game of one-upmanship. Unless Reardon got a good look at her. Since he was rising from his pole position and swaggering toward them, that could happen any minute now. She glanced nervously at the one lantern sitting by the fire. They hadn't brought it forward—yet. She didn't want to wait around until they did.

If she addressed the marquess by his title, these men would instantly fall back, but he didn't want his identity revealed for fear it would lead to Blanche. Dillian wouldn't endanger Blanche if he wouldn't. The worst they could do was arrest him for insubordination or some such. She just didn't want to think what would become of her once Reardon disclosed her identity as Whitnell's daughter. Dillian sighed and held her tongue. She would sacrifice whatever it took for Blanche.

"A damned Yank and a bloody sailor, or I miss my guess," Reardon drawled as he strolled up.

"Captain, actually," the marquess responded in the same flat drawl.

"And what's this you've got behind you?" Reardon nodded his feathered shako in the direction of Dillian.

The marquess checked behind him as if he'd forgotten anyone followed. He shrugged his shoulders beneath his long coat with disinterest when he turned back around to face his interrogator. "One of my cousin's tenants. He's taking some livestock back for Mellon. I fail to see any reason for holding up our journey in this fashion. If you're the officer on duty, then tell your men to remove themselves from my path. The earl isn't a politically active man, but he might raise himself to action if he hears how the queen's forces are being used. If the queen's forces they are," he added with malice.

Dillian breathed a sigh of relief. She'd never heard of Mellon, but if Effingham threw around a title, they'd escape soon enough.

Reardon's voice held the same note of amusement as Effingham's had earlier. "Do we refer to the Earl of Mellon? And what would a blamed Yank know of such an illustrious personage?"

"He's my cousin," the marquess responded quite affably. "And he's damned glad to see the back of me. So if you're meaning to keep me here, you'll hear from him soon enough. I have yet to know the reason for this little blockade. Am I accused of smuggling American brandy?

Of riding the wrong horse before Derby? Just exactly what is the infraction?"

Reardon wandered a little closer to Dillian. She could feel his sharp gaze take in her broken-down nag, her homespun smock, her lack of baggage. She just prayed the baggy breeches, smock, and filthy hat hid enough of her to pass inspection. Reardon might be idle and effete, but she had never thought of him as dumb. She held her breath and stared off into space like a dim-witted know-nothing.

"I'm looking for a stolen heiress," Reardon said casually, his gaze seemingly probing beyond Dillian's loose smock.

Effingham laughed. "For that, I'll gladly dismount. If you find her beneath my saddle, I'll happily turn her over to you."

Reardon shrugged and finally let his gaze return to the marquess as he sauntered in his direction. "Ride this heiress, and the duke will revive drawing and quartering just for your benefit. Go on with you. I've better things to do with this night."

Dillian sighed with relief as they silently rode past the soldiers and took the crossroad leading even farther away from Blanche. Reardon had no reason to know that his former officer's daughter was now the companion of the missing heiress. She had dropped her old identity entirely when she'd moved in with Blanche. Blanche just referred to her as a distant cousin on her mother's side. She'd taken her mother's maiden name of Reynolds. He could not possibly make the connection. Reardon had no reason to recognize her. Why, then, did she have the uneasy feeling that he'd seen through her disguise?

They rode well out of sight and sound of the soldiers before taking a path through a farm gate and finally striking out over the fields in the direction of Hertfordshire and Arinmede.

The marquess didn't seem particularly talkative, and Dillian had no desire to share her thoughts, either. She just wanted to reach Blanche as quickly and safely as possible. Even if Reardon suspected her identity, he'd have no reason to follow her, no reason to associate her or the "damned Yank" with Blanche. Nothing else mattered.

They rode for hours, through fields and woods and finally on the roads that would take them to the manor. They stopped at a posting inn to refresh the horses and themselves. When the marquess returned with ale and food he'd persuaded from a sleepy scullery maid, he quaffed deeply of his mug and regarded Dillian with a look that made her uneasy. She made a show of brushing down her weary horse.

"Why do I get the feeling that officer back there knew something he shouldn't?"

Dillian tried shrugging nonchalantly as he did. She wasn't very good at it. "You were the one doing the talking. I played dumb as you told me."

"Your servants call you Miss Reynolds, but Lady Blanche called you Whitnell. If I'm harboring a fugitive, I'd like to know of it."

Damn his agile mind. He couldn't possibly know the truth. She didn't know the truth of it herself. He just jumped to remarkably odd conclusions using exceedingly few facts. Dillian gave up her pretense of knowing what she was doing and sipped the ale he handed her. She made a face at the bitter taste, but she needed something to wash down the night's dirt.

"I'm not a fugitive, if that's what you're insinuating. I'm just exactly what we've told you, Blanche's companion. What my name is isn't relative."

Effingham bit into his bread and cheese and chewed thoughtfully. He'd taken off his ridiculous hat, and Dillian watched as a hank of dark hair fell across his brow, almost in his eyes. She couldn't imagine why she thought of him as an aristocrat. He ate common fare as if accustomed to it, dressed like the worst rabble, and had the conversational delicacy of a hedgehog. But she read aristocracy in the long lines of his patrician nose and square jaw, the jut of his cheekbones over hollowed cheeks, the arrogant mannerisms bred into him from birth. His father and grandfather might have stayed one step ahead

of the law, but they'd never forgotten their breeding.
They'd passed it on to this man.

He finished his fare and gathered their tankards to
take back to the kitchen. Only then did he reply. Giving
her a stern look from beneath a thin line of dark eyebrows, he said quite forcefully, "I don't give a damn
who or what you are. I just won't have my home or my
people harmed in any way. Remember that."

Dillian found herself trembling as she remounted. She
didn't think the Marquess of Effingham made threats
idly.

Blanche watched with amusement as the breakfast
cutlery disappeared up Michael's sleeve and reappeared
in places like the flower vase with her morning rose. He
retrieved a fork from his pocket and a spoon from her
hair. Of course, the faint gray light of dawn from the
window made it easy for him to hide the gestures that
produced this sleight of hand. She gazed wistfully out at
the first streaks of light on the horizon and waited for
the orders to cover her eyes with the scarf Michael had
given her to replace her bandages. She could still see
little more than shadows and light out the window, but
she probably couldn't see more than that if her vision
were whole. Darkness shrouded most of the landscape.

In here, she could easily distinguish the white linen of
Michael's shirt and admire the way it draped his broad
shoulders. She had scolded him for improper attire, but
he'd only grinned and produced the rose from his shirt
cuff. She could see his grin and the rose, if only in outline and grayness. He refused to light a lamp.

"Never look so gloomy, my lady. You can see the
flower upon the table and the sun's light in the sky. That
is far more than your physician expected. Time will give
you the rest," he said gently as he handed her the silk.

Verity slipped from the still shadows of the corner to
tie the scarf around her mistress's head. She had very
properly chaperoned these morning sessions, but she remained so quiet neither of them knew of her presence
until times like these.

"I cannot sit here like a great lump of pudding for

the rest of my life," Blanche protested as the scarf turned objects into dim shadows. "Take me to Dillian, at least. I'm worried about her."

Her irritating footman laughed. "Worried about the she-devil? You would do better to worry about the marquess. He's too much a gentleman to cut out her tongue, and he's lived too isolated these last years to remember how to tame a shrew. You must smooth his ruffled feathers when he returns."

"Dillian isn't a shrew," Blanche objected, without emotion. She could tell he was preparing to leave, off on whatever odd projects he entertained when not with her. She shouldn't be depressed at the departure of a servant, but the day stretched long and boring ahead of her.

"You may ask his lordship's opinion on the matter when he returns. I expect him shortly. In the meanwhile, I have errands to run, places to go. I bid you adieu, my lady."

She heard the distance in his voice. The fact that he actually bothered to say farewell told more than she wanted to know. He was leaving. She frowned. If he was her servant, he couldn't leave without her permission. "I haven't given you leave to go," she informed him coldly.

"Neither have you given the night leave to turn to day, but so it has. Be kind to the marquess, my lady, and he will willingly die for you. You are two of a kind."

She didn't hear him go, but she knew when he left. He took the sun with him. Blanche didn't give in to the urge to ask her maid how he had gone. She preferred thinking of O'Toole as a dandelion seed wafting on the wind, alighting where the breeze took him.

That thought didn't make her any less restless.

"You say she's gone to France? That's impossible! Blanche wouldn't go alone, and I know for a fact that her companion is still in Hampshire."

The duke paced a dark library lined in mahogany shelves, paneled in burled walnut, and furnished in the heavy satinwood of a previous generation. The magnificently carved ceiling—also in burled walnut—showed the talents of an artisan long since dead, who most probably had spent his entire life carving on just this one project. The chamber reeked of ancient wealth, prestige, and favor.

Wearing a scissor-tailed morning coat, the slender intruder inspecting the shelves seemed oblivious to his impressive surroundings. He flicked a speck of dust from a leather-bound cover and lifted a book from the shelf to admire the contents, speaking idly as he did so. "For a fact, now? And will you not be needing my services any longer, then, Your Grace, that you know more than I do?"

The duke glared at his irritating employee. O'Toole had the maddening habit of behaving as if he were to the manner born. Only another duke should have the arrogance to ignore Neville's concern and fury and go about reading other people's libraries. O'Toole should be trembling in his shoes right now, not perusing a volume of Chaucer.

"Are you telling me that Dillian isn't in Hampshire any longer?"

O'Toole looked up with a pleased expression on his mobile countenance. "Very good, Your Grace. Now all you need do is believe it, and we'll make some progress this day, after all."

Neville ground his teeth and wished for a pistol. Instead, he opened his desk and produced a small sack of coins. "How much?"

"If I'm to follow them to France, it will take that and more, I wager." O'Toole eyed the sack of coins dubiously.

Neville pitched the coins at him and watched as his hired detective caught it smoothly and disappeared it into his capacious pocket. "Hire another operative to follow them. I want you to do something else for me."

The duke refused to allow himself pleasure as he noted the surprise in his hireling's eyes. He'd debated this moment for days now. He'd just decided to act.

"I want you to investigate the parentage of Blanche's companion, Dillian Reynolds. I want you to look into any possible relationship between Blanche's father, Lord

Albert Perceval, late of the Queen's Hussars, and Colonel Harold Whitnell, also known as Colonel "Slippery" Whitnell of the same unit."

O'Toole slid the Chaucer volume back on the shelf and approached the massive mahogany library table, where the duke stood. "To what end, Your Grace?"

"Treason, O'Toole, treason."

Fourteen

Gavin turned to check on his traveling companion and watched as she straightened her shoulders the instant she saw him turn around. Nothing told him more clearly how she must have slumped in the saddle without his observation.

Dawn cracked on the horizon, and because of the hours going out of their way, they hadn't even reached the boundaries of Hertfordshire yet. She must be saddle sore and exhausted to the bone, yet she forced herself to sit upright and give him that cocky look from behind fine eyebrows that said she had as much energy as he. On his own, Gavin would have continued on to Arinmede. He had an urgent desire for the protective custody of his home. But Miss Whitnell hadn't had the dubious experience of riding in the saddle for days on end, nor the callused toughness from sailing the sea on little more than hardtack and ale. He had those strengths. She didn't.

He sighed and allowed her to bring her mount beside his. "We have our choice of sleeping in the fields or stopping at the next inn. The horses need rest, and so do we. Neither choice smacks of propriety."

She gave him a look of blatant disbelief. "Since when have we considered propriety? I for one would prefer a decent breakfast and not whatever inedible contents you carry in your pockets. I vote for the inn."

Nothing shy about her. Gavin shook his head and proceeded onward. He had no particular desire to ruin the lady's reputation should anyone uncover her identity, but he wasn't inclined to save it in the usual way, either. If she thought to trap him into marriage by her boldness, she would find herself gravely disappointed. Somehow, Gavin thought marriage was the last thing on the lady's mind.

They found a tiny inn in the next village, stabled the horses, and breakfasted on ham and eggs before Gavin inquired into rooms. The proprietor wadded his pudgy hands into his soiled apron and nodded knowingly. He'd scarcely acknowledged Gavin's scarred face or odd attire since their arrival.

"Got just the thing for you, your lordship, our best room. The lad can stable down with the horses."

Gavin seemed to have developed a sixth sense where his companion was concerned. He felt her freeze and wait with bated breath for his reply, even though she stood behind him. He had half a mind to agree to this arrangement. That would teach her a lesson for insisting on following him around like a pet dog. Heaven only knew, he didn't need her company. He liked living alone. He liked traveling alone. He didn't need anyone, but he particularly didn't need this pint-size keg of trouble. But even if his mother hadn't been much of a lady, she'd taught him how to treat one.

Giving Dillian a venomous look to keep her tongue dried up, Gavin gave a curt nod. "The lad stays with me. He's less likely to get into trouble that way. He can fix a pallet on the floor."

Wielding his authority like a sword, he swung past the proprietor without giving him time to question or protest. The pudgy man ran after him, directing him up the stairs. Gavin scarcely needed directions. The inn had only two upper rooms: the common room with a dozen narrow cots, and the "best" room for visiting dignitaries or anyone else wealthy enough to spend more than tuppence for clean linen.

At least the room faced west so the morning sun didn't cast a discerning light on the dust balls under the bed and the cracked pottery at the bedside. Gavin jerked the limp muslin curtains over the room's one window to hide the rest of the room from light. He'd prefer not seeing his companion's expression when faced with this predicament.

The door shut behind the innkeeper. Gavin waited, but she said nothing. Finally, he heard her moving around, and he gave in. As much as he liked pretending he was alone, he couldn't resist seeing what she did now.

She had the heavy coverlet from the bed folded up on the floor in front of the door. As he watched she dropped one of the bed's bedraggled pillows upon it. They had both taken advantage of the necessary before coming upstairs, but bathing facilities had been nonexistent. She looked dubiously at the cracked pitcher and bowl, then glanced back at him.

"I think I'll wait until we reach Arinmede to wash," she said without preface.

"Excellent thought." He eyed the lumpy quilt with distaste. He'd slept on worse, but he didn't relish repeating the experience. His side ached and had grown stiff. The wounds of war weren't always gallant or romantic, just painful. He sat down in the room's one rickety chair to remove his boots. "I don't want to be seen near the manor before dark. I'm figuring we're only a few hours away. It will get hot in here before then."

To his surprise, Miss Whitnell sat down on the pallet to remove her boots. He had assumed she would appropriate the bed. She must have taken his words below literally.

"I'll sleep there," he informed her curtly.

"Not with me, you won't." She pulled off her boots, then glanced down with disgust at her rough homespun smock. She didn't say a word, but the glance was sufficient to tell him she wished she could remove it. Gavin imagined it irritated her tender skin. He didn't want to contemplate the tender skin in question. Without thinking, he pulled off his fine linen shirt and threw it at her.

"I'll turn my back so you can put it on. It will be a sight more comfortable than that ungodly thing you're wearing."

Instantly, Gavin wished he'd had the sense to turn his back on her before he'd thrown the shirt. Her eyes widened with alarm and hidden interest as he bared himself to the waist. He'd quit looking in mirrors years ago, but he saw himself in her eyes. He'd never been given to fat, and he'd worked hard all his life. He supposed he'd built muscles that the average aristocrat didn't possess, and the scar on his side probably had an entertaining effect. Gavin felt a familiar stiffening in his groin as he recognized the scarcely disguised interest widening Dillian's eyes. The knowledge of her desire lit a raging flame to his.

He turned his back on her. He needed a woman, but not this one. He'd learned to live without feminine companionship. He would continue doing so. He could see strings aplenty tied to this piece of baggage. He certainly didn't need a permanent ball and chain.

But her admiration burned a place in Gavin's gut that wouldn't go away. He hadn't realized how he'd missed that kind of look. He'd been recipient of them often enough before the damage to his face. He knew when a woman liked the way he looked. He'd been arrogant enough to accept their admiration as his due, the one thing he'd been given in this life to his advantage. The looks of horror his scars had received had hurt him more than he wished to admit. Gavin had known his vanity then, and it disgusted him as much as his scarred face disgusted his previous admirers. Dillian's unabashed look of enjoyment rekindled something that he didn't need anymore. Or so he told himself.

"I'll sleep on the pallet," he said abruptly.

"Don't be ridiculous. You're too big. I'm decent now. You can turn around."

He'd hoped for a glimpse of her wearing nothing but his shirt, but she'd rolled up inside the quilt, where he could see nothing but a mop of curls and her elfin face. When he turned back around, she quickly flipped over to present her back to his nakedness. Gavin almost chuckled. He had the wild desire to flex his muscles for her appreciation. He'd never particularly doubted his masculinity, but he felt its full potency now, reflected in the eyes of this one woman.

Instead of entertaining his pride, Gavin took Dillian at her word and climbed into the bed. The morning already promised warmth. He didn't need the cover she'd appropriated. "You'd make a great guard dog, Miss Whitnell.

Anytime you wish to leave Lady Blanche's employ, you're welcome in mine."

She didn't deign to reply, but Gavin fell asleep with dreams of Miss Whitnell in nothing but his shirt dancing through the rooms of his head.

"Here's your shirt back." Dillian reluctantly handed the item over. Her reluctance had little to do with the disinclination for donning the scratchy homespun and more to do with the fact that she disliked seeing that fascinating expanse of chest covered. She couldn't remember ever seeing a man's bare chest. The marquess had scars on his torso also, but they interested her less than the play of muscles beneath his skin as he reached for his clothing, or the sprinkle of dark hairs across his chest that tapered into a thicker mat as they dropped below his navel. Even the thatch of hair beneath his arms seemed mysterious and fascinating. She wondered if he was ticklish.

"Like what you see?" he asked in amusement when she didn't divert her gaze quickly enough.

She flushed and turned away as he pulled the shirt on. "There are enough pompous asses in this world without creating another one," she answered enigmatically. She was twenty-five years of age but she felt sixteen again, flustered and perspiring and uncertain where to look.

"You could be right about that, but I'm willing to allow you to test your theory anytime you wish. Until then we'd best get ourselves out of here."

He strode briskly from the room, fully clothed again, right down to his impossible coat and hat. The proprietor waited below, bowing obsequiously as the marquess pressed the requisite number of coins on him.

"Anytime, guv'nor. You're welcome back anytime. We keep our traps shut and respect our patron's privacy."

The marquess didn't reply but strode out into the late afternoon warmth in the direction of the stable. Dillian scampered to keep up. She found his moods impossible to sort out. One minute he jested, the next, he clouded up like a thunderstorm. She might as well follow a tempest.

On the theory that the first strike worked best, she taunted, "The innkeeper never noticed your pretty face. What's the point in keeping that blamed hat pulled down over it in this heat?"

"Heat?" To her surprise, he sounded amused. "You call this heat? It's warmer than this in the dead of night in a Georgia winter."

Dillian gasped as he turned, grabbed her by the waist, and threw her up in the saddle. The hard grip of his hands around her waist left her breathless, which he no doubt intended since he continued talking without waiting for her reply.

"Your friendly innkeeper expected adequate payment for keeping his mouth shut. He thought you my catamite. In comparison to that, my pretty face is little cause for comment." He threw himself into his saddle and jerked the reins to trot his horse from the stable into the sunshine, throwing a coin in the direction of the stable boy who had saddled the animals.

"A cat what?" Dillian stared at his broad back. His tone indicated grim distaste, yet she heard irony in his words.

He looked over his shoulder at her. "I suppose that's something else they don't teach ladies. You've lived in this world how many years? You can't be as innocent as you seem."

Dillian scowled as he faced the road again. "I've lived long enough to distrust all men. I suppose he must have thought us capable of some kind of perversity."

"Very good," floated over his shoulder as they rode out of the yard. "Reflects intellect and innocence at the same time. You're quite good at this game, Miss Whitnell. Why hasn't some man snatched you up before this? Or does the change of names have something to do with a hidden husband?"

She wanted to hit him. If she had a gun, his broad shoulders would make an inviting target. "The innkeeper was quite right, my lord," she shouted back at him. "You are perverse."

He chuckled and continued on in silence.

This time, Dillian kept a close eye on the road they took and the places they passed as they approached Arinmede Manor. If for any reason they must flee this place, she wanted to know in which direction.

Dusk became dark as they reached the village nearest the manor. The local tavern spilled light and song, but all else appeared quiet. Dillian noticed the marquess took the back roads around town rather than the more direct path down the main street. She supposed it wise to conceal the fact that the marquess had left his lair for any amount of time. He wouldn't want his appearance in Hampshire connected with his departure from here.

He'd discarded his great coat and broad-brimmed hat at dusk. Now he withdrew his cloak from his bags and threw it on. The night had cooled considerably, but Dillian thought the change of clothing more for disguise than warmth. Both coat and cloak were distinctive enough for people to notice, but few would connect the two, unless someone got a close look at the marquess's face. He made it a point to let no one get that close.

"Surely, you don't think someone will have noticed our comings and goings," she said as she rode her mount up next to his.

"I've learned it's best to take no chances. Your garb is nondescript enough not to call attention. I would prefer that the rumors confirm the Marquess of Effingham haunts only the streets of Arinmede."

" 'Haunts' is right," she grumbled. "You creep around like a ghost. Where's the point, I ask you? You're lord of the manor, provider of all you survey. People would worship at your feet did you display yourself. What have you to hide?"

"Perhaps I would prefer not to be worshipped," he answered dryly.

Even as he said it, a slight feminine figure walking along the path gave a shrill shriek and dashed into the nearest doorway as they rode by.

"Well, that was certainly illuminating." Dillian stared at the house where the woman had entered. Frightened faces peered around the shutter and watched them until they rode out of sight. She returned her gaze to the marquess's stiffly proud back. "What did you do, threaten them with hell if they didn't behave?"

He gave one of his mirthless laughs. "I don't speak to them at all. The feeling is mutual."

She had an upbraiding for his attitude on the tip of her tongue when a scream of sheer panic split the silence. The village was small, and the reason for the scream easily discovered. An orange flame shot through the thatched roof of a cottage on the next road over.

The sight of fire froze Dillian into motionlessness. A night of roaring flame flared instantly in her mind's eye, and panic ate at her. Not so the marquess. He spurred his weary nag down a side street and disappeared from sight before she could follow.

Dillian had no difficulty following once she recovered herself and set her mount after him. She did have some difficulty fighting her way through the narrow street as the entire village poured from their doors, buckets in hand, while excited children raced up and down screaming "fire" at the top of their lungs.

As she worked her way closer to the source of flames, she found the populace nearly motionless while a young mother screamed and wept in the street before the burning cottage. From her vantage point on top of the horse, she scanned the building, searching for the reason for this inactivity. Her breath caught in her throat at the sight.

The damned marquess had climbed a rickety ladder up to the burning roof of the cottage and now hurled hands full of thatching at the street in some insane effort to break through the roof. It didn't take long for Dillian to figure someone must be in the loft, and the stairs below were already lost in flame. Her breath came in short gasps of panic as memories of a similar incident assailed her.

Only the angry murmurs of the mob brought her back to the moment. She could hear the curses, the fear, the panic rippling through the crowd as the cloaked figure on the roof rained smoldering thatch upon their heads. They remained motionless in the street, letting the fire burn rather than aid the marquess. They despised what they feared, and they feared this man they didn't know. To them, he was no more than a black shadow seen infrequently and then only in darkness, a menacing figure who lived in a haunted mansion. Dillian couldn't imagine what they thought the specter on the roof was doing except saving the lives of the people inside, but they offered no help.

Leaping from her horse, nearly breaking her neck in the attempt, she hastily grabbed a bucket already filled with water, ran up to the cottage and splashed it on the nearest eruption of flame. She slammed the empty bucket into someone's waiting hand and grabbed the next. The young mother at the foot of the ladder continued wailing as she watched the man frantically digging a hole through her roof.

Gradually, the crowd came to their senses. An older man snapped orders, and a chain of people formed between pump and flames. He displaced Dillian at the head of the chain, giving her an odd look indicating her disguise had come awry. She glanced down at herself and saw where she'd splashed water and soaked the tunic. Even with the binding, her breasts swelled against the damp cloth. So much for hiding herself.

She left the bucket brigade to their work and elbowed her way through the crowd to the wailing woman. Other women crowded around, trying to comfort her, but her cry of "My babies! My babies!" would pierce the hardest of hearts. Dillian's stomach lurched as she gave a quick glance to the roof. Smoke seeped through everywhere, and small sparks glittered against the darkness. Only the prior night's rain kept the entire roof from exploding in flame. She couldn't tell if the marquess made much progress.

"Angel of death, that's what he is," some woman grumbled beside her. "He's come to take their souls away."

Similar sentiments echoed around her, and fury at such foolish superstition replaced panic as Dillian shoved to the front. The young woman was near hysteria, but Dillian grabbed the arm of an older woman who seemed to have her wits about her. "Get him a knife, saw blades, an ax, anything to help him," she ordered.

The woman looked surprised, then thoughtful as she glanced at Dillian's improper attire and heard her lady-like accents. With a nod of her head, she whispered to another woman beside her. Word spread through the women rapidly, and soon several broke into a run down the street in search of the needed implements.

"Daughter of the devil!" screamed one of the more hysterical women in the crowd, pointing at Dillian.

"Don't be ridiculous. I'm a friend of the marquess. If you want those children saved, you must help him. Bring me some water." Dillian's impatient response caught the ear of someone a little more sensible, and a bucket eventually appeared.

The bucket weighed more than she could reasonably carry, but she attempted it anyway, hauling it in one hand while she maneuvered the precarious ladder with the other. Effingham wasn't even aware of her presence as she splashed the water over the entire area where he worked. At the first touch of water, he looked up, cursed, and returned to his efforts.

Someone hastened up the ladder and handed them an ax. Dillian grabbed it and shoved it beneath the marquess's nose. He offered no thanks but began hacking at the remains of the roof beneath the hole he'd created. The faint sound of crying seeped through the cacophony around them.

More buckets and more tools followed. The marquess yelled at one of the men on the ladder to get Dillian out of there. When she saw that the man intended to stay and help, she went willingly. The stench of smoke and burning wood choked her into near insensibility. It was too much like that other night, too close to that disaster. Her frayed nerves couldn't withstand much more of the strain. The crying rang louder in her ears as she escaped, shaking, down the ladder.

A cry of "He'll kill them all!" met her ears as she climbed down. Without thinking, Dillian swung around and slapped the terrified woman across the mouth.

"*You'll* kill them all!" Dillian shrieked back, not believing she said these words, not believing her own voice as it came out of her throat. "You'll kill them by standing here doing nothing in your narrow-minded prejudice. If you won't help, then get the hell out of here!"

Her fury and near hysteria made an immediate impression. Someone led the woman she'd slapped away. Others stared at her in fear. One tentatively began the climb to the roof with a bucket in hand. The hysterical mother unwrapped herself from her consoling friends to grab Dillian by the arms and plead, "Don't let him kill my babies! Help them, please!"

Even as she said it, a tower of flame shot through the hole in the roof where the Marquess of Effingham worked.

Fifteen

Dillian didn't hear herself screaming as the black-cloaked figure disappeared through the roof behind a wall of flame. She only heard about it later when the marquess gave her one of his wry looks and commented on her fine set of lungs. Right now, as he disappeared into the inferno, she felt only the hands of a plump village woman holding her back while the waiting crowd grew silent.

The men continued pouring water on the dying flames downstairs. A few brave souls scampered up and down the ladder, dousing the sparks in the thatch as quickly as they appeared. After that one brief spurt, the fire apparently died to a smoking, steaming sizzle. Finally, after what seemed hours of waiting, a hoarse shout echoed from inside.

"I'm handing them up. Someone come get them!" The clipped American twang sounded oddly resonant among the slurred accents of the villagers.

The man already at the top of the ladder hurried to the edge of the hole and reached down, straightening a moment later with a limp bundle in his arms. A murmur passed over the crowd, and another man hastened up the ladder to take the child. A minute later, an even smaller bundle appeared though the burned thatch. The hysterical mother already cuddling one child broke into sobs of relief as the second one let out a healthy squall as he was carried down the ladder.

She still cried, "My babies, my babies!" but this time the note in her voice was that of relief.

Dillian waited. No more bundles appeared. The man on the roof scurried down as if his duty had ended. She looked around. The women banded together and led the weeping mother and children away. The men returned to their bucket brigade, dousing the final trails of fire. No black-cloaked figure reappeared on the roof.

She approached a gray-haired old man who seemed only to watch. "Shouldn't someone fetch a ladder to help the marquess out?"

He looked at her as if she spoke a foreign tongue.

She turned to a man coming up beside her and repeated the question. This one looked dubiously at the smoking, gaping hole in the roof, and shrugged.

She couldn't stand it another minute. Effingham had just risked his life rescuing a stranger's child, and they made no effort whatsoever to see to his welfare. All her hysteria, panic, and fear erupted in an explosion of rage as she shouted at the crowd. "He could die in there! If you cowards will do nothing for him, then someone must!" And with a strength she hadn't known she possessed, Dillian scurried up the steps to the roof, caught the ends of the ladder, and heaved it up after her. The men below stared at her in astonishment. One sidled off to retrieve a ladder thrown down in the street in the confusion. Dillian didn't linger to watch. She hauled her burden over the roof to the gaping hole.

"My lord, are you down there?" she called into the smoldering stench of wet thatch.

"Do I have somewhere better to go?" he asked dryly through the hellish fumes.

Even when she was worried sick about him, he made her want to slap him. "I can think of an appropriate answer," she called back, "but half the town is listening, so I'll refrain. I'm lowering this ladder. Watch out that I don't skewer you with it."

Someone climbed onto the rickety roof with her, but she ignored him. No wonder the marquess avoided a town full of superstitious idiots like these. She wouldn't blame him if he never darkened their doorsteps again. Had she breath enough left to tell them so, she would, but she was having difficulty breathing. She blamed it on the smoke, but the tears streaming down her face and the sobs choking her throat didn't help.

Dillian lowered the ladder through the gaping hole and felt Effingham grab it on the other end. The man beside her gently pushed her aside, holding the upper rungs so it didn't fall through the weakened supports. She thought he muttered something about the marquess "ought to fly through the roof," but she ignored that also. She didn't breathe evenly again until she saw Effingham's dark hair and soot-blackened visage appear through the scorched thatch.

He immediately caught sight of her and scowled through his coughing. "You have no business up here. Get down where you belong."

"Why, of course, your mighty lordship," Dillian replied with all the sarcasm she could summon through waves of relief. "I'll go down with all the other peasants waiting to watch you fly through the roof of your own accord." And with that retort, she scrambled backward until her feet reached the new ladder, and she let herself down and out of his sight.

The man holding the first ladder gave his lordship's scarred, scowling face a single look and moved backward also. "Reckon I'll do the same, your lordship." As he reached the roof's edge and safety, he grew a little bolder and added, "But if that's your lady down there, my lord, you're a braver man than I am if you come down anytime sooner than dawn. She has a tongue to blister the fur off a cony."

To the astonishment of those waiting below, the black scarecrow of a figure on the roof erupted in pealing tones of belly-deep laughter.

"You didn't have to tell them I was a war hero recovering from my injuries," Gavin groused as they rode their mounts into the stable.

"No, I could have confirmed their fears that you're a vampire who walks the night and sucks their blood."

Gavin gave her an evil look as she climbed from the horse on her own. The glance showed him how her damp shirt clung to her tempting curves, and he had to turn away to work on his saddle. Damn and blast the male reproductive instincts, he cursed as he slid the saddle off. They surged to the forefront at the most inopportune times.

"That's the most ridiculous thing I've ever heard of. Where do they get tales like that?" Gavin tried keeping his mind on their running argument. It was the only thing saving his sanity at the moment.

"What should they think?" Dillian asked indignantly. "You hide up here for months on end. No one but your servants ever see you, and you barely speak to them. You live in a crumbling pile already reputed to have ghosts. You don't introduce yourself to society. Your only contact with the village is with the money you send down for supplies. I can't think of a more effective means of breeding suspicion."

"As long as it means I'm left alone, I don't care what they think," he answered curtly. The emotions of the evening had affected him more than he could wish, but he wouldn't let her know that. The hysterical cries of the young mother, the whimpers of terrified children, and Miss Whitnell's frantic screams chased around and around in his head, and he couldn't get rid of them. He kept glancing over his horse to see if she still stayed on the other side. Her concern had shaken him. No one but Michael had offered any concern for him in a long time.

"Well, just fine and dandy. You keep skulking around this monstrosity, and they'll keep thinking you're a vampire. Some night they'll march up here with burning torches and try to put a silver bullet through your heart, or something else equally dire."

Gavin watched her savage attempts to groom his horse. He might do better to save the horse's hide and drag her out of here. "Leave the horses. I'll call Mac to finish up here."

He noticed she didn't argue with this command. Grooming horses apparently didn't come under a lady's list of accomplishments. She put the curry comb back and strode off toward the manor, her hips swinging furiously beneath the damp tunic. Gavin nearly swallowed his tongue watching the rhythm of the sway.

"You have no reason to worry over my eventual fate, Miss Whitnell," he responded as he caught up with her.

He had to end this madness once and for all. "You and Lady Blanche will be nowhere in sight should it happen."

She stomped up the steps and tried opening the massive door. When it didn't budge, she beat upon it. Gavin leaned over her head, wrapped his fingers around the edge, and gave a mighty pull. Ancient oak creaked and heaved outward. Even the damned doors in this place were backward.

She didn't thank him for his assistance but glared at him as he followed her into the darkness of the hall. "I suppose you'll insist on throwing us into the streets again. It's no matter to you that we'll all be burned in our beds."

"No, no more than it is no matter to you if the citizens of the whole damned town come after me with torches. You have your problems, I'll take mine."

"You are the most impossible, irritating man! We can't possibly leave until Blanche is safe. I categorically refuse to leave. I'll clean your kitchens, repair your draperies, pacify the villagers, whatever you want in exchange for our residence here. Make your choice, but don't even think about turning us out."

Gavin wouldn't have been half so amused had she pleaded instead of yelling at him. As it was, he found the turn of the conversation quite stimulating. He had half a mind to tell her what he required in exchange for her residence here, but a shadow beneath the stairway came forward before he could voice his lecherous thoughts.

"I wouldn't answer that one if I were you, my lord," the shadow spoke, coming into the puddle of light from the candle at the foot of the stairs. "She's like to skewer you with her tongue if you try."

"Will you quit that 'my lord' business, Michael? It irritates the hell out of me. And what are you doing lurking in the shadows at this hour? Where is Lady Blanche?"

Light danced off the reddish glints of his brother's hair as Michael leaned against the newel post and regarded both of them. "The two of you look like bats fried in hell. Did they burn down the Grange, too?"

Gavin wiped idly at his face with his handkerchief

while Miss Whitnell scrubbed hers with the back of her sleeve. She left more smudges than she removed. He had an overwhelming desire to scrub her face for her, but he conquered it by concentrating on Michael. "No, just a house in the village. Miss Whitnell, why don't you go up and wash and check on Lady Blanche?"

He could see the urge to do so leap eagerly to her eyes as she took a step toward the staircase. Something in the atmosphere must have given them away, however. She shook her head resolutely, crossed her arms, and turned her glare on Michael. "What's wrong? Why were you waiting for us?"

Michael raised his eyebrows and turned questioningly back to Gavin. "What's wrong with this picture? You're supposed to seduce the duchess, not the she-devil."

As much as he loved his younger brother, there were times Gavin could easily strangle him. Actually, he thought he could strangle him more often than he could love him. He didn't have to do either at the moment. Despite her evident exhaustion, his companion practically went up in flames beside him.

"She's not a bloody damned duchess, and if I have any say about it, she never will be! If anyone tries seducing her, I'll personally see their throats severed!"

Gavin couldn't remember being so amused in a long time. The daring Miss Whitnell barely reached his shoulder. Her thick curls had fallen in damp ringlets about her very feminine neck, and her monstrous tunic clung to a figure too slender by half. And she threatened two men twice her size and strength. Not only did she threaten them, she used damned foul language in the process. Idly, without giving his words much thought, he said to Michael, "Obviously, a military background there, wouldn't you say?"

To his surprise, she turned white as a sheet and started for the stairs.

Michael gave him a sharp look as Dillian hurried stiffly upward. "I think you just hit her sore toe with a sledgehammer."

He may have wished upon occasion to silence her quick tongue, but Gavin had never meant to hurt her.

For the first time in a long time, he felt someone else's pain, and an awful guilt that he had caused it. He remembered Dillian's anxious, soot-blackened face peering down from the thatch of a burning cottage as she foolishly tried to rescue him. He heard her screams of terror as he fell through the roof. Not once had she ever looked at him as a monster or treated him as anything else but another human being. Even his title meant little to her. She'd left him a rose, for pity's sake. And he'd done nothing but gripe and complain and slam her feelings into the ground. He'd kept to himself for so long, he'd forgotten how to respond to the concerns of others.

He felt an ass, but he was helpless to do anything about it. He didn't even know what he'd said that had sent her fleeing like that. With resignation, Gavin turned back to his brother. "All right, what's the bad news?"

His usually overconfident, ebullient brother looked suddenly uncertain as he listened to Miss Whitnell's footsteps hurry down the upper hall. It occurred to Gavin that Michael and Miss Whitnell would make a very good pair. The thought thoroughly depressed him, but he didn't stop to consider why.

"I think we'd best discuss it together," Michael answered slowly. "The ladies may provide more enlightenment than I can."

"I don't suppose it can wait until morning?" Gavin asked wearily.

Michael shook his head. "You don't think the she-devil will wait until morning to see the duchess, do you?"

Of course not. Both women would be awake way into the night catching up on the wrongs committed by a couple of useless bachelors, scheming how best to keep the manor as their hiding place. He must have baked what was left of his brains to let Michael bring the women here in the first place. They'd be damned lucky if a couple of fathers didn't show up with shotguns.

"You *are* going to get them out of here?" Gavin demanded with suspicion.

Michael looked resigned as he glanced upward. "Not easily."

* * *

Dillian hurriedly found Blanche's room, barely knocking before entering. She found Blanche sitting at the table in darkness, her eyes unbandaged as she stacked a deck of playing cards into a swaying card house. A gust of air caused by the door opening toppled the cards.

"Drat it, O'Toole! Must you choose now to make a grand entrance?"

Momentarily amused, Dillian glanced around for Verity. The maid wasn't in sight. Frowning again, Dillian answered, "I'm sorry if my company disappoints you. I left O'Toole downstairs arguing with the marquess."

Blanche leapt from her chair and ran to hug her cousin, stopping only when she caught some glimpse of Dillian's disarray. "My stars! What have you done to yourself?"

Immense relief swept through Dillian as she realized Blanche could see her, even in the darkness. "Your eyes! They're undamaged, then?"

"Even if they weren't, my nose never lost its sense of smell." Blanche sniffed and picked fastidiously at the damp tunic clinging to her companion. "You'd better go wash and find clean clothes."

Clothes. She hadn't packed clean clothes. She'd been so damned afraid the marquess would leave without her, that she had completely forgotten anything but a suitable disguise for following him. Dillian sighed. "I haven't even got my boy's clothes. I left them at the Grange. I'll go get that dress I found."

"Let me call Verity for some warm water. You can just wear one of my robes for now. Tell me all about it. I'm so horribly bored sitting here like a turnip. Is it safe for us to leave yet?"

"I doubt it." Dillian watched with interest as Blanche tapped on the door between hers and the next room. Had Blanche expected O'Toole and told Verity to leave? That didn't make good sense. She didn't inquire as the maid answered the rap. The idea of warm water and scented soap wiped all other thoughts from her head.

"Couldn't we light a lamp in here?" Dillian inquired as Verity hurried to fetch the requested water.

Blanche drifted toward the window. "O'Toole thinks I should wait until my eyes have healed more. He makes me bind them in the daylight, although he's given me the prettiest scarf to use instead of those awful bandages."

All Dillian's protective instincts reared up, but she said nothing inflammatory. She would watch and see for herself first. "How much can you see like this?"

Blanche shrugged. "Probably as much as you can. What do you see when you look around?"

Dillian hadn't thought of it that way. She looked around. The moon shone faintly through the windows, creating more shadows than it illuminated. She could see the outlines of the bed, dresser, table, and wardrobe. She could see Blanche silhouetted against the glass. She could guess at the other odd shapes scattered across the furniture. "I see what you mean. If you could see those cards you were stacking, you're seeing about everything I am."

Blanche let out a sigh of relief. "Thank goodness. I worried Michael lied to me. It's hard to remember how much one can see in the dark. I felt like I moved through a shadow world."

"It is a shadow world." Dillian gratefully took the pitcher of water Verity carried in. Within instants, she had the filthy tunic and breeches off and scrubbed her skin with the delicately scented soap Blanche used. She wondered if Verity had thought to bring this with her clothes or if Blanche had requested it of O'Toole, but she didn't ask. She regarded the relationship between her cousin and the footman warily, but she knew better than to tread on uncertain ground without looking before she stepped.

They discussed the Grange and the events that had taken place while they were separated as Dillian washed and donned the robe Verity found for her. Neither of them indicated any surprise when the peremptory knock echoed on the bedroom door.

"Here comes our eviction notice," Dillian sighed as Verity hurried to let in the marquess and O'Toole.

Sixteen

Carrying a candle, Gavin nearly retreated from the bedchamber and slammed the door on the seductive sight within. If nothing else proved he had wandered too long from civilization, his reaction to one extremely feminine figure in a silken robe did. Not only did blood rush to his groin, but his palms broke into a sweat and his heart raced with an unseemly beat. He blew out the candle.

It didn't matter. He still could only focus on that one slender beam of white in the darkness. He smelled the soap she had used to wash, damn it all. His mind had taken leave of his senses. He'd had his share of women in the past. There had once been a time when he could have just crooked his finger and had any number of them at his feet. Their heady perfumes hadn't loosed his brains, but one whiff of this termagant's soap, and he was ready to crawl on hands and knees and beg for more.

That thought didn't appease his already black mood any.

"All right, Michael, have it out. Our agreement was to check the security of the Grange and send the ladies home. Once we verify the guards at the gate are doing their job, the Grange should be safe enough. You can accompany their carriage to reassure yourself, if that's the problem." Gavin stood as far from the slight figure in white as he could. He noticed with interest that the lady had drifted to the corner closest to Michael, but he didn't speculate on that. Michael had never shown much interest in women, and they generally returned the favor. The lady no doubt sought to get as far from Gavin as

she was able, and in so doing ended in Michael's corner.
If he thought she could see his scowl, he would turn it
on her and drive her screaming from the place. With
any luck, the noisy baggage she called companion
would follow.

With only two chairs and a bed for seating, they were
one too many. Michael gallantly offered Lady Blanche
a chair while Dillian appropriated the bed. Gavin could
scarcely tear his gaze away as he realized she meant to
sit cross-legged among the covers, pulling the thin silk
of her robe around her. He couldn't keep from staring
at the juncture where her legs must meet beneath the
robe. Then she darted a gaze in his direction and more
discreetly curled her legs under her. For good measure,
she tugged a blanket around her waist. Gavin gave a
mental gasp of relief, but refused the remaining chair.
He crossed his arms over his chest and watched Michael
lean back against the table in his favorite storytelling
posture.

As Michael spoke, Gavin quietly contemplated the
thickness of the rope and the number of turns he would
make in it as he wrapped the noose around his brother's
throat and hung him from the highest yardarm. The situation Michael had embroiled them in was tense enough
without complicating it further.

"My lady," Michael nodded his head gallantly in
Blanche's direction, "you will forgive me for questioning
your companion, but if I am to protect you, I must know
the truth." When Blanche offered no objection, he
turned toward Dillian. "Miss Reynolds Whitnell?"

The figure in white merely stared at him, waiting for
more.

"The servants call you Miss Reynolds, but your employer calls you Whitnell. I assume both names are
yours?"

"Assume what you like," Dillian replied insouciantly.

Gavin could sense the tension forming in his brother's
seemingly idle posture. Michael played the part of devil-
may-care Irishman to the hilt, but his brother was no
more Irish than he was careless. Their lives often enough
had relied on Michael's keen wits and acting ability.

Gavin doubted if anyone ever saw the real man beneath his brother's facade. Sometimes he doubted if he even knew him. That might be the reason he'd never strangled him.

Michael stared at the ceiling as he spoke. "I will assume both names are yours through your family. Since Whitnell is the one you hide, I assume that is the one most people would recognize. Lady Blanche's mother was a Reynolds."

Gavin had the amazing feeling the air in the room had just frozen to ice. He watched both women. Neither moved an inch. Neither responded. Michael continued as if he hadn't expected a response.

"Lady Blanche's father had a bosom companion in the military, a certain Colonel Whitnell. From all reports, the two men were so inseparable that they died together at Waterloo."

Perhaps he imagined it, but Gavin thought he saw the termagant's shoulders wilt just a little. Having kept himself absent from company for so long, perhaps he had become alarmingly sensitive to the moods of others. He felt as if the ice in the room now dripped with sorrow.

Michael turned to Lady Blanche. "I am trying to help you. Your secrets won't go beyond this room. But if I'm to stay one step ahead of your enemies, I must know more than they do."

Lady Blanche began to speak, but Dillian overrode her. "What can a mere footman do? Don't be presumptuous. We're perfectly fine here. We will pay our way if the marquess is willing to wait until the funds are available. You need not know anything else."

Gavin considered stepping in to protect his brother from the lady's shriveling tongue, but Michael scarcely needed protection. He merely crossed his arms in a stance similar to Gavin's own and said without inflection, "The duke has investigators searching for the relatives of Colonel Whitnell and is even now verifying that Lady Blanche's mother and Colonel Whitnell's wife are sisters. Obviously, the various branches of your respective families are not very close."

Lady Blanche responded with a sigh, "They did not

even speak. Neville's family stayed in London and disapproved of everything my father did, probably with some cause. Neville never had reason to know anything of my mother. The fact that she was a Reynolds was scarcely a family secret. She came from a respectable family. He just never put two and two together before. Why does he do so now?"

"Blanche!" Dillian exclaimed with irritation. "You have no reason to tell him any of this."

Gavin watched with amazement as the delicately fragile lady turned her chin up in defiance at her older cousin's admonishments.

"He is trying to help, Dillian. We cannot do it all on our own. If I choose to trust him, it is my own decision."

Apparently so astounded she couldn't reply, Dillian actually held her tongue. Gavin gave both women credit for good sense. He couldn't remember ever giving a woman other than his cousins credit for sense of any kind. Perhaps the English were a different breed, after all.

"Thank you, my lady," Michael answered, throwing Gavin a quick look. When he received no support from that quarter, he continued, "Rumors of treason are currently circulating London connected with the name of Whitnell. If the relationship between the colonel and Lady Blanche's father is a close one, then the tar can spread. We wouldn't wish that to happen, would we?"

Gavin watched with more than a little amazement and delight as the slender female on the bed erupted into a towering inferno of rage.

"That's not true!" The blanket went flying as she leapt to her feet. "My father died for his country! He damned well lived for his country! He would never do such an obscene thing. They lie! Tell me who says such tales, and I'll . . ."

Since the lady seemed prepared to beat the information out of Michael, who offered no defense, Gavin thought it prudent to intrude. Stepping forward, he grabbed Miss Whitnell by the waist and hauled her against him before she could throw herself at his brother.

Gavin knew his mistake at once. An armful of warm

squirming female flesh nearly drove him to the brink right here in front of all and sundry. Rather than drop her as he ought, he jerked her up against his chest until her squirming suddenly halted. Perhaps the heat burning through him singed her sufficiently to recognize her danger. When he looked down, he met her eyes staring upward. He didn't see fear in them, but in the darkness, he didn't try reading what he saw there. He merely lowered her to the floor now that she had quieted.

"Attacking your defender is not very sensible, my dear Miss Whitnell," he murmured in a tone that surprised even him. He could feel the others staring, but the fact that Dillian didn't back away held his interest more.

"I will not have my father maligned," she replied in a voice that strove for dignity but was not quiet steady.

"And so we will not. We merely seek the truth. Rumors do not circulate without reason. What would someone gain from maligning your father's name?"

She finally backed off, steering a wide path around Michael to sit on the edge of the bed. "My father made enemies as freely as he made friends. He had a rather forceful nature."

Which he evidently passed on to his daughter, Gavin added to himself. His silence forced her to continue. Michael and Lady Blanche left the conversation to them.

She clasped her arms around her as if to keep from shivering. "I can't think of anything anyone would gain other than venting their anger. And what is the point of that now that he's dead? And what does any of this have to do with Blanche?"

Michael finally spoke. "Perhaps it has nothing to do with Lady Blanche. Perhaps it has to do with you."

The room fell silent. The lady rose from her corner chair to sit beside her cousin, hugging her awkwardly. Dillian didn't seem to want the comfort but sat still for it. Gavin noticed she turned her gaze to him instead of Michael. He didn't want her turning to him. He didn't want any part of this. He retreated into the darkest corner beside the door and let Michael handle it.

"They burned Blanche's home to get at me?" Dillian finally asked, not hiding the incredulity in her voice.

Blanche's clear high voice surprised them all as she finally entered the argument. "That doesn't make sense. Everyone there knew Dillian as Miss Reynolds, a distant relation of my mother's. They had no reason to associate her with Colonel Whitnell."

"It didn't take me two minutes to figure out the relationship," Michael answered dryly. "Someone desperate enough to burn down a house full of people is quite capable of seeing through such a thin disguise. Why is it you felt compelled to hide the relationship?"

Gavin noted with interest the way the two women looked at each other first before sending some silent communication that nominated Dillian as the one to reply.

"For several reasons, none of which have anything to do with this. As we said before, Neville's father disapproved of everything Blanche's father did. My father's friendship was undoubtedly one of them. My father had a certain . . . notoriety. He came of good but not wealthy family. The hussars are a rather expensive regiment. His manner of supporting himself came into question upon occasion, but as far as I am aware, he never did anything dishonest."

Gavin wanted to know how her father managed to support a wife and daughter, but Michael intruded first.

"He gambled," he said flatly.

Dillian nodded and said defensively, "Everyone does."

'Could he have left creditors of which you're unaware?" Gavin surprised himself by asking that. He knew too well about creditors, only from the other end of the stick.

Dillian sat still as she contemplated the answer. "It's possible, I suppose. I didn't see my father often, and he certainly never discussed his business affairs with me. He's been dead for some years now, however. Why should anyone wait until now to seek revenge or whatever?"

"Because they have only now returned to the country. Because they have only now discovered who you are. There could be any number of answers. Who was your

father's man of business? Would he hold any notes without telling you of them?"

"My father handled his own business, not that there
was much of it. He spent everything he ever earned. I
didn't see anything that looked like notes in his papers."

Michael suddenly straightened. "You have his papers? Where?"

Gavin expected the response to be they burned with
Blanche's house. Instead, she shrugged and said, "Proba-
bly in London. I didn't know what to do with them, and
I got tired of hauling them about."

Blanche nodded. "You asked me to put them in the
vault, if I remember, but there wasn't enough room for
all those old journals. So we sent some of them over to
Mr. Winfrey. We should have asked him to have them
evaluated to see if they had any worth, but it didn't seem
important at the time."

Gavin could just imagine Michael's eyes rolling sky-
ward. He had the urge to shake both women himself.
Military men didn't collect books and papers and carry
them about if they had no value. His fingers fairly itched
to rifle through them already.

Michael answered with some semblance of control.
"We need to see those papers. Did you not look at any
of them?"

Blanche threw her cousin a swift look and replied,
"Well, they didn't seem any of my business, and Dillian"—she sent her cousin another look—"Dillian
doesn't have a fondness for paperwork."

Gavin rather suspected that was the understatement
of the year. Dillian might climb the roof of a burning
house or play ghost in abandoned dumbwaiters, but she
wouldn't be much inclined to scholarly pursuits. Rather
than consider how appealing he found her adventurous
nature, he said the first thing that came to mind, and
regretted it immediately after.

"I think we need to see those papers, or at least assure
ourselves that they're protected."

He wanted to bite his tongue the minute the words
escaped his heedless lips—he'd just trapped himself.

"I thoroughly agree, your noble lordship." Gavin

could almost hear the laughter in Michael's reply. "Shall we hop in the carriage and journey to London?"

Gavin growled a curse, and wondered if he could gnaw his hand off and escape the iron teeth of the snare. Dillian saved him from immediate reply.

"They're my papers. I'll fetch them. We have no assurance that's what the arsonist wanted to destroy. I want Blanche staying here, where it's safe."

Blanche kneaded her hands in her lap. "Dillian, that might not be so wise."

Gavin waited in silence. Michael did the same.

Dillian looked at her cousin. "Why not?"

Blanche looked at her hands. "I put the smaller things in the vault in the town house." Everyone waited silently. "I never use that vault. I have to write the numbers down that open it."

Gavin groaned inwardly, seeing where this led. Dillian still sat there expectantly.

Blanche turned her head to him as if looking for his absolution. Gavin merely waited. She sighed and murmured, "The numbers were written on a piece of paper I carried in my daily journal."

"Daily journal?" Michael and Dillian echoed each other.

Blanche nodded. "The one that the fire destroyed."

Seventeen

Blanche's declaration fairly well left them at wit's end.
The night grew late. They had all reached the edges
of exhaustion, and the general consensus was to sleep
on it and work out the problem in the morning. Only
Dillian knew the problem wouldn't resolve itself in the
morning without a push in the right direction. She'd seen
the look on the marquess's face. He would vote to throw
them all out of here and let them go to the devil without him.

She couldn't really blame him. She and Blanche were
virtual strangers who had disrupted his reclusive existence. He undoubtedly had better things to do than
chase around half of England saving them from unknown and possibly imaginary villains. She'd have
reached beyond irritation by now had she stood in his
shoes.

For herself, it wouldn't have mattered. She would just
have caught the next mail coach into London, retrieved
her father's papers and journals, burned the lot of them,
then dared anyone to come after her. But whoever or
whatever the arsonist was after had endangered Blanche.
Dillian wouldn't stand for that. She'd lay down her life
for Blanche. She considered her own life relatively
worthless, but Blanche had the whole world at her fin-
gertips. Blanche could make a difference. For the sake
of both their mothers, for her own sake, for Blanche,
she would see nothing happened to prevent her cousin
from taking her rightful place in this world.

And the marquess of Effingham held their future in
his hands.

From the shadows of the hall, Dillian watched the

marquess hurry down the stairs to his lair in that disreputable room he called a study. She'd heard Michael go
out the front door earlier. She couldn't imagine what
kind of hold a footman could have over a marquess to
allow him as much leeway as he had, but she didn't think
it would last much longer. Unless something drastic happened soon, Effingham would throw them out on their
ears in the morning.

Dillian had left Verity looking after Blanche on the
excuse that she would go to the room she'd made her
own. She would go there, but only to change into something a little more respectable than this thin robe. Then
she would confront the marquess.

The thin French dress wasn't much more concealing
than the robe, and Dillian shivered as she let herself
down the back stairs a little while later. She pulled her
borrowed shawl more tightly around her and forced herself forward. She didn't fear the servants hearing her.
She imagined an entire army could hide themselves in
this place and the servants wouldn't hear. No, she feared
the beast lurking in the gloom of that study down the
hall and how he could affect their lives.

She shouldn't think of him as a beast. He was a soldier. Upon occasion she had considered her father a
beast because of the life he led, but military men were
a different breed. She'd learned to deal with her father.
She could deal with the marquess.

She scratched briefly at the study door but didn't allow
Effingham the opportunity of denying her entrance. She
walked in before he could answer.

He'd lit the lamp on the desk. She had grown so accustomed to walking about in darkness that the light
startled her. The man standing beside the desk startled
her even more.

Rakish black curls fell in tangled disarray over the
marquess's brow, accenting deep-set dark eyes. A muscle
tightened in his jaw as he saw her standing there, and
the thin white scars of his cheek stretched thinner and
whiter, curling his lip up in an expression of mockery.
That look alone ought to make her shudder, but Dillian
couldn't resist letting her gaze fall to the open neck of

his shirt. More bronzed skin shone in the lamplight. The marquess obviously did not spend all his days hiding in his hermitage.

"You are going somewhere?" he asked with almost a pleasant rumble, eyeing her lacy gown.

That interpretation of her change of garments hadn't occurred to her. She had only meant to make herself respectable. This meeting hadn't got off to the best of starts. She clasped her hands in front of her and wondered why she was suddenly nervous. She had faced down Neville often enough, and he was a bloody duke.

She ignored his question and plunged right into the topic at hand. "I've come to beg," she said with as careful a tone as she could muster. She didn't want to beg, but she would—for Blanche.

Effingham's stiff stance relaxed somewhat as he lounged against the desk and crossed his arms. Dillian hated it when he did that. It made him seem enormous and important and intolerably bored with the whole proceeding. She hated it when he didn't even respond but waited for her to continue without giving a clue as to how he felt.

"Blanche is my only living relative," she continued boldly. "She is young, and the duke's family is rather overpowering. I've protected her from them these last five years, but I don't think I can protect her from a murderer. If the villain is actually after me, I must leave her at once. I just can't leave her unprotected. I thought, if I could go to London and find my father's journals, I could take them to someone in authority, and they might know what to do with them. Perhaps they could discover who threatens us."

The flickering light played over the marquess's scarred cheek. Dillian thought he may have deliberately turned the damaged side of his face to her. She almost felt grateful that he had chosen this side to show her. The other side was too handsome by far, and she didn't need any added distraction.

"You have a higher opinion of authority than I have," he replied enigmatically, his dark eyes shadowed as they watched her.

That wasn't the reply she wanted. Doggedly, she pushed a little harder. "My father had a great many friends in government. I will find someone to listen. It may take a little while. I'll have to open that vault somehow, and Blanche's solicitor isn't too fond of me, so he'll likely stall. But I can do it. And once I make someone listen, perhaps I can get them to protect Blanche. It's just that, until then . . ." She waited, hoping he would understand and make the offer she wanted. He didn't.

She finally doffed the demure plea and glared at him. "Damn and blast it, Effingham! Help me out a little. Blanche is no trouble at all. You'll not even know she's around. She can pay you well. She has a maid now. What more do you want?"

"Did you by any chance live with your father in a military barracks?" he asked with satirical interest.

Dillian clutched her fingers into fists, closed her eyes, and prayed for strength. If only she were a man, she could just run her fist into him and release some of this frustration. Bloody damn hell, anyway!

Fighting for control, she opened her eyes and glared at him. "My mother died when I was twelve. After that, my father's idea of companion for me was anyone who owed him a favor. I can ride a horse like a man, shoot like Manton, fence with the best of them, and even know boxing, although it's relatively useless due to my size. Does that answer your question?"

She thought he smiled. Since this side of his mouth had a permanent upturn, she couldn't tell for certain. Either way, she wanted to kick him.

"Yes, I believe it does. It answers many questions, not the least of which is why you're not married by now. You must scare these milksop aristocrats to death."

Dillian thought she might tear her hair out in rage and frustration. Better yet, she'd like to tear his. "What has that to do with anything? You're a bloody damn aristocrat, for pity's sake. Do I scare you?"

He considered that a minute, looking her over thoroughly as he did. Dillian suddenly realized she didn't shiver from the cold, she shivered from the way he made her feel. No man had ever made her feel like this before.

The masculine interest in his eyes made her recognize herself as a woman. Her breasts suddenly felt immense. They ached. A tingling feeling settled into the place below her belly, and it grew stronger the longer he stared. With shock, she realized what was happening to her. She stared at him in incredulity. Why, of all men, must it happen with this one? A bloody damn Yank with a soul from hell, and she wanted to know what his arms would feel like around her!

She knew what his arms felt like around her. She wanted to know more.

As if recognizing the sudden flicker of desire in her eyes, the marquess said gruffly, "Come here."

She blinked. He didn't move. He didn't say more. He just waited. Dillian moved one foot forward, then the other, stepping within arm's reach of him. Perhaps Effingham wasn't as calm as he pretended. His knuckles appeared white where his hands bit into the upper parts of his arms.

She didn't jump or even flinch when he finally reached out one hand and tilted her chin upward. Unable to read the opaque depths of his dark eyes, she just held her breath until he lowered his mouth to meet her own.

It was bliss, sweet bliss—moist heat and hard pressure and a tingling fire sweeping from her head to her toes. Dillian inched forward until Effingham grabbed her waist and hauled her up against him. His mouth crushed even more firmly against hers, leaving her gasping for breath. When her lips parted, his tongue thrust in, and she melted.

She caught his shoulders to keep from sliding right through his grasp and down to the floor. She had no muscles at all, just liquid fiery heat racing through her veins and obliterating all else. He explored the insides of her mouth, creating a hollow in her insides. He tasted her lips, outlined them with his kisses, then drew her back for more, until she met his tongue with her own, and she nearly cried with desire.

She knew his hands took unspeakable liberties, but she ignored them as she stood on tiptoe and carried the kiss deeper, losing herself in the sensation of heat and moisture, the taste of brandy, the impossible pleasures his lips commanded. Not until he caught her bottom in both hands and pulled her up against him did she fully connect what their tongues did with what their bodies wanted. When she felt the length of him pressed against her belly, panic raced down all the trails the heat had left, and she wrenched her mouth away.

He didn't release his hold on her buttocks. She still felt him intimately pressed against her through their clothing.

A hot flush of embarrassment flooding her cheeks, Dillian stared at the V of his neck exposed by the open shirt as his voice rumbled somewhere over her head. She had difficulty focusing on his words. They sank in slowly.

"I have no intention of marrying anyone," he was saying, "so if that is your ploy, you'd best be gone now, Miss Whitnell."

Dazed, still confused, Dillian let her gaze drift upward to meet his eyes. They didn't seem as cold as his words. They looked as heated with desire as her own must. "I hadn't thought . . . Oh." She could actually read his mind, she thought. Or perhaps she had been on the receiving end of this kind of proposition once too many times. She didn't know why this one felt different, but she didn't run from him as she had the others.

"Cleaning your rooms and mending your draperies isn't enough, is it?" she forced herself to ask as coolly as she could.

This time, it was his turn to look startled. Perhaps she had read him wrong. Perhaps he hadn't even realized what he asked until she pointed it out. His lips curled in a snarl, and then he thought better of it.

"You don't know what you're saying," he said gruffly, dropping his hands, waiting for her to step back. She did, only because she couldn't keep her balance this close without falling against him.

"I think I do. If that's what it costs to protect Blanche, I'm willing to pay the price."

His shirt had opened even farther, revealing the dark hairs on his chest. The proximity of all that potent maleness made her belly churn. She didn't debate whether with fear or desire. She said what she had to say without giving herself time to think about it.

"I have no wealth to support a mistress," he said curtly.

Dillian glared at him. "I didn't ask for money. You offer something I want. I offer something you want. It's fair trade. It's done all the time."

"Not by innocent twenty-two-year-old misses."

"I'm twenty-five, and what makes you think I'm innocent?"

That took his breath away. She saw him watch her warily now, with a hint of speculation. She drew herself up to her full five feet, two inches, and met his eyes boldly. "I'll move into the big chamber upstairs. It's up to you."

She walked away while she still could. Her legs trembled like jelly. She feared she would fall on her face before she reached the door. He said nothing, did nothing to stop her. She opened the door and walked out, closing it carefully behind her. She still couldn't stop trembling. She waited for a roar of rage, a smashing of glass. She heard nothing.

He must be considering it. Dillian forced her shaking legs up the front stairs to the main bedchamber, the lord's chamber that occupied the better portion of the front hall in the older part of the house, where the ghosts walked. She felt like a ghost herself. She couldn't believe she'd done this.

The chamber loomed dark and icy as she entered. A huge mahogany tester occupied the raised dais at the opposite end of the room. A fireplace filled the left wall, but no warm fire welcomed her. Perhaps she should start one. Perhaps she should run like hell and get out of here.

She'd left Blanche's silk robe upstairs. She wished for its protection now. What did one wear on an assignation? She had only this one gown, and she couldn't afford to have it torn from her back if the marquess entered in a steaming rage. She didn't think he would, but he had a temper she couldn't predict. She'd caught him by surprise. He just hadn't pieced together all the

details yet. He would. Then she would see if he took it
as insult or temptation.

With frozen fingers, Dillian unfastened her gown and
hung it neatly in the wardrobe. She had no corset or
chemisette, just her chemise and stockings. The stockings
were too fine to risk. She carefully unrolled them and
looked around for somewhere to store them. She didn't
like leaving her undergarments lying about. They should
be washed, but she didn't want them dripping somewhere he could see.

She finally placed them in the wardrobe with the
dress, then crawled into the immense bed and pulled the
covers up around her. Perhaps she should find a flint
and light a lamp. She couldn't bear facing what she
planned. She left the lamp dark.

Shivering in the damp air, Dillian waited for the sound
of footsteps on the stairs. The old house creaked and
groaned as it settled down for the night. She thought
she heard the wind sigh through the passage behind the
walls. A faint light beat of rain pattered against the
windowpane.

The spot where she lay grew warmer. Dillian tried
imagining what the marquess would do to her, but the
room held enough ghosts without creating more. She
had never meant to marry anyway, and had always been
curious about what happened between a man and a
woman. She could salve her curiosity and save Blanche
at the same time. Virginity was a dispensable commodity
she couldn't afford forever. She liked the idea of giving
it to someone who made her feel like a woman and not
an object. It was much better done this way, with desire
on both sides. Far better than selling herself as wife for
a thousand pounds a year and the respectability of a
name to a man she couldn't respect or admire much
less desire. Once Blanche deeded her the Grange, she
wouldn't need a husband at all. This would work. She
knew it would.

She was still trying to convince herself of that as she
fell asleep with the tower clock on the landing wheezing midnight.

*   *   *

In the room below, the marquess heard that same wheezing chime, only he could gain nothing so restful as slumber. With the heat of lust racing through his veins, he would find no sleep tonight, not even with the help of the brandy bottle at his side.

Just the image his mind conjured of chestnut curls spread across lacy pillows made his blood boil. He needn't continue the torture any further by imagining the bedcover slipping off a creamy bare shoulder, revealing glimpses of those soft globes he longed to touch so much that his fingers actually tingled. Tingling fingers didn't compare to what happened to the rest of him. Gavin adjusted his position in the hard chair for the fiftieth time that evening, seeking some relief from the discomfort.

He'd been without a woman too long, his loins told him, but he'd quit listening to that part of himself long ago. Fingering the scar on the side of his face, he stared into the dying flame of the lamp. She'd grown up surrounded by randy young soldiers, he told himself. She had as much as admitted that she was no longer innocent. She had offered herself. Why shouldn't he take her up on the offer?

But it was just that offer holding him back. He'd seen the fear and courage, the determination to protect her young companion at any cost, even at the sacrifice of her reputation. Gavin wanted to believe that he scorned human sacrifice, but the truth was that he admired her courage too much to accept it. His admiration created this ridiculous urge to protect her, if only from herself.

He knew the urge to be ridiculous. Dillian Whitnell needed no man's protection, certainly not his. But just for a little while, he pretended that she needed him, and him alone. Just for a little while. His better sense would return soon enough.

Eighteen

The sun streamed in Blanche's window when Dillian finally made her appearance there the next morning.

Verity brushed her mistress's hair, and the light shone like spun gold through it. Dillian felt a veritable dowd beside her cousin's elegance, but then, that feeling was nothing new. The feeling that she fell beneath her cousin's contempt, however, was completely alien to her.

Dillian looked around for any sign of the marquess or the odious O'Toole, but they had mysteriously absented themselves. The marquess had never appeared last night. Only she knew how she had soiled and humiliated herself with her offer. The worst part of it was that she would do it again.

In saving Blanche, she would lose her cousin forever. Dillian didn't harbor any foolish illusions that she could hide the fact that she had become a man's mistress. But she wouldn't think about it now, in the bold morning light. He hadn't come to her. Perhaps he had decided she wasn't worth the invasion of his privacy. Perhaps she had misunderstood him entirely, and he didn't desire her at all. In that case, she must find alternative plans.

"Where is everyone?" she asked as casually as she could, taking a seat at the table and helping herself to tea from a pot Verity must have scavenged somewhere.

"O'Toole rode out early this morning. I haven't seen the marquess." Blanche turned her head in her cousin's direction. She wore the scarf O'Toole had given her over her eyes, but Dillian saw it was thin enough to allow light and shadow. "What will we do, Dill?"

Dillian took a sip of tea and stared out at the lovely morning. Even the overgrown brambles seemed appeal-

ing in the sunlight. The hideous rows of towering evergreens hiding all traces of civilization beyond seemed
more like a friendly hedge in this light. A patch of sunlight between drive and house beckoned for a bed of
roses. She'd never been much of a gardener, but she
found the idea appealing right now, more appealing than
what she'd offered to turn herself into.

"Wait on the marquess and O'Toole," she finally answered with a certain amount of gloom. "There must be
some way of persuading them to let you stay here while
I go into London. Did O'Toole give no hint of how we
might manage it?"

Blanche rested her chin on her hand while Verity
rolled her hair up into an elegant knot on top of her
head. "He gave no hint that we would have to leave.
Do you really think the marquess will throw us out? He
seems a little gruff, but not exactly heartless."

"You haven't seen him swing a sword capable of beheading three people at once," Dillian grumbled. "Do
you recall the vines beneath your windows at the
Grange? He climbs them as if they're a ship's rigging.
The man climbed down inside a burning house to rescue
two children he didn't know. He's not heartless. He's
insane."

Blanche's mouth turned up in amusement. "And this
is the man you think I should marry?"

Dillian shrugged. "He could certainly protect you, but
no, you're right. You ought to have someone aristocratic
and sophisticated, someone who can stand up to Neville
on his own ground, not just beat him into a pulp. Although the latter does hold some appeal."

Blanche sat back and sipped at her cup of tea, an
accomplishment she managed quite gracefully despite
the blindfold. "I rather had an impression of the marquess as an aristocratic, extremely reserved gentleman.
Do you tell me he's a ruffian?"

Dillian stared out the window. She could see him now
in gentleman's waistcoat and frilled linen, again in open-
necked shirt and trousers, or with a black cloak streaming behind him as he rode a massive—stolen—stallion.

She shook her head in despair of ever describing him. "He's not like anyone we've ever met."

"Neither is Michael," was Blanche's surprising answer.

Dillian looked up sharply. "Michael is a conniving varlet and most likely a Captain Sharp as well."

"He visits me every day and brings me roses that I can smell and touch. He thought of this scarf. He teaches me how to play cards and make coins disappear. Want to see a penny disappear?"

A purely rhetorical question, Dillian assumed, since Blanche promptly lifted the coin from the table, covered it with her fist, then opened her empty palm. A quite clever trick, one she might have questioned at another time, but not now, not with her impending doom hanging over her head. And Blanche's, from the sounds of her praise of O'Toole. Blanche was not easily impressed. Leaving her young cousin in the company of a charming rogue when she was extremely vulnerable had not been a wise thing to do. She would make O'Toole leave with her when she traveled to London. Better that Blanche fall for the marquess than his wayward companion.

"Make Neville disappear like that, and the two of you will have accomplished something," Dillian responded unhappily. "In the meantime, be sensible, Blanche. He's a charmer, not an eligible suitor."

Irritably, Blanche shoved away from the table. "I know that. Why can't Neville be more like Mr. O'Toole? Why do all the nice men have to be unsuitable?"

Now, that was an interesting question. Because the suitable ones were spoiled rich boys? What did that make the marquess? Dillian shook her head, not wanting to follow the direction of her thoughts. "You haven't met all the nice men yet. Give it time."

Blanche's slender fingers drifted to the raw burns upon her cheeks. "I'm not certain I have any time left," she answered sadly.

Blanche's reply haunted Dillian's thoughts the rest of the day. She had more than enough to think of while simultaneously trying to find the marquess and avoid him, without wondering what the wretched O'Toole was up to now. They were supposed to have had some discussion today on how to get those papers. Why couldn't men keep promises? Probably because they weren't as important to them as to herself.

Complaining to herself didn't make the day pass any faster. Dillian built card houses with Blanche and explored the manor further while Blanche napped. She listened for the sound of the marquess's voice wherever she went, but found no trace of him. She tried not to think about Blanche's plantive words, but they played over and over again in her head whenever she let her mind wander.

Blanche with all her wealth and beauty had been the target of every fortune hunter in the kingdom in the past. Scarred, she would still be no less a target, but also an object of pity. The thought revolted Dillian. Blanche had a brilliant mind, a sunny character, and impeccable morals. Any man would be blessed to have her without the wealth or looks. Maybe that's what they should do, disguise Blanche as a poor woman.

Then she would go unmarried for the rest of her life, Dillian thought savagely. Any way she looked at it, Blanche must buy herself a husband. She ought to at least have the opportunity to buy one she liked. The ignoble thought did not make Dillian any happier with herself.

Frustrated at her impotence, Dillian cleaned the master chamber, added a few more paintings she scavenged from the rest of the house, and wandered into the walled garden in search of more roses. She didn't know if the servants could see her from here. From what she could tell, they primarily stayed in the kitchen on the other side of the house. At this point, she didn't care what they thought. If Effingham meant to throw them out, what difference did it make?

Obviously, the men thought their own pursuits more important to abandon them like this. Or perhaps they had their own idea of how to get rid of the women invading their lives and had set about it without consulting them. Either alternative seemed likely given their arrogance. Dillian hated depending on anyone, but she could do nothing until she knew Blanche was safe.

Dillian helped Verity steal dinner from the pantry that evening, and they feasted royally on the meal neither man returned to eat. Perhaps the servants thought the marquess crept into the pantry at night to clean out the larder. Whatever the reason, the roast came to the table almost warm, and the potatoes melted in their mouths. They had even stolen a bottle of wine from the cellars and lifted their sagging spirits considerably by polishing it off between the two of them. Verity rightfully refused to drink any. She would have to guard her mistress through the night.

Half a bottle of wine didn't exactly make her foxed, but Dillian felt considerably better than she had all day when she traversed the dark halls to her room that night. Not until she reached the third floor and the bed where she had thrown the silken robe did it occur to her she had promised the marquess to sleep in the main chamber. What if he came home tonight looking for her?

That thought nearly paralyzed her into inaction. The wine soured in her stomach, and she glanced desperately around the candle-lit room to make certain he didn't lurk in the shadows. She had made an offer, the only offer she could make considering her nearly penniless state. Could she renege on it? Could she afford to let any chance of saving Blanche get by?

She couldn't. Blanche had ruined her life to save Dillian and the rest of her household. Blanche had delayed her marriage to promise her homeless cousin a future once she held her inheritance in her hands. Dillian simply couldn't take and take and never give. She could do this one simple thing to ensure her cousin's safety.

At least, it seemed simple the night before when Effingham had held her in his arms. Now with the cold light of another day shining upon it, her senses returned. She obviously hadn't thought this through clearly the night before. The consequences of surrendering her reputation loomed enormous, but not so enormous as the physical act itself. She didn't know if she had enough courage to go through with it.

Theory was one thing, action, quite another. But Dillian had learned to take action at an early age. She had roughly trod over all odds, discarded all doubts, lied, cheated, and generally did whatever necessary to protect herself and her loved ones. She could do the same now. With determination, she picked up the robe and returned down the stairs in the direction of the main bedchamber.

She knew the instant she reached the second-floor hall that the chamber was occupied. She saw the flickering light beneath the closed door, sensed a warmth that hadn't been there before. Wrapping the robe around her arms and holding it before her like a shield, she tiptoed closer, listening, hearing nothing.

The old door creaked as she pushed it open. The heat from a blazing fireplace engulfed her. The heavy scent of roses perfumed the air. Candles illuminated every corner of the room, decimating the shadows, and flickering light played rainbows across a crystal decanter beside the bed.

The bed. With widened eyes, Dillian stared at the bed. The marquess waited there, lounging—fully clothed—upon pillows she had gathered from all over the house. He had his boots crossed over the wine satin bedcover she had found in an old trunk. The candlelight didn't completely erase the shadows created by his strong cheekbones, but she could see the glitter of obsidian eyes from beneath dark curls. He had one arm crossed over his elegant frock coat, propping up the other, which held a fluted glass to his lips. He appeared as frozen as she felt, and she daringly closed the door behind her.

"I've given you a chance to reconsider your offer," he said finally, swinging the glass between his fingers. "I don't think you fully understand the consequences."

Gavin attempted to feel as cold as he sounded, but he had too much wine in him. He blamed it on the wine even though his loins tightened at just the sight of the seductive sway of the lady's hips as she made a hesitant step forward. In that ancient high-waisted gown, she was all curves instead of the slender stick of today's fashion. Some lower part of his mind taunted him with how those

curves would feel in his hands even as his conscience
strove to warn her of the treacherous shoals ahead.
There could never be more between them than this lust
that throbbed through him now, and for all he knew,
that could all be on his part and the result of long
abstinence.

He had spent this past day and night fighting his ridiculous urge to protect her, to keep her from throwing
herself away on someone as worthless as himself. He'd
finally lost that battle, but still his conscience demanded
he warn her. That she showed no sign of repulsion even
though he'd made certain she could see him fully for the
kind of man he was made him admire her even more.
Or desire her even more. He was beyond the ability
to differentiate.

He wanted her with every aching fiber of his body.
Something deep inside his mind continued screaming at
him to remember who she was, but it made no difference
any longer. He recognized her as a well-bred English
lady despite her appearance. He also saw her as a
woman with the immense generosity and intelligence to
see beyond his scarred face to something in him even
he no longer believed existed. She obviously thought him
a man of character, one worthy of her trust.

He was about to prove her wrong.

"More than likely not," she answered his question
about understanding consequences. Her voice sounded
slightly huskier than usual. Gavin couldn't decide if she
looked terrified or delighted. He'd made certain she
could see him, knew fully what she would have to look
at when she woke in the morning, but she didn't tear
her gaze away as other women did. He found it impossible to second-guess this little termagant.

"You can turn around and walk out now, or start removing your clothes," he answered without any gallantry
at all. These last twenty-four hours had been pure hell.
He couldn't summon any more gallantry. The fool
woman had no clue what she asked of him. He'd have
to make her see it before they went too far or before
either of them developed any more sentimental notions.
Still, the possibility that she accepted this as mere lust

kept the heat rising. Gavin wanted her so much he could taste it. He needed her. Hell, he needed a woman, period. It just so happened this one appealed to his more prurient instincts.

Beneath his glare, she hesitated. Then dropping the robe over a nearby chair, she slowly raised her hand to the bone button at her low-cut neckline. Gavin watched with fascination as the button slid easily from its hole. He turned the empty wineglass to his lips and kept his gaze fastened on her as she undid the second button. She'd accepted his challenge and prepared to face him down. This was one battle he didn't mind losing. Something in his gut clenched as the third and fourth buttons fell open, and he glimpsed something white and lacy beneath.

He could see far more than that from this vantage point. She didn't have the winter white skin of so many women in this country. The flesh rising above those lacy undergarments swelled with a creamy richness he wanted to lick. He told himself he should have eaten more dinner, that his always ravenous hunger needed appeasing, but he didn't have a taste for roast pork tonight. He wanted cream. Already, she'd won the battle. Or lost, whichever the case might be. His conscience disappeared entirely beneath the boiling tide of his desire.

Dillian hesitated again before reaching for the long slender sleeves, and Gavin heard himself growling with impatience. This time, he thought he detected uncertainty and a moment's trepidation before she rolled off the sleeve. Good. Let the little witch have second thoughts. And third.

But the moment those sleeves slid off her fingers, he forgot even those few good intentions. The chemise beneath the bodice barely concealed the full rising curves of her breasts. Had an artist sculpted a goddess he could not have created more perfect femininity, and no corset supported all that wealth of loveliness. It was entirely natural. Gavin's fingers itched to touch.

Motionless, he continued watching as she pushed the dress from her hips. It puddled on the floor, leaving her clad only in the skimpy chemise and stockings. He could see right through the thin material where the firelight silhouetted the juncture of her legs. She wore no pantalets. Gavin reached to unfasten the flap of his breeches before it cut into his straining flesh.

He had only one last weapon left in his arsenal with which to halt this charade. In a voice hoarse with lust, he demanded, "Do you know how to protect yourself?"

Her look of startlement, followed by a furious flush from the tips of her ears to the full curves of her breasts made him wince inwardly, but he didn't relent. He gazed mercilessly at the hard points of her nipples against thin cloth while waiting for her reply.

"I thought you would know."

The husky sound of her voice surprised Dillian as much as her reply. As a lady, she shouldn't know about these things. But she'd absorbed a great deal from her masculine companions over the years, more than they'd ever realized she'd understood. Whores had ways of protecting themselves from the eventual results of their couplings. She'd just never learned what they were. The thought of creating a child with this man lying here so coldly watching her left a chill in her middle, but she supposed these matters should be attended to. He'd already made it plain he had no wealth to support her. She couldn't expect him to support a child.

His scowl at her reply made her cringe. Her humiliation deepened as he growled, "I didn't bargain to teach lessons." He jerked his head in the direction of the dressing screen in the corner. "I found vinegar in the pantry, but no sponges. I'll be careful this first time. You can use the vinegar to cleanse yourself afterward. Now, take off the rest of those clothes."

The heat of his gaze on her skin burned more warmly than the fire, creating an exquisite sensitivity that made her feel as if scorched by flame. The utter humiliation caused by his words completed her decimation. She hoped the fire's light concealed her flush as she reached for the ribbons of her chemise. Her fingers trembled while scraping across newly sensitive skin, arousing her breasts to a heavy ache as she loosed the first ribbon.

She'd not thought to stand before him like this, in a full blaze of light. She'd imagined the cover of darkness concealing her sins. When she glanced up to see the man in the bed unfastening his breeches, she thought she might burst into flames of embarrassment, but she couldn't turn her gaze away. Somehow, he held her spellbound.

The part of her mind still functioning told her she must go through with this. She had come this far, surely she could make herself go farther. Miraculously, she had gone beyond humiliation already. The bulge threatening to push the marquess's breeches completely open held her fascinated, much as a snake fascinates its intended victim. She had caused that bulge. He couldn't help himself any more than she could. The notion gave her enough courage to untie the second ribbon and let the chemise fall.

The filmy material caught on her breasts, and she tugged at it until it dropped to her hips. She watched the involuntary muscle behind his breeches lurch dangerously, and her hand flew to her throat. The touch of her own hand against naked flesh caused another nervous jerk. Gritting her teeth, Dillian tore her gaze away from his breeches and watched the marquess's eyes. The blatant need there tore her into tatters. He would never let her stop now.

Effingham moved more quickly than Dillian thought possible. One minute he lay sprawled idly across the satin covers, the next he unfurled like a striking snake, catching her about the waist, hauling her down on top of him. The chemise fell, unnoticed, to the floor.

The part of him that made him male, now fully uncovered, pressed hot and heavy between her bare thighs.

Nineteen

The frill of Effingham's shirtfront bit into Dillian's breasts. The buttons of his unfastened breeches pressed into her bare thighs. None of those material things had as much effect on her senses as the heated flesh pushing at that tender juncture. She couldn't imagine how this coupling business worked, but this juxtaposition of bodies told her more than she wanted to know. Her first instinct screamed for her to scramble out of this bed and flee down the hall.

But then the marquess pulled her mouth down to his, and the sensations of heat and wine and the moist demands of his tongue overpowered all rationality. His hands clenched her bare waist, but the power of his kiss held her more surely than his hands. The urgency of his lips made Dillian feel devoured, needed, desirable. It opened a well of yearning she hadn't known existed inside her. A longing to please consumed her. She wanted to know where his kisses led. She wanted things she couldn't put a name to, so she kissed him back as thoroughly as she knew how, hoping he would teach her, hoping she could satisfy his cravings as well as her own. The mortification he had imposed on her earlier faded into nothingness. Common sense evaporated. The intoxicating man beneath her became her entire world.

A large hand encompassed her breast, and Dillian gasped at the sensation of being held there. It almost distracted her from the pressure between her thighs— almost, but not enough. She opened her legs wider to kneel more comfortably astride his hips, and his groan matched her own when they came in contact like that. She froze.

The marquess slid his other hand between them, touching her where they connected, and her gaze darted to his. His dark eyes watched her every move, and Dillian suddenly felt very naked, very vulnerable beneath his gaze. He could see right into her soul, but he still wore all his clothes.

The hard control in his voice as he spoke brought her swiftly back to earth.

"I'm going to put the candles out before we burn the house down around our ears. If you're having second thoughts, get out now while you still can. I won't stop once I come back to this bed."

Effingham shifted her to one side and raised himself gracefully, tucking his thickened member behind his breeches as he reached for the nearest candle. Dillian felt cold all over as she watched him walk around the room, coolly snuffing out flames with his fingers. The shadows of darkness followed him, filling up the places the light had conquered. His shadow loomed ever larger as he came around past the fire. From here, he seemed enormous. She had to remember she bedded a monster, a man who despised the society she knew. She had no idea where this would lead other than to eventual abandonment. She must be mad. She ought to heed his warnings and run.

Instead, she pulled the satin covers down and climbed between the cool sheets, clinging to the memories of a lonely, misunderstood man who risked his life for a stranger's children, a man who could turn back an angry mob without loss of life. Somewhere beneath the guise of beast existed a man who could teach her the ways of love, even if he could not love himself.

The marquess left a single lamp burning as he approached the bed, and Dillian could see he had begun unfastening his shirt. When he drew it over his head and flung it to the floor, she suppressed a gasp. She hadn't noticed the particularly ragged scar decorating his ribs before.

She thought the gleam in his eye might be sardonic as he reached for the band of his trousers, but she would never totally understand the moods of this man. When he stepped out of the pants, she realized he had just made himself naked for her as she had done for him. He didn't do it to expose his beauty, however. He did it to expose his ugliness.

She didn't seek physical beauty. She didn't know what she sought other than Blanche's safety. She wanted to cower into the pillows as Effingham kneeled on the bed's edge, but she wouldn't let him see fear. That's what he expected to see. Reaching beyond herself, thinking only of him, Dillian held out her arms and welcomed him to her embrace.

She avoided looking as his manhood stiffened. That part of him still frightened her. But the caress of his fingers on her breast as he lay down beside her thrilled her beyond any joy she had ever experienced. She arched upward for more, and he rewarded her with a slightly one-sided smile. She clung to the bleak look of pain and desire in his eyes, searching for something more, something too deeply hidden for him to reveal.

"You may despise military men, madam, but you're as brave as any soldier," he praised her gruffly. "And too trusting by far. Come here. I'll not wait any longer."

He frightened her with those words, but Dillian came into the strength of his bare arms as ordered, not knowing the meaning of retreat. Effingham lay beside her and kissed her mouth while caressing her breast. Then, when she relaxed, he bent and took her nipple between his lips.

Dillian nearly arched from his arms as the electricity of that touch shot through her. The marquess growled his approval of this success and moved on to the other breast, caressing the first one with agile fingers until Dillian thought she would melt into a puddle of hot wax. The scent of snuffed candles drifted through the room, mixing with the musky smell of his skin and their combined ardor. The worn sheet rubbed against her back as he pressed her down, but she only noticed the strength of the arms and legs pinning her against the mattress.

The marquess's lean elegance disguised his sheer physical power. Dillian couldn't move unless he let her. She raised her arms to the hard curve of his shoulders, and he pressed more kisses to her mouth in return, but they both knew these gentle caresses merely prolonged the inevitable. The heat of desire throbbed through them in every place flesh touched flesh. When he inserted his knees between her thighs, she stiffened, but he caught her hands between his and bent to lave her nipples once more. This time, her legs parted of their own accord, to ease the stabbing ache of desire between her thighs.

He held her wrists firmly, covering her mouth with his until she writhed with the depth of his kiss. Her powerlessness made her tense, but then he lifted himself to kiss her breasts once again, and she relaxed, giving herself up to the pleasure. That's when he impaled her.

Dillian screamed but found her screams drowned by Gavin's mouth. He filled her so completely she thought she should surely burst, but he held himself still until her torn tissues adjusted somewhat to the invasion. All her stomach muscles pulled taut, protesting his blunt intrusion. He kissed her again, and the warm familiarity of those kisses slowly reassured. When he did no more, Dillian looked up into the whitened scars of his face to see him watching her.

"You'll regret this one day," he said somberly, giving recognition to what she had just surrendered. But then he kissed her again, and Dillian closed her eyes and let sensation overwhelm thought.

He caressed her breasts to peaks of excitement, then moved inside her, until the moisture lubricating them made his thrusts more than bearable. Dillian clung to his muscular upper arms, raised her hips, and felt him shudder with need. This time, he thrust so deeply she thought herself torn asunder. Then he jerked completely from her, and spilled his seed into the sheets.

She felt strangely bereft as he jerked and trembled atop her. She should be grateful that he had taken this precaution, but she felt empty and abandoned, useless somehow. Bereft. And soiled.

She wanted to turn away but couldn't. Effingham held her too firmly pinioned with his weight. She became more aware than ever of the bronzed torso looming over her, of the thin lines of scars that marked his otherwise magnificent chest, of the heavy weight pressing her deep into the mattress. She felt the heat emanating from him, noted the trail of dark hairs between his flat male nipples down to his navel and beyond. She found it difficult believing that the Dillian Whitnell she knew lay in a naked man's bed, thoroughly ruined, but she could feel the stickiness of her own blood if she needed proof. She fought back tears of shame. She never looked back and never cried.

He rolled aside but held her down with one strong arm across her breasts. His fingers played with the peaks until she felt that restless stirring within her womb again.

"I thought you had at least some experience," he muttered roughly.

"I've been mauled before," she answered without thinking of the coldness of this reply. The coldness wasn't for him, but for the other men who had made her feel as if she were no more than a horse to be petted or whipped as the mood took them. And perhaps it was a little bit for him, for the dissatisfaction she felt right now.

"I didn't maul you," he reminded her. "The first time just isn't pleasant. The necessity for caution didn't help. I'll show you how to fit yourself with sponges soaked in vinegar next time. If this is the life you mean to take up, then you should know how to protect yourself."

She felt humiliated, abased, reduced to a whore off the streets. "There will be no other after you," she ground out through clenched teeth. "Let us keep this to the immediate. Must I use the vinegar now?"

Dillian knew he stared at her, but she couldn't look at him again. The place between her legs ached abominably. How many more times must she repeat this performance before he grew bored with it?

"I think you're sulking because it wasn't as good for you as it was for me."

She heard laughter in his voice, and she wanted to punch him, but she refused to acknowledge his existence. The fact that he lay naked and half on top of her made that pretense a trifle difficult.

His hand strayed between her legs, caressing her gently there. Dillian couldn't help the involuntary reaction of her hips as they rose eagerly at his touch.

"After twenty-five years of abstinence, you must be more starved for this than I am," he murmured against her ear, just before he captured her mouth and kissed her again.

Dillian tried resisting. She didn't think she could take it again this night. Perhaps tomorrow, after she'd recovered. Not now. Not while she felt sticky and soiled and humiliated beyond redemption. But he wouldn't let her pull away. He coaxed his tongue between her teeth, filled her mouth with his breath until she needed him to breathe again.

His skillful fingers caressed her in places she scarcely dared touch herself. Her nipples hardened into tiny nubs beneath his lavish caresses. His mouth upon them caused multiple explosions in her blood. And his hand came back time and again to pluck and stroke sensitive tissues until she ached with the need for him inside her.

"My lord, please," she whispered, ashamed at her begging.

"Gavin," he ordered. "My name is Gavin. Call me by it."

Since his finger had slipped inside her to make her quake with the desire for more, she could scarcely argue. "Gavin," she whispered urgently.

"Very good."

Then he applied his finger more provocatively until she writhed and cried out and finally exploded into rolling spasms that left her totally drained and as boneless as a newborn.

"That's what I'll do to you when I come into you next time," he murmured against her ear.

Next time. He would do this again and again until she had no mind of her own, until he claimed her body and soul. Dillian could see it coming, but already he had sapped her will until she could offer no protest. She merely curled against his strong chest and let him hold her. His hand stroked her buttocks, and she felt his arousal. She ought to leap from the bed and run for safety. She merely fitted herself against him and smiled at his groan.

He took her again before he taught her the use of a vinegar douche. His withdrawal just as her body opened to receive his seed left her frustrated once more, but she made no complaint. She had no desire to carry anyone's bastard.

"Anglesey and Dismouth are thick as thieves. The earl is the older. He's guiding His Grace through the labyrinth of Parliament. Dismouth has his tentacles in every pie in town. He wants a place in the cabinet, and he's cultivated friends in high places. Even the Regent puts on his best behavior in the earl's presence, for fear he will get his allowance cut otherwise."

Dillian plucked idly at a loose thread in Blanche's bedcover. "What has this to do with anything?" she inquired irritably. She hadn't had much sleep. Her body felt a stranger to her. And she couldn't bear looking at the lean man lounging against the far wall. The marquess behaved as if they scarcely knew each other when he'd explored her more intimately than her own mother ever had. She resented his offhandedness, even though she understood the necessity for it. He left her feeling hollow inside.

Michael gave her an impatient look. "Pay attention. Dismouth has access to all the military high commands. Wellington is at his beck and call, and all the ambassadors who worked on the Treaty of Paris report to him. If there is anything in your father's papers, anything at all that might be of interest to him, Dismouth will know it."

Dillian glanced toward Blanche, who absentmindedly stirred at her cold cup of tea. Not finding any help in that quarter, she shrugged and asked the obvious, "If he already knows of it, why should he want them?"

"That is what we must find out," Michael answered with satisfaction.

"Wouldn't it be simpler if Miss Whitnell just collected the journals and turned them over to a solicitor?" The marquess didn't stir from his corner, but his energy still permeated the room. Even Michael turned around to glare at him.

"Don't be such a blockhead, your noble lordship," O'Toole responded with some irritation. "If there's something of value in those papers, it belongs to the lady. And if there's something treasonous in those journals, all concerned are dead and buried and there is no need for tarnishing either lady's name with it now."

"Then, I shall just go to London, persuade Neville and the solicitor to hand over the books, and bring everything back here," Dillian declared, tired of this whole game. She wanted it over. She saw no sense in any of it.

"And how do you mean to persuade the duke to anything?" the marquess asked with a trace of menace in his tone.

Blanche and Michael stared at him, but Dillian just gave him a malevolent glare. "I'll hold him at gunpoint. Is that what you want to hear?"

"I want to hear the end of this so I might get back to business."

The marquess spoke matter-of-factly, without the harshness of his words. Dillian still felt them like a blow to the belly. She sank back into the pillows on the bed and let the others carry on the discussion. She wanted just exactly what he wanted: this to be over so she could go on with her life as planned.

"If it's actually the papers they're after and not Lady Blanche, then it's possible they contain evidence of someone else's treason," O'Toole continued, spinning his list of possibilities, "someone willing to pay a very high price to conceal it. Burning down a house full of people is the act of a desperate man. If this man believes the papers still available, he'll stop at nothing to get his hands on them. We must be in a position to act quickly, if so."

Dillian idly contemplated burning down Blanche's town house and the solicitor's office, but she wasn't quite so desperate as that. She plucked at another thread and waited for the irreverent O'Toole to continue. She wondered why the marquess didn't knock the irritating footman flying, but she'd already decided O'Toole held something over the marquess that kept him from retaliating. She wondered what it was.

"How do you plan on obtaining the papers in the first place?" the marquess asked. "Let's deal with the problems one at a time."

O'Toole shrugged expressively. "I don't. I took a look in the vault yesterday. The papers aren't there."

Dillian didn't question the footman's larcenous declaration. A man who could make coins disappear in thin air could undoubtedly open vaults without a combination.

The room erupted in voices, all but Dillian's. A dizzying sensation spun her head back against the pillow, and the hollow at the pit of her belly ached as she finally met the marquess's eyes.

He didn't believe a word of her story, and he didn't care. His gaze told her he would make her pay for every minute of this confusion. She could see it in the way his glance insultingly swept from her eyes to her breasts to the place where his body had entered hers.

When Michael's announcement finally broke through the barrier of her flaming senses, Dillian accepted his decision as the punishment she deserved.

The marquess, however, wasn't so acquiescent.

When Michael announced, "His lordship and Miss Whitnell must go to London," the lounging figure in the corner erupted like a cannonball from its barrel.

"The hell I will!" he yelled at the room at large, before slamming from the chamber without a backward glance.

Michael calmly looked at Dillian. "He's a marquess. He's the only one who can move about in Dismouth's society. He has to go. You'll have to persuade him."

Dillian thought he looked right through her and knew every sinful thing she had done. The knowledge pierced her to the quick, and she slid from the bed and out of the room without examining her motives or intentions. She just wanted out from under O'Toole's knowing gaze.

No matter that none of this made an ounce of sense any longer. Whores lived in London. Why shouldn't she?

God certainly had a strange sense of justice.

Twenty

"I'll not make a bloody ass of myself flitting around ballrooms and salons and pretending I'm a damned aristocrat!" the marquess yelled loud enough to rattle the filthy chandelier, even though the two of them were alone in the room and stood only yards apart.

"You'll have Matilda up here looking to see if the ghosts have got you," Michael reminded him calmly. "I'd suggest you lower your voice."

"I'll damned well shout as loud as I choose, and to hell with the servants." Even as he protested, Gavin lowered his voice and stalked the salon. Protecting the women from discovery had almost become second nature.

"You'll have Miss Whitnell with you. She can tell you who's who and what. If the duke has the papers, then it shouldn't take long at all."

Gavin sent his brother a malevolent glare. With the skin of his scarred cheek drawn up and white, the look would have terrified a lesser man. Michael merely leaned against the wall, unperturbed.

"You just want us to leave you alone with Lady Blanche," Gavin accused him. "She's not your type, you know. You might as well bang your head against the wall. You would fare better if I stayed here and you accompanied the dauntless Miss Whitnell."

Michael gave his brother a knowing look. "I ought to at that. You would come flying after us within days. I've seen that proprietary look before. You've staked your claim, and you'll cut the balls off any man daring to come between you. Don't warn me about the Lady Blanche. You've grabbed a firebrand by the wrong end, and you'll be lucky to get away with your flesh still attached. Abstinence has made mush of your brains."

Gavin looked away. He didn't dare confirm his brother's opinion, but he felt the truth of it all the same. He had gone around in a state of near arousal all day, just thinking about the moments when he could get Dillian away from the others. Matilda had looked at him peculiarly when he'd included sponges on the list of supplies he wanted from the village. And he didn't even care. He meant to bury himself deep inside Dillian's welcoming heat and stay there all night. He needed that. He damned well deserved it after all this.

"Leave Miss Whitnell out of this," he said harshly. "I'm not going to London. You're much better at sneaking about than I am. You go. I'll stay here with the ladies."

"Sneaking is not what this is all about. We need information, information that only people at a high level can provide. The duke already recognizes me. He will make no connection between an eccentric marquess, Lady Blanche, and the papers he must have stolen from the vault. We have no other choice. You have to be the one who gets the papers out of him."

"He's probably already discovered they're nothing but a soldier's notes on the most potent apple punch, or a litany of the best whores in Europe. This is a wild-goose chase, Michael. I'll not suffer society for this nonsense."

"My father didn't need notes on whores and punch, he had an excellent memory." A slender female figure moved gracefully into the abandoned salon, her high-waisted blue gown floating almost as ethereally as the ghost supposedly haunting this place. Gavin felt his guts twist with the pain of desire. He had indeed gone too long without a woman for this one to sever his senses like this.

"Then, you looked at the papers? You know what's in them?" he asked sarcastically, in a futile attempt to distance himself from her.

"They're diaries of military strategy mostly. I glanced through them once, to see if I could find any personal information. He had maps and notes about this regiment and that. A lot of it was in a shorthand code he often used. I didn't see anything of any interest to anyone. The war is over. Of what use can any of it be?"

Michael and Gavin exchanged looks. Gavin knew even better than his brother what those notes could mean if read by the proper authorities. A detailed accounting of military strategy might make an excellent book for war aficionados, or lead to the public condemnation of incompetent officers who drove their men into losing positions and left them. Such papers could contain tales only dead men knew. They could also lead to the spoils of war, hidden while on the march and never claimed later. The possibilities loomed innumerable. Someone knew what those books contained and didn't want the information released.

"We won't know until we find the books," Michael pointed out. "If they're the reason someone intends you or Lady Blanche harm, we must find them first."

Gavin watched Dillian's eyes widen with a fleeting moment's fear, then shutter again. She didn't even know he watched. She had slipped back into that devious mind of hers and didn't know the rest of the world existed. He wanted to change that. He wanted all that brilliant intensity focused on him alone. He wanted to be the sole beneficiary of all that female loveliness. If he must sacrifice his pride and submit to the inglorious rounds of London society, he'd demand Dillian as his reward. He would become the center of her universe. Gavin liked that idea almost well enough to accept Michael's dastardly plans.

"And you have some fool idea that the duke will take me into his confidence and shower me with those papers?" Gavin asked, his tone demanding that Dillian look at him. She did, and he felt the impact of those long-lashed eyes all the way to his core. She regarded him with barely disguised hostility, but he knew what he could do to her with just a touch. He wouldn't indulge himself now, but he moved a step closer, just to remind her of the chemistry.

He smiled when she crossed her arms over her breasts and looked away.

"That's the easiest solution," Michael agreed. "Or you could discover their location and send for me. While you keep him distracted, I can ferret them out."

"And the only way I can do this is by going about in society?" Gavin held his gaze on Dillian while he spoke to Michael. He kept his voice low and caressing, and she rewarded him with a shiver as she avoided his eyes.

"You also need access to the cabinet heads once you uncover the papers and discover their contents. We need to know which man is best for our purposes."

Gavin sensed his brother's look of curiosity, but he ignored it. He reached and tucked a loose curl behind Dillian's ear. Her hair always looked as if she'd just climbed from bed. He liked it like that.

"And Miss Whitnell? What shall we do with her?" Again, he directed the level of his voice at her. She began running her hands up and down her arms as if to warm them.

Michael didn't answer.

Gavin waited a moment, enjoying watching her, knowing she didn't know which way to turn. When Michael still didn't answer, he glanced up, to find the salon empty of all but Dillian and himself.

He cursed and glared at the unlit shadows of this tomb. His brother had the lazy habit of disappearing in the face of conflict. He glanced back down at Dillian who looked equally bewildered as she tried to figure out where the elusive O'Toole had gone. "Don't bother yourself. He'll appear again when he's ready. In the meantime, Miss Whitnell, what are your suggestions? Shall I take you to London as my mistress? I rather like the sound of that."

Color rose in her cheeks as she looked to the dust-covered furniture and not at him. "If that's what you prefer," she answered flatly. "But I rather think it would look odd if the Marquess of Effingham suddenly turned up with Lady Blanche's companion and began asking questions."

She'd certainly hit the nail on the head in no short time, Gavin admitted, disgruntled. He couldn't object to the idea of London too much if he knew she would adorn his bed at his beck and call. But her suggestion gave him images of a lonely bed while she gallivanted about London having the time of her life.

"Then, I'll leave you here," he threatened.

"That would suit me, but you don't know a duke from an earl, Anglesey from Dismouth. You won't know how to go about. I rather suspect O'Toole's etiquette was learned on the back of a mail coach. If you prefer to rely on it, then so be it. I'll not argue."

She didn't stalk off, although Gavin suspected she wanted to. She stood there, not looking at him, waiting for the slap in the face he would give her. He gave her what she expected, but he did it gently. He had no reason for unselfishness. She would pay his price. But he would try not to hurt her too badly in the process. Only as the words emerged from his mouth did he realize how thoroughly she had snared him.

"You'll go with me. We'll take separate residences and pretend no acquaintance, but you'll make yourself available when and where I ask. I'll be discreet." The words made it sound as if he were in control, but they both knew if he wasn't wiggling on her hook, he would have left her behind.

She turned back to him then, and really looked at him. What Gavin saw in her eyes had him quivering right down to his toe bones. Before she even spoke, he grabbed Dillian's arm and pulled her out of the salon, down the hall, toward the bedchamber. He would have her now and sort out those other issues later.

Reaching his goal, Gavin slammed the door behind them and dragged Dillian to the bed. Bending her unprotesting body backward over the high mattress, he plunged his tongue between her teeth. She whimpered slightly against his mouth but lifted her arms willingly enough to circle his shoulders. Gavin needed no further encouragement. Massaging her breasts with his hands, he rubbed his arousal against her, and felt her arch hesitantly against him. He hardened so rapidly, pain shot through him.

When he reached to pull her gown up, the door behind them slammed open again.

They both jumped, startled, their gazes swerving to see who stood there. The doorway was empty.

Dillian giggled nervously behind him. "Perhaps the lady is displeased with our presence."

Cursing, Gavin looked down into her pale face and frightened eyes and tore himself away. The pain of his arousal eased somewhat when he saw her move hesitantly to a sitting position, her fingers curling into knots in the bedcovers as she regarded him with wariness. At least she made no effort to run from him, nor did she look at him with disgust. He should be grateful for small favors.

He walked over and slammed the door shut. Not finding a bolt, he propped a chair against it. "You'll find sponges and the vinegar solution behind the dressing screen. Soak a sponge in the solution and insert it as deeply as you can. You'll have to learn the proper procedure now. We'll not have time for lessons in London."

Deliberate cruelty was the only way to protect them both. Once she understood this relationship had no future, he could offer her the small kindnesses he would offer a mistress. Until then he would obliterate any small hope she might harbor that he could offer her more. He should never have bedded a virgin. They mixed up emotions with lust.

Gavin tried not to feel guilty about those thoughts as he removed his clothes while she slipped behind the screen. She was twenty-five years of age, long past marriageable. She knew what she was doing. She benefited as much as he, maybe more so, from this arrangement. He had no reason to feel guilty over what was, after all, a business transaction. He didn't exactly bed a child.

But his ability to rationalize flew out the window the instant Dillian stepped from the screen wearing nothing but the silk robe she had carried in the prior night. Her nut brown curls clung to her pale cheeks. Her devastatingly blue eyes behind long lashes filled her face. And the white silk clung to every ample curve. Gavin drew her forward, pulling the robe aside and filling his hand with her breast. She shuddered, but the nipple puckered obligingly.

"Thank you," he muttered gallantly, assaulted by too many senses to say more before he bent and took that enticing plum into his mouth.

Her moan fed his needs. He eased her back against the bed while he filled her mouth with his tongue. Her robe fell open, and he plucked her nipples into readiness. She raised her legs of her own accord, circling his hips to bring him close. The silk still rubbed between them, hindering his access to the heated cavern of his goal. Gavin swiped the soft material away, positioned himself carefully, and thrust forward so quickly she bucked off the bed, taking him deeper than he thought possible.

Not until he'd spilled his seed deep inside her and began to harden again did he realize the trap he'd set for himself.

He'd found the only woman in the kingdom who could look on his grotesqueness without flinching, and he had turned her into a whore. She would never look on him with anything but hatred from now on. She would leave him the first chance she found. And he would be right back where he started again.

Gavin closed his mind against the image of long lonely nights tossing on the couch in his study, not considering them while he held the solution in his arms.

Dillian struggled briefly as he surged against her again, but Gavin subdued her quickly enough. She was as ripe as he was willing. They'd take what pleasure they could from that. Her shudders of ecstasy from their last joining still engulfed them.

Dillian lay still against the sweat-dampened sheets, absorbing the sensation of a man's heavy leg entrapping hers. She could feel his heartbeat and heard the sound of his even breathing. Those elemental signs of life stirred something deep within her, something she had to deny before the tear creeping down her cheek became a flood.

She would prefer denying the alien sponge, but she could feel the heavy flow of his seed against her thigh and understood its necessity. In just this brief time she had come to accept the naturalness of Gavin's body inside hers. Her womb grew taut and ready just thinking of him. She even understood now why women had children. She could easily dream up fantasies of taming the beast, revealing the gentle man inside. Turning her head, she traced the pale scars of his jaw, knowing the damage went deeper than his skin, wanting to believe she could heal it. She ached with a longing for completeness she'd never known before. She could even consider proudly growing round with his child if he asked it of her.

He wouldn't ask it of her. Dillian's fantasies snapped back to the dark corners of her mind, where they belonged. The marquess thought of her only as a vessel to ease his needs. He had made that more than clear. The sponge offered concrete proof of his intent. Its presence sickened her. If she thought too long about it, her own cooperation in this charade would sicken her. He had turned her into something obscene, and her stomach revolted at the thought.

She shoved Gavin's leg away and felt him stir, but she rolled from the bed before he could reach for her again. For her own peace of mind, they would have to establish some rules here. He couldn't just haul her into any available room and attack her like that again.

She slipped behind the dressing screen and rid herself of the abomination before scrubbing thoroughly, using the vinegar douche. She wished desperately for some of Blanche's perfumed water, then vowed to have it before she committed this act again.

Gavin sat bare-chested with his back against the pillows when Dillian emerged from behind the screen, fully dressed. His powerful shoulders silhouetted against the white linen made her pulse race madly but she ignored her more primitive instincts. She found that a trifle difficult while her gaze kept straying to the dark trail of fur on his chest.

"Don't ever do that to me again," she warned. "Even a whore deserves more respect than that."

She saw nothing in his eyes, only the mocking expression of his scarred features as he carefully regarded her.

"What does respect have to do with anything?" he

asked coldly. "We both had an itch, and we satisfied it. Or is that the problem? Did I not satisfy you enough?"

Dillian reached for the first thing that came to hand—the vase of roses on the dresser. Water drenched the rug as both vase and petals splattered dead center on his chest. Before he could even react to the first volley, she followed it with the brass candlestick, the ivory hairbrush, the Dresden figurine, and a half-dozen crystal, nearly empty perfume decanters. All bounced near or on the pillows and bed as her target leapt—roaring—from the sheets, covered in rose petals, stinking of old perfume, and bruised from brass and ivory.

Dillian didn't linger to hear his furious diatribe. Pulling back the chair blocking her exit, she escaped to the hall, slamming the door behind her. The satisfying crash rattled any remaining pictures on the wall.

Twenty-one

"If Dillian is to go about in society, she must have gowns," Blanche announced decisively. "She will protest, but you must see that she goes to my modiste. Madame will accept my credit."

"I would rather see her strung to the rafters," Gavin muttered, pacing the room with fists clenched, occasionally glancing out the window at the rapidly fading day.

"We must find a tailor for you, and you will need the carriage," Michael added, apparently enjoying the sight of his brother's discomfort. "A marquess cannot walk to society functions."

"The carriage is little more than a rattling heap of junk," Gavin fumed.

"Where will you stay?" Blanche exclaimed. "Dillian must stay in my town house, but that would not be at all appropriate for you."

"I have friends." Still growling, Gavin paced the length of the chamber once more. He bristled with energy and frustration.

"Mellon," Michael said knowingly. "The earl never uses his house. And your cousin refuses. Excellent idea. Gives you credibility."

"I don't want credibility. I want this over. I detest this invasion of my privacy. I have no inclination for skulking about glittering ballrooms for the amusement of London."

Blanche drifted from her seat and placed a placating hand on his chest. "You have been more than kind, my lord. I cannot begin to offer you all the gratitude I feel. I know this is a tremendous imposition. If I could think of any other way around it, I would gladly do so. But people's lives may depend on your actions. I cannot jeopardize my households by appearing in public. Dillian is very clever. She will find a way to complete this mission quickly."

Gavin's eyes blazed at this mention of the dragon lady who blew hot and cold and sometimes both at the same time. "She'd best, or I'll trade her to the duke for the papers."

Blanche smiled and patted him lightly. "Dillian is difficult, but she will grow on you, you'll see."

"It's almost dark. Where is the fair lady?" Michael raised a questioning eyebrow in his brother's direction.

"Pulling wings off butterflies, I expect. I'll tell Mac to bring the carriage around. If she doesn't appear, I'll let her find her own way."

The marquess stormed out, obviously relieved to escape the box they held him in. Michael and Blanche exchanged glances as she removed her scarf.

"Is he always so temperamental?" she asked hesitantly.

"Only when he's frothing at the bit. Your cousin must be keeping him on a tight rein."

"Dillian? She most always avoids men. The marquess isn't one to molest a lady, is he? Upon occasion some of my friends have tried, and she's cut them extremely cruelly. If there is any chance that . . ."

Michael waved her to silence. "Let them fight their own battles. Gavin's avoided women these last few years. No doubt any woman makes him uncomfortable."

Blanche blinked and regarded him carefully. "And you? Do you avoid women, too? You only linger long enough in my company to teach me amusing tricks, then you disappear again."

He dug his hands into his pockets and shifted uncomfortably as he stared at the window instead of at her. "A footman has no business in a lady's chamber. I'll see that our hero and the she-devil get off properly."

Blanche's lips turned up in a wry grimace as O'Toole quickly followed the marquess, leaving her to her own devices.

Biting her bottom lip, she gazed consideringly at the wardrobe hiding the secret passage. Idleness did not become her. She could see in the dark. Her hands had healed enough to use them a little. Why should she be the only one left sitting here?

With Mac driving the ancient barouche, Gavin clung to the overhead strap inside and stared at the woman on the bench across from him. She had wrapped herself thoroughly in an old shawl and pointedly gazed out the window, although darkness made all but the most distinctive shapes impossible to discern.

Before the war—before a pointless fight had turned his handsome visage into a caricature of itself—Gavin would have coaxed and wheedled Dillian into laughing. He knew how to turn a lady up sweet. Heaven only knew, he and Michael had survived on the kindnesses of ladies often enough. He couldn't do that anymore. Perhaps he had grown rusty. Perhaps whatever charm he had once possessed grew hard from lack of use. He saw himself back then as a feckless, useless piece of baggage. He didn't consider himself much more these days, but he didn't pretend to be more than he was, either. He didn't have it in him to offer sweet words, charm, or tenderness to woo her back.

But Dillian's silence disturbed him. Her senseless attack earlier had infuriated him, but life was too short for holding a grudges. He had said something, done something, that had gone against the grain. He understood that much, even if he didn't quite understand what he had said or done. Women had odd principles. Gavin could accept that. But he couldn't accept this stony silence between them.

Admittedly, now that she had released his ruthlessly suppressed desires, his main interest centered on getting her back in his bed again. He wouldn't be a man if he didn't think of the immense pleasure she had brought him and crave more of it. He didn't think he'd ever felt anything quite so good in all his days of philandering. But part of the joy had come from the fact that he knew he had given her the same pleasure she had given him. He'd thought they'd actually had an understanding of sorts. Dillian's withdrawal now displeased him if only because it proved him wrong.

The carriage hit a particularly rough rut, jostling them both in their seats. Dillian grabbed for the strap but made no comment. She released the edge of her shawl to hold on, and the heavy material sagged, revealing her lovely breasts straining against the ridiculously out-of-fashion gown. Gavin had some fond memories of those creamy globes. He had no desire to be denied access to them.

"I understand making love in a moving carriage is a provocative experience," he suggested idly. Just saying the words aroused him. He could imagine her kneeling over his lap with her skirts pulled up around her. He bit back a groan as his flesh grew stiff against his trouser seam.

"You wish to retrieve the vinegar and sponges from the valise?" she asked icily.

Since the valise rode on the outside of the carriage, it would require stopping Mac and answering a great number of ridiculous questions. Just the thought dampened Gavin's ardor.

"You would have to rely on me to withdraw." The cold-blooded discussion of such a topic drained the pleasure from it. This business of keeping a mistress took away a great deal of the spontaneity and pleasure he remembered from his younger days. He found himself craving just a little bit of her affection, a spark of her wit. He didn't want it like this, coldly businesslike. He was at a loss as to how to change it.

She finally looked in his direction, but the look was so icy, Gavin would have preferred it if she'd kept her gaze on the window.

"I have learned the hard way not to trust any man. No, thank you. Unless this is an order?" she asked with such heavy sarcasm that he almost called her bluff.

Now that they reached the toll road, Gavin released the strap and rested his hands on the knob of his cane. He held her gaze as best as he could under the circumstances. "Is that what it will require from now on? Direct orders? Shall I make appointments?"

She had the grace to blush and turn away. "I do not

know how these things are commonly done. If a man wishes an assignation, doesn't he make the arrangements?"

"I know extremely little about your rarefied London society. I prefer some semblance of spontaneity myself. I would like to take you on my lap right now and unfasten some of those buttons and progress from there." Gavin smiled grimly when he detected a deepening of her blush in the dim light from the carriage lantern. The carriage halted to pay the toll, so he heard her reply clearly.

"I'm not a whore," she murmured, clenching her hands into fists in her lap.

He ignored Mac's discussion with the toll taker outside as he carefully formulated his answer. "No, you're an extremely responsive woman who enjoys the physical pleasures of her body. Not many women are so fortunate. If I thought you did not like what I do to you, I would not bother you again. As it is, we could find some enjoyment in what would otherwise be a tedious journey." The carriage jolted back to motion as he spoke.

"I still feel like a whore." She didn't speak loudly, but she kept her fists clenched so tight her knuckles turned white.

Gavin considered her words carefully, looking for some way to ease her natural reaction. Men had little difficulty falling into bed with any woman who offered. Why, in blazes, did women insist on carrying around all the guilt? Groping for the right words, he asked, "Are you saying the only way you won't feel like a whore is if I force you? You would feel better if I order you over here and pull you into my arms against your wishes?" Gavin admitted to himself that he wasn't adverse to doing that at this point. He wanted her, and he didn't have patience for playing games. He would take her in whatever way she preferred. It just would have relieved his conscience and bolstered his pride if he thought she wanted him also.

He should know better by now, he thought grimly. What woman would want a monster like himself?

With fascination, Gavin watched as Dillian's eyes widened and fastened on him as she absorbed his words.

He could almost see her thoughts as they played across her face. He'd give her credit for that much: she wasn't unintelligent. She caught on quickly.

"That's what I'm asking, isn't it?" she asked quietly. "I'm asking you to take all the responsibility so I can continue playing injured maiden. I'm sorry."

Gavin heard her reply with amazement. He had never expected such an admission and certainly not an apology. After all, she *was* an injured maiden. He had all the experience on his side, and he had taken advantage of her. By accepting equal responsibility, she placed herself in the same position with him. He didn't know if he liked that idea or not.

"Does that mean you'll come sit beside me of your own accord, or do I still need to pursue you?" he asked with interest.

She knitted her hands together and studied his face a moment, then obligingly dropped the shawl, picked up her skirts, and rearranged herself on the sagging seat beside him. The narrow carriage bench barely held two, and he sat nearly in the middle. He could feel the heat of her thigh squeezed against his.

Gavin met her upturned gaze as he pulled down the window shade. "Would you prefer it if I doused the lantern?"

She traced the ridges of his scarred jaw, and he flinched, but she didn't seem particularly revolted by the irregularities. "It took a particularly vicious person to do this to you. I didn't think men in battle had time for such things."

Gavin caught her slender waist and hauled her on to his lap. He began unfastening her bodice buttons as he spoke. "I never claimed sainthood. That set of scars didn't come from battle. It came from a man who thought I'd seduced his betrothed. At the time, I was better at guns than rapiers."

She inhaled sharply as his fingers slid beneath her bodice to cup her breast. He sighed with contentment at the heavy warmth of her against his palm. He needed this, though he didn't analyze the reason why. He just needed the soft warmth of human flesh and the rhythm of her pounding heart. Gavin relaxed and stroked the malleable peak, finding it already aroused.

"Did you seduce his betrothed?" she asked with interest, delaying the inevitable result of their rising ardor.

Gavin shrugged. "It worked a little both ways, I suppose. She was young and lovely. He was a middle-aged, balding, paunchy merchant. In those days, I didn't deny any willing woman."

"Stupid."

He tweaked her breast, and she gasped. He covered her mouth with his, and she drank him in hungrily. Yes, he'd been stupid. He didn't tell her how stupid.

Gavin threaded his fingers through her hair and tilted her head back to see her eyes. "After the duel, her reputation was in shreds. I went back to do the honorable thing and offer her marriage. She screamed in horror at the sight of me and ran away. I heard later that she married the bald merchant."

Dillian had the nerve to give him a saucy grin. "You went back covered in bloody gashes and scared her to death. She deserved her bald-headed merchant."

He could correct her, but he didn't. He liked this version better. He'd been a bastard, no doubt, but he'd been an honorable one. He just hadn't thought his face that important at the time. He'd learned differently soon enough.

"I suspect you need spectacles, Miss Whitnell, but I'll be satisfied that you don't run screaming from my presence." Gavin unfastened the ribbon of her chemise and allowed himself to gaze with satisfaction on the portion of her breasts revealed. He pushed the soft material aside and caressed her nipple. He loved the way she arched instinctively into his palm for more.

"I may not scream in horror, but I don't promise not to scream in outrage," she warned, but her hand made its way to his chest and tugged at the fastenings there.

Enjoying the badinage, he pushed her bodice off her shoulder. "Outrage is acceptable." He took her mouth again, drowning all the years of loneliness in the welcome he found in her response. His soul craved her acceptance, her comfort, her understanding. His body

craved the release she could give him. He only acknowledged the latter.

Gavin scarcely heeded the scream of the horses as he
trailed his kisses from Dillian's mouth to her breast. She
was making small moans against his ear that provoked his
senses and sent him to new heights of arousal. He had her
gown eased up to her knees, and his hands climbed higher.
He didn't have time for screaming horses.

Screaming horses. The carriage jerked to a halt, nearly
tumbling them both from the seat. Gavin hastily shoved
Dillian back on the bench and reached into the pocket
of his cloak for his pistol. He kept a solid grip on his
cane with the other hand. A flick of the wrist would
release the deadly sword blade hidden there, but he preferred that method of fighting as a last line of defense.
He leaned over and pushed the window shade aside.

"Can you see anything?" Dillian whispered. He
sensed her pulling her bodice back in place, and Gavin
cursed. If Mac had just hit a tree stump, he'd have the
driver's head. His loins hadn't stopped throbbing just
because of this little delay.

"Stand and deliver!" a masculine voice roared from
the side of the road.

"Oh, for pity's sake." Disgusted, Gavin gauged the
distance between himself and the mounted figure at the
edge of the woods. The pistol had a short range. He
needed to get closer. "The bastard must be desperate to
rob a carriage as pitiful as this one."

"You don't think it's one of Neville's men looking
for Blanche?"

"I think it more likely a blockhead too foxed to see
straight." Grabbing his cane, Gavin staggered from the
carriage door, pretending to fall to his knees as he
climbed out. His hand found several small pebbles and
a good-size rock. Under the concealment of his cloak, he
deposited them in his coat pocket as he pushed himself
drunkenly to his feet again. Aware Dillian had unraveled
his cravat and unfastened his shirt, he figured he looked
the drunken aristocrat well enough. He lurched a little
closer to the mounted highwayman.

"Whatta hell you want?" he slurred his voice as he staggered toward the side of the road.

The highwayman had a musket aimed at Mac's head. His hired man-of-all-trades didn't have a lot in the brain box, but Gavin wouldn't see the poor sap shot for his service. He steered his course between the two men.

"Give me all your jewels," the highwayman demanded, a trifle uncertainly.

"Jewels!" Gavin roared, flinging one side of his cloak dramatically over his shoulder. "If I had jewels, did you think I'd ride about in this moth-eaten piece of tin?"

The musket swerved uncertainly in his direction. With deadly precision, Gavin palmed the larger rock in his hidden hand, aimed, and sent it flying at the horse's nose.

The horse screamed in fury and reared, flinging its unsuspecting and obviously incompetent rider to the ground. Gavin reached for his pistol with satisfaction—until he heard the decidedly feminine screech behind him.

"Get your hands off me, you loathsome cowardly cur!"

"Stop her clapper and get her out of there!" a man's voice shouted from the far side of the road.

With a roar of rage, Gavin leapt to the carriage step, hauled himself to the top, and launched himself at the shadowy figure on the other side daring to lay hands on Dillian. They went down in the road, scuffling, while another mounted man in the shrubbery screamed his curses.

Gavin had his hands full and couldn't reach the pistol in his cloak. He grabbed the other man's neck cloth and tried throttling him, but his assailant carried more weight. He broke Gavin's hold and flung him to the ground, pinning him down with his bulk. Gavin freed one arm and aimed for the testicles. His punch swung wide, but struck a soft belly and caused a howl.

As he dug his fingers into any soft spot he could find, Gavin felt the swish of skirts beside his face and cursed mightily at the fool woman who couldn't stay where she belonged. He tried shouting at her to get back, but the miscreant had him by the throat. He drove his knee upward and unsettled the other's man position, but he couldn't get out from under in time to grab Dillian.

With surprise, Gavin felt a tug at his cloak and found

himself nearly smothered in skirts and petticoat. Since his assailant had both hands in his lapels while pounding him into the ground, the action confused him. Perhaps he'd banged his head one too many times. The wild boar riding him roared some more in an incomprehensible tongue, but even as he released Gavin's coat to reach for feminine skirts, Dillian darted out of range.

Taking advantage of the other man's distraction, Gavin flipped him back over and slammed his fist into a fat jaw with the same motion. The bulky figure beneath him collapsed. Before he could leap to his feet and grab Dillian, he heard the roar of his pistol.

The third man screamed in agony, and galloping hooves soon followed as Gavin shook himself off and rose to his feet. With complete astonishment he took in the sight of the lady in frail, old-fashioned skirts aiming a pistol with professional expertise toward the edge of the highway where the mounted thief had stood just moments before. All that could be seen or heard of him now was the pounding of hooves in the distance.

"Damn good show," he muttered before turning to wrap his cravat around the downed highwayman's wrists. "Mac! Have you got the other one trussed?"

"Was I supposed to?" a plaintive voice cried from the other side of the carriage. "He done rode away, and the devil be with him is all I say."

"I'll second that notion," Gavin muttered, searching through the unconscious man's pockets, finding nothing of interest.

"I believe they were after me," Dillian said quietly from beside him.

Quietly. Dillian never did anything quietly. With a jerk Gavin jumped up and caught her where she swayed. She grabbed his rumpled coat and buried her head against his chest. A surge of protectiveness startled him as he cradled her small form against his much taller one. Michael was the one who defended the hurt and helpless. Gavin had never concerned himself with anything except survival. But still, he held her, absorbing her tremors of fear. It felt right somehow.

He kissed her curls and stroked her slender back. "I believe you are right. This doesn't bode well at all."

Dillian looked up suddenly. The paleness of her face struck him to the heart.

"Blanche! If they know I'm with you, they'll go after Blanche!"

He couldn't disagree with that assessment, either.

Twenty-two

Huddled in her shawl, Dillian sat beside the marquess on the driver's seat as he urged their one horse down the road. The other horse carried Mac to the manor to warn Blanche and Michael of the attack.

Gavin's focus seemed entirely on their one decrepit horse, but she sensed his awareness of every sound and motion around them. She felt the same awareness. They couldn't afford a repetition of the earlier attack, and two of the highwaymen still roamed loose.

At the same time, though, Dillian's awareness centered on the man beside her. He continually surprised her. She still felt awestruck by the swiftness of his attack. How many men would have been both quick-witted enough to stone a horse and strong enough to strangle an assailant twice his size? With the pistol in his pocket, he could have easily dispatched the third man had she not done it for him. She regarded him with some awe.

"I suppose I am in your black book again," he commented, finally breaking the silence between them.

"Oh, certainly. I always disdain marquesses who can fell two thieves at once. Very bad *ton*," she answered airily.

"Good. I've always disliked ladies who can shoot. That makes us even."

"I told you I could shoot. I'm also an expert marksman at archery, but I failed to bring my bow. I'm not quite so good at fisticuffs, however," she added regretfully.

"Don't ask me to give you more lessons. I still have bruises from the candlestick. I'm debating the wisdom of arming you when we reach London. On one hand, I want you able to protect yourself from any more such attacks, but on the other hand, I don't want the blamed weapons turned on me."

"I never aim a pistol at the person who gives it to me," she said carelessly. "Unless provoked," she added as an afterthought.

Dillian thought the rusty rumble from his chest might be laughter. She smiled a little herself. The attack had terrified her more than she'd realized. The first strains of relief were just fighting their way through. "What will O'Toole do when he gets your message? If Blanche isn't safe at Arinmede, where can he take her?"

The marquess stayed silent for a while. Gavin, she amended to herself. She had every right to call him Gavin. She called Neville by his given name as an insult, refusing to use his title. But despite all his eccentricities, the marquess struck her as a very noble marquess. She had difficulty thinking of him as a person like herself.

"I'm not at all certain that they want her. It's a possibility, I suppose. They meant to kidnap a lady. They could be a trifle confused as to which one. I just have the feeling that they knew who you were."

"That's probably because the one you've got trussed up yelled 'She's the one.' The other man cursed quite nicely after that. Shouldn't we question him now?"

"If we were back home, I'd have him nailed to a tree by now. Unfortunately, as Michael continually points out to me, I'm a bloody aristocrat here. I'm supposed to abide by the law. We'll find the magistrate in the next town and question him there."

"Where do you call home? Is it near the sea? I can't imagine how you became a sailor."

The horse whickered as a hare darted across the road, but the animal didn't have the energy to protest more than that. They continued plodding down the dark lane. The marquess shrugged offhandedly at her question.

"I grew up on the road. We never stayed in one place long. My father had wandering feet, and my mother wouldn't let him wander without her. The wilderness of Kentucky appealed to me in my ill-spent youth, but we didn't linger."

"Your accent isn't quite American, but it's not English, either. I suppose that's because you traveled so much?"

"My father's accent was very definitely British. He used it to advantage quite frequently, claiming to come from English aristocracy, inserting himself into the best society when we had money enough to get his suit cleaned." Gavin laughed shortly. "I thought he'd made the tale up. I didn't realize he really was the grandson of a marquess. I suppose my accent combines the worst of his and my mother's. She came from Virginia."

He abruptly cut short any further description of his parents. Now that he'd finally opened up enough to talk, Dillian didn't want him stopping. "Is your mother still alive?" she asked carefully.

"No, she died when I was fifteen. My father died a few years before. We made our own way after that."

"We? You have brothers or sisters?"

He hesitated. Dillian hated it when he did that. She knew he edited whatever he told her next to suit her ears. She considered punching him, but they were getting along too well to disturb the peace over such an innocuous question.

"Michael is five years younger. He went where I went. It may not have been the smartest thing to do. I probably could have found a family to take him in, but . . ." He shrugged. "Michael's always been an odd duck. I didn't think he'd fit anywhere else. I don't know if I did him any favors, though."

"He's your brother?" she asked incredulously. She couldn't think of two people more unalike. Gavin was tall, lean, and darkly handsome in a formidable way. Michael was slight, auburn-haired, and charmingly good-looking, with a smile that could light candles if one believed it. She preferred Gavin's straightforward curtness.

He shrugged. "That's a matter of opinion. You'll have to ask Michael. As I said, he's an odd duck."

"He calls himself O'Toole," she argued, puzzled. How could one not know if someone was a brother or not?

"He calls himself a number of things. We stayed with a family named O'Toole several times. They had a passel of redheaded kids and spoke with a brogue wider than the sea. Michael rather fancied himself as one of them. The father was an Irish charmer. I've punched him more often than not for insinuating our mother would commit adultery, but the truth was, she and my father fought like cats and dogs. She followed him around the country, but they didn't always live together. They left me behind often enough. She came home with Michael one of those times."

"But he's at least your halfbrother, and your mother was married to your father at the time. He has every right to call himself a Lawrence. There are certainly enough families in London where every child has a different father, but the married name sticks."

Gavin gave another short laugh. "You haven't seen the Lawrences. We all look alike. The family traits are very distinctive. That, more than anything, has convinced Michael he's not our father's child. The fact that my mother claimed to have found him under a cabbage leaf and denied giving birth to him didn't help matters any. My father called him our little orphan. Of course, both my parents were liars extraordinaire. They were perfectly capable of denying his birth so they could deny adultery. He's my brother as far as I'm concerned. Michael's opinion is another question altogether."

Dillian lapsed into silence. She hadn't meant to unbury so many secrets. She'd led an unpleasant childhood, but at least she'd had a mother who loved her until she died and a home to call her own until her father died. She'd resented her father's preoccupation with soldiering. His companions had raised her as much as her father had. He'd left her destitute and homeless because he'd never cared enough to provide for her should he not live forever, as he'd apparently expected to do. But she didn't think her father had ever lied to her or denied her existence.

"Sometimes, our lives seem to be some celestial joke, don't they?" she mused aloud.

She sensed his grin in his reply. "Celestial? Or satanic?"

"Well, considering where we're likely to go when we die, I suppose the devil is in charge now. But that doesn't explain our childhoods."

He gave her a quick glance as the carriage rumbled

into the darkened streets of a small village. "You'll not go to the devil for a little carnal pleasure, I assure you, or most of mankind would inherit hell."

Dillian liked the way he said that. His voice took on a velvet timbre that licked along her spine and made her feel his words in the bottom of her stomach. She didn't dare look at him. His thoughts would follow too close to her own. She'd never thought she would anticipate the pleasure of lying naked in a bed with a man, but she wanted that now. She wanted Gavin touching her.

Instead, he halted the horse outside an inn where one room still shone brightly and the sounds of merriment echoed from within.

Gavin swung down from the driver's seat, then held his hands out to catch Dillian as she picked her way down from the high perch. He held her waist briefly, but put her aside as soon as her feet touched the ground. She wanted more, but she couldn't expect it. He already slogged through the swampy morass of a courtyard toward the inn, leaving her to follow as she would.

Cursing ungallant Yankees and their one-track minds, she hurried after him. She didn't deceive herself into thinking the arrogant marquess would take a room at this lowly inn and enjoy her company for the night. No, the damned man had decided to find a magistrate, and magistrate he would have, whether he had to raise one from the dead or a warm bed to do it.

When she finally caught up with him, he already conversed with the innkeeper. Absently, he caught her waist and held her by his side as if she belonged there. She wanted to smack him, but the innkeeper must think her his wife or his doxie. She preferred the former, and wives didn't generally smack their husbands.

The innkeeper nodded his head toward the tavern, and giving a respectful tug of his forelock to Dillian, he lumbered toward the light streaming from the attached room. Gavin remained where he was, proving himself too proud to enter a common tavern. She supposed he adopted the pose on purpose, but she didn't like it much, not any more than she liked the hood with which he concealed his face.

"Let go of me," she hissed when the innkeeper disappeared into the other room.

Gavin hugged her tighter, and raised his hand to caress the lower curve of her breast. "Not likely. If it weren't for our friend out there, I'd have you upstairs and in bed so fast you wouldn't know what hit you until I came inside you. Prepare yourself, woman. I'll have you before this night's over."

"You're a disgusting, immoral, perfectly obnoxious lecher with no sense of decency, propriety . . ."

The innkeeper reappeared trailing a disheveled, slightly drunken man of middle age. His rotund figure spoke of many nights in this tavern, but his eyes twinkled with interest rather than drunkenness as they perused the odd couple at the inn's entrance. Only then did Dillian realize how her ancient gown and Gavin's hooded cloak must appear to others. Damn and blast the man, he had her dressing as archaically as he did.

"Caught a knight of the road, have you?" the magistrate asked, nodding his head knowingly. Or perhaps his head just naturally bobbed.

"I wish to question him. I suspect he and his cohorts intended to kidnap my wife." Gavin placed Dillian proprietarily next to the inn desk and prepared to walk out, leading the magistrate after him.

Dillian refused to remain where placed. She hurried in their paths.

As the two men strode toward the carriage, her gaze caught on a furtive shadow near the paddock. With a shout, she directed their attention toward a man mounting a horse just on the other side of the fence.

"That's him! He's getting away!"

Gavin cursed vehemently as he raced toward the paddock, pulling his pistol from his pocket as he did so. The magistrate wandered with curiosity to investigate the waiting carriage, but Dillian already knew what he would find: nothing. She broke into a run across the muddy yard as Gavin grabbed the mane of the nearest horse and hauled himself upward, riding bareback as he took off after the fleeing figure.

A pistol barked, and she could see the flash of a firing

pan against the night sky. A third horse and rider broke out of the shadows, following the escaping prisoner. To Dillian's horror, she saw Gavin's horse rear and fling its rider to the ground. The last she saw of him was his dark cloak billowing against the night sky.

Screaming, she raced in his direction, forgetting the magistrate, forgetting the escaping highwayman, forgetting whoever it was who had freed him. She saw only the specter of Gavin's body flying through the air, smashing into the ground at an awkward angle. She saw the horse trotting back toward the barn and food. She couldn't see Gavin.

Ignoring the tears streaming down her cheeks, she cried, "Where the devil are you, you stupid man!" as mud sloshed over her slippers and up her dress. The paddock was worse than the courtyard. She slid and barely avoided landing seat first in the mire. Recovering rapidly, she raced toward the place where she had seen him last. "I'll kill you if you're not dead already," she muttered, hitting a particularly smelly pile that wasn't mud. She wanted to kill him. She wanted to die. She couldn't imagine how they would fare without the marquess helping them. She didn't want him dying on her account. She damned well wasn't finished with him yet.

She didn't know how much of this she muttered as she climbed the other side of the fence and found his cloaked figure pushing out of the mud on the far side. She just heard his chuckles and fought the urge to shove him back down again.

"You gamble-gated clod, I suppose you think this is funny!" She stalked toward him, placing her hands on her hips rather than grabbing his hair and pulling him up to hug him to death. She had never learned a great deal about expressing affection from her father's friends. She did know a great deal about insulting them into getting up when they were down.

"Immensely funny." Then with a strength Dillian hadn't expected, Gavin grabbed her arm with his muddy hand and jerked her down on top of him. "Absolutely hilarious." Pushing her flat on her back in the mud, he kissed her until she could say nothing more.

Twenty-three

"I can't arrive at Blanche's town house wearing this," Dillian muttered, picking at the coarse cotton skirt irritating the flesh above her stockings. A decent petticoat would have helped. The maid they'd bought the garments from apparently wasn't given to wearing undergarments.

Gavin gave the sagging neckline of her bodice a look of interest, and she sent him a baleful glare. He apparently enjoyed the show so much he forgot to keep his hood pulled around his face. Her nipples ached in response to his heated gaze.

"I rather like it," he replied, turning his attention back to the horse as the carriage rolled down the road in the broad light of a new day. "I'm having second thoughts about our plan. I think I would much prefer taking you with me as my simple country mistress. I wonder if Mellon has decent bathing facilities in his London house?"

Dillian sent him a look meant to be angry, but she flushed all over as she followed the direction of his thoughts. The simple pan of water they'd stood in last night to cleanse the mud off had led to some activities she hadn't thought possible. She had taken a shameless man to her bed. And her bath. The memory of him standing there naked, dripping water and soap, still aroused her. She wouldn't imagine what he could do with a real tub.

"I would be of little use ensconced in your bedroom as a mistress and nothing more," she said scornfully, then blushed even more as she realized what she'd said. Stupid. Stupid, stupid, stupid.

He gave her a laughing look but didn't take advantage

of the opening she'd left him on the number of "uses" he might find. She liked his eyes when they laughed like that. They looked brown now and not the deep black she'd thought them. "I'd be of little use to Blanche," she amended hastily.

"And I wouldn't get much done, either," he admitted. "So we'll put ourselves in cousin Marian's hands and hope for the best."

Traveling in daylight, with the constant traffic of horses and wagons on this main highway, they had little to fear of the prior night's highwaymen. But as they drew close to the mudflats on the outskirts of London, in sight of the brown smog hanging over the city, Gavin pulled the carriage off the road. Dillian looked up at him questioningly.

"My cousin lives in an area well traveled by the *ton.* I don't want it generally known that I've arrived in company with a woman. Stay inside the carriage until I can send a maid out for you. The two of you can exchange shawls or whatever, and you can come in the house carrying one of your bags, as if you were the maid returning to the house after fetching something I'd sent for."

Dillian gave him a scathing glance at this role of maidservant, but she saw no better alternative. Reluctantly, she allowed him to help her down from the driver's seat and install her inside with the shades drawn.

The exchange went as smoothly as planned, the maid remaining inside the carriage while a groom drove back to the mews to park it. Dillian assumed she slipped from the carriage then and returned to the house while she and Gavin faced the amused and heavily pregnant Marian Montague, the marquess's cousin.

"My word, the two of you look like something from a village costume ball. Gavin, you cannot go about London in that Gothic cloak. You look like a smuggler escaped from Cornwall. And those trousers!" She covered her mouth to hide her laughter, and shook her head when the marquess growled and stormed around the room, examining her enormous collection of bric-a-brac.

"I didn't come here to become a fashion plate. This is serious business, Marian. Now, put a cap on it.

Miss . . ." He hesitated over the name he should use but remembered the one they discussed in time. "Miss Reynolds is your only concern. There must be no appearance of a relationship between us, so you cannot be seen together. We merely want your advice."

The strangeness of the situation had kept Dillian silent. She felt like a peasant next to Marian Montague's dark loveliness. She could very definitely see the Lawrence resemblance to Gavin. No pink-and-white miss this. Rich brown hair dangled in elegant curls around a complexion of creamy tan, accenting a wide rosy mouth that laughed frequently. She liked the dancing highlights of eyes that matched Gavin's almost exactly.

Throwing his anxious, pacing figure a quick look, Dillian dived into the conversation without permission. "I need only get to Lady Blanche's house. She keeps a caretaker and his wife to look after things. I can send one around to the modiste. I just cannot conceive of how I can communicate with his lordship. I do not go about in society on my own. I can see the solicitor, and I'm certain Neville will storm the threshold at some date so I may ask about the missing papers. But how will I get word to Lord Effingham?"

Dillian felt odd calling Gavin by his title. She had scoffed and called him beast and other names, but she had never addressed others when speaking of him. The intimacy between them was so fresh in her mind, that she felt awkward retreating to this formality. From the fierce dark look he sent her, she assumed he felt the same.

"I damn well will not go about in society if you're not there," he growled. "And I'll not skulk about the back alleys of London getting to you." He turned his glare on Marian as if her pregnancy at this time was done just to annoy him. "Since you can't go with me, you must find some other means of introducing Miss Reynolds to society."

Laughing eyes darted from Gavin to Dillian and back again. "Of course, dear cousin, anything to appease the angry beast. I really wish Reginald were here. He would love to see this. The hermit of Effingham forced from

his lair by a woman. Is Lady Blanche quite as beautiful
as they say?"

"More so, Lady Mairian," Dillian answered quietly.
"She is as beautiful on the inside as the outside. I will
do anything for her."

The laughter left their hostess's eyes as she regarded
Dillian more carefully. "Just Marian. I do not use my
honorary title. Lady Blanche must be a saint indeed if
you wish to sacrifice yourself for her. Personally, I think
sacrifice highly overrated, but I understand the concept.
Since we have agreed it is best that we give the appearance of never having met, I cannot offer any of my family or Reginald's as your introduction. Perhaps we can
ask my half sister's husband if he knows of someone.
That would be sufficiently distant, wouldn't it?"

"I hate to impose . . ." At the militant gleam in Marian's
eyes, Dillian accepted her proposal. "I think that would
work. He wouldn't be a complete stranger to Lord Effingham, in that case, so it would make sense if such a person
introduced us in public. We can take it from there."

Gavin interrupted. "A caretaker and his wife isn't sufficient protection. I want a burly footman at every door,
around the clock. And you will need a maid to go about
with you. You're not to leave here until they're hired."

"That is the most ridiculous—"

"You'll do it, or I'll move in with you," Gavin threatened. "No more burning houses or kidnappers. You get
the papers. I'll make the proper connections. We get the
papers to the connections. Then we'll get the hell out of
here. That's it."

Both women stared at him, but he remained adamant.
Dillian felt an odd fluttering in her midsection as she
translated the look Effingham fastened on her. She'd
become his property, and he protected what was his. She
hadn't bargained for this. She didn't know if she liked
it. She just knew she'd run up against an elemental force
that she couldn't control any more than she could control the wind or fog.

"I've brought you the lady's maid you requested, miss."
Dillian looked up with irritation at the hunchbacked

footman Gavin had evidently hired off the street. Unkempt black hair hid his face, and his clothes hung like sacks from his arms and legs. She didn't intend to stay long enough to buy livery for his hirelings, but she wished she had some excuse for clothing this beggar. She wished she had some excuse for throwing him out. Something in his manner was not only too familiar, but too obnoxious for a servant. Still, if Gavin thought him competent, she couldn't quarrel. Only one other footman had appeared for the job. That scarcely made for adequate protection in a house this large.

She'd thought the service would send over several maids for an interview. Evidently a temporary position attracted few interested applicants. Dillian would have preferred waiting until the modiste had finished pinning the gown she wore, but the faster they got this over with, the better she would feel.

"Show her in, Grimley." Dillian gestured to a place among the bolts of cloth and scattered accoutrements, where the maid might stand without scattering the modiste's haphazard arrangement.

Dillian thought her eyes might fall out when the apparition appeared in the doorway. Even the modiste stopped to stare at the newcomer. Her assistant gave a gasp, then a little giggle. The apparition merely stood where placed. Grimley stood in the doorway, rubbing his hands with satisfaction.

"Indira Muhammed, miss," he announced proudly, as if he'd sought her out himself.

The figure cloaked in white robes and veil didn't move or say a word. Suddenly, the very bizarreness of the situation struck Dillian. The modiste kneeled at her feet, staring, her mouth full of pins. The assistant buried her giggles in a bolt of spectacular peacock blue cloth. The unsightly footman in beggar's clothes and hunched back preened like the most supercilious butler she'd ever encountered. And the lady's maid—the lady's maid that was to rig her out in the height of fashion, dress her hair, guide her in the rigors of society—that lady's maid, stood before her in white sheets and covered head to toe in veils. Unless the whole world had gone mad, something was seriously amiss.

Battling hysterical laughter Dillian focused her sharp gaze on the obnoxious footman pinning him in place as she spoke to the modiste. "Madame, if you and your assistant will leave me now, I would like to talk to the maid alone. You should find tea in the sitting room."

The footman's eyes widened, and he began to back out beneath Dillian's furious scrutiny.

"Grimley, keep your posterior where it is. Don't move a muscle."

As the modiste and her assistant departed, chattering laughingly, Dillian turned her gaze to the passive white-garbed maid, but her words were for the footman. "Grimley, shut that door—now."

As soon as the door shut, she stepped down from the chair, dragging her half-pinned hem through the debris of fabrics and lace. "Blanche, so help me, if that is you, I'll scalp you alive. And if that wretched excuse for a footman is O'Toole, I'll go after him with a butcher's knife, I swear I will."

The laughter from behind the veil was very distinctly Blanche's.

"See, I told you, Michael. Dillian has eyes like a hawk. It would never work." The figure in white threw back the veil, revealing the fading burns of Blanche's fair cheeks and eyes undisguised by bandages or scarf. She blinked rapidly in the daylight, then adjusted the veil slightly to shield her eyes.

The hunchbacked footman collapsed cross-legged amid the billows of petticoats and netting scattered across the settee. Shoulders straightened, he lost the hump and a few dozen years. Dancing eyes regarded the disarray and the two women in its midst. "But wasn't it worth the try? The expression on her face was worth its weight in gold. I'll treasure it always."

Dillian grabbed a pair of sewing shears and came at him with points upended. "I'll murder you, O'Toole. I'll cut your throat and slice you into little bits and mail what's left back to your brother."

His eyes went wide at this mention of Gavin. "Damn

you, Whitnell, where'd you hear that piece of nonsense?
I have no brother."

She grinned malevolently. "Oh, no? Want to keep it
quiet a little longer? Or shall I broadcast it to the
streets? Gavin won't mind."

"That's not funny. I didn't figure you for a spiteful
witch." Michael turned to Blanche, who listened with
amazement and curiosity. "I'll leave you in her hands.
I'll be about. If you need me, just call loud enough.
Someone will hear and get word to me."

He stood to go, but Dillian planted herself in front
of the door. "If that means you'll have the household
permeated with your spies, forget it, O'Toole. Or shall
I call you Lawrence? It makes no difference to me, but
Blanche deserves better. How dare you endanger her by
bringing her here?"

O'Toole halted and regarded her warily. "Is that what
this is about? Blanche? Did you seriously think I would
do anything to endanger her?"

Lilting laughter drifted from the other side of the
room, where Blanche wrestled with the ungainly veil,
trying to remove it from her hair. "I wrapped myself in
sheets and went down and told the cooks I needed to
visit the nearest coaching inn. They went into hysterics,
but the one called Matilda patted my hand and said
she'd see I got into town. I almost got away without
him knowing."

"Matilda's practically blind. Half the time, I think she
believes Gavin is the late marquess. She probably
thought Lady Blanche the marchioness dressed for a
ball." Michael relaxed his shoulders somewhat and eyed
the shears in Dillian's hand with interest. "Could you
really use that thing like a sword?"

"I'd rather have a sword," she replied grumpily,
throwing the shears on a heap of material and retreating
to the settee. "I'd rather you dressed me in gentlemen's
clothes, gave me a sword and pistol, and let me go after
Neville. This is ridiculous." She glared at Blanche.
"What the devil did you think you could do here dressed
like that?"

Blanche shrugged. "When Mac came racing up telling

Michael you'd almost been kidnapped, I figured I had to do something. I couldn't think of a better way of disguising myself."

"Your eyes? Don't they hurt? It's bright in here."

Dillian noted Michael already moved toward the draperies, pulling them closed even as they spoke. The veil had served two purposes then: disguise and bandage.

"I can see," Blanche replied defensively. "It stings a little, but I'll live with it. I can't go around in scarves for the rest of my life."

"You could go around blind the rest of your life," Michael said harshly. "If you must do this your way, you have to keep the veil on. I told you that."

Blanche stuck her tongue out at him, then draped her head in one of the pieces of shimmery see-through material. Dillian wasn't certain she could believe her eyes. Blanche never did anything so improper. Blanche had no idea what kind of ideas that gesture might give a man. She turned quickly and caught enough of Michael's expression to know the notion hadn't escaped him. She'd seen that hungry gaze on Gavin's face often enough.

This couldn't be happening. At least, Blanche didn't seem aware of her footman's feelings. Or did she? Of course, if O'Toole was really a Lawrence, he wasn't precisely a footman—although being the bastard brother of a bankrupt marquess didn't raise his desirability any great extent.

She couldn't think of the consequences of the impossible while faced with the very real danger presented by Blanche's appearance. Turning her mind back to the immediate, Dillian idly poked at the pins sticking her. "If I'm the target of this murderer, we're endangering Blanche by keeping her anywhere near me. And if she's the target, it won't do at all having her where everyone knows her."

"No one notices ladies maids," Blanche protested. "I'm perfectly safe here. And you're much better off with me instead of some incompetent servant the kidnappers might bribe."

The idea of using Blanche as her maid horrified Dillian. Her opinion apparently carried to her face, because

Michael hastily intruded before she could offer her objections.

"If the villains have figured out you were traveling with Gavin, then Arinmede is a prime target. Blanche couldn't stay there any longer. It will be much easier protecting the two of you together."

Dillian frowned, distracted by this new topic. "I don't understand how anyone could know I was with him. It doesn't make good sense. I think they just wanted a woman, and I happened to be there."

"You went past a tollbooth, didn't you?"

Dillian shrugged. "I believe so. Mac handled the transaction. Lord Effingham and I were inside."

"Did you keep your voices down? Could anyone have overheard you?"

She tried to think back. "I don't know. We were fighting at the time. I don't think we spoke much. What difference would it make? A toll collector isn't likely to know me."

"But if he had a soldier demanding the names of every occupant of any carriage that passed, he might pay closer attention than you expect. If you didn't deliberately keep quiet, or if Mac didn't keep his gob shut, he'd know a lady traveled in the carriage. The carriage has the Effingham crest. Everyone knows the marquess keeps no company. A lady traveling with him would raise suspicion."

"A soldier could have just demanded that I get out and introduce myself. He wouldn't have to send highwaymen to drag me out, screaming, in the middle of the night."

Even Blanche's eyes widened before Michael said out loud the thought that followed.

"If the soldiers take orders from Neville, and he's the villain, they wouldn't want a kidnapping traced back to him, would they? They'd hire someone else to look into the matter."

Twenty-four

Soaking his abused muscles in the Earl of Mellon's luxurious bathtub, Gavin found his thoughts drifting over ideas he would never have considered just a few weeks ago. Women did that to men, messed with their minds until they could no longer think straight.

Just a few weeks ago he'd had only one goal: scrape, squeeze, and dig enough money out of the estate to buy the lands surrounding Arinmede so he and Michael would never starve again. So far, he hadn't found the owner of those lands, so he'd invested in lucrative funds until he did. The manor itself was a worthless ruin. Any money spent there would be a foolish waste of his few precious resources. The antiques and paintings and other valuables that his predecessor had left to rot had provided an unexpected gold mine, thanks to his cousin's husband, Reginald Montague. Reginald could turn a crumbling volume of poetry into filthy lucre.

But now Gavin sat here contemplating aching muscles and old age. He had barely turned one more year than thirty, but he felt the stiffness of old injuries, knew he lacked the agility that had saved his life more than once. He'd let Dillian's screams distract him from trussing the first villain, and his fury at her near abduction had made him careless with the second. He'd only had his wits and strength to keep him alive all these years, and both seemed on the wane. He'd been humbled before, but not like this.

He could blame Dillian, he supposed. Women, unwittingly or not, had been the downfall of many a man; he could attest to that. Had Michael just left well enough alone and allowed the two women to find their own way, he would now rest happily at the manor without a care in the world beyond himself. They had a permanent roof over their heads for a change, although Michael didn't like spending much time under it. They had good food in their bellies. They didn't need to chase about London looking after two females. But the instant the women hit their lives, he wound up with aching muscles and a mind that couldn't fasten on one topic longer than two minutes, and now he was expected to gallivant around London like a bloody marquess.

Gavin sipped the brandy one of the earl's thoughtful servants had provided, setting it back on the table beside the tub as the warm liquor slid down his throat. He even found himself contemplating the pleasures of living like this all the time, of having Dillian in the tub here with him. Lord, but that thought made still another muscle ache. Gavin eyed his rising flesh ruefully. He'd start having foolish notions about marriage soon if he didn't get rid of this obsession with the blasted little termagant.

He relaxed against the high tub back. He wouldn't have to worry about marriage with Dillian around. She had her own obsessions, and they weren't about him. She'd made that clear enough. He'd met women with fixed ideas before, but they normally fixed them on marriage. Dillian had her mind fastened on the Grange and keeping Blanche out of Neville's hands. He and the termagant made a good pair, if he did say so himself. With her mind firmly fastened on her goal, she didn't have time to contemplate his myriad faults, but she accepted the pleasures he could give her without too many qualms. They could each work off their physical needs together while pursuing their own goals. Gavin liked that arrangement better than any other he'd ever considered. Except, somehow, Dillian had diverted him from his goals to hers.

He didn't like the idea of making a circus of himself by appearing in society. Scowling, Gavin reached for the towel. He'd much rather corner the duke, grab his lapels, and shake the papers from him, then threaten him within an inch of his life should he come near the women again. He supposed that kind of behavior only worked in the uncivilized environs he'd inhabited as a youth. Here in civilized England, the duke would no doubt call out His Majesty's Royal Guards or whatever and have Gavin and everyone else arrested. He really should learn more about the powers of a marquess.

That gave him a mission more to his liking. To hell with these women and their scheming. He'd talk to Reginald. As the younger son of an earl, Montague knew about these things, or he'd know who to ask. Idly, Gavin wondered if his American scorn of aristocracy had thrown away opportunities he didn't know about. If he had the bloody title of marquess, he might as well make the most of it.

With that decisive action in mind, Gavin threw himself out of the tub and prepared to dress.

He accepted the shirt handed him without thinking, then jerked to attention and swung around. Scowling, he confronted the man who didn't belong there. "How the hell did you get past that overdressed prick at the door?"

Without his black wig and wearing the earl's livery, Michael merely shrugged. "Don't rely on the earl's servants to protect your back. They're soft. Dismouth is hosting a small soiree next Friday night. You and Miss Whitnell will have invitations. Have you seen a tailor yet?"

The white lines crossing Gavin's jaw tightened as he glared at his brother. "I'm not wasting good coin on foolish frippery just to dance attendance on these fashionable fribbles. I'll have Reginald get me into White's. I can do just as much there as at any party. Let the ladies play games. I mean to get the business done and over."

"Anglesey doesn't go to White's. Half the cabinet you wish to meet doesn't go there. You would have to join every gentlemen's club in town to meet everyone. Every last one of them will be at Dismouth's soiree, however. Wear your cloak, an eye patch, and boots if you like, but get yourself there. We must establish your consequence so we can get those journals into the right hands if it becomes necessary. I've got my hands full keeping those two females corralled."

Gavin looked down at his unshod feet. "I could use a

new pair of shoes." Then he returned his glare to Michael. "But I'll not wear those ridiculous knee breeches."

"Fine. You won't be the only one. You can introduce yourself to Lady Darley today so she can formally introduce you to Miss Whitnell on Friday. She's expecting you. And I've made up a list of the best tailors—"

"Out!" Gavin roared, pointing at the door. "I'll not meet any damned Lady Anything. I'll not be pricked and prodded by man milliners. I'll buy a pair of shoes and show up at your party, and that's the extent of it, although what in hell I'll do when I get there, I can't fathom. I can just see me stabbing an oyster and inquiring over the dinner table as to the whereabouts of Colonel Whitnell's diaries." This last he muttered as he buttoned his shirt and reached for his trousers.

When Michael didn't immediately leave as ordered, Gavin looked up with another scowl. "And what did you do with Lady Blanche that you can be here deviling me?"

"The lady decided of her own accord that she wished to aid her cousin. The only way I could hold her was to hog-tie her, so I let her have her way." At the alarmed look in Gavin's eyes, he added hastily, "I brought her lady's maid with her. At least they're all under one roof now where I can keep an eye on them."

Gavin slammed his fist against a wall, and the bedroom door immediately popped open to reveal a nervous servant asking if he wished anything. The man flinched and retreated when Gavin turned his glare on him. Satisfied that he hadn't completely lost his touch, he sat on the bed to tug on his well-worn boots. "And you've got the lady right where the duke can find her. You'd have done better to hog-tie her and hide her in the passage back at the manor."

Michael picked up a silver-backed brush from the dresser and tossed it idly in the air, catching it with one hand, throwing it to the other, heaving it back in the air in a repeat pattern. "You're the one with the touch for ladies, not me. And what did you mean by telling the she-devil I'm your brother? She'll hold that over me until my dying day." A fine tooth comb joined the brush in an airy dance.

"You *are* my brother. Put those damned things back and get out. The idea of those two loose in London gives me cold shivers. Someone should keep an eye on them."

Michael juggled a snuffbox into the twirling pattern of brush and comb, squinting at the objects as he did so and ignoring the marquess. "You're the one looking after the she-devil, not me. I brought you a damned duchess, and you settle for a penniless witch. I'll never understand your thinking, your noble lordship. You like penny-pinching?"

Gavin stood up, grabbed the hairbrush from the pattern, and flung it at his brother. Not missing a beat, Michael caught it and flung the snuffbox at Gavin. Cursing, the marquess caught it and flung it back to the dresser.

"I'm not playing games with you. If your Lady Blanche is everything you say she is, she'll find a more attractive, younger suitor than me. I don't need a wife moping around all day asking when I'm taking her to London. Damn and blast it all, Michael, get your hide out of here and back to those women!"

Michael carefully caught the brush and comb and lay them on the dresser. "If the she-devil turns out to be the offspring of a traitor, her reputation will be ruined, and it could very well bring Lady Blanche's down with it. The lady will have to marry her duke, then, and Miss Whitnell will be out in the cold. Think about that carefully, brother mine."

Gavin growled something irritable as he looked in the mirror to tie his cravat. When next he looked up, Michael was gone.

Cursing the cravat, the empty room, and his brother's insinuations, he reached for his coat. He had no desire at all to contemplate what would happen to Miss Whitnell should their plans fall through and the duke threw her out of his cousin's household. He only wished to contemplate how soon he could climb into her bed again.

The depressing possibility that it might not be for a long time sent him stomping down the stairs, leaving the

Earl of Mellon's staff quivering in their shoes as he
swept out in a swirl of cloak and a menacing growl for
his carriage.

"They are my papers, Mr. Winfrey. They belong to
me personally, left to me by my father. I wish them
returned now." Dillian repeated the same words she had
already said in as many ways as she could say them,
trying to get through to the bespectacled solicitor shaking his head across the desk from her. She thought she
might leap from her seat, grab his spectacles, and grind
them into the floor if he took them off and polished
them one more time.

"I'm sorry, Miss Reynolds, those books were brought
in by Lady Blanche for safekeeping. I can only release
them to Lady Blanche. I have already explained this.
Should Lady Blanche be forthcoming, I will more than
happily turn them over to her."

"Lady Blanche was nearly murdered in her bed!" Dillian shouted. "Do you really think she will present herself in public for someone to try again? What if I bring
a letter from her?"

She thought she saw a gleam of interest in his bespectacled eyes. She wished she could glare at him like Gavin
could. She wanted to see him pale in fear.

"There is some concern as to the lady's health, you understand. If you could bring her in, just so we may ascer-
tain that all is well and she is not being coerced . . ."

"Coerced!" Dillian couldn't stand it any longer. She
rose from her respectfully humble position in the hard
chair and paced the wooden floor. She wore one of
Blanche's bonnets and a pelisse that almost matched one
of her old gowns. She had striven for a look somewhere
between menial companion and respectable lady. Her
angry pacing now more resembled the colonel's daughter. "Did you think I would have her kidnapped? Did
you think her so hen-witted as to be coerced by the likes
of me into anything? Did you think at all, Mr. Winfrey?
If you will not hand over my papers, I shall hire a solicitor of my own and sue you for slander and theft. I want
my papers, and I want them now." She leaned over the

desk as she imagined the marquess would have done and glared at the solicitor.

Since she merely stood five-two and possessed half his weight, the solicitor did not look impressed. "You may do as you see fit, Miss Reynolds, but I shall certainly tell His Grace that I do not find you a suitable companion for his young cousin."

Dillian straightened. "You do that, Mr. Winfrey. And I shall tell Blanche that Neville is certainly not a suitable husband. I have already told her that you are not a suitable solicitor. I think she will believe me now."

She wished for Gavin's cloak as she swirled around and stalked out of the stuffy office. She could not believe the man wouldn't give her her own papers. They belonged to her father. He had no right holding them. Neville must be behind this. Perhaps she should confront Neville directly. She much preferred immediate action to planning and scheming.

Still fuming, she almost smacked into the marquess as she stormed into the street.

He caught her elbows before they crashed, then glanced up at the sign on the door behind her. "I take it you were not successful."

She jerked her arms from his grasp. "I shall have Blanche give him notice at once. London is full of solicitors who will be eminently more accommodating. Let go of me. We are not supposed to know one another. Did you think to beard the lion yourself?"

His lips curled in amusement, and she wanted to smack him for that. The marquess didn't look any more fashionable than he had at the Grange, but he did wear a curly-brimmed beaver hat which made his darkly sardonic face even more fascinating. Beyond her fury, she found herself melting beneath his gaze again. She hadn't considered the hows and whens of their next bedding, but that expression on his face made her think of it now. She tried desperately not to blush.

"I had thought a reasonable discussion between gentlemen a possibility, but now I see I must resort to more drastic measures. You have no doubt turned him into an obdurate mule with your ranting and raving. What are you doing out here alone? I thought you had more sense than that."

"I'm not alone, and it will spoil everything if we are seen together or if you show any interest in my affairs. Now, leave off, Effingham. I'm not completely incompetent."

His eyes narrowed, but he tipped his hat with his cane and walked off as if they had just bumped into each other and apologized for the inconvenience. When Dillian turned to watch him go, she noticed the attention of several ladies along the street drawn toward his tall figure. With his scarred features turned toward the buildings beside him, they saw only the handsome countenance and arrogant stride. They ought to see his ugly character, she thought spitefully, proceeding toward her waiting carriage.

"Well, what did he say?" Blanche asked eagerly as Dillian climbed in and the carriage rolled on.

Blanche still wore her ridiculous veil but the sheets had been replaced by a nun's habit. She now wore a pair of wire-rimmed spectacles and white powder covering the red scars barely visible beneath the veil. Dillian grimaced at the disguise, but in the darkened carriage, her cousin couldn't see the expression.

"He will not release the journals unless you ask for them. I do believe he thinks I have kidnapped or murdered you. I am willing to believe that even should you appear in person, he will call you an imposter."

Blanche warily touched her cheeks. "Surely, I will not look so different that he wouldn't recognize me. He must know I will have scars."

"You won't," Dillian said steadfastly. "You will be fine as fivepence in no time. That is neither here nor there. I believe he is thoroughly in Neville's employ. You must find a solicitor of your own."

Blanche looked doubtful. "He has never given me reason to distrust him. He just has my best interests at heart. I should go in and show him I'm alive."

"Looking like that?" Dillian asked skeptically. "He'll have you committed to Bedlam. The marquess ought to commit that brother of his to Bedlam. I can't believe he talked you into that hideous disguise."

Blanche shrugged, in a careless gesture much like one Michael used. "If I cannot go about as myself, I must go about as somebody. If no one sees my hair or scars and I hide behind spectacles, they'll never recognize me. People only see the outer trappings."

"That sounds suspiciously like O'Toole talking, but for once, he is right. People are idiots." Dillian lapsed into a sullen silence.

"Do we see Neville now?" Blanche asked with curiosity.

Dillian sent her a sharp look. "Why bother? He will no doubt tear the door down as soon as he hears I'm in town. I give Winfrey three hours to locate him and get him the message. Shall we go shopping and leave him to tear the house apart alone?"

Blanche considered their options. "I think that might be best. Neville has a terrible temper when roused. We'll give him time to cool off. Perhaps O'Toole can pour some brandy down him until we return."

Dillian looked delighted for the first time that day. "I knew you had a brain behind that pretty face, my lady. Shall we stop at Gunter's first? I think a celebratory ice is in order."

Dressed again in a black wig, hunched back, and carrying a gnarled walking stick, O'Toole answered the furious pounding on the door. Deliberately opening the well-oiled door as if it weighed two tons, he had time for a good look at the unwanted visitor.

The young duke had the look of a harried man. His elegant gray frock coat had come unbuttoned at top, and his cravat had a wrinkle in it. He had one hand fisted about his expensive beaver hat, and the other clenched in his trouser pocket, throwing the tailored lines into disarray. He glared at the unsightly footman answering the door.

"I've come to see Lady Blanche," he announced, shoving the door open wider when the servant made no effort to do so.

"What's that you say?" O'Toole cried, cupping a hand around his ear.

"I've come to see Lady Blanche!" Neville shouted back, shoving his way into the entry.

"Baby Ann? Ain't no Baby Ann here. You've got the wrong door. No knocker up, if you look rightly. Don't know why you'd be calling for a baby, anyhow. Screaming damp critters they are." O'Toole hobbled behind the duke as Neville ignored his ramblings and headed for the stairs to the private floors.

"Blanche!" Neville shouted into the echoing emptiness of the household.

Wide-eyed, the caretaker's wife scurried out of his way as he stormed down the main hall, O'Toole tottering as fast as he could after him.

"Which is Lady Blanche's room?" Neville demanded, suddenly swinging on the servant behind him.

"Doom? We'll all meet our doom, right enough," O'Toole nodded sagely. "Ashes to ashes, dust to dust, that's the way it is. Can't say that you're old enough for that, though," he looked at the duke doubtfully.

Uttering a curse, Neville swung around and threw open the nearest door. He proceeded down the hallway, flinging open doors on unused chambers still in dustcovers until he came upon one littered in a chaos of gowns and petticoats, bolts of cloth, and sewing implements. Striding in, he began tossing things about in an apparent search for something.

"Here, now! You can't go doing that to the lady's things! I'll have the watch down on you now if you keep that up! Looka there, now! It'll take the maids days to clean through that. Out with you, now, you young scamp. There ain't no Baby Ann here." O'Toole swung his gnarled stick ineffectually at the young lord, beating him about the knees.

Neville kicked at the stick as if it were a pesky kitten and continued working his way through the room, ravaging the antique secretary thoroughly, no longer attempting to communicate with the obviously deaf footman.

"Damn her! There's got to be some clue as to where

she's gone. They have to communicate somehow." Slamming a desk door shut, Neville waded through the debris to the bedchamber next to the sitting room.

"Call the watch!" the doddering butler shrieked behind him. "Call the guards! The devil's in the lady's chamber! I'll lay him low, I will! Just fetch the watch, you layabouts!"

The stick beat about Neville's shoulders now as he sent perfume bottles and cosmetic cases tumbling from the vanity with each jerk of a drawer. With another curse, he reached behind him to grab the stick and fling it across the room. "Get lost, old man. I'm looking for my cousin."

"Cookin' for a dozen! Bedlam, that's where you belong, sir! Bedlam! Be gone with ye now. Out! Out!" O'Toole grabbed a candlestick and flourished it like a sword in the duke's face.

Racing to the doorway at the sounds of shouts as they entered the front hall, Dillian nearly collapsed with laughter at the tableau she discovered upon reaching her bedchamber. O'Toole pranced and danced like some demented puppet, flourishing his candle sword, screeching at the top of his lungs, while the noble duke just looked ill-tempered and impatient.

"I think I just may keep you around as court jester." Dillian laughed at her ranting footman as she strolled into the chaos that had been her bedroom. "Hello, dear Neville. How are you doing today? Would you like me to show you how to use that powder duster? Just a little to your cheeks to take away that furious red might do the trick."

The hunchbacked footman leapt and wailed a little longer, but at a brisk gesture from Dillian, he hastily departed.

Neville glared and started to follow the servant, but Dillian blithely blocked his path. "She's not here, your noble grace. She's not anywhere you can find her. She's somewhere safe and happy." Wickedly, she added, "And a romance just might lurk in the offing. Wouldn't that be lovely, now? We couldn't have a June wedding, of course. She'll want time for the burns to heal. But July, perhaps. Don't you think July a nice month for a wedding?''

Neville looked as if he might throttle her. Dillian had some difficulty standing still before the awful murder in his eyes, but she had to give O'Toole time to spirit Blanche to safety. She refused to retreat.

"Oh, by the way, would you happen to have the papers Blanche stored for me in the vault?" she asked casually. "They belonged to my father. I thought I might write his memoirs now that Blanche may safely be married in a few months."

"I don't know anything about your bloody papers, Miss Reynolds. You're her damned companion! Why aren't you with her? Do you work with this villainous lover to see her reputation ruined beyond repair? How much does he pay you to stay away? I'll double it. Just tell me where the hell she is!"

"My, my. A little testy, are we? You may pay me anything you like, but the only thing that will get me out of here and back to Blanche is those papers. Your nasty-minded solicitor won't give me the books that Blanche left with him, and someone has stolen the papers from the vault. That does not look very good, now, does it?" Dillian omitted the fact that she and Blanche couldn't open the vault if they wanted to but their eccentric footman had fingered it open easily. As he'd said, the only contents were a few of Blanche's baubles.

"What does not look very good is your blackmailing me to get them. I know nothing about your bloody papers, but I'd like to know who you really are, Miss Dillian Reynolds. Just exactly what connection is it you have to Blanche?"

Dillian batted her eyelashes. "Why, the very best, to be sure. Now, if you will excuse me, a lady must keep her reputation, you know. Entertaining you like this in my bedchamber could lead to all sorts of improper speculation. You wouldn't wish to be shackled to a penniless female, now, would you?"

She stepped into the hallway, giving Neville room to pass. At the far end of the hall, O'Toole waited to guide their visitor out.

"Now, remember, Your Grace," Dillian called after the cursing young man as he strode down the hall. "Find those papers, and we'll talk!"

"I'm going straight to Bow Street!" he yelled back. "You can't kidnap an heiress in this country and get away with it."

Well, actually, they could, Dillian thought as she waited for the sound of Neville departing. It would be extremely easy to spirit Blanche out of Neville's incompetent hands for as long as they liked. The problem lay in the fact that without access to Blanche's funds, they would run out of money before they could go far.

Twenty-five

"Tell me again why I'm doing this," Dillian muttered as Blanche stuck still another ribbon into her unruly curls in a vain attempt at creating a sophisticated coiffeur. Still fearful of encountering one of the myriad pins that had adorned the bodice of her gown just hours before, she scarcely dared breathe.

From the doorway, O'Toole answered, "Because if you don't, his noble lordship will storm through the crowd like a vengeful god breathing fire and smoke and will terrify everyone into fleeing before we find out anything."

Both women turned to glare at the man lounging—uninvited—against the door jamb. Blanche responded first. "You have no business in here, Mr. Lawrence. Go on with you, now."

O'Toole crossed his arms over his chest and smiled. "I like it when you call me that. It makes me sound respectable." Since he still wore the hideous black wig and servants' clothes, he looked a great deal less than respectable.

Dillian didn't bother looking at either of them. They quarreled and spat like children, and she didn't have the patience for it tonight. "Expecting me to stop his lordship from storming through society is a little like asking me to halt Napoleon's army. Just exactly what am I supposed to do: trip him up? Shoot him down? Grab his finger and bite it? Will he even wear proper attire or will he appear shoeless and in a cloak?"

"He had shoes made," Michael responded brightly.

Dillian groaned and rolled her eyes heavenward.

"That means he's wearing that shapeless American coat and trousers, doesn't it? And the cloak, too?"

Michael shrugged. "He threw me out. I can't say." He sent Dillian a shrewd look. "It's not his clothes he's worried about."

With a gesture of impatience, Dillian brushed Blanche away from her hair. She glared at Verity to keep the maid at a distance. "I know, but most men are fools. However, I have no intention of telling your lordly brother that the ladies swoon at his feet for reasons other than the scars. I should think his good looks have spoiled him enough."

Michael chuckled and relaxed again. "Keep that up, and I might grow to like you. It's wounded vanity that makes him bark and growl."

At the remark about vanity, he sent Blanche a speculative look. In the privacy of Dillian's chamber, she had removed her concealing headdress. In the mirror Dillian could see the raw red of her cousin's injuries, but they seemed to heal well. Blanche appeared oblivious to their observation. She merely patted Dillian's curls one more time and stepped back to admire her handiwork.

Dillian spoke where her cousin didn't. "Blanche has no vanity. She barks at you because you're annoying."

The person in question looked up in surprise at finding herself the topic of conversation. "What did I say? When did I ever bark?"

Dillian grinned at the confusion suddenly marring O'Toole's arrogant features. She patted Blanche's hand reassuringly. "It's quite all right, cuz. You may test your growling abilities on O'Toole all you like. I don't like leaving you here with him. I want you to lock your door, keep Verity at your side, and not come out until I am home."

Blanche looked startled, then colored along her hairline as she glanced at the man in the doorway. He whistled innocently, but Dillian had begun to understand the enigmatic Lawrences a little too well. This one might claim no relationship, but the dangerous gleam in his eye had a very familiar quality to it.

"Mr. Lawrence won't harm me," Blanche answered,

still with an air of uncertainty. "You told me he's the marquess's brother, didn't you?"

"She lies, I lie, he lies. Who's to say who or what I am?" Michael answered airily. "But I swear upon the golden chalice, my lady, that I have never harmed a female in all my life. You are safe with me." He made a gallant bow accenting his words.

"The carriage's come!" the caretaker called up the stairs.

Michael frowned. "Your servants need training, my lady. I'll take care of it."

He turned and disappeared from the doorway. Dillian listened for his departure, but he moved on soundless feet. No wonder he succeeded in disappearing and appearing like that. She wondered how he learned the trick.

"Hurry, now. You can't keep Lady Darley waiting. Let me see how you look." Blanche stepped back as Dillian stood up. She adjusted the wide blue sash beneath the bodice, pulled the ivory lace overskirt out slightly to the side so it fell more gently over the ruffled hem, and nodded happily. "You look absolutely grand, Dillian! I knew you would if I could ever get you into a decent gown. You'll have all the gentlemen swooning."

"Who would want a gentleman who swoons?" Dillian grumbled, catching up her skirt and heading for the hall. "I would still prefer a sword if my task is to keep the marquess from beheading half the guests. At least I would stand a chance, then."

"Your task is to introduce him to the proper people, and you know it, Dillian," Blanche said as she followed her to the hall. "You may only pretend to be my companion, but you know everybody I know."

"My father knew everybody, and see where it got him. Perhaps I should call in his guards and ask them to carry swords when the marquess is about." Dillian spoke mostly to herself as she trailed down the stairs. She did know a lot of people. She just hoped when Lady Darley introduced her tonight, they would accept that Blanche's companion had always been an acceptable, if impoverished, part of society. She just prayed none of her father's disreputable friends would recognize her should they have finagled their way into an event of this sort. They might wonder why Colonel Whitnell's daughter now called herself Miss Reynolds. She had never met them in Blanche's company. Surely, she wouldn't be so unlucky as to meet them tonight.

Lady Darley smiled gently as Dillian bounded into the carriage. An older woman of indeterminate age, she was the widow of some relation of Viscount Darley, the husband of Marian Montague's half sister. Dillian didn't attempt tracing the family tree but merely accepted her as one of the numerous single females flitting around the edges of the *ton.* Her graciousness recommended her more than her relations.

"You are very kind to do this for me," Dillian said as she settled herself into the carriage seat.

"Not at all, my dear. I so enjoy shepherding a new young lady about. It makes me feel young again. The gentlemen will be all over themselves to meet you tonight. 'Tis a pity it's not a ball so I could enjoy watching you dance."

"A lady as lovely as yourself must spend more time dancing than watching," Dillian answered in the same spirit. She had not much practice at politeness, but she had seen Blanche do it often enough. Surely, she could survive a single night of it.

Lady Darley smiled and tapped her with her fan. "You will do very well, my dear, very well."

Dillian doubted that, but she kept her doubts to herself. Butterflies danced in her stomach, and her fingers clenched in knots in her lap, but she wouldn't admit nervousness to anyone. At the grand old age of twenty-five, she had nothing about which to be nervous. She had gone past "on the shelf" to ape-leader. She meant only to act as friend to a man who had no knowledge of society. Or civilized society, in any case. Just because that man was her lover . . .

Good Lord, she couldn't even think of that without burning hot all over. How did women learn to be so blasé about such things? She knew married women took lovers all the time. They flirted with them publicly. Surely, she could manage acting quietly as friend?

She had all the time the carriage waited in line to stew in her own burning juices. The earl evidently had invited half the *ton* to clear all his obligations at once. Dillian felt surely it must be midnight and the marquess would have come and gone by the time she and Lady Darley descended to join the throng entering the earl's home. Knowing Gavin, he had walked and didn't wait for this processional nonsense.

Of course, then again, he may not come at all, Dillian thought as she gazed around the crowd in search of his rather distinctive form. It would be just like the irritating man to drag her into this mob and then decide not to appear after all.

The Earl of Dismouth nearly swallowed his false teeth when Lady Darley introduced Dillian as Miss Reynolds. He'd met her as Blanche's companion, not as a social equal. She hoped that was the reason for his startlement. Dillian wondered how Michael had obtained her invitation, but she merely smiled politely at the old man and murmured something insignificant. She didn't like the way those cold gray eyes followed her even after she left the reception line. Neville kept very poor friends.

She didn't see Neville, but he no doubt had found a smoke-filled room in which to politick. She thought it might be amusing if he saw her here, but she wouldn't count on that for the evening's entertainment. With growing interest, she scanned the crowd.

"'Tis a pity Lady Marian can't come tonight, but there's Jessica, her sister, and Lord Darley, her husband. Have you met them yet?" Lady Darley waved to a lovely blond young lady and her small but elegantly dark husband. Her relations, Dillian assumed.

She soon found herself in a circle of laughing, chattering young people. Neither Jessica nor Lord Darley spoke much, but their presence drew others, and Dillian's acquaintance with them led others to accept her as one of them. She didn't dispel that notion with her usual cynicism.

A whisper rolling across the room and a sudden diminishing of noise levels turned heads toward the entrance. Dillian hid her gasp behind her fan as she followed all gazes to the sight calmly strolling through the doorway. She shouldn't think "calmly." He appeared calm. Wearing a white satin-lined cape and an elegantly tall black hat that enhanced his strikingly lean figure garbed now in black and white evening clothes, the Marquess of Effingham regally outshone any other gentleman here. Doffing his cape, he swung it and his hat to the nearest servant as if accustomed to doing so in front of a large assembly every day. But Dillian knew the effort it took. Though he held himself proudly, not disguising his scars, she could tell by the stiffness of his shoulders that someone coming up from behind could knock him flat on his face. Every muscle in his body moved tautly as he stepped down from the entrance and joined the deteriorating reception line.

"Who is that?" someone whispered behind her.

"My word, I don't know, but I mean to find out," a female voice replied.

"Effingham," Lord Darley said with conviction in Dillian's ear. "Shall we go meet him? That is your purpose here tonight, is it not?"

Dillian didn't have the tongue to answer. She thought perhaps she'd swallowed it. She took Lord Darley's proffered arm and gratefully let him guide her through the milling mob. The Marquess of Effingham in starched cravat, evening coat, and angle-length pantaloons stretched taut over muscled legs left her speechless. She knew what he looked like naked, for heaven's sake! Why should his elegance now play such havoc with her feelings?

Because he looked just what he was: a marquess. A man far above her reach. Dillian almost felt resentment when Darley finally approached him and offered the public introductions necessary for their deception. A real marquess would have reason to lift his eyebrows in disdain and turn away from such as her. She couldn't believe she'd had the audacity to berate a man like that and order him about as she had. She must be all about in her brain box. The Marquess of Effingham could walk through this room and make heads tumble with just a curt look if he desired. He didn't even need his sword. That dark angular face and those devastating nearly black eyes would do the work for him. The elegance of his clothes spoke of his power to do so.

She almost trembled as she held out her hand. Accepting her fingers in his, Gavin ruined the effect by raising a quizzical eyebrow and with that mocking smile tugging at the corner of his lips, asking, "Should I kiss it or shake it?"

Dillian fought to keep from bursting out laughing. Darley chuckled beside her. Effingham gave her an evil look, made a quick bow over her hand, then proprietarily placed it on his arm. He proceeded to look her over thoroughly, from her unruly curls tamed by the ribbons, to the daring décolletage of her gown, to her slipper-shod feet.

"You clean up very well, Miss Reynolds. You may introduce me around." Giving Darley a brief nod, he said, "You're looking well, Darley. Don't let Jessica tease you into anything I wouldn't do."

He damned well considered himself the Prince Regent, Dillian thought, grinding her teeth in an effort to keep smiling as Gavin kept firm hold on her hand. "I'm certain Lord Darley is better able to make suitable introductions, my lord," she said, attempting to pull her hand away.

"And I'm equally certain Darley would rather bask in his bride's smiles than mine," Gavin returned quite affably. "Isn't that so, Geoffrey?"

The viscount looked a trifle uneasy as he gazed back and forth between the scarred and formidable visage of the marquess to the determined jut of the lady's delicate chin. Not being a man of resolute nature, he answered honestly, "Jessica's a deal prettier than you, Effingham, I'll grant you that, but Miss Reynolds is right, you know. It's not seemly to appear too much in her company so soon after introduction."

The marquess smiled grimly, and Dillian decided immediately that she liked the viscount. Few other men would have made such casual reference to Gavin's looks without fear of retribution. She decided to rescue him from the decision she'd forced upon him.

"Since he's an American, they'll understand he hasn't quite learned the proprieties."

Darley looked relieved, if slightly amused. "Americans are notoriously uncivilized, granted. I'm certain you'll be in good hands, Effingham. Marian will have your neck if you do aught else."

"It's a damned good thing there aren't too many Lawrences left in this world," Gavin agreed, before looking down at his small companion. "Although the Reynolds might have produced one or two equally well matched." He glanced back at the viscount. "I'll worry about my cousin. You just keep your own lady in line."

Dillian didn't like that gleam in Gavin's eye. Or rather, she liked it altogether too well. She felt all slithery inside when he looked at her like that, and she needed all her concentration to keep her wits about her tonight.

She heard Darley say something in parting. She realized she stood alone beside Gavin with probably all of London staring at them. She had no idea how to move, what to say. She only knew the pressure of his hand against hers, the hard muscle of his arm beneath his evening coat, and the tension streaking back and forth between them. Her fingers bit into his coat, and he glared down at her.

"All right, termagant. Where do we start? Shall I growl at your duke first? Glare at the earl? Gnash my teeth at a few cabinet ministers? Just precisely why have you exposed me to this scene?"

Darting a nervous gaze to the curious stares around them, Dillian desperately tried to remember their purpose here. She watched a gloriously gowned young matron fan herself hastily as Gavin turned his mocking look and scarred features in her direction following her impertinent stare. Why had she exposed him to this appalling scene?

Because of Blanche. Because someone had tried harming Blanche, and they must find out who and why. If Neville was the culprit, they had to know which of these people were his friends, and which they could trust. And if her father's journals were somehow involved, they must know who could help them get the journals back, and who they could trust with them. A lowly Miss Reynolds had no means of learning these things. A Marquess of Effingham did.

The whole scheme became perfectly clear to Dillian all at once. It gleamed bright and golden in her head. Why on earth hadn't she considered it before?

With a brilliant expression of innocence, Dillian announced, "You needn't gnash your teeth at the ministers, my lord, you must smile at their ladies."

Twenty-six

"I've heard such appalling rumors! How is dear Blanche faring, Miss Reynolds? Will she return before the Season ends?"

Dillian translated this as "Is she horribly scarred and ever coming back?" but she maintained her polite behavior and smiled dutifully at Lady Castlereagh. "She is doing much better than expected, my lady. The doctor recommended a change of scenery, and she has taken a villa in the south of France for a while."

Having satisfied herself on that topic, Lady Castlereagh turned her attention from an upstart nobody like Blanche's companion to a more immediate interest. "Lord Effingham, I've heard so much about you. Why have you not introduced yourself before this?"

Dillian admired Gavin's stiff bow. The mocking curl of his lip didn't extend to a smile, but Lady Castlereagh didn't know that. Dillian had already introduced him to the wives of the prime minister and the home secretary. She could tell Gavin had lost some of the hard edges of his fear, but he remained wary. He had reason. Behind his back, people whispered and wondered, and gossip flowed without his having done so much as introduce himself to their society. She'd seen pity in the eyes of some, revulsion in others. People preferred perfection. It made them more comfortable. Still, more than one hopeful miss had come forward at her mother's urging. Dillian preferred keeping him steered to the powerful peeresses, the women behind the men, and away from eager young hopefuls. She didn't explain the reason for that to herself.

"As a newcomer to this country, I had much to learn,

my lady. And an estate that needed to be set to rights. It seems the time has come for learning a little more than my rural abode can provide. It is my great pleasure to make your acquaintance. I, too, have heard much about you."

All he'd heard about Lady Castlereagh was her abominable penchant for gaudy jewels, her husband's powerful position as foreign secretary, and her domination of ticket vouchers for Almack's, Dillian thought spitefully. But he didn't need to know more than that. If a question arose about the patriotism of Colonel Whitnell, Lord Castlereagh was the man in position to quench them. Gavin needed to meet the man. Castlereagh was also in a position to introduce the marquess to Wellington. Dillian could not, without risking revealing her father's identity. Wellington would know her father was no traitor. Once they found the journals, he might be the man to receive them. Gavin would be in a position to know by then.

"Miss Reynolds, would you mind greatly if I borrow the marquess for a little while? I have several people to whom he really must be introduced." Lady Castlereagh claimed Gavin's arm and had effectively dismissed Dillian even before she had given her agreement.

The lady didn't reckon on Effingham's stubbornness.

Politely removing her hand from his coat, the marquess bowed respectfully and replaced it with Dillian's. "I beg your pardon, my lady. I will gratefully call upon you so you may make any introductions you like, but Miss Reynolds has promised to aid me with some unfinished business. My regards to your estimable husband."

Without further ado, Gavin tugged Dillian through the crowd.

She tugged back. He walked too fast. She had no intention of making her debut in society by being dragged like so much fodder about the room. The marquess turned and gave her an impatient look as she placidly caught up with him. He glared. She smiled. He growled and pulled her in the direction he had set himself.

"Would you care to tell me where we are going?" she asked as politely as she could while engaging in this tug-of-war. "If you wish to meet Neville, he's no doubt in one of those antechambers off to the right."

"I don't wish to meet Neville. I don't wish to meet Wellington. I don't wish to meet another damned soul. This is a pointless waste of time. We'll find the damned journals and then decide what to do about them. I don't know why I let the lot of you talk me into this."

"Because you thought we'd back down when everyone screamed in horror and ran from the room. You thought you'd be back at Arinmede the next day." He jerked her through the open French doors and without fighting back, Dillian had to follow. She continued relentlessly, "Only now you're discovering you're not the creature of horror you thought, and it disagrees with you. My sympathies, my lord. Did you merely borrow those clothes from the earl so you need not waste your coins on them?"

He dragged her to the stone wall surrounding the balcony, out of the light from the room they'd left. "I bought them so I would not shame you, more fool I," he growled.

Dillian had only time to catch her breath at the sight of the glitter in his eyes before he had her surrounded and pulled up against his chest, his mouth grinding demandingly into hers.

She didn't fight him. She knew the futility of fighting the inevitable. She could feel the desire surge between them, the power and elation of it as they succumbed to something far beyond the meaningless social amenities forced upon them this last hour. Her arms circled his shoulders, and she clung tightly as he drew her upward into his embrace. She gladly surrendered to the heat of his mouth, welcoming the invasion that followed. She understood the need pouring between them as she understood nothing else.

Gavin set her aside so quickly that Dillian's fingers still clung to his coat. Cool spring air rushed between them, chilling her heated skin. She jerked her gloved hands back and ran them up and down her bare arms for warmth. She stared back at him through the darkness, trying to divine his intentions, too frozen by the swiftness of their separation to think coherently at all.

"Who is this Lady Blanche everyone speaks of?" he demanded, in a tone not his own.

Dillian stared, wondering if he'd gone mad or if she'd mistaken him for the wrong marquess. She had her back turned toward the doorway, but as she glanced away in confusion, she caught the shadow of a movement near the glass. Understanding dawned at once, and she made a play at shrugging her shoulders offhandedly.

"A young friend of mine, my lord. A house fire left her exceedingly distressed. As I told Lady Castlereagh, she has gone to France to recuperate. Why do you ask?"

"Probably because he knows you're a liar, Miss Reynolds."

The Duke of Anglesey strolled onto the balcony, eyeing them with displeasure. He stood only half a head taller than Dillian, yet he confronted Gavin with all the confidence of a man certain of his place in life. His fashionably tailored frock coat and exquisitely tied cravat should have put Effingham's careless attire to shame, but "exquisite" and "careless" presented two entirely different worlds in Dillian's eyes. She disliked dandies in general, Neville in particular, and she had discovered a growing fondness for antiquation in dress. Give her Gavin's cape any day over Neville's fashionably tied neck cloth.

"Why, how charming to see you, too, Neville. Surely, you've grown an inch since I saw you last, although it does seem all in your head. Effingham, here's the man you seek. Anglesey, the Marquess of Effingham, Gavin Lawrence. I'm certain the two of you have much in common, so I'll leave you to yourselves."

Gavin lost count of the number of subtle and not so subtle insults Dillian managed to wedge into this little speech before she attempted to escape. He caught her arm before she could flee. He couldn't take his eyes off her in this crowd. He wouldn't have any more near abductions hanging over his head. He would see her home, and with any luck, into her bed before this night ended. He wouldn't trust this bloody duke for two seconds.

"I'm not difficult to find," Neville responded coldly. "You have an odd manner of seeking me." He turned his hard glare on Dillian, as if the fault lay with her.

"I allowed Miss Reynolds to distract me. I apologize. Would it be possible to call on you someday to speak on some business matters inappropriate for discussion at this time?" Gavin kept his hand firmly on Dillian's arm, although she did her best to twist it away.

"I cannot imagine what we have to discuss, unless you have some means of coercing my cousin's whereabouts out of this fiend in female clothing," Neville replied arrogantly.

As the duke turned to leave, Dillian cried after him, "If you do not return my father's papers I'll see that Blanche never speaks to you again!"

Gavin didn't know whether to slap his hand over her mouth or admire her courage. Already puffed up by his own consequence, the duke puffed even more with fury. He swung around and glared at Dillian to the extent that Gavin thought of jerking her behind him for protection.

"Those papers were in Blanche's safekeeping. You will see them if and when she returns to claim them."

"Those papers are my property! That is thievery!"

Several people had drifted to the open doors at the sound of rising voices. Gavin gave Dillian's arm a tug to apprise her of the situation, but she merely turned her hostile glare in his direction. Before she could say more, Gavin interceded.

"I dislike intruding on what is apparently a family argument. If you will excuse me . . ." He dropped Dillian's arm and started in the direction of the door.

"Far be it from me to interrupt your little coze," Neville said snidely. "Miss Reynolds is no relation of mine. You are welcome to her." With that, he strode briskly from the balcony, disappearing behind the drapery within.

"He has those papers," Dillian complained bitterly, staring after him. "If there is anything in them, Dismouth will know soon enough, and then all the world will know. I can't afford a solicitor to sue for them."

"There are other means of obtaining what you want. Let us get out of here before we provide any more free entertainment." Gavin steered her toward the glass doors, but she resisted. He had no grand desire to return to that hothouse full of overblown orchids, either, but even his American manners told him they couldn't properly sneak out through the gardens. He despised being gawked at, but knowing the evening had finally ended and he had only a few more minutes until freedom made it easier. He glanced at her impatiently.

She stared at someone just beyond the crowded circle near the doors. "Reardon! I cannot let him see me."

Rather than follow her glance, Gavin scowled. "If you keep any more secrets, they will surely spill all over the floor one of these days. We will simply march through the crowd and out the front door. He's not likely to notice."

"You don't understand! Reardon is one of my father's friends. He'd see me at once and expect to be greeted, but he knows me as Whitnell, not Reynolds. It could get extremely sticky should anyone overhear." She lowered her voice. "He was one of the soldiers at the crossroads that night. Neville has apparently hired him."

Gavin thought she made things unnecessarily complicated. She ought never to have called herself Reynolds in the first place. He could see no reason why it mattered one way or another what people called her. Michael called himself anything that came to mind, and no one cared overmuch. He didn't think he had much hope of telling Dillian that.

He'd accomplished all he'd intended to accomplish here tonight. Society knew him now. He could make his own inquiries from here. With a sigh of resignation and a burning desire to get out of here and into Dillian's bed, Gavin took the matter into his own hands. "Faint," he ordered, reaching down to lift her from the ground. "Close your eyes and go limp." Without further warning, he caught her behind the knees and picked her up.

He didn't give Dillian time to call him all the names

undoubtedly flying to the end of her tongue. Wisely heeding his words, she collapsed in his arms. Perhaps women could faint from embarrassment. Gavin didn't think Dillian much capable of it, but she put on a good show as he strode into the shocked crowd carrying his limp burden.

Lady Darley and several other matrons hurried to his side, exclaiming in hushed peeps much like baby birds. Gavin didn't attempt to translate their protests. "The lady fainted. Show me where to take her while someone calls for her carriage."

They led him down a path opening directly through the crowd. Gavin tried ignoring the shocked stares, the words whispered behind gloved hands, but he felt as if all the world stared at him. He resented becoming the object of such attention, but he merely set his jaw and continued on his chosen path. If they needed a tame lion to stare at, so be it.

Lady Darley came to his rescue, leading him into a small salon while sending a servant hastening for her carriage. "What happened? Lay her down here, if you please." She indicated a backless divan.

"No doubt corset's too tight," Gavin responded wickedly, feeling Dillian stir in his arms. "Mustn't wear them often, I suspect."

Dillian skewered him with her glare as he lay her down, but she held that fiendish tongue of hers while Lady Darley remained present. "I am quite fine, now, thank you. You may stop hovering."

"Now that we have made complete spectacles of ourselves, I think we best depart." Gavin turned to Dillian's chaperon. "Lady Darley, if you wish to enjoy the remainder of the evening, I will gladly escort Miss Reynolds home. I have no desire to linger any longer."

Too shrewd to miss the looks the young couple gave each other, knowing the entire meeting had been set up deliberately for some reason beyond her knowledge, Lady Darley shook her head disapprovingly. "There is sufficient talk as it is. I think the evening shall be most boring after this. I'm ready to retire if Miss Reynolds is. We thank you very much for your concern, my lord."

Gavin bowed gallantly before the knowledge in her eyes. "We are most grateful for your help, my lady. If you are certain you wish to depart, I will find my own way home."

"I don't suppose you'll explain any of this?" she asked with interest, searching Gavin's face for clues.

"Someday, perhaps, my lady, although you must ask Miss Reynolds for answers. I give you good day, then." He bowed and walked out of the room, counting it one of the harder chores in his life. Dillian lounging defenselessly on a sofa made Gavin's blood run cold and hot at the same time. He had no intention whatsoever of letting her leave this house without his protection. Neville had looked fit to kill, and he still didn't know how this Reardon person fell into the scheme of things.

Miss Dillian Reynolds Whitnell had a lot to explain. He had every intention of sticking close to her side until she explained it to his satisfaction.

Twenty-seven

"Did she deny it?"
    "I didn't ask. All the evidence is clear." The Duke of Anglesey looked disgusted as he crossed the study and helped himself to another glass of brandy. "I can't believe I was so blind. The daughter of Colonel Whitnell living in my own household! My word, she had enormous nerve living so boldly under my nose. What in the name of heaven could she possibly hope to gain?"

Dismouth snorted. "Anything and everything. She has a comfortable position and access to an extremely wealthy heiress. You said yourself that she has alienated your cousin's affections and kept the two of you apart. There's no telling what other mischief she is about. Whitnell was a notorious troublemaker. There's no doubt the daughter is the same. Has your operative sent word as to your cousin's whereabouts?"

The duke shook his head and took a healthy sip of the liquor before speaking. "They've traced her to the south of France, according to the reports I've received. That's the same as Miss Rey . . . Whitnell said this evening. I can't imagine who Blanche travels with, other than her maid. I have someone else working on that angle."

"For all you know, your men are off after a red herring. Whitnell could very well have your cousin under lock and key somewhere. She may have set the fire deliberately for her own purposes. This works out very well for her. If she can keep Lady Blanche hidden until she turns twenty-one and continues her influence . . ."

Neville set the glass down hard and paced the carpet. "I can't believe Blanche so weak-minded. She is young, yes, but she is not stupid. She must know what is happening. Unless she's painfully hurt . . ." He gritted his teeth and swung around to face his older companion. "What in hell can I do?"

The earl stared thoughtfully into his own glass. "Well, there are those papers you removed from the vault. Your Miss Whitnell seems most eager to lay her hands on them of a sudden." He looked up to watch the young duke's expression. "If they're Whitnell's, they may contain information valuable to the government. For your cousin and for the security of the country, we should possibly take a look at them."

Neville set his jaw and glared out at the night sky through the study window. "They are not mine to dispose of as I wish. I handed the ones I found over to my solicitor for safekeeping, thinking they belonged to Blanche. He is not likely to give them over without Blanche's permission. Winfrey has the stubbornness of a mule when it comes to moral authority."

Dismouth tapped his fingers together. "Then, Miss Whitnell should suffer equal difficulty in obtaining them?"

For the first time that evening, the duke managed a half smile. "She would need two dragons and a platoon of knights to pry that old bastard out of his position."

Gavin already knew the sword he would use on his own personal dragon, although slaying her wasn't precisely his intention. He might occasionally contemplate cutting off her tongue, but he had no desire of otherwise ending a relationship that afforded him such pleasure.

He could think of no other good reason why he should lurk in a dark London garden on a windy spring night. He'd already scouted the front and decided he couldn't gain access from there except through one of the two doors: the belowstairs servants' entrance or the main entrance. The likelihood of one of the servants letting him in was small, and he had no intention of giving Michael more ammunition for his quick tongue if he should answer the main door.

The house shared inside walls with two other town

houses, leaving any access impossible from the sides. So now he stood in the garden behind the mews, contemplating the lighted windows above. He must be mad.

A silhouette crossed the lighted path of a second-story window. Since their charade required that he have no apparent knowledge of Lady Blanche and her companion, he'd not seen the inside of this protective prison where the women hid. Gavin didn't think much of Michael's precautions. He'd seen only one old man checking the downstairs locks. No one guarded the outside. With a good ladder, he could climb inside in a flash.

Unfortunately, he didn't have a ladder. And he could tell from the shape of the silhouette that it was Dillian standing near the window.

Damn, but he hadn't performed such contortions to get to a woman since he was a schoolboy. Anyone in their right mind would simply give up and go home. He knew how to live without a woman. He'd had lots of practice lately.

He just kept remembering how she looked lying there on that divan, the frail folds of her fancy gown falling to the floor, her face flushed and anxious as she watched the door for the appearance of her own personal demon. Dillian Whitnell might have the courage of a lion, but she had the physical vulnerability of any other woman. Since at the moment, Gavin considered her *his* woman, he meant to protect her.

He also meant to climb into her bed, but that was another matter entirely.

He would accomplish nothing by hiding in the shrubbery. Just as he'd decided to fling pebbles at the lighted window, the figure pulled the draperies across and disappeared into the interior.

Cursing, Gavin sought some means of gaining entry to that floor without pounding on doors and waking the entire household to his lecherous inclinations. No vines conveniently lined the solid, vertical walls. He could possibly look for some access from the roof of the neighbor's house, but he had no means of lowering himself two floors to the window he wanted.

Just as he concluded he would have to search the

mews for a ladder, he noticed a shadow furtively flitting from an ornamental boxwood to a hideous stone urn. Jaw setting grimly, Gavin pulled his black cloak more firmly around him for concealment and slipped behind a rose-covered arch.

The shadow skirted the house foundation much as he had done earlier in search of some means of entrance. Unlike himself, this person showed no evidence of avoiding doors and windows. He located the shadow near the rear door.

Gavin crept closer. He couldn't stop the intruder from entering the interior without following. He didn't possess Michael's ability of walking noiselessly, but the spring grass concealed his footsteps well enough, as long as he avoided the graveled walkway.

An overly tall hedge concealed the rear door briefly as he skirted around it. When he reached the shadows on the other side, the furtive figure had disappeared. Cursing, not knowing if the intruder had somehow entered the locked door, Gavin slid behind the stone urn—and nearly knocked down the intruder hiding behind it.

Finding his arms suddenly filled with squirming round curves, Gavin grinned and leaned against the urn for support while wrapping his captive even more firmly against him. He couldn't have mistaken the identity of his captive were he blind, deaf, and senseless. Her curves fit most fortuitously into all the right places. "Had I thought you so eager for my company, my lady," he murmured into her ear, "I would have notified you of my arrival much sooner."

Dillian followed her outraged gasp with a thump of her small fist against his chest. Gavin squeezed her more tightly against him, trapping her dangerous arms between them. That maneuver denied him full access to her lovely breasts. He made up for that lack by lifting her so the hollow between her thighs fit neatly against that part of him which welcomed her most.

Gavin felt her stiffen at the intimacy he forced upon her, but then nature had its way, and she relaxed, molding herself more securely into his embrace. Just that little surrender sent all his senses blazing, and he had to restrain himself from finding the nearest level surface to take her on. He had treated her crudely enough in the past. He would maintain some measure of gentility for the moment. Besides, he enjoyed the sensual pleasures of touch and smell and anticipation almost as much as the actual act. He breathed deeply of Dillian's lavender scent.

"Are you still wearing that gown you had on this evening?" he asked hoarsely, seeing the daring neckline in his mind's eye as clearly as if she stood before him in lamplight.

"No," she whispered hesitantly. "I took it off before I realized someone lurked in the bushes."

Gavin released her sufficiently to glance down at her shadowy figure. He could see something loose and flowing about her ankles. He threw his cloak back over his shoulder, freeing his hand to run over the silken material covering her breast. "You're out here in your nightrail?" he asked in astonishment mixed with a sudden surge of lust.

She hid her head against his chest and nodded.

Gavin played that notion through his head and chuckled. She could have called Michael and told him an intruder lurked in the yard. Instead, she had dashed outside wearing only her nightrail. He gathered her a little closer and wrapped them both in his cloak to keep her warm. "You knew it was me," he said with certainty.

"You don't have to be so blamed arrogant about it," she answered huffily. "Who else would be foolish enough to attempt scaling bare walls?"

Relaxing his shoulders against the monstrous urn and holding her close, Gavin shook his head, still chuckling. The little termagant had begun to grow on him. He found himself rather liking her prickly defenses. He preferred her mischievous laughter when they were in accord, but that didn't happen often enough to suit him. He'd settle for the heat generating spontaneously from their bodies as they stood together like this. He knew if he touched her breasts, she would be as aroused as he was.

"Consider it a compliment that I so desire your lovely

self, I'm prepared to scale walls for you," he murmured against her hair, allowing himself the pleasure of running his hand up and down her ample curves beneath the soft material of the gown.

She pulled her head back and glared up at him. "You didn't mean to . . ."

He heard the shocked tone of her voice but ignored it. "Of course I meant to. Shall we go in now or do you wish to explore the possibilities of this garden?"

Her small fist beat a tattoo against his chest again. "You wretched pig! In Blanche's home! Have you no decency? Would you shame me before all the world? Why do you just not claim me your mistress before all the *ton* and make it easier for yourself?"

Gavin sighed and settled her tirade by closing his mouth across hers. She didn't struggle long, he noted. Dillian had an unpredictable temper, but her physical desire blazed as strongly and hotly as his own. He took a seat on the stone bench surrounding the urn and eased her nightrail up so she straddled his lap. He'd prefer a warm bed to cold stone, but he would take what he could get. She tasted of strawberries, he decided as he dipped deeply into the sweetness of her kiss.

"Gavin, don't," she whispered when he gave her a chance to catch her breath. "We can't . . ."

For answer, he suckled her breast through the thin wisp of her nightrail.

She melted, almost literally melted, sliding into his lap and nearly falling from his knees before he caught her. He didn't think he'd ever felt such intoxicating pleasure with a woman in his life. Her responses not only made him ache with desire, they restored something missing inside him, gave him back some shred of the confidence he'd lost. Not all, perhaps. He might never return to the arrogant, cocksure bastard he'd once been, but he had no wish to return to his previous life in any form.

"Gavin, you can't possibly . . ."

He drank in her sigh of pleasure as he pulled her skirt up and caressed her lightly, luxuriating in the simple pleasures of heated skin, crisp curls, and welcoming moisture. Instead of beating him with fists, her hands now slid beneath the shirt she'd unfastened. When her fingers sought and played his nipples, Gavin nearly took her then and there. She learned exceedingly well and much too quickly. That knowledge delighted him even more.

As he reached for the buttons of his trousers, she stiffened. He'd thought her beyond the protesting stage, and he threw her an anxious glance. She wasn't looking at him but at something over his shoulder.

"There's someone there, in the shrubbery!" she whispered, leaning to speak against his ear.

The little wretch was perfectly capable of saying the like to distract him from his purpose. His fingers caressed her intimately, reminding her of his ownership of this particular part of her. She shivered and moved against him instinctively, but her gaze remained fixed on something over his shoulder.

Hell and tarnation, he swore silently, turning slightly to look where she now pointed. She hadn't lied. A man slid from the rose-covered arch, creeping toward the rear door.

"I didn't fasten it behind me!" Dillian whispered.

Gavin muttered a filthy imprecation and carefully set Dillian aside on the bench. The cold stone should cool her off. He rather thought his own loins might petrify into permanent stiffness. Still, he eased himself around the urn and prepared to fling himself upon the intruder when a second-floor window flew open and a veiled head leaned out.

"Dillian! Are you out there? Come back inside at once!"

The intruder shot through the shrubbery, scaled the ornamental boxwood, leapt from a wrought-iron table to the top of the brick wall, and disappeared on the other side.

"Get back inside the house!" Gavin shouted, not following the thief's path but heading for the gate to the mews.

"No, don't!" Dillian threw herself at him, clinging so he could scarcely move. "He might have a weapon. He's too far ahead of you. Let him go."

He had no experience with clinging women, nor any patience with them. Shaking her off, Gavin ran to the gate and out into the mews. Looking both ways, he could discern no running figure. Stables and discarded trash littered the dark alleyway. The man could hide anywhere. Without knowing in which direction he went, he had little or no chance of finding him without a small army. She'd safely distracted him until the culprit got away.

Cursing with angry frustration, Gavin slammed back through the gate and grabbed Dillian's arm, dragging her toward the house. "Why in hell did you stop me?" he demanded. "I could have nabbed the varmint, and we might have had a few answers around here. I sometimes wonder which side you're working for, Miss Whitnell."

"Nabbed the varmint?" she repeated with distaste, dragging on his arm rather than running to keep up with him. "How very expressive. Let me go, my lord. I'm not one of your minions to be thrown about of your own accord."

He threw open the door and jerked her inside. The door slammed behind them, echoing through the nearly empty household. "Do you prefer it to think I am one of *your* minions?" he asked furiously. "Am I only to do as you bid? Just precisely what game are you playing here, Miss Reynolds Whitnell?"

Blanche was running down the stairs, her eyes wide with terror. Michael already stood in the front hallway, arms crossed over his chest as he observed Gavin dragging Dillian in her nightrail down the corridor.

Oblivious to their audience, Gavin continued shaking his captive. "It's about time I had some honesty from you. I want the whole story, or I'm washing my hands of this whole damned deal."

To the astonishment of all, Dillian jerked herself out of Gavin's grasp, picked up the skirts of her nightrail, and started up the steps. "Then, go, my lord. I have no further use for you at all."

She left everyone standing in the hallway, gaping, as she departed with the injured dignity of a royal princess.

Twenty-eight

Dillian kept her head high and her shoulders back just as her military companions had taught her those many long years ago when she had childishly wanted to run and hide and weep until her heart broke. She wouldn't let hasty words wound her. She would hold herself above insults. And if physically challenged, she would fight with every ounce of her strength. Effingham should rejoice that he hadn't actually lifted a hand to her, or she would have bitten through it.

She even resisted slamming the door behind her as she retreated to her room. She clenched her fists and fought against the tears swimming in her eyes. She wouldn't think of the things the blamed marquess had done to her, of the intimacies she had allowed, of the way he made her feel special each time he looked at her with desire. Shame swept through her as she remembered what they had almost done in the garden. She had pretended all along that she had done those things for Blanche, but she'd lied to herself. She had done them because she wanted Gavin's arms around her, wanted his kisses, wanted him in her bed.

She was indeed her father's daughter.

Flinging herself across the bed, Dillian buried her head under the pillow. Her father had taught her to turn her back on the past and always look forward. She tried doing that now, but only a bleak emptiness marked the path that lay ahead. She ought to pack her bags and walk out, leave everything behind and start over. That was the simplest course.

That was the course she had chosen five years ago when her father had gone off to war and left her penniless again. She had taken her mother's name, sought her mother's family, and started a new life. What life could she start now?

She didn't want to start all over again. The first time hadn't been quite so wrenching. Her father had ruined his name so many times that she hadn't despaired of leaving it behind. She'd lived wherever he'd left her, with whomever would take her in. She'd not made any long-term friendships that way. It had seemed glorious starting out all over with a new name, a home, a friend, and family. Leaving all that behind now would break what remained of her heart.

Besides, she couldn't desert Blanche.

Dillian let that determination sink in. Her father certainly hadn't provided a model example of the rightness of his way of thinking. Perhaps turning her back on the past and moving on with her life wasn't the ideal method of dealing with problems. It certainly seemed the easiest solution, but that didn't make it *right*.

Drying her tears on her pillow, Dillian contemplated her alternatives. Regardless of anything else, Blanche was her friend. Blanche had saved her life, saved her meager savings, taken her in when no one else would. She simply couldn't desert Blanche. Not even her father could be that callous.

So if she didn't desert Blanche, how could she protect her? The wretched Lawrences had taken over Blanche's life in the interest of protection. After her outburst downstairs, Dillian supposed the marquess would use this opportunity to run back into hiding. She couldn't say the same for his younger brother. Michael seemed a singularly determined young man.

She owed neither man any explanation. Michael could stand guard at the door all he liked. Gavin could go hide in his cave. That left Dillian to produce the journals and any secrets they might uncover. Without Gavin to help her, she must decide what to do with them after she'd read them. She didn't think she had much chance of calling on Wellington without the marquess to vouch for her.

What if they were wrong, and the journals held no

secrets? What if Neville had truly decided to just murder Blanche rather than wait around for her to cut him off? That intruder tonight wouldn't be fooled for long if he worked for Neville. He'd know Blanche disguised herself and hid here as her maid. She must get Blanche to safety first, then go after the journals. She should never have let Blanche stay in London.

She reached that decision just as she heard her cousin's light footsteps on the floor outside her room. Scrubbing at her tearstained cheeks, Dillian leapt from the bed and began searching through her few personal articles. By the time Blanche had knocked and entered, Dillian had her old brown round gown in her hands and was ripping at the hem.

Blanche stood there worriedly just inside the doorway, watching Dillian rip at the old dress. "Are you leaving?" she asked in a small voice.

"No, you are." With firm conviction, Dillian produced the hoard of coins she had sewn into the hem during those hours she had watched over Blanche in the physician's home. She gathered them up and dumped them into a small pouch she kept at hand. "I think there is enough here to take you and Verity to France, in truth. If Michael insists on accompanying you, he can go as coachman or whatever for propriety's sake, but he'll have to pay his own way. It shouldn't be for very long. I'll send for you just as soon as I'm sure it's safe."

Michael appeared noiselessly in the doorway. "And you're after thinkin' the likes o' the lady will reach Dover without notice, be ye? Will you be sendin' the army with them, p'raps?"

"Stifle that nonsense," Blanche answered crossly. "Dillian may be right. if I'm not in England, Neville can't touch me. I'm quite capable of living quietly for a few months. That way I'm no danger to anyone."

Michael shifted himself from the wall and entered the room. "Your duke has men crawling all over Dover and into France looking for you. With or without the burns, you aren't exactly invisible. Someone is bound to notice you. If you go anywhere, it should be in the opposite direction. Have you any friends in Scotland?"

Blanche's eyes lit with hope. "Yes, I do. As a matter of fact . . ." She stopped and shook her head as her glance fell on Dillian. "Neville knows all my friends. He will already have notified them. They would simply send for him the moment I arrived. I'm sorry, Dillian. Do you know of anyone?"

"I do, but I don't know if they can be trusted any more than I can trust Reardon. If Neville can hire an army, he can hire anyone. It's not as if old soldiers are given much in retirement pay," she said bitterly.

"Reardon? Who is Reardon?" Michael asked with suspicion.

"None of your blamed business. None of this is any of your blamed business. Why don't you go away and leave us alone? Even that mule-headed brother of yours has sense enough to know when he's not wanted." Dillian turned her back on the too knowing eyes of Michael and sat down at the vanity to unpin her disheveled hair.

"That's not the way I'm seein' it, colleen. Gavin knows when he's wanted all right. He's just a mite contrary when it comes to givin' in. He'll come back. The two of you might as well sit here and tat doilies or whatever until he does." He eyed the bag of coins. "If you're going to spend money, spend it on hiring a few extra guards around here."

Dillian tucked the pouch carefully beneath her, out of sight. She took a brush to her hair and glared at Michael's reflection in the mirror. "Go away, O'Toole. We have better things to do than tat doilies or talk to you." She didn't dare speculate on what he meant about Gavin knowing when he was wanted. If that wretched excuse for a marquess had told O'Toole anything . . . She simply wouldn't think about it.

She watched Michael's expression in the mirror as he turned to Blanche. Something in his gaze caused a painful tug on her heart, and she closed her eyes against it. No one had ever looked at her like that. The bloody marquess had looked at her with desire. Lots of men had looked at her like that: like she was a plump pudding begging to be devoured. She rather thought that like young boys who could never get enough food, men could never satisfy their craving for women. But lust had nothing to do with what she saw in Michael's eyes when he looked at Blanche.

The impossibility of the match made her speak harshly. "Out, O'Toole, or I'll scream bloody murder and call for the watch."

When she opened her eyes and looked in the mirror again, he was gone.

From over her shoulder she heard Blanche whisper, "Why can't anything be easy anymore?"

Michael idled the next hour or so by carrying up buckets of water and rope, locating hammers and nails, keeping the curious caretaker and his wife quiet, and watching out all the downstairs windows. When Gavin reappeared carrying a large sack beneath his cloak, Michael opened the front door for him instantly, then returned to rigging the rope over the door.

Gavin eyed the arrangement approvingly. "I'd hoped to find buckets here. I had to steal most of this lot as it was. Lazy merchants don't keep gentlemen's hours around here."

Michael tied the rope end to the door latch, tested the rigging by opening the door and watching the bucket tilt precariously, and nodded. "Just don't go running in and out without unfastening it." He disabled the rigging temporarily so they could get out without drowning.

"I'm bloody well not going anywhere. You are. I can finish up here. I want you over at the solicitor's office. Be a beggar or a king, I don't care, just get in that office and find the journals." Gavin emptied his sack in the middle of the hall floor and sorted through his collection of oddities.

"As you pointed out, it's the middle of the night," Michael reminded him. "Unless you have breaking and entering in mind, I may as well stay here for now."

Gavin threw him an impatient look. "Then, go break and enter if that will get them any faster. If the journals are the key, let's find out. I've had enough of games. I want this over."

Michael leaned against the newel post and contemplated his brother's tightened jaw and the flashing anger of his eyes. Gavin looked every inch the Lawrence he was at the moment. The Lawrences were known for their dark coloring: complexions, eyes, and hair. They were also known for blazing tempers and outrageous arrogance. Gavin had all that and more. The white scarring on his cheek did not deflect in the least from the stormy expression that matched the one Michael had frequently seen on his father's visage. Fortunately, their mother had more aquiline, aristocratic features, which she'd passed on to her eldest son. They made his haughty look haughtier, but much more handsome than his father's. Women forgave a handsome face a lot of things. Unfortunately.

"Finding the journals won't end a thing, you're aware," Michael said conversationally, watching as Gavin selected a long stick and measured it against the front window.

"Are you still here? Must I do everything myself?" Gavin answered with irritation, not turning away from his task.

"What difference will it make when you discover Miss Whitnell's deep dark secrets? It won't make her a different person. She'll still be a cantankerous she-devil, and you'll still want to climb between her sheets. She's been good for you. She's got you out of the house and back into the world for a change. So why do you keep growling and behaving like a rabid animal when she's around?"

Michael watched with interest as Gavin's knuckles whitened around the stick he whittled to fit the window. He fully expected his brother to launch himself at him any minute now. He frequently trod the narrow line between Gavin's fury and patience. Sometimes he slipped too far on the wrong side. The topic of the luscious Miss Witnell drew that line narrower than usual. Michael waited for the eruption to follow.

Instead of exploding, Gavin merely set down his stick, walked across the floor, grabbed Michael by the shirtfront, and lifted him from his feet. "You will not refer to the lady in that manner again. Do you understand?"

Michael hid his grin and nodded solemnly.

Gavin threw open the door and pitched him into the street.

A moment later Michael heard the sound of his own contraption being fastened to the front door latch. So much for getting back inside anytime soon.

Grinning and dusting himself off, Michael whistled as he wended his way merrily down the darkened city street.

Dillian heard the tapping and scraping below and wondered what the devil O'Toole had decided to do at this hour. Unable to sleep, she pulled on her wrapper and went out to peer over the stairwell. The sight of Gavin in shirtsleeves, his cravat pulled off, and his buttons unfastened to expose his chest nearly sent her fleeing back to her room. The sight of the sticks and hammer in his hand kept her glued to the floor.

She couldn't see where he went with them. He disappeared out of her sight toward the rear of the house. The quiet tapping and scraping resumed.

She had no desire to ever speak to the man again. She didn't even want to be in the same room with him. If she never saw him again, she might eventually forget what it felt like lying naked in his arms feeling his body filling hers, hearing his whispered words against her ear. Eventually. The day she died, perhaps.

If she went back down there, he'd either insult her again, or kiss her back into his bed. She didn't want either alternative. But she couldn't sleep knowing he wandered the lower hall. She sat on the top step with her elbows propped on her knees and her chin in her hands, and debated her choices.

Gavin found her there sometime later, curled up and sleeping on the landing. He tried regarding the dark fall of curls against her pale cheek coldly, but he couldn't. She had berated him, teased him, laughed with and at him. She had worried about him. Behind that sharp tongue and lovely curves lay a woman with all the tender emotions he'd been deprived of all these years. They spilled generously from her in every word and action.

She'd surrendered her innocence to his selfishness just to save a friend. She hid secrets, yes, but she wasn't the only one. Perhaps, if he felt generous, he could possibly believe that she had thought she protected him by keeping him from running after the thief. Women had had stranger notions in his experience.

With a sigh of exasperation, he laid down his tools and lifted her into his arms. She'd fall down the damned steps if she lay there much longer.

She stirred in his arms as he carried her down the hall. Her arms went around his neck as if they belonged there, and Gavin pressed her a little closer, enjoying the warmth of her against his chest. She buried her face in his shirt and murmured something sleepily. The moment jarred something previously untouchable inside him, and he held back a gasp against the knifing pain. It did no good yearning for what he could not have.

Carefully, Gavin lay her against her rumpled sheets, fearing if she woke she would scream and flail at him again. He really didn't want her screaming at him anymore. He just wanted to hold her against him and feel her body next to his.

He'd never known how cold loneliness could be until he had to cover Dillian up and walk away.

The north wind howled through his soul as he closed the door behind him.

Twenty-nine

Wearing an elegant beaver hat, a frock coat of such fit even the Beau could have found no complaint, and stockinette breeches held secure by straps inside knee-high Hessians, Michael Lawrence "O'Toole" made a polite nod to the clerk in the first office and proceeded up the dimly lit stairs to the next floor.

The clerk downstairs had every right to stare. No gentleman of such elegance ever stirred at this unearthly hour of the morning unless headed home after a night of dissipation. The frock-coated gentleman lightly ascending the worn stairs not only showed no sign of dissipation but moved with the quickness and grace of a skilled athlete. The clerk shook his head in amazement and returned to his own particular cubbyhole.

Upstairs, Michael scanned the row of locked doors, their glass panels dark at this hour. Finding the one he sought, he removed an object from his pocket, fiddled idly at the lock, and a few seconds later, the door opened to welcome him.

Humming softly to himself, he gave the door as polite a nod as the clerk downstairs and sauntered into the office. Gray light seeped through a filthy window illuminating a clerk's tall desk and stool, walls of books, a few battered wooden desks, and another door at the rear.

As if he owned this office, Michael strolled to the rear door, fiddled casually with the latch, and swung it open with a light twist of his wrist. Dropping the small tool into his pocket he wandered through this larger room, admiring the heavy draperies covering the floor-to-ceiling windows as he pulled them back to let in light, poking about among the avalanche of papers cascading from shelves, files, and desk, and generally assessing the room's contents. Finally deciding on a towering wooden file cabinet in one far corner, he systematically worked his way through the drawers until he unlocked the one he wanted.

Admiring the drawer's contents as he fingered through them, he kept one ear open for the sound of early arrivals. Voices carried up the stairwell easily, giving him more than enough time to open a leather satchel he'd discovered in his earlier perusal. The contents of the drawer fit neatly into the satchel, leaving a bit of space for a few other objects that caught his discerning eye.

Still humming a slightly wicked sea chantey, he closed the satchel and strolled out of the office, neatly locking drawers and doors behind him. On the landing, he lifted his hat to a clerk just arriving, sauntered on down the stairs and out to the street. He was whistling "Black is the Color of My True Love's Hair" by the time he summoned a hackney and settled onto its torn leather squabs.

Dillian woke to find herself in bed still wearing her wrapper. Puzzled, she lay against the pillows, trying to remember the events of the previous evening. The incident in the garden made her blush heatedly, but it also made her exceedingly restless. Throwing off her covers, she sought her slippers. Only then did she remember Gavin moving about the hall below as she watched from the upper landing.

She didn't like thinking he had found her and carried her to bed. Surely, he hadn't played so free with her, or he would not have stopped at just leaving her in bed with her wrapper still on. Knowing the extent of the marquess's lust, she could imagine what would have happened had he entered her chamber unchaperoned. She must have wandered back to bed on her own and fallen asleep waiting to see what he would do.

That didn't quench her restlessness to any degree. Washing and donning one of her old gowns, Dillian listened at Blanche's door, heard no one stirring, and hastened down the stairs. She found no sign of Gavin's presence in the long hall below. The scraps of wood and tools he'd scattered across the carpet were nowhere to be seen. She started to check behind the floor-length draperies but discovered a footman leaning his chair against the front door. He blinked sleepily at her, then leapt to his feet and moved the chair back where it belonged.

She'd never seen the man before. Her only attempt at hiring servants had resulted in Michael and Blanche's appearance in dreadful disguises. Perhaps the caretaker had found someone. The footman blushed slightly at her continued stare and crossed his hands behind his back, taking on a formal stance of guarding the front hall.

"Who hired you?" she asked with more curiosity than anything else.

"Earl of Mellon, miss," he answered promptly.

The Earl of Mellon. The name rang familiar, and Dillian narrowed her gaze. "Does the earl not keep his own house to guard?"

The footman started to shrug, thought better of it, and said crisply, "Yes, miss, but I was told to come here."

She didn't see much point in asking by whom. She knew. Without continuing the discussion, Dillian drifted toward the dining room to see if any hint of breakfast had appeared. To her astonishment, she found a place set at the table with a lovely yellow rosebud in a crystal bud vase set beside it.

Since Blanche had brought no servants with them, the caretaker and his wife had more than enough to do without setting tables and cutting flowers. Meals had been taken as Dillian and Verity found them. Blanche had little notion of the kitchen's location and relied on her maid and companion to serve her whatever they rummaged from below. They usually ate in their rooms rather than in this formal hall. Dillian contemplated the place setting and wondered if the caretaker's wife had decided Lady Blanche ought to receive more respectful service.

No, that couldn't be it. They'd kept Blanche disguised and hadn't informed the servants of her presence. Dillian stared at the rose with perplexity. Surely, not . . .

Gavin? She looked around the room for some trace of him, but better sense won out. Granted, she had teased him once with a rose by his bedside, but Gavin didn't possess the romantic instincts to repeat the gesture. Michael must have placed this here for Blanche.

Reaching that conclusion, Dillian wandered on toward the kitchen stairs. Before she got past the ornate pilasters at the end of the room, a maid scampered through the doorway bearing a tray of steaming dishes. She bobbed a curtsy at Dillian and hurriedly began arranging silver serving dishes on the sideboard.

A maid? Not even stopping to question this new arrival, Dillian turned around and retraced her steps back up the stairs to Blanche's room. Knocking rapidly, she let herself in at the first sound of someone stirring on the other side.

She nearly tripped and fell over with shock when a man's broad, naked back rose from the lacy pillows.

One dark eyebrow cocked inquisitively as Gavin peered over his shoulder. "You could have waited until I answered," he muttered gruffly, running his hand over his unshaven jaw and shoving his hair out of his face.

In utter shock, Dillian ran her gaze around the pink and white lace-filled room, then returned it once more to the totally incongruous image of muscular, bronzed male flesh rising out of it. White silk partially covered the dark hairs of his chest as he turned over. Pillows with pink-embroidered roses and hearts framed the black mass of his curls as he sat up against them. A canopy of white lace tied back with pink ribbons shadowed the strong angles of his jaw and the mocking curve of his mouth.

It was one shock more than Dillian could take this morning. Laughter bubbled up from somewhere inside her, laughter she hadn't released in so long it practically hurt as it soared upward through her throat and escaped through lips she didn't bother covering. She held her stomach against the ache and bent over with the force of her howls, collapsing on the nearest chair as Gavin gave her a scowl and threw his long—very naked—legs over the side of the bed. The image of a man's hairy legs in Blanche's maiden bed brought more gales of laughter.

A genuine smile even curved Gavin's lips as the silken coverlet slid to the floor, revealing a neatly crocheted pink blanket beneath. When Dillian breathlessly pointed out the fluffy slippers beneath his feet, he lifted one with his big toe and admired it, casually heedless of his nakedness—until he stood up and crossed the room toward her.

Dillian abruptly stopped laughing.

She backed toward the door, uneasy with the sensations rippling through her when confronted with this large, lean, decidedly naked man approaching her with a determined look in her eye. She didn't dare lower her gaze any farther than his obstinate, and neatly cleft, chin. "No," she said adamantly, although he hadn't offered a word.

"Then, get yourself out of here quickly, Miss Whitnell, before I do something rash," Gavin answered mildly. "I generally bite the heads off people who laugh at me, but I'm willing to make an exception in your case only because I can think of many more pleasant things to do with you."

To Dillian's surprise, she didn't take his advice and run. Something in the way he mentioned people laughing at him made her hold her ground. She pressed her hands back against the solid wooden door and dared to meet his eyes. "Did you decide yourself above being an object of humor when you became marquess or before that?"

He halted in front of her, his broad bare feet not inches from where she stood. His hand instinctively rubbed his scarred jaw, but the curve of his lip no longer mocked as he regarded her carefully. "Michael laughs at me with impunity. I haven't beheaded him yet."

"Why is that, do you think, my lord?" she asked daringly, forcing him to look deeper into himself and away from the touchier subject of why he hadn't taken off her head.

He saw through her ploy quickly enough. Placing a hand on either side of her head, he pinned her in place. "Not for the same reason I didn't take off yours, I can

swear. Now will you get out of here and let me get
dressed, or will you join me in a tumble on that confection of a bed?"

She didn't have to look down to know he was well
prepared for the tumble. Gulping, she edged toward the
door latch. He lifted the arm barring her way. "Tell me
where to find Blanche, and I'll be on my way."

"Very sensible," he agreed, retreating a fraction to
grab a pair of trousers thrown across a chair, holding
the cloth in front of him. "I would hate to profane that
maidenly bed with what I have in mind right now. You'll
find your lady on the next floor up, where an intruder
wouldn't expect to find her."

Dillian opened the door slightly, poised for escape,
but she couldn't resist one further look back. "The
rose?" she asked, almost wistfully.

He grinned, making his dark eyes twinkle. "I'll let
you guess."

Dillian soared out of the room on winged feet. She
couldn't believe just that laughing smile could make her
feel this way. In a moment, she would be sensible. In a
moment, she would realize that the Marquess of Effingham had no business in this house, that he couldn't
possibly have put that rose there, that she would have
to call the watch and have him thrown out before he
committed something disastrous. She would remember
his insults, remember his rotten behavior, and she would
scream bloody murder until he threw up his hands and
went back to his Gothic ruin. In a moment. Not just yet.

Of course, in a moment, she remembered she was the
penniless daughter of the infamous Colonel Slippery
Whitnell, and the feeling went away without her ever
having to consider the other points. She made a suitable
mistress for a marquess. She could never be anything
else. That smile meant nothing more than his desire to
see her in bed again as soon as possible.

By the time Dillian found Blanche, leaden shoes had
replaced winged feet.

Gavin winced as he looked in Blanche's enormous gilt
pier-glass to adjust his neck cloth. The reflection staring

back at him was an alien one. In his attempt to suit
society's idea of a gentleman, he wore a dark blue super-
fine frock coat with a gold embroidered waistcoat of
white silk and fawn nankeen trousers, all of which cost
him a small fortune out of his own pocket. He ought to
bill the ladies for his expense. The wretched starched
neck cloth wrapped around his throat until he feared to
lower his head, but its pristine whiteness served as con-
trast to his already dark coloring, making him look more
savage than civilized. He hadn't bothered having his hair
trimmed, and it curled about his neck in almost as unruly
abandon as Dillian's. If he didn't do something about it
shortly, he'd have to tie it back in a ribbon. Though he
didn't recognize the elegantly clothed creature framed
by Blanche's gilded angels, he didn't see the monster he
expected, either.

Standing back, Gavin gave the cloth one more adjust-
ment and surrendered. The man staring back at him
didn't precisely look English, but he didn't look as deformed as he had expected. He rubbed at the scars, but
somehow Dillian's casual acceptance of them had dwindled them to just scars, not the grotesqueries he'd seen
them as. He still fought the urge to pull a hat down over
his face to conceal them in shadow rather than reveal
them glaringly in the broad light of day, but he clenched
his jaw and ignored the urge. He had plans for this day,
and hiding in dark corners wouldn't accomplish them.

As he ran lightly down the front stairs, he felt an
eagerness for Dillian's approval of the new Marquess of
Effingham. Last night hadn't counted. They'd had other
concerns at the time, and no time for exchanging personal opinions. He wanted to see the light of approval
in her eyes before he ventured out into the world.

"Do you know where Michael is?" The voice he
sought drifted upward from the front salon.

"Not since you threw him out of your room last
night," Blanche replied lightly. "You really shouldn't be
so mean to him. He's making this whole thing a great
deal more fun than it would have been otherwise.
Wouldn't it be wonderful if he would fall in love with
you, and the two of you could marry and live happily

ever after? You could have the Grange to live in and
raise a dozen little O'Tooles. You deserve that kind of
happiness, Dill."

Gavin froze on the bottom step.

Dillian's words echoed laughingly through the hall. "I
can picture it now with a dozen little imps disappearing
and reappearing at will all through the house and stable.
I would need put bells around their necks. Don't lend
your dreams to me, Blanche. I'll not ever marry."

Gavin was already heading toward the back of the
house, bypassing the front salon, as these words followed
him out.

Of course she would marry. Blanche had been entirely
right. Dillian ought to have a half-dozen little cherubs
running about her feet, making her laugh, keeping her
busy and out of trouble. She was meant for sunshine
and laughter. He couldn't picture her haunting the side-
lines of London society in the shadow of her cousin, but
he could see her swirling in circles on the green grass
with her face turned toward the sun and her skirts billowing around her. Mischievous elves belonged in the
country, not the city. A mischievous elf like Dillian
might possibly be the perfect solution to the imps of hell
that kept Michael wandering.

He'd never given Michael the kind of home he'd
needed. Michael had a nature as wide and generous as
Dillian's. He needed a home, love, and support. He deserved a laughing woman on his arm and in his bed.
Gavin had only offered him darkness and scorn, a life
of hand-to-mouth existence. He'd thought a roof over
his head and food in his stomach would suffice, but not
for Michael. He'd known that. He just hadn't acknowledged it. Michael had abilities and needs more spiritual
in nature than Gavin's. He didn't need food or shelter
or even women so much as he needed love and joy and
happiness. And Gavin certainly couldn't give him any of
that. Dillian could.

He let himself out the rear door into the gardens, then
into the mews. It wouldn't do for anyone to see him
parading around Lady Blanche's town house anyway.
He'd only sought to stay and protect the women while

Michael uncovered the journals. Now that he'd brought in the Earl of Mellon's servants, the intruder would have a difficult time of entering without notice. He'd find more security to reinforce them after dark. They wouldn't need his presence any longer.

He had some inquiries he needed to make, a few introductions to arrange, some information he needed to ferret out. Michael should return soon to keep the women out of mischief.

One troubling thought lingered long after Gavin left the garden gate: Michael deserved better than a woman soiled by his brother.

Thirty

Lieutenant the Honorable James Reardon sprawled inelegantly in a rear booth at White's. At this hour of the day nothing stronger than coffee sat on the table before him. His companion occasionally rattled his newspaper as he perused it, but the lieutenant didn't take the hint. He sipped at his coffee, kept a close eye on arrivals, and continued his monologue.

"I mean to find her, Martin. I thought one of you would look after her. I can't believe you lazy louts went about your own business and let her disappear like that. I should never have stayed in Vienna so long. Damn it all, if it hadn't been for that bloody cannonball . . ."

"The bloody cannonball could have killed you, but it didn't. It could have crippled you, but it didn't. All it did was give you an excuse for lingering with a certain well-endowed countess in Vienna until you perfected your waltz again. Don't give me that faradiddle, Reardon. If you'd had any concern for the girl, you would have written."

Reardon glared at the slightly balding man in the booth across from him. "You're a fine one to speak, Martin. You came back to a comfortable position, a few thousand pounds of your own a year, and a wife with a family to keep you well to grass in the future. You don't have to scrape on what little can be squeezed from a lieutenancy. Why didn't you see how she fared?"

Martin sipped at his coffee and glared over his spectacles at his friend. "I did. She was nowhere to be found. Hawley and the major joined up again when Napoleon came out of Elba rattling his sabers. Timmons and Shelby were in the Americas catching cholera in the swamps while the navy burned Washington. Who was there to ask? If I could have found Whitnell's papers, I might have found a letter or two to locate her, but you'd already ordered them shipped, and you weren't to be found. They found nothing on his body. I did all I could under the circumstances. I saw him decently buried. He didn't have relatives to speak of that I knew besides his daughter. Damned if I know what else I could have done."

"Timmons and Shelby and the lot shouldn't be difficult to find now. Have you asked them? Timmons showed her how to ride a pony. She's always had a fondness for him."

Martin set the newspaper aside with an exasperated glare. "She don't know his relations. How would she reach him? You're all about in your head, Reardon. I don't know what you're talking about. For all the chit doted on you, you never gave her a second look. She's no more feathers to fly on than you have."

Reardon growled something irascible, drained his cup, and kept his attention focused on the door. "I made sure no one else touched those papers. Her father meant her to have them. I just hope she received them, and they're not sitting around the War Office somewhere. Whitnell raked his share of coals in hell, but that daughter of his meant a lot to him. He meant to take care of her."

"He had a damned rotten way of showing it, is all I say," Martin muttered, returning to his newspaper.

A tall, lean figure elegantly garbed for this hour of the day suddenly detached himself from the table behind Reardon, rising to stand over their booth much as Gabriel must stand before the golden gates. Reardon glanced up in surprise, taking in the rapier-destroyed cheek before sitting a little more upright at the sight of ferocious dark eyes.

"You speak of Colonel Whitnell, I assume?" the stranger inquired with exaggerated politeness and an American drawl.

"Can't see that it's much of your business, old chap," Reardon replied arrogantly. "Eavesdropping can get a fellow thrown out of here."

"Vilifying a lady's family and speaking ill of the dead ought also, but I've noticed British rules are a little more lax than ours," the stranger responded with equal arrogance.

"See here, you interfering bastard, I ain't said anything against the lady . . ."

"Shut up, Reardon," Martin said pleasantly. "You were flapping your gob in a dozen different directions, as usual." Turning to the stranger, he inquired, "The Marquess of Effingham, I presume?"

Gavin nodded curtly. "I wish to learn more of Whitnell. You served with him?"

Another gentleman wandered up in time to hear this question. Pounding Gavin on the back, he shook his head in mock dismay. "Don't go asking these fellows about Whitnell. They worship the ground he walked on. If you want the real truth about the bastard, let me tell you a tale or two."

Reardon shoved from his seat and glared at the newcomer. "Get your royal ass out of here, Dunwiddy. You don't know a thing about the colonel. All you remember is the time he threw your scrawny little rear over the wall for tattling to the dean. You aren't worth the spit to polish his boots."

"The only thing I tattled to the dean was the method the lot of you used to cheat on the exam. Whitnell's main asset was his ability to slip through every damn crack in the rules. He was a bounder then, and he was a thoroughgoing rotter when he died!"

Gavin eased away from the altercation as several more gentlemen added their opinions of Colonel Whitnell's character. The boundary line in the fracas became immediately clear: his men would stand behind him with their dying breath; all others maligned his character beyond repair.

As he turned away, he noticed the Earl of Dismouth sitting in one corner watching the debate with interest. He caught Gavin's eye and reluctantly, Gavin strolled over. He didn't like the man's looks. Dismouth represented the epitome of everything about the British class system that Gavin despised. Undoubtedly brought up in the best families, in the best schools, trained to civil service for the good of his country, he had the arrogance of his station with very little understanding of the people he meant to govern. Idly, Gavin wondered if he'd even walked through the town his title represented.

"Started a bit of ruckus over there, didn't you?" Dismouth made a lazy gesture toward the chair across from him. "Believe we met last night, didn't we? Effingham, isn't it?"

"Dismouth." Gavin nodded curtly, taking the seat offered, not answering any of the obviously rhetorical questions.

"What interest can an American have in Colonel Whitnell?" the earl asked idly, sipping at his morning libation as he set aside his newspaper. "As far as I'm aware, the scoundrel's bad habits never extended to that particular continent."

Gavin signaled a waiter, taking his time before replying. He had learned many things in his lifetime. One of them was to hold his tongue until he'd thoroughly considered his reply. When another cup of coffee appeared before him, he returned his attention to the earl.

"I have heard rumors," he answered casually. "A man in my position takes an interest in his surroundings. It's beneficial for survival where I come from."

The earl scowled and signaled to have his cup refilled. "Learning about a man dead these three years or more isn't likely to benefit anyone, unless your interest is in the daughter. She's penniless, you realize."

Gavin shrugged and sat back in his chair. "To my knowledge, I've not made the lady's acquaintance, but thank you for warning me. An heiress is more to my taste."

Interest finally warmed the earl's cold eyes. "An heiress? You wouldn't happen to have a particular one in mind?"

"I've not been about in society long enough to sort them out. As I said, I'm just feeling my way about. Curiosity is one of my besetting sins. I keep hearing the name Whitnell whispered about. For a man dead three years or more, it seemed odd." He nodded in the direc-

tion of the still vociferous argument across the room.
"He still engenders strong opinions."

Gavin watched as the earl's expression grew serious,
apparently over some inner debate. When the man
spoke again, he listened as carefully to what wasn't being
said as to what was.

"Wellington nearly lost Waterloo," the earl finally answered in a low voice meant to indicate secrecy. "You
really should take up your place in Parliament, Effingham. We need fresh blood to keep us awake. You
Americans have different ways of looking at things that
might stimulate some refreshing debate. We keep much
of national policy to ourselves, sometimes to our detri-
ment. Did the country know how close we came to being
part of Napoleon's dominions, the uproar would be
enormous."

Fustian, Gavin muttered to himself. This man no more
cared about public opinion than he wanted to give a
vote to women, Catholics, or nonlandowners. Gavin kept
his thought to himself. "You have sufficient uproar on
your hands as it is," he said idly. "I shouldn't think you
would want to stir more debate over Wellington's incompetency at this date. They'd likely stone you."

"Precisely what we wish to avoid, but if the real truth
about Whitnell got about, we'd have no end to it. The
churls are up in arms as it is. If they should hear their
great national hero would have lost the war through the
influence of a man like Whitnell, who should never have
served in his majesty's finest troops—well, I shouldn't
wish to be around when that happens. The last time a
mob in London got angry, they nearly destroyed several
streets and everyone on them. An old lady just riding in
her carriage died in the riot, and the merchants they
stripped went bankrupt. And that was just over the
hanging of a wretched thief who once served in the navy.
I shudder to imagine what would happen if Wellington's
victory is desecrated by idle tongues. I wish I could lay
my hands on the scoundrel who started these rumors
about Whitnell's journals."

"You are saying his journals expose Wellington as an
incompetent officer?"

Dismouth shrugged offhandedly. "I am not saying anything except that Whitnell worked closely with the general and was in possession of almost as much power as his superior officer. I believe you have heard of Whitnell's reputation. Is that the kind of man who could successfully lead troops into battle?"

Gavin had seen enough of war to know that was precisely the kind of man to lead men into battle. Dismouth's story had enough holes to shoot a squirrel through, but in his experience, government officials never told the whole truth when a half would suffice. In any case the tale held no interest to him, other than the mention of the journals.

"I take it Whitnell left journals that would expose Wellington?" Gavin asked without interest. "Why doesn't someone just burn them?"

"Interesting you should ask that." The earl sat back in his chair. "Whitnell's daughter worked as a companion to a lady whose house burned to the ground one night."

"The daughter had the journals?"

"We don't know. She may have read them and stored them somewhere for safekeeping."

Gavin rose from his seat as if bored with the whole thing. "Then, perhaps you ought to join forces with Lieutenant Reardon over there. He seems to think finding the daughter is of some importance. But penniless companions are of little interest to me."

"Then, I wouldn't continue seeing Miss Reynolds if I were you," the earl answered snidely, returning to his newspaper. "That is the alias Miss Whitnell currently uses."

Gavin briefly contemplated grabbing the man's cravat and pounding his smug face against the nearest wall. On second thought, he wandered into the outer room and waited for a certain Lieutenant Reardon to extricate himself from the shouting rabble. Now that he wore the disguise of British nobleman and haunted their vaunted halls, he may as well put his new persona to use.

Dillian adjusted her dull brown bonnet to cover the last recalcitrant curl, and refused to look at her reflection in the hall mirror. She knew she looked like a brown sparrow. She didn't need the mirror reminding her.

"I wish you wouldn't go, Dillian," Blanche said worriedly. "I would rather you waited for Michael or the marquess. They may have found out something you should know first."

"What could they possibly find out?" Dillian asked scornfully. "That Winfrey won't release books that belong to me? I already know that. That Neville is too determined to have his own way to help us? Unless the marquess has untold sums hidden away somewhere with which to hire barristers to sue your solicitor, I cannot fathom what they can do."

"Appealing to your father's men will accomplish little more," Blanche pleaded. "You know few have funds enough for themselves. What can they do?"

"I don't expect them to supply funds. I only wish to see if they know anything of the contents of the journals. I still cannot believe there is anything of value to anyone in them after all these years. It should be perfectly harmless going down to the War Office and asking for the direction of my father's friends."

"If you are the one those men meant to kidnap, then I see nothing harmless about your walking the streets alone!" Blanche finally released her anger as she glared at her cousin. "At least wait until Michael returns so he can go with you."

"You set far too great a store in a man who disappears without a word for days at a time. I do not have such confidence in him."

"Then, take Verity with you," Blanche protested a Dillian resolutely headed for the stairs. "You cannot go about the city alone."

"Balderdash," Dillian replied succinctly. "My reputation will scarcely be salvaged by the accompaniment of your country mouse. Besides, I go as Miss Whitnell. I was raised by those soldiers I go to see. You are the one with a reputation at risk. Keep Verity close."

She sailed down the stairs in one of her old round gowns, every bit the country mouse she called Verity. The footman's eyes widened in surprise as he opened the door for her, but Mellon's servants were well trained. He made no comment upon the lady of the house going out into the world as a veritable dowd. Of course, he didn't realize the true lady of the house was the maid disguised in scarves above stairs.

Dillian disliked leaving Blanche alone and vulnerable should Neville return, but she could not bear to sitting idle another minute. In her experience other people never applied themselves to her problems as thoroughly as she did. And if the villains were actually after her and not Blanche, it was better that she use herself as decoy to keep them as far away from Blanche as she could.

She found a hackney waiting on the next corner. Peering up at the slovenly driver, she asked if the carriage was taken. She didn't like the driver's bleary eyes as he glared down at her, but she had little choice at this hour. They'd left Blanche's carriage back at the village.

When he nodded and took up the reins, she pulled herself inside the narrow confines of the interior, cursing the low quality of help these days. Or perhaps he thought her so lacking in coin as to be not worth the effort of helping her inside.

When they turned right instead of left at the next street corner, Dillian thought perhaps she should knock and remind the driver of the address. But she had not gone to the War Office in years. Perhaps the streets had changed or the driver knew some better route.

But when he turned right again, she knew they were headed in a circle, and she pounded the driver's door with her gloved fist.

He ignored her as they maneuvered around a coach and four holding up traffic so its occupants could descend with their myriad packages. Dillian was tempted to open the carriage door and leap out, but she feared falling beneath the feet of the other horses, or those of the gentlemen riding behind them. She waited until they passed the obstruction, then pounded again.

The driver pulled into a narrow alley and stopped.

Fuming, Dillian threw open the door and prepared to depart, hanging onto her reticule without any intention of paying the madman a shilling. Before she could put one foot on the step, an elegant figure in beaver hat and tails gently shoved her back inside and climbed in after her.

He beat upon the driver's door with the head of his walking stick, and the carriage started up again.

Enraged more than frightened, Dillian turned to let the intruder have a piece of her mind, until her gaze encountered laughing green eyes and a familiar, if irritating, grin.

"Well, Miss Whitnell, it seems you are incapable of even the most basic common sense. I could have been the duke or Dismouth or any number of ill-wishers. Do you have no sense of self-preservation at all?"

Fury diminishing to cool anger, Dillian opened her reticule and produced the small pistol her father had designed for her. Aiming it directly at O'Toole's black heart, she answered calmly, "More than you do, it seems, Mister Lawrence. Shall you order the driver to continue my way, or shall I?"

Thirty-one

"Very good!" Michael admired the pretty pistol in Dillian's hands. "You and Gavin are two of a kind, after all. Personally, I have little use for weapons, but I understand their necessity."

Michael shifted his position slightly, removing his tall hat, straightening his coat. An instant later Dillian discovered she held nothing but thin air.

While she gaped at the place where her pistol should be, Michael continued as if nothing unusual had occurred. "Of course, Gavin swears he has given up heroics for investments, but we both know better than that, don't we?"

Dillian glared at him. "Speak for yourself. I have found very little heroic about his attitude."

Michael lifted an inquiring eyebrow. "Spoken like a woman scorned. I had thought the interest more on Gavin's side than yours. You do not seem one of those soft women who swoon about romantical fantasies."

Dillian sat back in her seat and refused to look at him. She wanted her pistol back, but she wouldn't let him know that, either. "I am in no way romantical, and I despise military men, so I can assure you I have no romantic interest in your brother. I spoke only my honest opinion. The marquess is too self-centered and arrogant for heroics."

Michael toyed idly with his beaver hat for a while before replying. "You despise military men? I thought you practically raised by soldiers."

Dillian clutched her now nearly empty reticule. "That is precisely what I mean. They are not family men. They are fine fighting companions, but they are not . . ." She stopped, realizing she would reveal entirely too much if she continued.

But Michael had no difficulty following the path of her thoughts. "Of course, they are not the type of men you wish to become romantical over. You would prefer a man who looks after his home and family rather than one who goes marching off to war."

"Exactly." Said that way, she couldn't deny it, although she had no intention of becoming romantical over anyone.

Michael smiled and propped his feet against a ridge in the opposite wall. "You describe Gavin perfectly. All his life he's attempted to put a roof over my head and keep me under it. He doesn't realize the failure is mine and not his. Now that he owns his tottering castle, he invests every moment of his time in holding onto it so we'll both have a home to call our own. Given my nature and the state of the castle, I'd definitely call that heroic."

"I suppose marrying an heiress to keep his castle is also heroic?" Dillian asked with a bite of sarcasm.

Michael began whistling as he glanced out the window to check their location. Satisfied, he returned to the conversation with a smile. "That was my idea. Not very good at romance, am I?"

"Romance is vastly overrated," Dillian answered coldly. "I suppose someone like Blanche can look forward to it. She deserves someone to love and who loves her in return. Since she can have her choice of men, she has more opportunities than the general population."

The smile disappeared from Michael's eyes. "You're quite correct in that instance. But does that mean the rest of us must settle for practicality instead of love?"

Dillian gave him a sharp look. "What difference does any of this make? Where are we going?"

Michael leaned lazily against the squabs, crossing his arms over his chest. "I thought perhaps if we circled the city for a few days, I might keep you out of trouble until Gavin has time to solve all our little mysteries. It would give him an opportunity to woo our lady also, but I see now that isn't likely. He'll no doubt come after me with his sword if I don't return you promptly."

Only because he doesn't like sharing his possessions, Dillian thought spitefully, but she had sense enough to hold her tongue on that one. "I'm certain that would be the heroic thing to do," she answered instead.

Michael gave her a look of curiosity. "I suppose I can understand why you're fighting what you feel for him. I just didn't think you mercenary enough to consider wealth more important than character."

"O'Toole, will you please just have the carriage halt and put me down somewhere? Anywhere. I see no reason to continue this nonsensical conversation."

He whistled lightly to himself. "That bad, is it? And I wager Gavin hasn't got a clue." He remained silent a moment longer, as if monitoring some internal debate. Finally coming to some conclusion, he slapped his hat back on his head and handed back the pistol. "He hasn't told you about the scars, has he?"

Dillian accepted the pistol, sliding it into her reticule without interest as she regarded Michael's expression. "He has. What difference does it make?"

Michael made a sharp whistle of surprise. "I didn't think he had it in him." He turned and studied Dillian a little more closely. "You're not his usual sort at all. I haven't decided if that's for the better or worse." He sat at an angle so he could observe her better. "I don't suppose he told you the full tale? Gavin's not one to brag about his exploits."

"I scarcely think seducing another man's betrothed is anything to brag about," she said tartly.

Michael shook his head. "Now, that's a lie. He's up to his old tactics, scaring you off, he is. You don't scare easily though, do you?"

Considering that a fool question, Dillian didn't reply.

Michael nodded as if she had. "Good. Gavin's as hard-headed as they come. He delights in terrifying innocent misses. Justifies his laziness in staying locked up. If he didn't put you off with that tale, nothing will. He got those scars for more heroics."

Dillian's head jerked up from her contemplation of her gloved fingers. "Heroics? It happened in the war, then?"

Michael shook his head and tut-tutted. "Gavin only joined the navy because we were living on the coast then, and the British had the arrogance to think they could blockade us into starvation. Then they took to firing on civilians, and Gavin took strong objection. Don't get me wrong, he enjoyed besting the devils, but his main thought was protecting our home at the time. He thoroughly disliked the navy, but he did what he thought necessary to protect what was his."

That made sense. Not only did Gavin possess a finely honed instinct for protecting what was his, but he apparently lacked any innate ability for killing. She remembered Gavin riding hard after the men who would have endangered the Grange. He hadn't killed them, no more than he had hurt the highwayman who attacked them or the trespasser he'd caught. Gavin had the soul of a peacekeeper, not a fighting man. He wouldn't go off to war for the glory of it. That knowledge eased her somehow, but it didn't change matters any. She didn't say anything.

She didn't need to. O'Toole had evidently made up his mind to spill it all before he thought better of it.

"Gavin was a handsome fellow back then. He had the ladies standing in line, but once he made his choice, the others ceased to exist as far as he was concerned. She came from a wealthy family. The parents didn't approve, but the lady was determined. She swore she'd wait for Gavin until he returned from war."

Dillian didn't want to hear this. She stared out the carriage window. They did seem to be circling the city.

"When Gavin returned home, he found his beloved betrothed to a wealthy older man. He didn't confront her, didn't let her know he'd returned. He merely set about finding out as much about the man as he could. What he discovered wasn't very pleasant. He took the evidence back to the lady's father, thinking even if the lady no longer loved him, she should be protected from her own foolishness. Her father had Gavin thrown from the house."

Dillian could see it easily. America was no doubt little different from England. From things Gavin had said, she knew they'd grown up poor, that his family—despite their claim to aristocracy—were little better than charlatans living off the labors of others. Families preferred lineage and wealth to good looks, high hopes, and good intentions.

"Gavin finally sought the lady. Apparently, she thought him easily satisfied with her bed without the honor of his name. She didn't believe his warnings. He should have left it at that." The note of bitterness in Michael's voice was unusual, and Dillian cast him a quick glance. His expression revealed little, which said a lot in itself. Michael's features generally mirrored his mood.

"But, no," he continued, "Gavin had to be heroic. Instead of bedding the lady at her invitation, he sought to protect her by exposing the truth about her suitor and challenging him to a duel. The man chose rapiers, a nicety Gavin never learned with our rambling upbringing. Swords, he understood. Not rapiers. He went out anyway."

"The man savaged him," Dillian said quietly.

"Tried to cut his initials into Gavin's face, to be exact. Their seconds eventually put a halt to it. That wasn't enough for Gavin. Wearing an example of the bas—" He cut himself off and substituted "bully's." Dillian realized then that Michael never used the curse words so common to others. ". . . of the bully's cruelty," Michael continued, "Gavin insisted on appearing before his lady friend bearing the bloody scars as proof of the man's character. It seemed the wealthy widower she meant to marry had lost several wives in the past, not necessarily to natural causes."

Dillian hid a gasp and shudder. She knew the rest of this story. She could feel Gavin's anguish when he held his heart in his hands in a desperate effort to keep the woman he loved from harm, only to have his heart thrown back at him with hysterical shrieks of horror. A tear trickled down her cheeks at the thought of a man so tenderhearted, so courageous, even after all he'd gone through. This story rung much more true than the one he'd given her. She recognized that now. His beloved's shrieks of disgust at his ruined face would have decimated what remained of Gavin's pride.

"You don't have to tell me the rest," she said quietly. "How soon after that did you leave for England?"

"We couldn't earn the fare immediately on Gavin's earnings. We had to wait until some of his investments made returns. We've not been here a year or so. We simply left town and started wandering again after that little episode. It wasn't easy for Gavin making a living with a face like that. He worked on ships mostly. He could have caught one to England anytime, but he wouldn't go without me, and he wanted a little extra so we didn't arrive completely penniless. Gavin's a bit of a fool sometimes."

"Yes, I suppose he is. I've always considered the heroes of legends quite foolish. Just think of Lancelot, Tristan, Hamlet, any of them. They died for naught. Even had they lived and triumphed, their ladies would no doubt have turned into fat, overbearing harpies in time. Heroism simply isn't worth the effort," Dillian stated flatly, sitting stiff and straight against the seat. "If you really intend for us to circle the city forever, I would like some nuncheon soon."

Michael laughed, then laughed some more when he saw her stony face with the tear streak down it. "You're good, She-devil," he spluttered, gasping for breath, then laughing again. "You've very good. Harpies, indeed! Quite definitely harpies." He chortled, holding his side from the effort of containing himself.

Dillian fought back a smile at his foolishness. She hadn't thought she liked the mock Irishman, but she was coming to understand him a little better. Of course, she would no doubt like anyone who defended Gavin. That thought frightened her just a little.

"Nuncheon?" she asked, arching her eyebrows.

Moderating his laughter to a broad, admiring smile, Michael nodded at the window. "Would you care to share it?"

Dillian glanced out to see they had stopped in a tangle of carriages before White's. Just as she was about to admonish him for the impropriety of thinking she could dine there, her gaze fell on the two gentlemen in serious discussion outside those famous bay windows.

The Marquess of Effingham and Lieutenant Reardon.

Blanche stood in the doorway to the dining room and watched her silverware disappear up Michael's coat sleeves, reappear from his pockets, and waft through the air half a dozen pieces at a time as he contemplated the mural of the goddess Diana hunting a stag on the wall. He knew she was there. He just didn't see fit to acknowledge her. That fact and the disappearing silverware told her something troubled him. He had an odd way of concentrating on problems.

"Did you find the journals?" she finally demanded.

A silver candlestick joined the forks and knives. "Are all the patients in Bedlam lunatics?" he asked enigmatically, still not looking at her.

"It's better to ask if all lunatics are in Bedlam. The answer is no. Will you at least tell me what is happening? Dillian isn't speaking to anyone since you brought her home."

The first part of her reply brought a smile to his lips, and the candlestick reappeared on the sideboard. One by one, the number of pieces circling in the air dwindled. "You should thank me for that. I'm certain Gavin would, should he deign to make an appearance. Somehow, we have to bring those two together. Gavin needs a woman in his life."

"I can assure you that Dillian would tell you quite unequivocally that she doesn't need a man in hers. I am beginning to understand her decision. If you don't put those silly toys down and tell me what happened today, I shall go to Winfrey and demand he release those journals at once."

Michael's smile turned sad as the last fork disappeared, whether into his pockets or coat sleeves or the sideboard remained unclear. "Too late, my lady. It seems your solicitor suffered a small loss this evening when his office went up in flames. I understand they're blaming someone with a smoldering cigar."

Blanche gasped and lowered herself into the nearest

chair. She stared at him in mixed perplexity and horror. "That can't be true. Neville wouldn't do that. All our papers are in that office." As she realized what she'd just said, she fell silent, her mind quickly darting to all the legal documents that encompassed: wills, deeds, powers of attorney, everything that governed her life and Neville's. She stirred uneasily and glanced to Michael, who still studied the mural. "What will that do to the estate?"

"I'd ask Gavin that if he would put in an appearance. He's not studied much British law, but he has a fine grasp of the legal system. Perhaps duplicates are filed elsewhere."

Blanche nodded uncertainly. "Surely, they must. I believe I've heard wills are filed with some court for public record. I'm certain I've seen copies of some deeds . . ." At Anglesey, in Neville's possession. She closed her eyes and swore to herself. Dillian was right. She was much too trusting. Her eyes flew open again as she frantically tried to remember where she'd put the deed to the Grange. Surely, she hadn't . . . She almost certainly had. She kept the papers to her mother's property with her in the house that had burned. She had counted on Winfrey keeping copies.

Crushed, more depressed than she wished to let anyone see, she rose from her chair and started out of the room.

"They'll think they're safe now," Michael called softly from behind her.

Blanche hesitated, then shook her head. "No, they won't. They didn't go after Dillian to get the journals. They went after Dillian because they thought she knew what was in the journals."

Michael stayed slouched in his chair as he watched her swish gracefully from the room. Why must she be as intelligent as she was beautiful?

Thirty-two

G avin didn't bother lurking in shadows looking for a less intrusive way of entering the house this evening. He strode up to the front door of Blanche's town house and pounded his fist against the panels, since the lady hadn't hung out the knocker. To hell with London society. To hell with the Duke of Anglesey. He'd had enough playing games. The time had come for direct action.

Michael appeared more promptly than expected, this time dressed as himself instead of one of his more disreputable characters. Gavin recognized the glare in his brother's eyes and ignored it, pushing past him toward the stairs.

"She locked herself in hours ago," Michael called after him. "And she has a gun."

Why didn't that surprise him? Gavin didn't lose a step as he took the stairs two at a time. He'd had a bloody awful day hanging around the rarefied atmosphere of London's gentlemen's clubs. He was in no mood to tolerate defiance now.

As he approached Dillian's room in this richly carpeted, elegantly furnished home of a duke, Gavin knew a moment's hesitation. Perhaps he had stayed too long from civilization, after all. He had no right whatsoever to storm through someone else's home as if he belonged there. Nor did he have any right to demand entrance to a lady's bedchamber. True, the four of them had dispensed with formality while hiding in the upper floors of Arinmede, but that didn't mean the rules of civilized behavior no longer applied. If he walked in there now, he branded Dillian his mistress for all to see.

It wasn't lack of civilization that drove him. It was a burning need to see Dillian. Shocked at this discovery, Gavin halted halfway down the carpeted hall. Most of the grand chambers in his ruin of a home had never seen carpeting. Apparently, even the humble halls in the duke's house sported them. What in hell was he thinking of coming here like this?

As he hesitated, Blanche slipped from the room he knew as Dillian's. She glanced at him uncertainly, then looked back at the door behind her. Apparently reaching some decision, she closed the door without warning the room's occupant of his presence. Gavin wondered what that signified, but he thought the lady might tell him as she drifted in his direction.

She didn't wear her scarves or veils in candlelight, and in the flickering light of the wall sconces, he could readily see the raw burns healing on her cheeks. She had discarded the bandages on her hands, but the damage was still too severe to conceal beneath gloves. He imagined she must feel a great deal of pain, but the relief of her returning sight kept her brave enough to ignore her other injuries. For now.

"I don't think she's in a humor for listening to reason right now," Blanche stated bluntly when she stood before him. "Dillian is usually the most rational of creatures, but she's up in the boughs now. I don't know what is between the two of you to make her so, but I would not think it wise to go in there."

"Even with a chaperon?" Gavin asked wryly.

"I don't think a chaperon is much protection for either of you. I suppose I ought to be shocked at the idea of sending you in there at all, but somehow, in relation to other events, it seems rather insignificant in the scheme of things. Talking reason to her appears more important."

"She's on a real tear, then?"

Blanche nodded. "I gave her all my jewels to take to the cent-per-centers in the morning. She has decided you are no longer trustworthy."

Gavin gave a vivid curse that caused his hostess to wince, but he didn't linger to hear her admonishments.

He strode down the hall and slammed open the door Blanche had left unlocked.

Dillian started up from her packing with a surprised jerk that quickly became ire when she saw him. "We no longer have need of your services, my lord," she informed him coldly. "Therefore, you no longer have any right to mine."

Gavin slammed the door closed and stalked across the room. "Services? Is that what you call them? When I put my tongue in your mouth and you melt in my hands, that's a service? When I lay you down in my bed and you shiver with desire, that's a service? Don't lie to yourself any more than that, Miss Whitnell. Did I want your 'services' right now, I could have them, and you would have no more right to complain than I."

"You arrogant, conceited oaf!" Dillian flung the flimsy muslin gown she held at his head. "Do you think you need only crook your finger, and I will fall at your feet?"

Gavin swiped the flimsy cloth from his face and threw it on the floor. "I'm not so foolish as that. You have the will of a stubborn mule. I would have to do far more than crook my finger, and falling at my feet is not the result I would want in return. But since we cannot have what we both want with your cousin waiting anxiously in the hall and my brother, no doubt, clinging to the ledge outside your window, we shall have to settle for something a little more rational than our own physical desires."

He watched with curiosity as the anger went out of her like air from a deflated balloon. A more experienced woman would have accepted the challenge, played the seductress, then walked out, leaving him cold and aching. But Dillian was too new to her sexuality to know her own powers, and too honest to deny the blunt truth of his words. For a moment Gavin's hopes soared at this unspoken admission of desire. Then he remembered himself, and returned to his mission.

His gaze fell on the trunk she packed, and Blanche's warning came back to him. "You're planning on going somewhere?"

"We're leaving. Blanche's injuries will heal soon

enough. I think we can conceal her until she's twenty-one. Then she can hire another solicitor, take control of her funds, and do as she likes."

"With Winfrey's office destroyed, Neville can wreak havoc in the courts in those six months. He could have himself named Blanche's guardian, declare her incompetent, claim he's discovered a new will, any number of things, and the courts will quite willingly accept the word of a duke over a mere woman."

Dillian stared at him through eyes grown wide with horror. Gavin regretted terrorizing her, but he had no intention of letting her out of his sight. He feared the duke was the very least of their worries.

When she didn't say a word, he continued, "You'll have to trust me. I have nothing to gain from any of this."

"Nothing besides a rich heiress or the influence of a powerful duke," she replied bitterly. "You need only turn us over to Neville to win a friend for life and all the cash reward you could ask. Blanche and I can offer you nothing until year's end."

Gavin scowled, struggled with his suffocating cravat, and took the wing chair beside the fireplace, completely ignoring the fact that he crushed the tails of his evening coat. "I suppose you have no reason to trust me over anyone else. What must I do to convince you that I have no interest in anything but your safety?"

She regarded him with scorn. "Go back to complaining of what a nuisance we are and return to your Gothic ruin."

Well, he couldn't ask for a more honest reply. With a sigh of exasperation, he studied her. She wore a dreary brown gown designed to deflect the eye from all her most estimable physical assets, diminishing her worth to spinster companion again. Unable to agree to her wishes, having no ready solution to the problem, he diverted the subject.

"I like that gown on you. It keeps anyone else from the pleasure of knowing your loveliness but me."

She scowled and turned her back on him as she pulled another dowdy creation from the wardrobe. "That ploy won't work. I'll not don a fancy gown just to spite you. I'm Blanche's companion, and I dress the part."

"Well, I need the aid of the dashing Miss Whitnell to solve our problem. The dull Miss Reynolds won't do."

"I went to Dismouth's as Miss Reynolds," she reminded him, folding the gown tissue paper. "Miss Whitnell is far more likely to carry pistols and curse like a trooper."

"Even better." He smiled with delight at the image. "I don't suppose you had the modiste make one of those military riding habits for you? The ones with all the buttons and the shakos to match?"

"They went out of style two years ago," she said scornfully. "Blanche has one she scarcely ever wore. She looked ridiculous in it."

Gavin noticed she was watching him out of the corner of her eye now, so he'd finally captured her interest. Settling himself more comfortably in the chair, he had the sudden realization that he'd not once concerned himself with the effect of his face or his appearance on the general populace since he'd got involved with solving this mystery earlier in the day. Thoughts of Dillian and her danger had erased any trace of his self-consciousness. He was setting himself up for a tumble, but he found himself enjoying a sense of purpose for a change. He felt alive again, not some rattled ghost hiding in shadows.

"Pity," he commented. "It would look good on you. I don't suppose you could do some female magic on it and make it fit you by tomorrow, could you?"

Dillian's amused glance told him he'd made some male faux pas, but he accepted it gladly if she looked at him again.

"Not unless some magic fairy could take three inches off the bottom and add it to the top," she answered without any hint that she'd taken umbrage at his ignorance.

Gavin measured her with his mind's eye and nodded reluctantly with agreement. Blanche was one of those willowy beauties who wore clothes well but possessed nothing beneath for a man to grasp. He much preferred

Dillian's shorter stature and bounteous charms. She'd snap his head off if he told her so.

"All right, then, did you have some fancy walking dress made up? I want to take you out tomorrow morning, and I want us to look every inch the dashing couple."

Gavin loved causing that look of perplexity. He'd just about decided he owed Michael a great deal, but he didn't owe him Dillian. He would fight until his dying breath to keep this delightfully opinionated, immensely challenging woman. She might not want him. He could live with that. But he'd damned well fight to hold her until she said so. Just deciding that made him feel better.

"I cannot be something that I am not," she protested. "I am not dashing. I am just plain Miss Whitnell. Should I play the part of anything else, I will make a laughing-stock of myself."

"I know the feeling," he answered dryly, casting a glance at his starched cravat and pulling at it with distaste. "That's why I thought the military outfit would make you feel better. You could even carry your pistol in your pocket, if you liked. I'll have horses, so we can ride, if you prefer. Personally, I think you're dashing in that gown, but I will admit that society operates under one blind eye and a terminal case of stupidity, so we needs must knock it over the head before it sits up and takes notice."

Gavin could see her biting back a grin. He felt better and better about himself as he sat there, watching her flower beneath his gaze. He'd not entirely lost his way with women, then. All he needed was a woman with sense enough to look beyond the scars. She didn't want to trust him. She didn't want to trust herself. She planned on running and hiding, just as he had all these years. He would teach her to confront her enemies with pistols drawn. He could see already that she warmed to the idea, that she recognized something of the truth of his words.

"What, exactly, did you have in mind?" she asked carefully.

*   *   *

"I feel like a blithering idiot," Dillian muttered the next morning as she stepped out of the house wearing a walking dress of delicate lavender and twirling a matching parasol, complete with ruffles and bows.

"You look like a porcelain confection, the kind people sit on their mantels and admire," Gavin admitted. His gaze slipped to the cleverly designed neckline, which gave glimpses of soft curves while still concealing them with gauzy ruffles. "But I'm a man who would rather touch than look."

Dillian sniffed. "I daresay you've broken your share of porcelain in the process." As they proceeded to the carriage he'd procured, she gave him an equally appraising look. She feared he had gone far in debt for this day's elegance. In his high starched cravat, gold silk waistcoat, and fitted blue morning coat he looked every inch the aristocratic marquess. His high-crowned hat did nothing to conceal the scars, but he made no attempt to keep his face averted. In fact, he met her gaze boldly, waiting for her approval. The look in his eyes nearly took her breath away, and she had difficulty continuing the conversation until she retrieved the ability to breathe. "You are looking unusually uncomfortable this morning," she finally discovered breath to say. "How do you find wearing shoes again?"

The flash of white teeth against bronzed skin almost sent her into transports once more. Dillian looked away as he helped her into the carriage so she might retain some of her thought processes for a few minutes more. The realization that she was about to enter an enclosed carriage with this man and no chaperon suddenly made her nervous. She remembered very distinctly what had happened the last time they rode together like this. She had sworn she would not demean herself again. That didn't mean she had achieved total resistance to Gavin's physical presence.

"Quite comfortable, thank you very much," Gavin replied as he swung in beside her. "The ability to dress as I choose certainly recommends living as a hermit."

Dillian stared straight ahead, struggling not to notice her reaction to the lean figure lounging lazily so close to her she could feel the heat of his thigh. She admired the polish of his newly shod feet as they sprawled in front of hers and fought stray thoughts about how his toes looked when bare. She wouldn't linger long on toes.

"I told you last night that you need not remain here for our sakes. You are quite free to return to haunt your hovel anytime you like."

Gavin had propped a walking stick with an ebony knob between his legs, resting his gloved hands on it as he looked down on her from his lofty height. She watched those hands tighten around the knob, but his voice remained pleasant as he replied.

"I have decided there is more money to be made by an occasional public appearance," he drawled. "I have heard no end of interesting investment possibilities these past days in the clubs. I mean to look into several of them."

Dillian darted him a quick look of curiosity. "You have money to invest?" She immediately regretted the crassness of the question and cursed her wayward tongue.

He merely looked down at her with that half-mocking grin teasing the corner of his mouth. "Did you think I spent it all on wine, women, and cards?"

She crossed her arms over her chest and sent him a disgruntled glance. "If you had any to spend, it went on food and cooks and fuel to heat that monstrosity in the winter. It certainly didn't go into planting your fields, which would have been the most sensible investment."

"The fields aren't mine to plant," he answered quietly. Then knocking on the carriage roof, he ordered the driver to stop.

Dillian didn't have time to question him before the earl's footman leapt to lower the steps and open the door. She wondered what Gavin had ever done for the Earl of Mellon to allow him so much freedom with his personal servants and equipment, but she refused to ask. She had some recollection of a mention of his cousin Marian marrying into the family. Nobility had too many connections to ever sort successfully.

"This is Bond Street," she whispered in puzzlement

as she took his arm a moment later. "Whatever are we doing here?"

"Walking together in public. I believe that is Lady Castlereagh over there." He tipped his hat brim with his walking stick and nodded to the viscountess across the street.

Dillian gripped his arm tighter, forced a smile to her face, and greeted one of Blanche's suitors as he passed by. The man nearly tripped over his own boots as he recognized Blanche's once dowdy companion, then hastily went on his way after his admiring greeting met Gavin's scowl. Dillian wanted to feel delight at walking this very public, very aristocratic street on the arm of a handsome marquess who offered such jealous protection. She should be floating on air. Once upon a time she had dreamed silly dreams of wearing elegant gowns, twirling parasols, and chatting gaily with handsome men. She had been a silly young girl then. She didn't have such foolish notions now. The Marquess of Effingham did not stroll the streets of London for the sheer pleasure of it, and he did not scowl for jealousy. He simply didn't wish his plans interrupted.

"Could you please explain exactly what it is we're doing so I might act the part?"

"You are acting the part quite well. You might wish to look upon me with doting admiration," he added after a moment's consideration. "But I will not ask too much of you."

Dillian could tell when he laughed at her, and she pinched his arm through the layers of coat and shirt. Gavin didn't flinch, but he did turn a mirth-filled look at her. The blatant admiration in his eyes nearly reduced her to breathlessness again. Why in the name of all that was good was he doing this to her? Hadn't she made it plain enough that she had no desire to act as his mistress now that this charade had ended? The journals were lost. They would never know now who might want them. He could do nothing further for her. She and Blanche must hide until they had funds to buy their safety.

Gavin had promised the person they met here today would aid them in that. He needn't be so confounded mysterious about it. And he needn't look at her as if he would devour her like one of his cook's meat pasties.

Dillian didn't have a chance to respond to his audacious statement. A familiar figure wending his way through the crowd ahead stopped her heart, and she tugged urgently on Gavin's arm. "We must get out of here," she demanded, attempting to steer him into the nearest haberdashery.

"Nonsense. Here comes the man I want to see." Gavin held himself firmly in place, ignoring her cries of protest.

Dillian considered dropping his arm and running, but she could already see it was too late. Her father's most promising recruit and closest confidante had already seen her. Lieutenant James Reardon was about to expose Miss Dillian Reynolds as the daughter of Colonel Slippery Whitnell for all of London society to see.

Thirty-three

"Dillian! Thank God. I've hunted all of England for you." With a pronounced limp, Lieutenant Reardon hurried through the crowd and grabbed Dillian's hands. All around the people stopped, stared, and blatantly eavesdropped as the young couple met under the black glare of the terrifying marquess. Just Effingham's malevolently scarred features stopped them. His threatening scowl had onlookers holding their breaths with fear and anticipation.

"Reardon," Dillian responded stiffly. "Have you met Effingham yet?"

To the astonishment of all, the marquess held out his hand and shook the young lieutenant's proffered one. Deciding they wouldn't see a soldier beheaded immediately, several members of their audience drifted off.

"We're acquainted," Gavin informed her. "He's the gentleman I wished you to meet today."

Dillian gave him a hostile glare. "You might have told me so I didn't succumb to failure of the heart."

Gavin raised a quizzical brow, making his visage all the more sinister. "I hadn't realized your heart was involved."

She smacked his shin sharply with her folded parasol. "That's not what I meant." Reluctantly, she found Reardon. "I had no idea you looked for me. Why ever should you do so?"

"I promised your father to look after you, but I've been confined on the Continent until recently. I'd thought some of our other acquaintances had seen you by now, but when I returned here, no one knew anything of you. I've been frantic with worry." Reardon still held her hand and searched her face anxiously. "My neglect is unforgivable. I can understand if you will no longer speak to me."

Dillian jerked her hand back. "Don't be ridiculous. I am perfectly fine. I'm quite capable of looking after myself. Goodness knows, I've done it most of my life. Don't enact a Cheltenham tragedy for my benefit." She sent the marquess a questioning look. His scowl had disappeared, but he still watched them cautiously. She thought she should give his shin another whack, but she generously refrained. "What is this about, my lord? Why do you wish us to meet?"

Seeing something he didn't like in the marquess's manner of looking at her, Reardon demanded angrily, "Yes, what precisely did you have in mind? If you've harmed one hair of this lady's head . . ."

"Cut line, Reardon," Gavin murmured without inflection, his gaze still searching Dillian's face. "The lady is capable of making her own decisions. Shall we repair to somewhere a little less public now?"

"We could have met somewhere a little less public," Dillian hissed as they wandered a few streets to the park.

"Not for my purposes," Gavin informed her as he found a bench they might share without half of London listening in. "All this secrecy is damning. You English are too blamed closemouthed. It's time we strip this nonsense to the bones for everyone to see and put an end to it."

"I beg your pardon," Dillian answered huffily. "I see nothing nonsensical about trying to protect myself and Blanche."

"Anglesey knows you're Whitnell's daughter," Gavin said coldly. "You are not protecting Blanche from anything by continuing this charade of being no more than a hired companion." He turned to Reardon. "Now, tell her why you're looking for her and why you're working for Anglesey."

On the opposite side of Dillian, Reardon looked puzzled but obliged. "Your father told me he left your inheritance in the papers I sent back to you. I thought you sufficiently provided for so I did not worry as I should have. When I returned six months or more ago and could find no trace of you, I became increasingly concerned. I knew those papers contained some defamatory material. The colonel had a habit of working out his angers by jotting down notes defaming his superiors, delineating their incompetence in rather deadly accuracy, commenting upon situations that should otherwise have no interest to him." He shrugged apologetically. "You know as well as I, Dillian, your father had as much pleasure from stirring trouble as from drinking ale. He never subscribed to the officer's creed of 'taking care of their own.' He looked at things from an enlisted man's mentality, and he relentlessly found fault with the aristocrats around him, despite the fact that he was one of them. He made a lot of enemies."

Dillian played with the ivory handle of her parasol. "I'm aware of that. But he was quite frequently right. That earned him more enemies than anything else." She sent him a scathing look. "The dukes of Anglesey have not exactly been his friends."

Reardon adopted a stubborn look. "As an officer, I'm required to obey orders from my government. If I'm told to report to the Duke of Anglesey, I do. The man is distraught over the disappearance of his cousin. I can see nothing wrong in looking for her. You are following in your father's footsteps if you hide her ladyship from her cousin."

"Balderdash. You are feathering your nest at the expense of a lady," Dillian answered scornfully. "Neville wishes to force Blanche into marriage. He may have also given someone the idea he wished the lady dead. He is the only one who benefits from her death or that tragic fire."

"Devil take it!" Reardon roared. "You cannot accuse the man . . ."

"That's enough, children," Gavin intruded curtly. "You will attract an audience again." He removed the parasol from Dillian's grip before she could strip the handle from it. The childish argument had relieved his concerns to some extent. Dillian treated the handsome lieutenant as a nuisance of an older brother, not as a

long-lost lover. He was inclined to feel lenient as a result. "You are perfectly aware that you and the journals,
not the Lady Blanche, could have been the target of that
fire. Reardon will help us discover the truth."

Dillian appeared only moderately pacified. "My father
has been dead for years, and no one has made an attempt on my life before. But in the last six months,
someone has shot at Blanche as she rode through the
woods, damaged the axle of her carriage so it overturned
on a particularly perilous road, and set fire to her home.
I cannot see these 'accidents' as coincidences."

Reardon looked alarmed, but Gavin merely asked, "I
assume you were with her at those times?"

Dillian's eyes grew wide as she immediately took his
meaning. "Surely, not! Surely, someone wouldn't risk
harming Blanche to get at me?"

Gavin waited for her to reach the inevitable conclusion on her own. Reardon appeared properly horrified,
but a shake of the head kept the lieutenant from speaking. Dillian's fingers clasped and unclasped in her lap as
she allowed this to sink in.

Finally, she gave Gavin a pleading look. "I will have
to leave her, won't I? Just for the sake of safety."

Reardon couldn't contain himself any longer. "I
thought you said they wanted the journals, not Dillian!
By the devil, if anyone . . ."

Gavin made an imperial wave of his hand. "That
could very well be, in which case, they think themselves
safe now that the solicitor's office has very conveniently
burned to the ground. Not a particularly creative
thinker," he commented. "That does not mean they believe Dillian knows nothing of the journal's contents."

Dillian gestured in exasperation. "Shall I make a public announcement of my incompetency as an heiress?
Perhaps I can convince the world I cannot read. I daresay Reardon knows more of those journals than I do.
They were written almost entirely in code. I can't imagine what my father thought I would do with them. If
he'd left stock or notes or anything of financial value in
them I would have noticed."

Reardon smacked his forehead. "Code! Of course. He

wrote the blamed journals in code. I should have remembered. Gad, hack a man's leg to pieces and his mind goes with it. Lord, I'm sorry, Dillian. And now it's all gone. Gad, I've made a muck of it."

"You made a muck of it when you hired on with Neville," Dillian answered coldly. "Now I suppose duty requires that you go back to him and announce that I'm definitely Whitnell's daughter and I've got Blanche hidden away for my own devious purposes."

"Rein that tongue of yours until I'm done here," Gavin warned her. "Reardon will do no such thing. Anglesey still thinks Blanche in the south of France. He's given the lieutenant orders to follow her there."

Dillian looked only moderately appeased. "Have a lovely journey, James. I understand France is quite nice at this time of year. Please take your time and enjoy it."

Gavin covered her mouth with his gloved hand and gave the violent objection in Reardon's face a look of warning. The younger man remained silent, but he still watched Gavin warily, with good cause. Looked at from the soldier's point of view, he saw a scarred sinister aristocrat manhandling a woman Reardon thought of as a sister, showing a shocking degree of familiarity. Gavin didn't care. With Dillian's life in danger, society's niceties eluded him.

"Reardon intends to return to the duke with confirmation of your identity, yes. It's pointless continuing the charade. You cannot spend the rest of your life avoiding the men who knew you and your father well." He released her mouth so she might speak again.

Dillian sighed and contemplated this announcement. "As the infamous Colonel Whitnell's daughter, I cannot continue as Blanche's companion, but I'm a danger to her life. I could not continue in any event." A look of sorrow crossed her face. "I would not see her reputation harmed, Gavin. Is there not anything we can do to prevent that?"

Gavin felt the now familiar tug on his heartstrings as he gazed into her pensive face. He had just handed her orders that meant she would no longer have a home and family or means of supporting herself, and she worried about her cousin instead of her own fate. He wanted to tell her she would never have anything to worry about, that he would take care of everything, but he knew the selfishness of that thought. She needed choices, not ultimatums. He cared too much for her feelings to force her into anything simply because she thought she had no choice.

Reardon momentarily came to the rescue. "Colonel Whitnell's daughter ought to possess the highest reputation known to society, as high as Wellington's. No shame should connect to Lady Blanche for keeping your company. Don't worry, Dillian, your father has friends. We'll see to it that your father's reputation is restored so you may hold your head up wherever you go."

Dillian patted his hand and gave him a stilted smile. "You are very good, James, but we both know my father was a notorious gambler, a troublemaker par none, and a devil-may-care rakehell. Even should you somehow clear these ridiculous rumors about his loyalty, you cannot deny what he was."

'When we are through with him, your father will appear a saint next to the real culprits," Reardon assured her.

Dillian looked at him with puzzlement, then turned to Gavin for explanation. He liked the notion that she believed him responsible for this turn of events. He didn't try dissuading her.

"Your father didn't keep his theories quiet. His friends knew his opinions on every subject. They are getting together this evening to put together a list of everything they remember. Your father often complained of high-level incompetence, but in latter days, he believed a conspiracy afoot. We don't know yet if he had evidence, but he believed the guns and cannon shipped to Wellington's troops were of a quality inferior to those ordered, that delays in shipping supplies were not entirely accidental, and that other similar events came from someone well paid to harm the cause."

"Treason," Dillian whispered. "That's not possible. Why wouldn't he have immediately reported it to his superiors?"

"Because his superiors could very well have been involved," Reardon answered for him.

And Gavin added, "And because there is some likelihood someone he knew well was part of it. Why else would he be suspicious when no one else was?"

Gavin caught Dillian's hand reassuringly when she recognized the possibilities involved. Her eyes reminded him of bruised violets when they turned to him.

"Surely, not Blanche's father?" she whispered.

Gavin shook his head, but Reardon answered. "Whitnell and Perceval were the best of friends. They wouldn't have remained so in that case. Since your father had no immediate family other than your mother's, and your mother's family was related to Perceval's, then the person he suspected could be familiar to both of them."

Dillian shook her head blankly. "My mother's family disowned her. They never moved in government circles in any case. Her parents died quite some time ago. Her only living family was Blanche's mother—" She looked up and turned from one to the other. "That leads us back to Blanche's father."

"And to his family," Gavin reminded her gently.

"Neville?"

Again, Reardon answered. "Neville's father. Neville was still at Oxford at the time."

"Oh, my word." Disbelief turned to horror. "Both my father and Blanche's died at Waterloo. Do you think . . ." She shook her head in shock and looked up at Gavin. "Neville's father inherited the marquessate with the death of Blanche's father. He would have inherited the dukedom if he hadn't caught the smallpox."

Gavin didn't hide the grimness of his tone. "If that's the case, then justice was certainly served by fate. But I wouldn't blame the man for Waterloo or fratricide, just greed. Neville's father was in a position to deal with military contracts."

"Along with the Earl of Dismouth, Anglesey's best friend," Reardon supplied, in case Dillian had forgotten.

"Neville's father's best friend," Dillian corrected. "Neville relied on his father's old friend for advice when his father and grandfather both died and he suddenly found himself duke. I never liked the man, but then, I never liked Neville."

"You never liked the power he had over Lady Blanche," Gavin corrected complacently. "You're a hard woman, Dillian Whitnell, but we'll forgive you. In the meantime, you're about to run off to France to meet your cousin."

"I'm what?" Dillian asked with incredulity.

"About to run off to France," Gavin repeated in a voice of firm determination. "You may take Blanche with you in whatever disguise you prefer. You are leaving the country immediately."

Before Dillian could say "Balderdash," Reardon joined Gavin's commands. "I'm going to announce that I've got the last of your father's journals. You know nothing of them."

Dillian looked from Reardon to Gavin. "Has it ever occurred to you to wonder," she asked with firm finality, "why no one has looked for those journals or endangered Blanche's life until six months ago—when James returned from the Continent?"

Without any further warning than that, she stood up and walked away, losing herself rapidly in the crowded boulevard ahead.

Thirty-four

Sitting cross-legged on the meager cot he had taken in the servants' attic, Michael narrowed his eyes over the pages spread before him and dipped his pen in ink. Sheets of expensive vellum from the desks below lay in a blizzard of white across the covers and on the floors, all covered with the same nearly indecipherable scratching

Ignoring the chaos he'd created, Michael continued scratching frantically across the sheet he worked on.

He glanced up only at a hesitant knock on his door. Looking around at the maelstrom of papers surrounding him, he unburied himself quickly, leaping to the floor and opening the door just a fraction.

His eyes widened at the sight of the fragile lady of the house in these narrow halls. Hastily, he stepped through the doorway and guided her toward the stairs.

"You have no business up here, my lady," he said bluntly. "If you wish to speak with me, you could have sent someone to fetch me."

"That's not any more proper," Blanche objected. "Dillian isn't here. I can't go sending for young male guests while unchaperoned."

Gavin would appreciate the idiocy of that speech, Michael reflected, but he didn't voice his opinion aloud. Gallantly bowing, he took the closed stairs first, as was proper in case the lady's foot slipped. When he reached the carpeted hall below, he held out his arm to help the lady on the last few enclosed steps. "Now we are on common ground. What may I do for you?"

"Dillian hasn't returned from her walk with Lord Ef-

fingham. Do you know if he meant to keep her away
this long?"

Michael rather calculated if Gavin could persuade the
lady to a room with a bed, they might not see the pair
for a week, but he supposed he ought not mention that
aloud. "If she's with Gavin, she's quite safe. You, on the
other hand, are an open invitation for evildoers. Take
yourself down to the library, set husky footmen at every
door, and I shall be down shortly with a task to keep
your mind occupied until she returns."

Her blazing smile of delight eased his discomfort at
sharing his usually secret activities. He had little practice
at sharing and much at keeping secrets. Perhaps it was
time he learned to share.

"You've talked to the little witch? What did she say?
Will she tell you where she's hidden Lady Blanche?"
Neville stood firmly behind his desk, for all intents and
purposes a calm man in perfect control of his destiny.
Only a man who knew him well might detect the note
of anxiety behind his question.

"She seems quite determined to have her father's papers, Your Grace," Reardon replied respectfully to the
man behind the desk, ignoring the older man in the corner chair. "She seems to believe they contain her inheritance, and she blames you if they're lost. She may have
some grounds for complaint, sir. I carried the last journal
in my kit and idled my convalescence by translating it.
With the aid of the other journals, I might determine
the names of the personages of whom he writes. From
what I can tell, those people would pay well to keep
their secrets."

"Blackmail? The fellow engaged in blackmail? Devil
take it, you are saying my cousin kept company with the
daughter of such a rotter all these years? She may have
found some way of holding Blanche hostage to her dirty
secrets! I will not have it! Hand over what you have,
Reardon, and I'll have the authorities after her at once.
Blackmail! It's inconceivable." The young, fair-haired
man behind the desk appeared moved to near apoplexy.

"Pardon, Your Grace, but the lady is entitled to her

inheritance, no matter what it contains. She may be completely innocent. So might her father. I never saw that either of them lived particularly well. Whitnell and Lady Blanche's father were close associates. The connection might be quite innocent. I have promised to hold the journal for the lady until she decides what to do with it."

"Under the circumstances, Reardon, that may not be entirely wise," a soft voice spoke from the corner. "You have heard what happened to the last two places where the journals resided? Perhaps you should commend them to safer hands."

Reardon turned to the speaker. "I do not wish to disagree with you, Lord Dismouth, but the lady thought she had placed the other journals in safe hands. Perhaps I will do a little better job of it."

Dismouth nodded politely in acknowledgment, and a few minutes later, Reardon found himself dismissed, unaware that his departure was watched from a window several floors below the one he had just recently occupied.

When Gavin knocked at the door of the Perceval town house later that day and Michael answered looking visibly distracted and covered with ink, Gavin grabbed his coat lapels, shoved him inside, and slammed the door after him.

"You have those blasted journals, don't you? I swear, I'll find a rope and hang you this time, Michael. If I can't find a damned tree limb high enough, I'll dangle you from the chimneys."

A picture in gauzy white drifted from the library, her golden hair straggling from her coiffure like moonbeams on her shoulders as she watched the two men with no visible sign of distress. Gavin noticed her hands were as ink-splattered as Michael's, but her words caught him more forcibly than her looks.

"Where is Dillian, my lord? It is most urgent that we speak with her."

"She didn't come back here?" Gavin shouted, dropping Michael instantly and running for the stairs. "Are you certain she didn't come back to hare off on her own? I counted on you holding her until I got here."

He practically flew up the stairs, long cloak flying behind him. Michael and Blanche took the stairs right behind him.

By the time they reached Dillian's room, Gavin had already stalked through it. Except that the maids had made the bed, it looked little different than the night before. The trunk still waited, partially packed, for its owner's return.

Gavin groaned and drove his hand through his hair as he stared bleakly at his brother. "Where is she?"

Looking thoughtful, Michael tapped his pen's quill to his lips. "Several possibilities arise . . ." He glanced around at expectant faces, shrugged, and led the way back to the hall. "I suppose a council of war is called for. Could we at least have tea before I famish?"

Dillian glared at the locked coach door as the coach ambled through the last remaining hours of daylight. She hadn't much liked thinking herself such an incompetent ninnyhammer that any pusillanimous henwit could come along and shove her inside a coach and abduct her. She didn't like thinking it, but it seemed to have happened.

If the brigands didn't stop for food soon, she thought she might starve to death. However, she would have a thing or two to say to the men who dared treat her this way, before starving.

She had tried pounding at the windows and yelling while they passed through busy London streets, but the clatter of wagon wheels, the shouts of street hawkers, and the noise of her own coach and driver drowned out any feeble effort she made.

Now they traveled along country roads, and she saw no one. If they would just slow down long enough to pass a farm wagon or something, she might break open the jammed window to lean out and attract someone's attention, but they passed no one at this time of evening. All the farmers had sensibly returned home to their nice, warm dinners.

Grinding her teeth in frustration, Dillian clasped her

fists firmly around her frothy reticule. She felt a fool in all this filmy lavender and lace, but she not only had her reticule, she'd hung on to her parasol. Her father's men had taught her to use whatever weapons came to hand. She need only wait until her enemy appeared.

As dusk drew on, they reached a village with a coaching inn, and her eyes lit with anticipation. Some of the joy died out of them a few minutes later when the driver jumped down and entered the inn alone. She scanned the empty yard looking for any sign of aid, finding none other than the saddled horse at the trough. If only she could reach the horse—

The driver reappeared carrying a bowl and a mug. Triumphantly, Dillian watched him crossing the darkening yard in her direction. Men were such fools, she thought pityingly. Just because she wore ruffles and lace, this poor idiot thought her so helpless that he dared approach her with his hands full.

Pulling the pistol from her reticule and holding her parasol aloft, she prepared to put an end to that spectacularly silly notion.

"You haven't slept all night," Blanche protested weakly as she watched the marquess don a fresh cravat borrowed from Michael's wardrobe. "You cannot go out there like that. You haven't even shaved," she added daringly.

"You could add his eyes are bloodshot, he looks gray as death, and a bit of a shade hungover," Michael added helpfully as he handed his splendid glossy hat to the man standing in front of the hall mirror.

"Thanks to you," Gavin growled. "You kept handing me that damned flask. She's not anywhere you expected, damnit! What do you think I ought to do? Go to bed and sleep on it?"

No one dared mention the obvious fact that Dillian had no actual connection to the marquess to demand that he do anything at all. Gavin owed her nothing. For all anyone knew, she'd gone tearing off on her own. They'd already sent messengers riding off to Hampshire and Hertfordshire, just in case. Effingham had done more than any one man could be expected to do for a female of small acquaintance. Both people standing here now made no such suggestion.

"You can't appear in the House of Lords like that, sir," Blanche said firmly. "You look like the Grim Reaper. They will run screaming in terror."

That image made him smile even more malevolently, that and the fact that the ever gracious Lady Blanche had just insulted him in her impatience. Gavin adjusted the hat on his head and drew his cloak more firmly around his rumpled coat.

"Be glad I do not wear the hood, my lady," he informed her coldly. Before they could throw any more obstacles in his way, Gavin grasped his walking stick, picked up the heavy satchel at his feet, and strode out, cloak billowing around him.

Michael sighed and grimaced as he turned back to the pale woman wringing her hands beside him. "I believe Gavin has just donned his hero hat, my lady. There is no reasoning with him once he does that. We can only hope to divert disaster. I will leave you with Cousin Marian while I find a safe depository for those papers. Get some sleep while you can. One of us will need it." He didn't wait for her protests but strode off to the library in a manner very similar to the man who had just left.

No one actually ran screaming from the stately halls of Parliament as the American Marquess of Effingham marched through them. A few observers may have looked for the army he appeared to lead, or at least anticipated drums and fifes. Others stepped out of his way, their eyes widening in horror as Effingham's grim face and burning dark eyes came into view. A low hum of interest grew to a noticeable murmur of alarm as word spread.

Uncaring of the sight he presented, Gavin strode through enemy territory with only one thought in mind—Dillian. If any of these effete dilettantes had harmed her, he would see them crucified. He couldn't bear thinking Dillian terrified, alone, and hurt. He cringed inwardly with horror and helplessness at just the passing thought of it. He refused to be helpless. He preferred rage. No man could touch what was his and live to speak of it. Rage carried him through these alien halls of elegant, whispering aristocrats.

He saw their haughty heads bend together and murmur in horrified tones as he passed. He grimaced terrifyingly at a guard who hurried to keep him out. Producing his card with the same flourish as a sword, Gavin shoved past the man and strode on.

Neville rushed toward him from the far end of the hall, but Gavin ignored his gesticulations. Michael had searched the duke's premises last night and found no trace of Dillian. The duke could suffer the torments of the damned along with everyone else. Gavin gave no preferential treatment.

He'd already sent word ahead. They expected him. They didn't know what to expect, he fully realized. He didn't care about that, either. He'd never had any notion of using his blasted title to stride into the most powerful house in England, walk in front of hundreds of the most respected, wealthiest, powerful men in the world, and fling their damned futures in their faces. But he would. For Dillian.

Gavin strode past formally wigged men in dark robes holding out their hands in greeting. Cloak flapping, he shoved past men who expected recognition. He'd disdained making a spectacle of himself in the past. He'd hid himself in shadows, protected himself from unwelcome notice, protected the innocent from his fearsome visage, but he protected no one now but Dillian. The American navy captain he once had been now arrived in his enemies' hallowed halls.

Arriving at last at the podium facing a chamber rapidly filling with robed aristocrats, Gavin slammed his satchel down in front of all the expectant, horrified faces, and threw off his hat so they could see him clearly. "I will trade all your dirty secrets, gentlemen," he announced in a voice that rang through the halls outside, "for the return of Miss Reynolds Whitnell. I don't give a good damn which of you sold out your country for the devil's coin. I want Colonel Whitnell's daughter re-

turned—whole and unharmed—within the next twelve
hours, or I shall have these journals published in every
bloody newspaper in the land!" He dumped the satchel's
contents on the table before him, spilling out a dozen
black-bound books.

From the ranks of the audience, at least three separate
sets of eyes watched the journals with special interest
and felt the marquess's scarred and terrifying visage
glowering directly at them. Not one of the owners of
those eyes dared rise and leave the room.

Thirty-five

The pistol blast spun her abductor backward when the parasol didn't quite accomplish the task. Dillian regretted the necessity of leaving the villain sprawled in the dust of the coach yard instead of questioning him, but she had no intention of allowing any of the rather large men rushing from the inn a chance to catch her. Fleeing for the saddled horse, she climbed the trough, ripped her lovely skirt, and threw her leg over the saddle. Shouts of pure amazement followed her out of the yard

She had watched the road signs carefully this time. She knew precisely where she was. She thought it kind of her abductor to go in a familiar direction. Kind, or the mark of treachery.

She wouldn't think about that. She couldn't believe Effingham would abduct her, not even for her own good. It was just coincidence that the coach had taken the road toward Hertfordshire and Arinmede Manor.

Concentrating on escaping, Dillian didn't notice the weary horseman sometime later resting his horse at a nearby creek. Any man with half an eye would notice her, however.

Gavin appropriated an office in the very center of Parliament's hallowed halls, in a room in full view of soldiers, guards, and any respected member who lingered outside the chambers. The satchel sat in the center of the desk, quite close to the place where he contemptuously rested his feet.

The first person who dared brave his scowl was a slight man of indeterminate age, bespectacled, and far from forbidding. He barely raised his balding head above the height of Gavin's shoes.

"I've come to say . . . That is, I regret what has happened to the lady . . . I had no idea. You see, it's all my fault, I'm sure. I just did what I thought best, as my father taught me. Now, I'm not so sure It's just that—"

Gavin impatiently slammed his feet to the floor and leaning over the desk, glared at his stuttering visitor. "Do I know you?"

The visitor gulped. "I apologize, my lord. I've been so distraught since the fire. I cannot keep my wits about me. I'm Winfrey, sir. Archibald Winfrey, Lady Blanche's solicitor."

"Do you know where I can find Miss Whitnell?" Gavin demanded.

"No, no. Not at all, my lord," the solicitor continued stuttering, worrying his hat brim between his hands. "That is just it, my lord. The lady cannot have her father's papers. I beg pardon for saying this, my lord, but neither can you. I had the papers all safe in my office, sir. I never meant to keep the lady from her fortune, if that's what they are. I simply protected them at the duke's behest. The lady asked for them, I know, but I did not realize—"

"You did not realize what you held?" Gavin asked menacingly. "For surely you realized you wrongfully kept the lady from what was hers."

"But, my lord . . ." the solicitor stuttered, backing away slightly from his fury. "The duke . . . Her cousin . . . You see, I thought to help—"

Gavin slammed open the satchel and waved a black book from its interior in the solicitor's face. "Is this what you came to see, Winfrey? Would you care to look inside it and verify its genuineness?"

Winfrey's eyes widened. "How did you . . . ? It's not possible. They all burned." He twisted his cravat as Gavin flung book after book onto the desk in front of him. "They're not even singed," he whispered in astonishment.

"Magic." Gavin smiled grimly. "One wave of my wand, and they're miraculously restored. If I must sit here much longer, I may resort to reading them. Perhaps you would care to tell a few of your clients that, Mr. Winfrey?"

The man backed out, still stuttering. Gavin gave a nod to a man posted directly outside, and a shadow followed the solicitor through the wide corridors of government.

This was going to be a damned long day, Gavin decided, returning his feet to the desk. He preferred action to sitting here like a duck ripe for the plucking. If he had to sit here much longer, he might just pull out his sword and go after the Duke of Anglesey personally. He wasn't a particularly patient man, and the idea of Dillian in anyone else's hands made him helpless with fury. He meant to destroy *something* before the day ended. It might as well be a duke. He concentrated on his growing fury and not the tearing hollow of fear for Dillian opening inside him.

A few hours later, Michael and Reardon appeared at the door of the chamber he'd appropriated. Gavin had entertained viscounts and dukes, the prime minister, and an assortment of other characters satisfying their curiosities or looking for his support in one cause or another these last hours. He wasn't in much humor to entertain his throwback of a brother and a man who'd left a lady penniless for the better part of two years. He glared at them both. Neither man showed a flicker of fear. They merely closed the door behind them.

"Montague has spirited Lady Blanche to safety," Michael informed him the instant the door closed. "He feared Marian would have the child early if he didn't do something drastic."

"Lady Blanche isn't in any damned danger. Dillian is," Gavin growled, flinging himself to a standing position and prowling the floor. "I can't bear sitting here any longer. I'll leave the blamed books with you. There's got to be some trace of her somewhere, and I mean to find it."

Reardon stepped in front of him, blocking him into a corner. "Forgive me, my lord, but I have to ask your intentions when you find her. Your public display has

made your partiality quite blatant. I will not have the
lady's reputation damaged further by allowing you to go
haring off after her."

Gavin's eyes narrowed dangerously. He ignored the
alarm in Michael's warning gesture. He saw only a
spoiled English soldier standing in his way. With murder
already raging through his veins, he didn't have patience
for politeness. He wrapped both fists in Reardon's gold-
buttoned coat and lifted the heavier man clear of the
floor.

"If you have any idea whatsoever," he spoke slowly
and distinctly, so there could be no mistake, "any idea
at all where Miss Whitnell can be found, you had best
spit it out now or you'll fly through that window within
the next ten seconds."

Since the window in question was several floors above
street level and the marquess commenced to counting
the seconds, Reardon squirmed uneasily in his grip.

Michael picked up two of the black books and juggled
them. "We know where she was seen last. Put your energy to something more useful."

Reardon sent Michael a look of gratitude as Gavin
instantly dropped his coat and swung his attention to his
brother, who now had two books and an ink pot circling.

"Where?" he demanded with such force the ink pot
should have shattered.

Slipping the books and pot back to the desk one by
one, Michael eyed Gavin's rage skeptically. "What do
you intend to do if we tell you?"

"It's a matter of what I intend to do if you don't."
The quiet fury of Gavin's voice spoke louder than his
earliest bellows. "You know what to do with these books
when I leave here. I've a man following Winfrey. You
two take care of the others. I'm going after Dillian."

Reardon still looked ready to launch another protest.
Michael averted the confrontation with a shrug. "Your
messenger saw her on the road to Arinmede late last
evening."

Cursing low and long, Gavin grabbed his hat and
cloak and swept out without so much as a by-your-leave
to the men remaining behind.

Taking full advantage of his cousin-in-law's extensive stable, Gavin had his mount galloping full speed toward the roads of Hertfordshire within the hour. He calculated Dillian had been gone well over twenty-four hours now. Anything could happen in twenty-four hours. His heart rode in his throat as he imagined what a gang of ruffians could do to a woman in just a few short hours.

But she was alive. The messenger had seen her alive and riding toward Arinmede. He thought he just might murder her when he found her. Why in hell had she gone to Arinmede?

Knowing Dillian, any of a thousand and one answers came to mind. He had no intention of fretting his brain to discover which one. He just needed to see that she was safe, and then he would murder her.

Not until he reached the sight of the overgrown pines lining the drive to his ruin of a home did Gavin think to wonder why he concerned himself at all with the wayward brat. He could have stayed in London, caught the thief and arsonist, and allowed Dillian to molder here until he had time to come back and pin her hide to the wall. No wonder Michael and Reardon had looked at him oddly. He was losing his mind.

Or some other more vital part of his anatomy, like his heart. He would consider that later. Right now he must figure out how to trap Dillian all over again, because he'd already figured out her main reason for coming to Arinmede. She could hide in there forever, and no one would ever find her. Except him.

The crumbling stable hardly seemed fit for his valiant horse, but Gavin quietly brushed the horse down, and gave him what oats he could find before slipping back through the midnight darkness. He glanced carefully over the house, finding no lamp burning but the one Matilda kept in the servants' hall.

Dillian was in there. She had to be. He couldn't think otherwise. Rage and something entirely foreign buzzed inside him as he slipped in the side door. He didn't stop to decipher the various emotions rampaging through him right now. First, he would get his hands on Dillian.

He must do this methodically or she would know he

was here and deliberately hide. He'd not find her for a
week that way. No, he had to think like Dillian. Where
would she hide if she didn't know her enemy or when
he would arrive?

Not downstairs. The servants might find her there. He
could check the dumbwaiter first, he supposed, but the
secret passage seemed a better bet. He just prayed she
hadn't found a passage that he hadn't discovered yet.

Gavin slipped up the back stairs and down the short
hall to the master bedroom and the nearest entrance to
the passage. Without a candle guiding his way, he could
fall over her. He'd left candles aplenty in the master
chamber. Just remembering that night Dillian had given
herself to him made him ache in more places than the
one easily aroused. He'd been a cad, but she'd been
more beautiful than any woman he'd ever known. He
wouldn't allow anyone else to hurt her, not even himself.

He found a candlestick in the holder just inside the
bedchamber door, along with the tinderbox. Trying to
make no noise, he lit the wick and cupped his hand
around the flame until it steadied. Then holding it high,
he stepped into the chamber, aiming for the wardrobe
and the hidden door.

Gavin didn't have to go that far. He found Dillian
sleeping in the middle of his bed, her dark curls tumbled
artlessly over her face, her lavender gown in tatters, and
one of his old coats clutched snugly against her breasts.

He wanted to scream at her carelessness. Instead, the
sight destroyed some barrier inside him, shattered it to
bits, leaving him wide open and vulnerable to this impish
sprite who had stolen his bed and his heart and, apparently, anything resembling his mind.

All thoughts of murder dissipated as he approached
the bed and her eyes fluttered open.

"Gavin," Dillian whispered, not moving from where
she lay. She looked up at the lean, cloak-draped figure
shadowed in candlelight. She could see the elegant
gleam of his white cravat against his bronzed skin, and
she smiled sleepily. "You only need an eye patch to
make a lovely pirate."

"I died a thousand deaths on the way out here," he

informed her dryly, sitting down to discard his shoes. "I think I ought to make you suffer a few of them. Would you at least tell me truly what the hell you're doing here?"

She made a grimace of disgust. "I was stupid enough to let someone abduct me. It was quite unpleasant, and I thought I might starve." She looked at him curiously as he stripped off his coat. "It seemed rather odd that they took me on the road to Hertfordshire."

"Or Bedford," he reminded her. "Or York for all that matters. Where is Anglesey?"

"Bedford," she admitted sleepily, her caution now diverted to another area. "What do you think you're doing?" she asked as he pulled off his shirt.

"Going to bed. I haven't had a wink of sleep in two days. Move over."

She moved over. And when the Marquess of Effingham lay sprawled, half-naked beside her, Dillian curled up next to the heat of him and promptly returned to the soundest sleep she'd known in weeks.

Dillian woke with her tattered dress tangled around her waist, lying spoon fashion within the curve of Gavin's long body, with his big hand proprietarily resting on her nearly bare hip. She held her breath, uncertain what to do, not wanting to wake him but not wanting to let him think her wanton if he should wake. Foolish notion, she scoffed to herself. How much more wanton could she be?

She knew she should break away when his hand began caressing her, but she couldn't quite find it in herself to do so. She knew herself as strong-willed, but his touch robbed her of all willpower. Perhaps he would stop with just a caress.

She must be getting addlepated. She knew Gavin as a sensual man with strong appetites. What had ever made her think he would stop with a single caress? She should have jumped out of bed the moment he climbed into it last night. His hand drifted higher to cup the mound of her breast, and the muscles in her womb clenched with desire.

"Gavin?" she whispered a trifle breathlessly as she felt the strength of his fingers through the layers of cloth.

"I want to love you properly," he murmured from behind her, his voice reflecting a hint of perplexity, "but I don't know how to go about it. If I let you up from here, you'll run, and I may never have another chance."

Dillian turned on her back and found Gavin's scarred face hovering over her, the uncertainty reflected there as well as in his voice. She'd never seen him uncertain. Gavin was a man who rode out into the world with clear purpose and a course of action. She couldn't believe she made him hesitant.

She traced the scar along his upper lip. "I need you," she whispered, disbelieving her own ears but knowing deep inside her that she spoke the truth. "Hold me?"

She watched the muscles in the broad shoulders above her relax slightly. He bent and kissed her nose, the corner of her mouth, and her ear. "I'll hold you forever, if I can. I warn you now."

She ignored the warning. Words meant nothing. The heat of his kiss as he finally pressed his mouth to hers meant everything.

She felt safe here. For the first time in her life, she'd found a place where she belonged. Dillian wrapped her arms around Gavin's neck and knew the protection of his greater strength. She wouldn't question the wrongness of what she did, or the possible results. She just needed the reassurance of his strong arms holding her, his hard body sheltering her, just for the moment. Just until she knew what to do next.

Gavin's tongue swirled inside her mouth, and every ounce of her yearned for more. Dillian arched into him, and felt his hand brush aside the featherweight of her gown and chemise to find purchase around her breast. She gave a moan of pure pleasure when his fingers finally sought the aching crest.

"I want all of you," Gavin said harshly, burying his face against her throat and nibbling at her there. "I can't pretend I'm a gentleman any longer. I'll not play the gallant, Dillian. I mean to take you and keep you."

She knew his words should alarm her, but his roaming

hands had aroused her to a plane beyond fear, and she didn't wish to be bothered with words. She could come to no harm while he touched her.

She still believed that minutes later when the remains of her clothes disappeared over the side of the bed. Gavin still wore his tight breeches, but his arousal strained so hard against the buttons that she couldn't bear letting him suffer longer. She couldn't believe her boldness when she reached to unfasten him, but she worked faster at his deep groan of approval.

When, between them, they had the buttons undone, Gavin murmured his ecstasies to her breasts as he pushed them together and devoted his attention to each in turn. Dillian quivered in delight as he suckled and stroked, then she nearly melted when he slid his hand down between her legs to stroke her there.

She had no understanding of the hold this ungentlemanly marquess had over her. A scarred beast, a military American, a man who scorned all she knew and loved, he ought to send her fleeing into the countryside. Instead, she opened her arms and heart and herself to him and took him inside her.

He drove deep, possessing her as he never had before. She tilted her hips to take him even deeper, and he held her there, not allowing her to twist away when their rhythm grew more forceful. As he pounded against her womb, the waves of sensation washed away all conscious thought. She rose to meet him as surely as the ocean met the sand. When the breakers finally crashed against the shore, she cried out at the rush of his seed carried on waves of ecstasy.

Only then did she realize what his warning meant. He had meant to claim her, and he had.

He'd planted his seed deep within her, where it could take root and grow. She might leave this bed carrying his child. In this, he had not protected her. Not this time.

She didn't know whether to weep for joy or dismay as Gavin's heavy body collapsed against her, trapping her within the confines of the feather mattress. She flung her arms around his neck and allowed him to kiss her into insensibility again.

Thirty-six

"Where do you think you're going?" Breathless from running down the front stairs, Dillian grabbed the belt she'd made of Gavin's cravat to keep her loose boy's breeches from falling. She'd stolen one of his shirts from the wardrobe, and the huge billowing sleeves made her an odd sight indeed. The maid dusting the front hall fainted dead away at the sight of her. Dillian didn't stop to concern herself. She wouldn't let Gavin get away without her.

Even seeing her flying from the house didn't keep Gavin from mounting the saddled stallion. He gave her a disapproving scowl as she grabbed his reins, but he softened enough to offer explanation of his departure. "I left Michael with those damned journals. It's time I found out who most needs them destroyed. Now, get yourself back inside the house, where you can't be seen. You know how to hide yourself well enough here. You should be safe until I return."

Direct and to the point. He didn't even raise an eyebrow at her ungainly attire. Dillian thought she could love a man like that, but right now she wanted to clobber him. "Those are my journals! I have every right to know what's in them. and I want to see the villain thrown in the darkest dungeon we can find. You go nowhere without me, Gavin Lawrence!"

He leaned over and pried her fingers loose of the reins. "I risked your life the other day. I don't intend risking it again. Get yourself back upstairs where you belong."

She smacked his hand and tangled her fist more forcefully in the leather. "You have stones for brains, Mr.

Lawrence! You risked nothing then, and you risk nothing now. I take full responsibility for my own actions. Let me go with you."

"Dillian, if you don't get your hands off those reins now, I'm coming down to take them off, and you won't like it if I do!" he threatened, catching her wrist in a powerful grip.

"You may spew pebbles from that stony brain as you will, Lord Effingham, but you won't scare me. Take me up with you at once, or I shall follow on my own." She'd thought he'd know that by now, but it seemed he needed reminding.

He glared, and before Dillian realized what he intended, Gavin swung down from the horse and gathered her up in his arms, holding her so close against him she feared to breathe.

"I'm not your father, Dillian," he growled against her ear. "I protect what is mine. Someone dared harm you. I will teach them and anyone else with similar thoughts that they can't get away with that. Don't get in my way, Dillian."

"I hate military men!" She tried screaming at him, but the words came out a whimper as she pounded her fist against his impervious chest. "Can't you see that if you must fight, I must fight beside you?" She didn't know where her anger had gone, but tears threatened to take its place. He would ride off as her father had and never return. She couldn't allow it. She just couldn't.

Her hot tears scorched through the cambric of his shirt as she buried her face against him. Her tears could destroy his defenses more surely than anger. Her words confused him. No one had ever offered to fight beside him before. He had just assumed it was his responsibility to defend those weaker than himself. Michael had found ways of working around him. No one else had ever tried.

"Dillian, I can do this better if I'm not worrying about you," he said gently, caressing her lovely disheveled curls. Her tears crumbled his remaining defenses, but he couldn't let her know that.

"You won't come back," she accused. "You won't! I want to go with you."

Gavin recognized that feeling of desertion all too well. He'd learned to overcome it, he'd thought. But he saw now that he'd merely isolated himself from everyone so they couldn't desert him, so no one could hurt him again. But her tears were killing him. He dearly wanted to keep her with him, to hold her close so no one could touch her but himself, to cherish her and protect this rare treasure he had yet to fully explore. At the same time, warning signals screamed in his brain. He couldn't risk her, even if he dared risk himself.

"Dillian, I'll come back," he told her firmly, lifting her teary face from his shirt. "This is my home, and I won't abandon it, or you. I'm asking you to trust me. Will you do that?"

The shimmering diamonds in violet eyes nearly undid him when she turned her face up to study his. She seemed so very intent, so horribly vulnerable. At the same time he saw her intelligence, knew her trust rested not on blind instinct but her experience and wisdom. He held his breath while he waited for her answer.

"Is Blanche safe?" she demanded.

"I should imagine she's on one of the Earl of Mellon's estates right now, surrounded by armed guards and my indomitable cousin and her husband. She's safe. You're not. You're the one they really want, Dillian."

She nodded reluctant agreement to this assessment. Her fingers traced Gavin's scars, caressing them gently, loving them with her touch. "I trust you," she finally admitted. "I just don't trust your brand of heroics. I want you back alive and in one piece, not on a stretcher or in a casket."

Hope wrapped a stranglehold around Gavin's heart. He hadn't dared hope— He still didn't dare hope. He had nothing to offer but an empty title and a Gothic ruin.

He smiled grimly. "I assure you, madam, that a weak-kneed politician and a duke or two are no match for someone who took on the British navy with little more than a leaky rowboat. If I know you're safe, I can concentrate on bringing the culprits to justice without distraction."

She released the reins and stepped away from him. She stood alone, straight and strong, and his heart cried out for her. "All right. I'll trust you," he heard he agree reluctantly. "But you had best keep messengers on the road night and day so I know you're alive. If I don't hear from you by tomorrow evening, I'm coming after you."

Her courage captured whatever part of his heart may have eluded her before. Tilting her chin, Gavin kissed her quickly, and swung himself back in the saddle before she tempted him to more. "With any luck at all, Miss Whitnell, I shall return here personally by then. Keep the sheets warm."

"If she hadn't had that blamed pistol with her, there's no telling what could have happened to her," Gavin raged as he stalked up and down the library in the Earl of Mellon's town house.

"We made sure she knew how to defend herself," Reardon claimed in his own defense.

Gavin swung around and glared at him. "She shouldn't *have* to defend herself," he shouted. "She should have friends and family looking after her. If His Majesty's bloody damned soldiers can't do it, then I will!"

"I'm not her bloody damned father!" Reardon yelled back. "I thought she was provided for. I didn't know the journals meant anything. Devil take it, I was in a hospital for a year! What did you want me to do?"

Michael flipped through a book tracing the genealogy of English nobility, adding more scratchings to the mounds of paper collecting on the desk. "The British are so predictable," he murmured, mostly to himself.

Reardon ignored him, but Gavin swung around to point an accusing finger at his brother. "Don't you dare leave here until I'm done with you. Every time I want to talk to you, you disappear. What did you find in those journals?"

Michael tipped his chair back, and tickling his nose with the quill of his pen, stared at the elaborate moldings on the ceiling. "I found Colonel Whitnell thought very highly of himself and not nearly so much of his superiors, except Wellington, of course. He and Lady Blanche's father, whom he calls Perceval regardless of which title he held at the time, enjoyed wine, women and song, not necessarily in that order."

Reardon scowled and threw himself into a chair, but held his tongue. Gavin reached over the desk and appropriated the stack of papers, shuffling through them rapidly, stopping occasionally to examine one more closely. "Go on," he said impatiently as he read. 'Don't make me read the whole blamed thing."

"Whitnell was extremely thorough. You have to give him credit for that," Michael continued, idly separating the quill's feathers. "He was in charge of munitions for a while. He kept records of what he ordered, what he received, and their disbursements. I don't particularly know what set him off, but he started writing friends back in England, inquiring into the manufactories of certain armaments. He had Perceval write friends in government concerning the actual expenditures to different companies. He apparently had lists and inventories comparing costs, invoices, and such. He hid those. They're not in the books."

Gavin had stopped reading, and Reardon stopped scowling. Both men watched Michael expectantly.

Michael shrugged. "He concluded the arms from certain manufactories were substandard for the actual items invoiced, that someone billed the government for two and three times the value of what actually was shipped, and that major amounts of government funds were siphoned into someone's pocket at the expense of Wellington's army. He speculated more than greed lay behind the plot, but he didn't succeed in proving it before he died."

Gavin's fist crumpled around the sheets he held. "Who? Damn you, Michael, who?"

Michael tilted his chair upright again and began scribbling on his notes some more. "Perceval didn't care much for his younger brother, but he refused to believe him capable of treason. He did grant that his brother might be involved in lining his pockets since their father had essentially cut him off from Anglesey. Dismouth and Perceval's brother worked together in the war ministry. Before you leap to any conclusions . . ." He held up his hand to keep Gavin from jumping to his feet. "There is no hint of Neville's involvement in his father's affairs. He was too young."

"But he would do anything to protect his father's name," Gavin growled, leaping to his feet anyway.

"His father left him nothing. Neville didn't even know who Dillian was until recently. Accuse him of attempting to murder Blanche, if you like, but not Dillian."

Gavin growled and returned to stalking up and down the library. "Dismouth, for certain. But why did he wait this long? The journals have been around for two years. Why did he wait until now to go after them and Dillian?"

Reardon stirred uneasily in his seat. "I returned to England about six months ago and started looking for Dillian. I'd ordered Whitnell's personal effects sent home after his death, and I thought to ensure she got them. I asked at the last place I knew she stayed, and they couldn't tell me, so I started asking some of the others who knew her. Dismouth might have got wind of it and started putting two and two together."

Even Michael frowned at the implausibility of this. "He wouldn't know the journals contained anything of interest. If he had, he would have traced them years ago."

"Winfrey!" Gavin shouted from the far end of the room. "Where did Winfrey go after he left me?"

"He's taken offices near King's Court. He went there," Reardon answered with a puzzled frown. "What does a useless old man have to do with anything?"

Gavin stalked back down the length of the library and slammed his fist against the table. "He had the journals and probably the files, too. Blanche said she'd given him the books and left the papers in the vault. Then Neville gave him everything in the vault. That gave Winfrey access to all the material he needed to blackmail anyone listed in those books."

Michael whistled. "The papers weren't with the journals. He must keep them on his person or somewhere no one else could find them. There's no telling how long he's been blackmailing Dismouth, maybe Neville, too. Only they didn't know who was behind the extortion. Reardon must have revealed something about Dillian's inheritance when he returned, and they decided Dillian was the culprit."

"Without those lists, we have no proof it was either Dismouth or the duke," Reardon cautioned him.

Gavin ignored the warning. "Michael, get those journals into the hands of the prime minister immediately. Make copies of those translations. Send one to the war ministry, one to the *Gazette,* and put the other in a damned bank vault if you must. Reardon, either keep Winfrey under observation or lock him up somewhere. Michael, work your magic with the duke. Don't let him out of your sight. Both of you find men to back you up. Have them follow anyone suspicious attempting to meet with either of them. I'm going after Dismouth."

"Winfrey is an old man! Let me go after the earl," Reardon protested.

"Dismouth is mine." Grabbing his cloak from a nearby chair, Gavin swung out of the room without a backward glance.

Cursing, Reardon stood up and glared at Michael. "Winfrey is an old man. I can have him locked in his rooms inside the hour. Who else should I go after?"

Eyes sparkling with mischief, Michael picked up the papers he'd been ordered to copy. "Gavin has no imagination. I think we can make much better use of Winfrey. Let's have him visit the duke."

Gavin had no difficulty learning Dismouth's direction. He expected resistance when he arrived there and had his speech prepared, but the butler let him in without a word once he produced his card.

"His lordship is not at home, my lord," the man announced ponderously. "He gives his apologies and asks that you accept this, sir." He handed Gavin a sealed letter on a silver platter.

An icy chill swept through him. Dismouth shouldn't have expected him unless he thought Gavin had uncovered his involvement in Dillian's abduction. The letter lying there in its pristine splendor screamed of guilt— and desperation.

But Dismouth couldn't have Dillian. Dillian was safe at Arinmede. The earl could threaten and bluff all he liked, but Gavin had Dillian. Knowing that, he tore the seal and swiftly read the letter beneath the butler's stoic gaze.

He read it again, cursed, and shoved it into his pocket. He glared blankly at the servant for a moment, trying to gather his shattered thoughts. Heart pounding, he could only focus on the danger to Dillian. Surely, the earl couldn't have located Dillian yet. The letter was all a bluff. But he couldn't take chances.

Aware that his sinister appearance frightened many, Gavin slammed his hat back on his head and scowled at the butler. "Did the earl take his carriage?" he demanded.

"Not that I'm aware, my lord," the man said stiffly, with a degree of uneasiness as Gavin continued glaring at him.

"I need to know his direction. Who is most likely to know it?" Aware that he insulted the servant by assuming he didn't know, Gavin watched the man draw himself up haughtily.

"I'm sure if I don't know, no other will," the butler replied with disdain. "He had a spare horse sent to the Doulton Inn. That is all anyone can tell you."

The Doulton Inn, on the Hertfordshire road. Gavin felt his insides freeze into a solid chunk of ice. Leaving the butler with a generous gratuity, he stalked down the wide stone steps to his waiting horse, his mind churning with possibilities. He couldn't believe Dismouth knew where to find Dillian. But as the letter crackled in his pocket, Gavin knew he'd shown his hand too plainly this time. At Gavin's appearance in Parliament with the satchel of journals, the earl had assumed himself undone. Dismouth couldn't know Dillian was at Arinmede, but he could discover Arinmede belonged to Gavin. Dis-

mouth would know by now that his hired kidnappers
had failed and on what road they'd lost Dillian. The earl
had taken a wild chance, but a successful one.

And he'd left Dillian alone, unprotected, unsuspecting.
Cursing, Gavin's first instincts were to ride hell-bent for
Arinmede. This time, however, he decided to err on the
side of caution. He stopped at Mellon's town house, and
finding Michael and Reardon already gone, he left messages in the hands of the servants with instructions to
hunt them down and deliver them. Then he borrowed
another of his cousin-in-law's expensive steeds and took
off flying into the evening gloom.

Thirty-seven

Gavin's burning desire for Dillian's safety screamed for a mad dash straight up the lawn and through the front door, but he'd learned a certain degree of caution lately. Concealed by the grove of pines and the shadow of dusk, Arinmede hid its secrets well. If he rode in there without care, anyone in the house would see him. Dismouth was clever enough to take advantage of that fact.

Cursing at the delay, Gavin dismounted, tied his horse behind a tree, and vaulted the crumbling stone wall to the manor lawns. He knew the extent of his boundaries well, knew every inch of the limited land he'd inherited. Overgrown hedges, weeds, and trees grown from seed scattered by wild birds covered almost the entire area that had once been elegantly landscaped lawn. He had no trouble slipping through the shrubbery unseen.

When he saw the first soldier mounted on guard duty at the drive, Gavin fought the urge to scream bloody murder and attack. This was his home. The woman inside belonged to him. Instinct demanded he defend them with his hands and his life. The sight of the second soldier off to the right stilled that insane flight of fantasy.

Dismouth had brought a troop of soldiers.

How could this happen? On what grounds could the earl enlist a troop of soldiers and post them on private property? How could Dismouth even know for certain that Dillian was here?

He couldn't. Dismouth had made assumptions. He knew Arinmede belonged to Gavin. He knew Gavin possessed the journals and sought Dillian's abductor. The earl would want to trade the journals for Dillian, but he would much prefer keeping his secrets. That would mean destroying Gavin and quite possibly, Dillian. In his position of power, the earl could doctor the journals, forge lies, manufacture evidence that Dillian and her father acted treasonously, that Gavin protected a traitor. Few would question a man they knew and respected over a woman and stranger they knew nothing about. Michael was quite right. The English were too predictable.

Gavin found his way back to the road with these thoughts pounding through his head. He hated leaving Dillian in the hands of a scoundrel, but he had to trust Dillian to take care of herself—as she had trusted him to do the same. He couldn't take chances by rushing in there now like a demented idiot. He needed help.

He couldn't wait for Michael and Reardon. He had no way of knowing when they would receive their message and how long it would take them to find horses and get out here. Gavin couldn't sit here and wait until they did. He needed help now, while he had the cover of darkness. He knew of only one place to find it.

A few weeks ago wild horses couldn't have dragged him into the village for any reason. With Dillian's life at stake, wild horses couldn't keep him away. Shedding his concealing hat and cloak, Gavin rode into town and straight to the inn. He entered the bright glow of lantern light, and stood before the crowd inside without cringing at the stares swinging toward him. Smoke from pipes and a badly ventilated chimney choked the air. Ale fumes and the stench of unwashed flesh wafted around him. The scent of fear and hatred reeked even stronger as the crowd recognized him and inched away.

Gavin used the sudden silence to his advantage. "A man who sold inferior guns to Wellington's army has my lady trapped in the manor," he announced to the room at large, his voice carrying easily through the low-ceilinged chamber. He hid his wince at the wariness and fear on the faces of the men turning toward him. He watched as some backed to a far corner, no doubt in the direction of the kitchen exit. Gavin held his temper and his pride, standing straight and tall for their inspection, reciting his tale without pleading. "This villain has brought soldiers who know nothing of his treachery to Arinmede. They have the manor surrounded so I cannot reach my lady. He wants the evidence I hold against him in exchange for her life, but I don't think he'll let her live once I give him what he wants. I must get her out of there, and I need help."

The room remained silent. Sweat beaded on Gavin's brow, and his fingers rolled instinctively into fists. Fury strained to beat obedience out of the sniveling cowards, but he needed their help. He couldn't command it. He had to ask for it. It went against every grain in him. He'd always done everything on his own. This time, he couldn't.

The innkeeper turned an unblinking gaze toward him. "What's in it for us?" he asked suspiciously.

" 'Enry, that ain't polite," another reprimanded. "If 'is lady is the one what 'elped save Emagene's young 'uns, we orter 'elp."

Gavin could see the argument forming on everyone's tongue. He didn't have time for argument. He appealed directly to their pockets. "I have been looking for the owner of the lands that once belonged to the manor, so I can put them back in production. Help me save my lady, and I'll use every power in my possession to buy back those lands and find work for anyone needing employment. No one will go without again."

Startled into silence, everyone in the room stared at him. A low hum of voices immediately followed the silence as speculations began. The lands around Arinmede had lain fallow for decades. The village had shrunk to nearly nothing for lack of any means of support. Those remaining lived in poverty or on the very edge thereof. Wild promises such as these needed careful consideration, but eagerness shone in every eye.

"What can we do?" the innkeeper asked, apparently acting as spokesman.

"I don't want anyone hurt. The soldiers have muskets, so you will have to stay out of their range and hidden as much as possible. If you take the old farm road behind the stable, the stable and darkness will hide you. I need a distraction that will give me time to get inside the manor. I suggest you carry torches and tinderboxes, light them when you reach the stable, and set fire to the haystacks, screaming and hollering like lunatics. I want them to think I'm leading the entire village to the attack. Once the soldiers start running after you, conceal yourselves in the woods. I just need time enough to get inside."

Gavin was aware of the incongruousness of his appearance in this dismal common tavern. He wore the elegant frock coat and cravat of a gentleman, stood taller than any man in here, wore shiny boots, and carried a riding crop. The men around him wore dirty smocks, greasy low-slung cloth hats, and pieces of leather wrapped in string for shoes. They didn't know he felt more at home with them than with the gentlemen his clothing imitated. He hadn't words to explain. He just knew what appealed most to their hearts and strived to break through to them. Gavin prayed the grim appearance of his face didn't affect the way they heard his words.

"You say the man inside is a traitor to His Majesty?" the innkeeper asked, again with suspicion.

"I lost my son in Wellington's army," someone else interrupted.

"I lost my damned arm in the army," a man shouted from the rear. "We ate weevils and dirt because the bloody nobles wouldn't spend their blunt on us."

"You had faulty muskets because of that man in the manor now," Gavin said quietly, his voice reaching over the grumblings in spite of the noise.

It took more persuasion, some coercion, and a great deal of wild promising, but little by little, the men in the tavern picked up their coats and hats, sought out their fellows, rounded up pitchforks and knives, and torches and tinderboxes, and slipped silently into the night after Gavin.

He'd never thought of himself as lord of the manor. He hadn't been raised to it. But he had some inkling of understanding of what it meant as these men looked to him for direction, not only for this moment, but for the future he promised them. He held their lives in his hands. He had a duty to protect them as he had a duty to protect Dillian. He'd never shirked responsibility before. He wouldn't now.

Gavin marched off in the direction of Arinmede, leading an unwieldy mob of villagers.

Neville Perceval, Duke of Anglesey, stared in dismay at the elegantly clad gentleman in gray. His hired investigator's hair gleamed auburn in the fading light, and despite his gentlemanly attire, the man momentarily appeared more leprechaun than real. The duke definitely did not like the flashing green of the man's eyes.

"You are telling me Dismouth and my father were the traitors, not Whitnell," Neville repeated in disbelief

"Correct, Your Grace." Michael showed no sign of impatience as he swung his ebony walking stick and took a seat without invitation. The soldier who had entered with him stood politely near the door, saying nothing.

"And Whitnell's journals are your evidence, and they didn't burn in the fire?"

Michael smiled graciously. "Thanks to myself, of course. I can also tell you where Lady Blanche is, but not until you've satisfactorily proved yourself innocent of recent occurrences. That's why we are here, Your Grace."

"Innocent!" the young duke said with irritation. "Innocent of what, may I ask? And who are you to act as judge and jury?" He sent a look to the soldier at the door. "Reardon, isn't it? Is the man mad?"

Reardon stood at attention. "No, Your Grace. The lady and her companion have been attacked on several occasions. One resulted in severe injuries to Lady Blanche. The most recent caused Miss Whitnell to fire a pistol to save herself. We have reason to believe the journals were the main cause of the attacks, but the fact that many of them involved Lady Blanche leaves your culpability in question, Your Grace. I apologize for the disrespect, sir."

"He apologizes for the disrespect," Anglesey muttered to himself, dropping back against his chair seat and covering his eyes. "Is my cousin safe and well?" he asked, without looking at the intruders.

"Safe and as well as can be expected," Michael answered coolly. "The fire has left some disfigurement, you will understand."

The duke uncovered his face and glared at his visitor. "And you think I'm crude enough to have her so cruelly burned?"

"Someone did," Michael pointed out logically. "You stand most to benefit."

Neville's eyes widened, and he rose from his chair. "Damn, you say!" he muttered as he strode around the desk. "And how do you figure that? She's worth a great deal more to me alive than dead."

Michael's expression didn't reveal a flicker of surprise. "It is quite common knowledge that the lady's possessions revert to Anglesey in the event of her untimely demise, Your Grace."

"It is also quite common knowledge that if she marries me, all her possessions come to Anglesey," the duke retorted. "I'd much rather have the lady than her possessions."

Something flashed swiftly behind the green of Michael's eyes, but his voice reflected none of it. "The lady doubts that, but that is not my concern. Who else benefits from her untimely demise besides yourself?"

The duke stiffened at learning of Blanche's doubts, but his mind willingly chased after the next question rather than the first. His jaw tautened as he considered it. "No one, directly. You understand that as a considerable heiress, Blanche is responsible for immense amounts of property as well as wealth. She has control over manufactories, borough seats, vicarages . . . The list is endless. Any number of people might prefer seeing that power in my hands rather than hers."

"Manufactories," Reardon repeated from the door.

"Borough seats," Michael said at the same time.

"Dismouth," the duke agreed in astonishment, raising his head to look at the other two men. "Dismouth inquired into the munitions factories once, and expressed interest in influencing Blanche in the matter of the borough seats. When I told him she refused my advice, he said no more, but he did occasionally express irritation with the situation. I believe he thought I lacked the backbone for dealing with my cousin."

"Doesn't Dismouth have a daughter in town for the Season?" Reardon inquired.

The duke began to look trapped as he glanced from one man to the other. "Lady Susan," he muttered. "But there's any number of females who hope to capture a duke," he continued defensively. "I sometimes feel like a particularly fine specimen of trout."

At that point Michael relaxed enough to grin. "Lady Blanche would appreciate the comparison. Reardon, bring in our friendly family solicitor."

"Winfrey?" The duke glanced in surprise to the door through which Reardon departed. He sent Michael a questioning glance. "Who in hell are you, anyway? And don't tell me O'Toole because I won't believe it. No damned Irishman would have troubled himself to dig so deeply into my affairs."

Michael's smile disappeared, and he shrugged. "No one of import, Your Grace. The lady required assistance, and I was happy to be of help. You wouldn't have received any extortion letters recently, would you?"

The duke didn't have time to reply before Winfrey stumbled through the open doorway, his hands tied behind his back. From behind his glasses, the solicitor glared at Michael as he heard the question thrown at the duke. "Of course not, you impertinent jackanapes. The duke has been all that is gracious. One does not extort money from benefactors."

Winfrey jerked from Reardon's grasp, straightened, and met the duke's startled look with pride. "Dismouth destroyed your father, Your Grace. I could only watch helplessly as he became more deeply involved with every passing day. I did not know his acts were treasonous until I translated the diaries. I do not know what I could have done if I'd known. The Percevals and Winfreys go back centuries, Your Grace. I could not have reported him."

"But you could destroy Dismouth without touching a

Perceval by extorting everything the earl owned," Michael said with delight. "A man after my own heart. Now, let us get down to business. There is the small matter of Whitnell's lists. And the deeds, Winfrey? What have you done about Whitnell's deeds? I believe you handled that matter also?"

Winfrey looked guilty for the first time. "I should have told the lady as soon as I discovered her identity, but she introduced herself as Miss Reynolds. There was some doubt in my mind, you understand, and I feared letting her have anything so dangerous as those diaries. She could have destroyed the family, sir. I couldn't allow that."

"What rot are we talking now?" the duke demanded to know.

Before anyone could answer, a footman in livery appeared in the library doorway. "A messenger, Your Grace. He wishes to speak with Mr. O'Toole and Lieutenant Reardon."

O'Toole and Reardon exchanged alarmed glances and demanded the messenger's immediate appearance.

When Gavin's message was repeated, three of the men in the room cursed. Michael said nothing but picked up his hat and disappeared out the door before any could stop him.

Thirty-eight

Garbed in a flowing lawn nightrail from one of the trunks, with one of Gavin's coats over her shoulders for warmth, Dillian gazed over the darkened lawns from her attic window. The soldiers still stood guard. She could see the occasional glint of their swords and the shadows of their movements as they patrolled.

She didn't think it very likely that Gavin had sent British soldiers to guard his home. While she contemplated her position, she chewed idly on the hunk of bread she'd stolen from the larder.

Earlier in the day, before the soldiers' arrival, she had amused herself by dusting Gavin's library. She hadn't worried greatly about the servants discovering her presence. From the thickness of the dust she assumed they didn't spend a great deal of time in this little-used room. Actually, she didn't spend much time in dusting, either. She just enjoyed examining the library's contents.

She heard the knocking at the front doors from a distance. Absorbed in an old illustrated text of *Gulliver's Travels,* she didn't pay much attention to the noise until it gradually sank in that one of the servants ran to answer the summons. Having no great desire to meet Gavin's staff or his guests while dressed like a ragamuffin, Dillian looked for a likely hiding place. The window seat served perfectly, until she glanced out the window.

Officers rapidly deployed red-coated soldiers across the shaggy lawns while a man in gentleman's hat and tails waited on the front steps. An officer pounded on the door for him. Dillian didn't recognize the officer, but she recognized the gentleman. Dismouth.

That didn't bode well at all. Torn between running to

hide in the attic and wanting to hear what the man said, Dillian took a middle course. She slipped down the back hall to the dumbwaiter and hid herself inside. She'd already learned this was where the servants stood to gossip.

"Says he's come to claim the place in His Majesty's name," Matilda grumbled a little while later outside Dillian's hiding place. "Can't imagine what His Majesty would do with a pile of stones like this."

"Reckon we should leave?" the maid whispered. "Did he say what was to become of us?"

Matilda grunted cynically. "If he's staying, he'll not wait on himself. You can be sure of that. I'll wait until his lordship returns, myself. I'll hear it from his mouth and no other's."

Dillian cheered in silent approval. She debated the wisdom of revealing herself to the staff and decided against it. They would be much less nervous not knowing of her presence. Besides, the explanations would be interminable, and she couldn't be certain they would believe her tall tale over an earl's.

When soldiers searched the house, however, Dillian panicked. She couldn't believe Dismouth knew of her presence, but surely he knew Gavin had the journals. What else could he look for?

She bolted for the secret passage. She disliked spending hours in the dark, but like the servants, she would wait for Gavin.

Except for one or two scattered about downstairs, the soldiers eventually left the house to stand guard outside. It had turned dark by then, but Dillian practically knew her way around this house blindfolded by now. She'd rummaged food from the pantry and retreated to the top floor, where she could observe the proceedings without being disturbed.

She sipped from her water glass and nibbled on bread and cheese while she contemplated the movements of the shadows outside. She didn't think she could make it across the lawns unnoticed, not in the ridiculous gown or any other attire she might find in the wardrobes. If she dispensed with the coat, she might make a good ghost, but her sense of humor flagged. She worried about Gavin.

Could they have locked him in jail for some infringement of the law of which he knew nothing—or more likely, of which he cared nothing? She didn't think he would take that kind of risk while her attackers remained at large. She rather suspected Dismouth's arrival had something to do with those blamed journals. She just prayed it had nothing to do with Gavin's disappearance. No messenger had arrived to assure her of his safety.

Her stomach churned unhappily at this knowledge, but she couldn't give in to doubt. Gavin had promised to return, and he would. She just need wait and watch until he did. She didn't know what would become of her when he did. She had told him she would be no man's mistress, yet he'd offered no promises of marriage. He wanted her in his bed, but from what she could see, men frequently suffered temporary aberrations of that sort. Nothing ever came of them but babies.

She wouldn't think about that. Dillian's hand instinctively covered her belly, but she wouldn't imagine a child growing there. She supposed she could force him to marry her if she carried a child, but that sounded a particularly unpleasant business. In fact, marriage didn't sound particularly pleasant. Men weren't to be trusted. She would have her mother's estate in six months time. She needed nothing else. She could rely on land to support her.

But she still worried about Gavin.

A furtive movement near the stable caught her eye. Surely, he wouldn't try going around an entire troop of soldiers by himself. Dillian's eyes widened at the thought. How else would he reach her? He had no connections to call on. The Earl of Mellon may have generously loaned him a house, but the earl was a retiring country gentleman who seldom took his place in Parliament. Surely, he would have no influence if the Duke of Anglesey and the Earl of Dismouth controlled these soldiers.

She definitely saw movement by the stable, and not

the stiff stride of soldiers, either. She could see more
than one shadow slipping from the trees. Michael as well
as Gavin? Reardon? What could they possibly do while
surrounded by soldiers?

She would have to lend a hand from inside. She
prayed those shadows represented rescue or she placed
herself in a load of danger, but she couldn't stand here
vacillating. She must grasp whatever opportunity
offered.

Pulling Gavin's coat more securely over her arms, Dillian tucked her newly loaded pistol into the pocket and
picked up the sword she'd removed from the library.
She preferred the lighter rapiers, but she could wield a
sword sufficiently well to slash and wound. She hoped
she wouldn't have to. She had no great fondness for
blood, hers or anyone else's. She'd never tried explaining
that to Reardon or her father's friends.

Dismouth had claimed the newly refurbished master
chamber, of course. She'd heard the servants on the
stairs complaining, threatening to quit if the "lady" appeared at this trespass. Dismouth had laughed at their
fears. He wouldn't laugh quite so hard if the ghost actually put in an appearance.

That thought made Dillian grin for the first time this
day. Slipping silently to the farthest wing of the house
and taking the servants' stairs down, she found the
chamber where Blanche had stayed not so long ago. The
soldiers wouldn't have discovered the secret passage yet.

Gavin had already found his point of entry. Concealed
by the branches of the overgrown evergreens, he awaited
only the opportunity. The shouts as the first fire took
hold alerted him to his chance.

The soldier nearest him turned with alarm, swinging
his musket as he searched the darkness for the source
of the noise. The shouts of his fellow troops followed
the first blaze of orange against the night sky. Without
another thought to his post, the soldier rushed to the
aid of his comrades.

Quite content with that state of affairs, Gavin pulled
his cloak closed, concealing his shirt and waistcoat. Slip-

ping from the dense evergreen branches, he walked quickly past the shabby shrubbery to an old oak that always rubbed annoyingly outside his study window. Hidden beneath its shadows, Gavin flung the rope he held over the lowest branch, knotted it, and began climbing.

He preferred avoiding the guards Dismouth undoubtedly left below. He couldn't imagine the earl lowering himself to sleep in the study for the servants' sake as Gavin had done. No, Dismouth would have taken the one decent bedchamber in the whole damned ruin. Gavin gritted his teeth at the thought of the bastard in the bed Dillian had prepared for them to share. He would slaughter the scoundrel for that crassness alone.

Gavin wasn't certain what he could do with a bloody earl once he caught him, but he would worry about that later. First, he would pry Dismouth away from Dillian.

He'd entered the wrong wing for using the secret passage. That wing overlooked the stable. It didn't matter. If Dismouth had posted a guard outside his chamber door, Gavin figured he could remove him easily enough. He had a great deal more incentive than the soldier did.

As he crept closer to the central part of the manor, Gavin noted no lights or guards. Checking down the stairwell, he saw a soldier leaning over the baluster, apparently trying to determine the source of excitement outside. The screams and yells were faint up here, but enough to cause alarm.

Grateful he didn't have to waste time on a man only following orders, Gavin turned to the master chamber.

He found the door locked, but knew from experience that it had no bolt. Without a qualm to the destruction he might cause his legs as well as the door, Gavin slammed his boot heel into the crumbling old lock. The door sagged open without resistance. Knowing he had only seconds before the guard rushed up the stairs, Gavin pulled the brace of pistols concealed beneath his cloak and shoved past the sagging panels.

Dismouth had evidently already arisen on hearing the sounds from outside. In the process of fastening his tight breeches beneath his shirttails, he leapt instantly for the sword resting against the dresser as Gavin crashed in. His breeches drooped, but the earl held the sword steady. Outlined against the uncurtained window, his fighting stance was easily discerned. Gavin on the other hand, blended in with the wood paneling behind him.

"Who's there?" the earl shouted, bracing his sword for an onslaught.

"Colonel Whitnell's ghost," Gavin answered dryly, quickly comprehending the other man's plight. One couldn't strike what one couldn't see.

The guard from the stairs rushed in with musket upraised. Gavin held out his foot and let the other man run into it. The soldier slammed nose first to the floor, his musket roaring into the ceiling overhead as it hit the floor with him. From down the stairs a woman's scream echoed upward. Janet, Gavin knew. He'd recognize her screams anywhere. When would the woman learn to stay in her room where she belonged?

"Effingham, is that you?" the earl demanded as the young soldier scrambled to his feet.

Gavin grabbed the soldier's musket. With a mutter of apology, he slammed the stock against the soldier's head, sending him crashing to the floor again.

The earl didn't wait to ask more questions. Brandishing his sword, he leapt in the direction of Gavin's voice and movement.

Gavin really didn't want to shoot the man. Each pistol carried one ball. He'd rather save them for more dire circumstances than this. He wanted the earl alive and well in a dark, dank dungeon somewhere. He dodged the sword blade and brought one of his pistols down hard against the earl's arm.

Dismouth roared with rage. From below, Janet screamed with fright. Other voices joined her, obviously wondering if they should brave the ghosts on the second floor to rescue the earl. Gavin longed to howl with laughter, but the earl hadn't realized he was outgunned yet. Swinging his sword wildly, the older man damned near disemboweled him.

"You're going to regret that," Gavin growled, lashing out with one fist, then kicking high with his boot.

The sword flew from the earl's hand with the first blow, and Dismouth bent, doubled in anguish, with the second.

At the earl's cry, a slender figure garbed all in white and wielding a splendid silver sword, stepped from the wardrobe. Gavin could see the ghostly image clearly, but he still blinked twice to make certain the apparition of the "lady" hadn't just materialized. The earl, on the other hand, only caught a glimpse of a white blur seemingly walking through a wall. He screamed in terror and stumbled toward the door.

"Very good," Gavin said approvingly, admiring the way the apparition drifted toward them, sword gleaming. "It sounds as if Matilda is about to brave the stairs. Don't give her heart failure, please. It's hard to find good cooks."

The sword glimmering in the lady's hand dropped abruptly to her side. "The damned thing's too heavy to hold up long anyway," she grumbled. "He's getting away." She nodded toward the earl staggering through the doorway.

Leaving Dillian guarding the fallen soldier on the floor, Gavin dashed after the earl, knocking him sidelong to the floor with a blow from behind. Gallantry didn't come into play with traitors and kidnappers, he reasoned. A pounding on the front door joined the voices of the servants amassing on the stairs, and he raised his eyebrows speculatively. Why would anyone bother knocking in this chaos?

He didn't concern himself with answering. Removing another piece of rope from around his waist, Gavin wrapped Dismouth's hands behind his back while the earl struggled for consciousness. The man had a harder head than the soldier's, apparently.

"Gavin, this one's coming 'round," Dillian called from the bedroom.

Cursing, Gavin knotted the earl's bonds tightly and rose to look for something to use on the guard. The sound of familiar voices from below halted him.

"Dismouth, are you up there?" Neville.

Gavin clenched his fingers into fists. He had no reason to trust the duke.

"Why isn't someone dousing the fire?" Lady Blanche's imperious demand followed the duke's call. "Reardon, have those soldiers fetch some buckets. Someone could get hurt."

Janet's hysterical screams from the stairs interrupted this voice of reason. "The lady! The lady's walking! I told you. Didn't I tell you? We'll all die in our beds!"

Gavin swung around to protect his back.

Dillian drifted through the hallway, peering down the stairs with curiosity at the noise emanating from below. She dragged the sword behind the long train of her over-large gown. She'd covered her hair in some translucent concoction of white gauze that did give her a certain ethereal appearance.

Cursing more violently now, Gavin jerked the half-conscious earl to his feet. "Go get dressed before they all get up here," he growled at his ghostly companion.

"Why is Blanche down there?" Dillian asked with more curiosity than fear.

"I daresay you can ask my brother that, whenever he deigns to put in an appearance. What happened to the guard?"

Dillian looked guiltily down at her sword. "I meant to hit him, but as soon as I raised it, he fainted dead away again. People seem to do that regularly around here."

Gavin couldn't help it. A chuckle rumbled deep in his throat. By the time Blanche and Neville pushed past the hysterical servants on the stairs, he held the earl with one hand and the stair rail with the other, trying to keep upright as the laughter rolled out of him. Dillian merely watched with amusement curling her lip as Neville nearly screeched to a halt at the sight of her ghostly apparition. Obviously not believing his eyes, he turned his gaze to the laughing marquess and his prisoner instead.

Amused, Dillian lifted her sword and flailed it through the darkness. "Dare to touch the hair on the head of a

marquess of Effingham, and I shall strike you dead!"
she wailed with what she considered quite dramatic flair.

Belowstairs, Janet screamed and fainted. In the light
of the lantern he carried, Neville blanched, but he could
scarcely ignore Gavin's renewed roar of laughter. It took
Blanche's scolding reprimand to set him back on course.

"Dillian! Stop that. You have the servants in hysterics." Coming up behind Neville, she added dryly with a
glance to the laughing marquess, "Not to mention Effingham. Is that the earl you have there?"

Events followed too quickly after that for Dillian to
keep them all straight in her head. Gavin evidently recovered sufficiently to turn Dismouth over to the duke
and the soldiers he'd brought with him. Someone led the
villagers in a water brigade to douse the fires. Since Michael was conspicuously absent from the debacle inside,
Dillian suspected he occupied himself there rather than
watch the duke and Blanche together. However it came
about, the fires were doused but the stables destroyed.
She ached at the realization that Gavin had deliberately
destroyed part of his heritage in saving her, but she
didn't know what she could offer him in return. She
owned nothing. Not yet, anyway. Maybe never.

Somewhere along the way Blanche brought the terrified staff under control, and soon gallons of ale and hot
tea poured from the kitchen. The men disappeared in
conference somewhere. Dillian wanted to hear what they
would do with Dismouth, but garbed in a nightrail, she
didn't have the courage for lingering. She wanted Gavin's reassurance desperately, but she had no right to ask
for it. When the house once more seemed under control
and Blanche suggested that they take her coach back to
London, Dillian didn't know how to refuse.

Her duty was to Blanche. Gavin hadn't asked her to
stay. No one seemed to know she existed any longer.
What else could she do?

To all intents and purposes, the adventure had ended.

Thirty-nine

For probably the hundred thousandth time in this past month, Dillian sat before the desk in the Grange study, poring over the antique script of dozens of legal papers scattered across the surface. She studied the dates and lined them up in order. She struggled over the legal descriptions, but the terminology meant nothing to her. She'd been told briefly what they meant, but the knowledge wouldn't sink in. It didn't make a great deal of sense when laid against her knowledge of her father.

She supposed if dead men could speak, one of them would come back and explain about the games of chance or the dissipation or the just plain incompetence that had led to someone parting with these deeds. From the looks of them, they had exchanged hands several times after the seventh marquess sold them. She would like someone to explain how her father had acquired them, but her father wasn't the only gambler in the kingdom. Or perhaps he'd used his military prizes to buy them cheaply from someone in desperate need of funds. She just couldn't imagine her father doing anything so sensible as sinking his money into land.

She sighed and stared blankly at the polished panel wall in front of her. The Grange was such a lovely, peaceful household, she could disappear in here for hours with no one the wiser. The place practically ran itself. With Blanche in residence, it needed no one else. She was bored out of her mind.

She wouldn't think about Gavin. He'd taken all the responsibility of turning Dismouth into the authorities. From what she could tell, he had also taken responsibility for seeing that the original journals never saw the light of day. The government had only Michael's translations and her father's lists of evidence. Michael's translations conveniently did not name Neville's father as Dismouth's partner in crime. Michael had made certain no stain besmirched the name of Anglesey or Perceval. She thought he protected Blanche more than Neville, but the result was the same. Actually, with Neville leading the soldiers that arrested Dismouth, the duke came out smelling more like a hero than anyone else. The newspapers had scarcely mentioned the Americans. Even Winfrey somehow escaped the wrath of government. No one had bothered explaining that to her.

Gavin hadn't bothered explaining much at all once he'd seen her safe and well. He'd disappeared into the murky halls of government, never to be seen again. Dillian didn't even know if he'd returned to Arinmede yet. The last she'd seen of him, they'd stood in the salon of Blanche's town house. He'd brought the Earl of Mellon with him, since Gavin's cousin had just given birth to the earl's latest grandchild. Gavin and the earl had exchanged polite pleasantries with her and Blanche, wished them a good journey, and left on their own business. It wasn't precisely the parting Dillian had anticipated.

She didn't know what she should have anticipated from a monster like Gavin Lawrence. He had no heart. She'd known that. He couldn't bed her in front of Blanche and the earl and everyone, so he'd shrugged her off just like an old coat. Or cloak. She wanted to run a silver sword through the place where his heart ought to be. Or lower.

She ignored the knocking at the front door. This was too early in the morning for normal visiting hours. The neighbors could gossip with someone else. She should find something useful to do around here to keep her mind off the impossible. If she would live at the Grange for the rest of her life, she must find some place in it for herself.

She scowled as the study door opened after a single knock. Turning to give the butler a scathing set-down, her eyes locked with somber green ones. O'Toole's eyes were never somber. Of course, on the other hand,

O'Toole never knocked. Maybe this was just a ghost of O'Toole.

He shut the door quietly behind him and scanned the papers scattered over the desk. To Dillian's surprise, she saw anger tighten his jaw and thin his mouth. She'd never seen the blithe O'Toole angry. She stared at him in wordless astonishment, waiting for him to explain his presence here.

"If I'd thought you the same corkbrained sapscull as your father, I would never have given you those wretched deeds," he announced coldly, proceeding into the room as if he owned it. The butler had taken his hat, and his auburn hair gleamed bright in the morning light from the windows as he leaned his palms against the desk and stared across at her.

"Thank you very much, sir. And just what would you have done with them, since they are signed by my father and belong rightfully to me?"

Michael grabbed one of the deeds and whirled off with it. "Do you have any idea how easy it is to forge a name? How simple it is to copy this antiquated script Winfrey uses? I could have done anything I pleased with them." He swung around and glared at her. "But I gave them to you. And you sit on them like a hen hatching eggs."

"What would you have me do with them?" she shouted back at him. "After that statement, I can't even be certain they are really mine. Are you sure you didn't just forge them for your own amusement? My father never had enough money in his life to buy this much land."

Some of the anger left his face as he regarded her with a little more interest. "Are you telling me that you've left Gavin going out of his mind tracing these deeds while you're trying to figure out if they're legitimate? Or if they're ill-gotten gains? Between the two of you, you haven't got a good pound of sense. I've been telling Gavin for a year now to just go plow the wretched fields and dare the owner to show up. He could have had a crop in already. And now you're wasting another year by mooning over right and wrong. The two of you belong together because you sure as certain don't belong anywhere else in this world."

Dillian heard little of this tirade beyond the mention of Gavin. Trying not to show her eagerness, she asked, "He's looking for the deeds? Why?"

"Stupid question," Michael replied in a good imitation of Gavin's growl. He slapped the deed he held back on the desk. "I have it on good authority that your father bought these quite legally from the late marquess. They were schoolboy chums or some such, and when the marquess found himself in financial straits at a time that your father wished to invest some of his gains—ill-gotten or not, I can't say—they came to a convenient arrangement. The marquess fully meant to buy those lands back. Unfortunately, he died rather unexpectedly before he could recoup his fortunes. I suspect the lands were not exchanged at fair value so much as for whatever your father had in his pockets at the time. The late marquess would have known Whitnell had no intention of farming them. Your father simply acted as a cent-per-center, probably with much better interest rates than the usual usurers."

"You're lying," Dillian said bluntly.

Michael grinned. "Prove it."

She stared in bewilderment at the assortment of deeds in front of her. She could prove nothing except that her father had in his possession the deeds to the extensive acreage around Arinmede. She had seen the journals and the translations. They had mentioned the deeds. They hadn't specified their location or from whom he had obtained them, but he had mentioned their existence. Michael hadn't made up the entire story out of whole cloth. Her father had left her an inheritance. He'd just forgotten to tell her that the deeds weren't with his other papers but in Winfrey's possession. And she hadn't known to introduce herself to Winfrey as Whitnell instead of Reynolds, until it was too late, until he was too busy blackmailing Dismouth with her father's journals.

She still didn't quite believe the legality of the deeds. Michael was quite capable of manufacturing them for his own purposes. But the deeds didn't interest her so much as Gavin's behavior. Michael still hadn't told her anything about his brother. She was far more interested in Gavin than his property.

"What did you expect me to do with this land?" she asked carefully.

Michael narrowed his eyes and glared at her over the desk. "I expected you to use your common sense, but it's obvious you have as little as Gavin. If you don't tell him you have them, then I shall. He promised those villagers he would put the lands into production, and they're expecting him to follow through. I'll not see him suffer because of your stubbornness."

Dillian ran her fingers through her already disheveled curls. "What am I supposed to do? Offer to sell them to him? Even should he have the money to buy them, he'll not have enough for plows and seeds and repairs and whatever. He'd go in debt over his head to put those lands into production. You know that."

He shook his head in disbelief. "You really are going to play the innocent for all it's worth, aren't you?" He propped his shoulder against the window overlooking the estate lawns. "He can't ask for you when he has no means of supporting you or a family. He's made some clever investments from his years in shipping. He's made a few profits. But he can't support a family by continuing to gamble everything he owns. He needs a steady income. Those lands would provide it. You hold his future as well as your own in your hands."

Dillian huddled against the tall back of the desk chair, wrapping her arms around herself in an age-old gesture of protection. "I'd willingly trade myself for those lands, but I don't want to tie him down for a lifetime he might regret," she said in little more than a whisper.

Michael threw her a quick look over his shoulder, then returned to studying the landscape. "You're the only chance of happiness he'll ever have. Without you, he'll rot away inside that moldering ruin, never coming out, eventually giving up and becoming a ghost to join the others. You returned him to life. Don't banish him to an early grave again." Almost too casually, he asked, "Where is Lady Blanche today?"

Dillian wished she could fully believe what he was saying, but Michael had a tendency to twist words to his own way of thinking. She stared thoughtfully at his back. "She's visiting one of the tenants who is feeling poorly. She asks after you frequently, but I have nothing to tell her."

He ran an ungloved hand over the window ledge. "There is nothing to say. Have she and the duke announced the date yet?"

Her own aching heart went out to him, but Dillian could only shake her head. "Neville will have to wait until she makes up her mind. Blanche has the heart of an angel, but she knows nothing of being a woman. She has all the time in the world to choose the man right for her."

Michael turned and gave her a wry smile. "If I were Neville, I'm not certain I would trust you to give that guidance. Once the scars heal, she'll have her choice of any man she wants. She could do worse than Anglesey."

"She could do better," Dillian declared. "They're first cousins. I don't approve of the match at all. But, then, I'm not her guardian." Dillian carefully stacked the sheets of paper in front of her into a neat pile. "I don't think the scars will ever quite heal," she said quietly.

"I wouldn't see her suffer the hell that Gavin went through," Michael answered firmly. "There should be someone in this world who can appreciate her beauty and goodness, someone who deserves a woman like her."

"And I suppose you mean to find this paragon?" Dillian asked dryly, rising from her chair. "And you call me a sapscull. She's too inexperienced to know her mind yet, but she's learning quickly. She'll want to see you. Ask Jenkins for her direction. You'll find her easily enough."

Understanding he'd just been dismissed, Michael gave the window one last lingering look, then strode toward the door. He gave Dillian a hard stare before he departed. "Lady Blanche is far above the likes of me, but if Gavin doesn't know about those deeds within the week, I'm telling him."

Dillian thought to say that a marquess of Effingham was far above the likes of her, but he was gone before she could get the words out of her mouth. She wasn't certain she believed them anymore, in any case. Perhaps wealth and titles did not make one person better than another. She stared thoughtfully after Michael's departing back as he took the walk outside her window.

Gavin Lawrence, eighth Marquess of Effingham, wiped the sweat from his eyes and gazed in frustration at the section of stone fence that represented a good day's work. He was wasting sums he couldn't afford in clearing up this crumbling ruin he called home just so he could keep his promises to the villagers. In the past month, they'd almost made the place appear habitable. Almost.

He glanced over his shoulder to the house behind him. Dark was descending and lights flickered in various windows, including those on the second floor. With a bribe of a little extra pay, he'd hired women willing to begin the chore of sweeping out decades of dust and spiders in the upper stories. He just didn't know what he would do with the empty chambers after they were cleaned. He'd had hopes, but they were dimming quickly.

Picking up the shirt he'd discarded earlier, Gavin threw it over his shoulder and strode back toward the house. He'd hoped the day's physical exertion would have exhausted the turmoil in his soul, but it was no more effective than a cold bath on his rebellious loins. He couldn't even force his mind to the task at hand. It kept wandering down the road to the idyllic pastures of the Grange and a certain tumble of chestnut curls and saucy grin.

He hadn't heard from her since he'd left London, but he hadn't expected to. A lady didn't write to a gentleman not her husband. She couldn't very well just drop in, uninvited, for a visit. He'd known that. He'd deliberately counted on it. If he kept her at a distance long enough, she would find someone who could keep her far more comfortably than he could. She'd had enough of hand-to-mouth existence. She deserved a real home and a family, not a crumbling ruin and a scarred beast who couldn't control his lust. What they'd shared had been just that. Lust would dissipate with time.

Only it wasn't dissipating yet. Cursing as his mind again wandered to how Dillian had looked when he'd first revealed himself to her the day he met her, how she'd defied him, laughed at him, done anything but turn from him in horror, Gavin entered the study in hopes of dispelling the memory.

The maids had torn down the fragile old drapery and scrubbed the windows until they sparkled. They'd stacked the old ledgers and books into some semblance of orderliness on the shelves and dusted every inch of remaining space. Candles illuminated the desk, and a small wood fire burned in the grate, dissipating any lingering mustiness. He would have to order the chimney cleaned before autumn.

Rubbing his perspiring chest idly with his shirt, Gavin finally noticed the vase at the edge of the candlelight. A single red rosebud nodded over the crystal lip. Every once in a while, a draft sent a flicker flashing across the cut crystal, creating more prisms of light. A yearning so strong he could barely stand against it hit him, and Gavin closed his eyes and clenched his hands into fists as he fought against the tidal wave of longing.

He wanted Dillian here. He needed her laughing eyes on the other side of that desk right now. He wanted her spinning in the chair, swirling the globe behind her, insulting him for his stupidity in wanting what he couldn't have. Then he wanted to haul her across the desk and strip the clothes off her and feel her clinging eagerly to his embrace. That's what he wanted more than anything else. He wanted her to come to him of her own accord, not because he forced her to it.

He might as well wish for a rainbow.

Plucking the rose from its vase, wondering which of the maids had developed the notion to place one there, Gavin blew out the candles and headed up the stairs, shirt and rose in hand. He couldn't make himself stay in the master chamber. Dillian's ghost haunted it now. Every time he entered he heard her voice, saw her drifting through with sword upraised, saw her as she stripped herself bare for him. He regretted that moment as much as he reveled in it, yet wanted to make it up to her as much as he longed to repeat it. He was rapidly becoming a madman. He needed her so desperately he created his own ghost.

As he passed by the closed chamber door, a flicker of light from behind the door caught his attention. No one should be in there at this hour. The servants all went to their own homes at dusk. He had the house practically to himself. He'd never felt lonelier in his life. Perhaps he should return to the sea. At least there he was guaranteed of company when he wanted it.

Reluctantly, Gavin crossed the hall and threw open the door. A blaze of light stunned his eyes, and he blinked and stepped back before he could take in the phenomenon properly. Once his eyes adjusted, he could see candles and lamps, probably everyone left in the house, illuminating every inch of furniture in the room. A fire danced in the fireplace, and moonlight streamed through the uncurtained windows. His gaze instantly swept to the enormous bed at the far end of the chamber.

Dillian sat there cross-legged, clad in diaphanous white silk, her chestnut curls bent over an assortment of old papers scattered across the covers. Gavin's heart rose in his throat at the same time as his stomach danced a nervous jig. What in hell was she doing here looking like that? And why was she studying yellowed old papers instead of looking for him?

He thought to yell those questions at her, but he couldn't get the words past the lump in his throat. Instead, he dropped his shirt on the floor and approached the bed with the rose in his hand. When she finally looked up, Gavin thought he might explode with the need created by her widening eyes and look of delight as she took in his state of undress. He dropped the rose on the papers in front of her.

"You've come to tell me there's a child," he said with more hope than he thought possible. If she carried his child, he was duty bound to marry her.

She smiled brilliantly. "No."

Hope shattered, he looked at her with wariness. "You've run away from home?"

She scooped up the papers around her and patted the bed. "No."

Gingerly, Gavin took the place cleared beside her. He could smell the rose now when he couldn't before. Or perhaps he just smelled the scent of her. He wanted to be satisfied with just having her close these few minutes, but he knew that would never be enough. He felt ready to rupture inside from keeping his hand to himself.

"Do you mean to tell me why you're here?" he asked with more than curiosity. At the same time he decided it wasn't just lust driving him. He wanted to ramble around inside her head for a while, a lifetime or so, perhaps. He didn't think forever would be long enough. How could he tell her that without scaring her away?

Dillian carefully held up the stack of papers in her hand, presenting them to him. Gavin didn't even look at them. He couldn't take his gaze away from the pink tint of her cheeks and the wonderful warmth of her eyes. He read things there he didn't dare believe.

"I've come to offer you a proposition," she said almost shyly. He'd never seen her shy. He didn't want to see it now. She needn't be shy on his account.

He took the papers and set them on a nightstand. "If the offer includes you, I accept," he murmured, leaning forward to brush her cheek with his lips. He'd be a fool to deny himself that small opportunity. When Dillian didn't protest, Gavin raised his hands to her curls. They were every bit as rich and silky as he remembered.

"You don't even know what the offer is," she protested weakly as he trapped his hand in her hair and captured the back of her head, tilting her face so he could reach her lips with more ease.

"If it includes you and a few lifetimes, who am I to object? I don't ask for anything more." He was drunk on her closeness. He didn't know what he was saying. It didn't matter. She took his kiss with the eagerness he remembered so well, and he nearly melted into a puddle of hot wax right there. She had the power to do that to him, to reduce him to nothing with just the heat of her kiss. Or the wink of her eye. It didn't matter. He would do anything to keep her here.

Catching his breath, Gavin pushed back enough to think again. He could see the desire burning in her eyes. She wasn't here against her will. She wanted this as much as he did. But did she want as much as he wanted?

"Are you offering me a lifetime?" he asked carefully, studying her expression with the experience learned at the hands of cruelty. He didn't feel deserving of her wit or beauty, but he wouldn't deny himself the opportunity of asking if she allowed it. "I threw out the vinegar and sponges. I don't want that anymore."

She bit her bottom lip and doubt flickered briefly in her eyes. "Does that mean you don't want me? I thought, if nothing else . . ." She made a helpless gesture.

Gavin's eyes lit with unholy glee. "You thought I might stop wanting you? Are you out of your mind? What proof do you require of my desire?"

She gave his expression a suspicious look, then glanced down at his lap. If she needed any proof of his desire, she could see it there easily enough. He was as rigid as a fence post. He loved the way her cheeks burned red when she met his eyes.

"You could have come after me," she said with annoyance.

"And what would I have offered you when I did?" Gavin threw his arm out to indicate their surroundings. "One bedchamber and a pile of crumbling stones? A penniless title? I'll not have you live the life my mother led, or the one your father left you to. I would give you a roof without holes over your head, walls that won't crumble, the knowledge that the children we create will have a home and support for a lifetime. I can't do that yet. I'm working on it. I can't ask you to marry me until I can truthfully promise that I can take care of you. You're offering me temptation right now far beyond my ability to resist." His gaze dropped longingly to the swell of her bosom beneath the clinging silk.

Dillian leaned deliberately forward, emphasizing the

arch of her breasts, defying him not to touch her. "Then, don't resist. You didn't give me your child last time, Gavin Lawrence. Give me one this time."

She saw the blatant longing in his face, the war of desire and honor in his eyes. She was being cruel by forcing him to choose one over the other, but she wanted to know he desired her before she gave him what he required. She had thought to trade herself for the deeds, but she really wanted his love.

Sheer anguish clenched his jaw into ridges. Sweat appeared on his brow as he sat back, not withdrawing entirely from her closeness but keeping out of easy reach. Gavin's gaze met and held hers in such a manner that Dillian stopped breathing.

"I'll not tumble you like a whore again, Dillian. I love you too much for that. I want you for my wife. I want you to learn to love me as much as I love you. After what I've done, I know it won't be easy. I'll work hard to earn your respect. That's what I've been trying to do. I'm looking for the owners of that land out there so I can turn this place into a home for you to be proud of. Give me a little more time. I'm sure I can do it. Just don't torture me like this, Dillian. If you had any idea of what this is costing me to keep my hands off you . . ."

Lord, she loved this man. He sat here and talked with earnestness of honor and respect when they both burned like flaming torches just looking at each other. She wanted to dig her hand into the thickness of the hair tumbling across his forehead. Her fingers itched to slide over the muscular ridges of his bare chest and to wrap themselves in the crisp dark hairs curling there. She wanted those large hands on her breasts again. She wanted to smooth the lines from his face, rub away the sorrow and anguish, make that mocking curve of his mouth turn into a real smile. She could do it. She had the power to do it. That knowledge thrilled her as much as the words of love she craved.

Rising to her knees, Dillian allowed herself the sensual pleasure of caressing his hair. When Gavin instinctively reached for her waist, she slid into his lap and sprinkled kisses against his bare shoulder. He smelled of male sweat and musk, and she tasted his skin in her hunger for his touch. She heard him groan, and his hands clenched tighter. She'd have to release him from his torment so she could have all that she wanted.

"I'll bring the deeds as dowry," she murmured into his ear. "All you need do is promise to love me forever, as I will love you. This ruin can collapse around our heads. We can raise our children in the fields. I don't give a fig. Just tell me you love me, and I'm yours."

He didn't stop for explanations. Beyond any possibility of holding back now, Gavin pushed her down on the bed and covered her with his body. "I love you, Dillian. I loved you before, I love you now, I'll love you for all our tomorrows. Don't ever go away again." In the gentle luster of candlelight they pledged their vows to each other more surely than if they stood in church.

Only when the last candle guttered out and the fire died to embers did he raise up in the darkness and leaning on his elbow over her, ask quizzically, "Deeds?"

Dillian's wild trill of laughter convinced the servants all over again that The Lady walked, only this time, the apparition laughed instead of wept. Surely, that was a sign of hope and a promise for tomorrow.